Caesar Ascending – The Ganges

By R.W. Peake

Also by R.W Peake

Marching With Caesar® – Birth of the 10th
Marching With Caesar – Conquest of Gaul
Marching With Caesar – Civil War
Marching With Caesar – Antony and Cleopatra, Parts I & II
Marching With Caesar – Rise of Augustus
Marching With Caesar – Last Campaign
Marching With Caesar – Rebellion
Marching With Caesar – A New Era
Marching With Caesar – Pax Romana
Marching With Caesar – Fraternitas
Marching With Caesar – Vengeance
Marching With Caesar – Rise of Germanicus
Marching With Caesar – Revolt of the Legions
Marching With Caesar – Avenging Varus, Part I
Marching With Caesar – Avenging Varus Part II
Caesar Triumphant
Caesar Ascending – Invasion of Parthia
Caesar Ascending – Conquest of Parthia
Caesar Ascending – Pandya
Caesar Ascending – The Ganges

Critical praise for the Marching with Caesar series:

Marching With Caesar-Antony and Cleopatra: Part I-Antony
"Peake has become a master of depicting Roman military life and action, and in this latest novel he proves adept at evoking the subtleties of his characters, often with an understated humour and surprising pathos. Very highly recommended."

Marching With Caesar-Civil War
"Fans of the author will be delighted that Peake's writing has gone from strength to strength in this, the second volume...Peake manages to portray Pullus and all his fellow soldiers with a marvelous feeling of reality quite apart from the star historical name... There's history here, and character, and action enough for three novels, and all of it can be enjoyed even if readers haven't seen the first volume yet. Very highly recommended."
~The Historical Novel Society

"The hinge of history pivoted on the career of Julius Caesar, as Rome's Republic became an Empire, but the muscle to swing that gateway came from soldiers like Titus Pullus. What an amazing story from a student now become the master of historical fiction at its best."
~Professor Frank Holt, University of Houston

Caesar Ascending – Ganges by R.W. Peake

Copyright © 2021 by R.W. Peake

All rights reserved. This book or any portion thereof may not be reproduced or used in any manner whatsoever without the express written permission of the publisher except for the use of brief quotations in a book review.
Cover by Laura Prevost
Cover Artwork Copyright © 2021 R.W. Peake
All Rights Reserved

For Jacqueline Peake Horton
July 28, 1927-July 3, 2021
Who taught me what being a Peake means

Foreword

When I sat down to write this story that began with the ending, it was done with the best of intentions; I never imagined that *Caesar Triumphant* would ignite an interest in my admittedly fanciful "What If" moment from history that, next to the untimely death of Germanicus, are two points in the history of Ancient Rome that I have spent more time than I should daydreaming about. And yet, here we are, but what *Caesar Ascending-The Ganges* represents is another quirk of mine, and that is my inability for any inner peace without finishing a story that I've created. It's something that literally keeps me up at night, and more times than I can count, I find myself cussing me out because my mind doesn't stop, at least until the story is told; the only way I can describe it is that it's like having an itch in my mind, and the only way to scratch it is to finish the story. Well, this is the culmination of that, and for my longtime readers and fans, as always, my sincere hope is that they enjoy this journey upon which Titus, Caesar, and all the other characters I've created are on as it nears the finish. In fact, this will ultimately become the fifth of what will be an eight-book series that imagines this world where Caesar actually heeds the warning to "Beware the Ides of March." Now, as I've learned over my own particular journey, my readers are keen observers, ready, willing, and able to catch my errors, whether it be historically driven, or a disruption in the details of the various plotlines I've created (which is actually a great thing that I appreciate a great deal), so right now, some of you may be thinking, "Holy crap; he's going to write TWO more books in this series?" The answer is, "Not really, but sort of," so allow me to explain.

When I wrote *Caesar Triumphant*, it had the (some readers would say "dubious") distinction of being my longest book, but beyond that, since I began with the ending of the story, over the course of the book, I mentioned past events in this fictional ten-year period that finds Caesar and his army at the literal edge of their known world. Now that the story is more fully fleshed out, anyone who begins the series with the first book will arrive at

Caesar Triumphant, and their likely reaction would be, "Huh? When did Pullus and the 10th besiege Ecbatana? I thought that was done by Octavian." And, they would be right, which is why I'm going to be releasing a Second Edition of *Caesar Triumphant*, but it will also be in two parts, with (hopefully) the various discrepancies sorted out, and the storylines for characters such as Hyppolita, Barhinder Gotra, and a handful of others who have become part of the story will be fulfilled. My intention is to release what will become the penultimate book in the series, tentatively titled *Caesar Ascending-The Han* very soon, probably around the end of September. The Second Edition of *Caesar Triumphant* will follow soon after that, and for those of my readers who are following the *Marching With Caesar* series, Volume XIX will be coming at the end of the year. Now, with that out of the way, I want to address something of a personal nature, and for those who don't care for their authors baring their souls, the story awaits.

It would be a massive understatement to say that the previous eighteen-plus months have been trying, on all of us, and for a variety of reasons, none of which I intend to discuss. But, as the saying goes, life goes on, and it's a part of our existence that, if we're lucky, that with all of our successes and gains, there are inevitably setbacks and losses that are painful to varying degrees, from the professional to the personal. I recently suffered one, in the form of the death of my aunt, who, even as I type the word, doesn't do justice to the role she played in my life, and to an extent, in the lives of those who enjoy books by Ron Peake.

Her name was Jacqueline Peake Horton; she lived 93 years, 11 months, and 15 days, dying on July 3rd.

However, she was so much more than that. She was Jackie, the woman who introduced a very angry twenty-year-old to a side of the family he knew nothing about; she was the person to hand that twenty-year-old the very first picture of his father, a moment when everything fell into place for him, when for the very first time in his life, he felt a sense of belonging.

I'm not going to go into the circumstances behind my birth and childhood, because now that I'm older, I recognize what a complicated and volatile situation I was born into, 19 days after my father, Jackie's brother, died in 1959, and my mom found herself in an impossible situation, one where she did the best she could under very trying circumstances.

Saying that I'm a bastard is such a gross oversimplification of the actual circumstances surrounding my birth, but I suppose that in the eyes of the law, that's what I am, which Jackie cared not a thing about. She was just thrilled that her baby brother, and the only male in the family, would continue the Peake line, and I will never forget when I got out of the car to meet her at her home in San Antonio. She ran to me and hugged me, but it wasn't until she handed me the picture of my dad that I understood why, and for the very first time in my life, as a father myself, I saw someone from my family staring at me who looked just like me, but it was so much deeper than that.

You see, I was the only person on my mom's side of the family who was born in the South at that time; other cousins came along later, but I was it, and while it's not very popular right now to be from the South for a number of reasons, some of them merited and some not, I was Southern in my outlook, never feeling fully understood or accepted by my relatives, all of them born in the North.

For example, I always gravitated towards the military, but aside from my maternal uncle, who was drafted into the Army in the '50's, military service wasn't something that my mom's side of the family did. Some would say I'm obsessed about things like honor, and personal integrity, that I can be touchy about being insulted, and that, while I don't start fights as a general rule, I'm also one who, as an adult, never walked away from one. I love conflict, and I always have, and it wasn't until I graduated as one that I realized that I had always been a Marine, despite not knowing that.

Sitting down with Jackie that first time, learning about my family's military service in which a Peake has served in every war our country has fought, resonated with me.

It was through Jackie and my growing knowledge of my family that I learned of the mystical power of blood and how, despite never knowing a thing about my people from the mountains of North Carolina, Scots-Irish to the core, I was and am thoroughly and unequivocally a member of my clan, even when I didn't know it.

The fact that she was married to a career Marine (although I never met him), probably had more to do with my choice of the Marine Corps than I realized at the time, but more than anything else, what I got from Jackie was acceptance.

Being the black sheep of a family brings with it a cost that it's taken me some time to understand; even now, I don't fully comprehend it, and it's to my eternal shame that there was a period of time where we fell out of touch, but it had NOTHING to do with her and everything to do with me. I always felt like an intruder, a stranger from without looking within, certain that I didn't belong, but I want to make one thing clear. It was my own demons that drove me away from her and all that the Peake name represented, never her.

I'm happy to say that, when I reclaimed the name that SHOULD be on my birth certificate when I began what will be my final career, and one that, as so many people told me over the last five decades, what I was born to do, it made Jackie very happy.

I'm a Peake, of Roan Mountain, whose family arrived here in America in the 17th century, who migrated to the wilderness of North Carolina in the 1730's, whose roots are buried deep in the mountains of Mitchell County, North Carolina.

And I wouldn't have known any of that if it hadn't been for my Aunt Jackie.

Now I'm heartbroken, because I should have told her all of this.

Semper Fidelis
R.W. Peake
August 15, 2021

Historical Notes

I never imagined when I began this story that I would find myself learning about ancient India, but here we are.

As always, I try to use the names for landmarks like cities, rivers, and mountains by the name they would have been known by back then, but what I've learned is that there's a further complication stemming from names changing over the millennia, and that's the fact that the Greeks, being the nosy little travelers they were, had names for these landmarks that were distinctly different than those used by the natives. Just one example is the island nation of Sri Lanka, which the Greeks called Taprobane, but was known to the native inhabitants as the island of Ravana, and as I usually do, I took a "hybrid" approach, and also as has been my practice, particularly for rivers, using the modern name in parentheses after my first mention of it. And, as anyone who has looked at a map of India knows, they have a *lot* of rivers.

Along with that challenge is trying to unravel the extremely complex history of ancient India, and as I said in my last book, *Caesar Ascending-Pandya*, I'm not doing it justice, and have grossly oversimplified the situation when it comes to the various kingdoms, but please accept my apology for this, because it's not done because I discount the importance of Indian history. After all, I spent three solid years of research of Republican Rome before I released the first *Marching With Caesar* book; to do India justice, I probably wouldn't have been releasing this book until 2025.

That said, I hope that I've captured the basic situation that Caesar and his army would have faced, and as I made mention at the beginning of *Pandya*, I have stuck with what is personal experience, and that is the distinctively different use of head gestures that the Romans encounter, as a theme to accentuate what I believe would be the challenge, even under modern conditions, of encountering a culture and people who don't have a common basis of understanding for even the simplest of things, like that nodding your head means yes to us, and shaking it means no, and in the First Century BCE, this could and probably would have caused profound problems.

The city of Madoura exists, and is known as Madurai today, but those more conversant with the history of ancient India might spot what appears to be a discrepancy, which is that it was part of the Pandya kingdom, not that of the Chola. I put it under the control of the Chola Kingdom for the purposes of the narrative, simply because the Southern Ghat Mountains, where an important event occurs early in the story, is west of the city. In my defense, I do reference that the control of this city has gone back and forth over the decades. Also, while it's not a perfect overlap, the Pandya and Chola were separate and competing kingdoms for a period of centuries, and a Karikala is considered the founder of what would become the Chola Empire. The story about how he came by the name Karikala is either because he suffered a severe burn to his legs as a youth, or because he singlehandedly slew an elephant with a sword, so I included both. There was no Prince Divakar, just as there was no King Nedunj, although Nedunj's father Puddapandyan was a real person who, like Karikala, is considered the founding father of the Pandya, although in Puddapandyan's case, it was a century after the story is set. The city of Uraiyur existed, and is now a suburb of Tiruchirappalli, in Tamil Nadu, as does the city of Chennai, which, thankfully, still goes by the same name. When it comes to the kingdom to the north, I use the general term of the Andhra, although this is also the beginning of the Satavahana dynasty, and for reference material, I used the book *History of the Tamils: From the Earliest Times to 600 A.D*, by P. T. Srinivasa Iyengar, although not to the extent that I probably should have, but I used this reference to base my decision on referring to what the Greeks called the Sornas as the Andhra, and the boundaries of that kingdom aligns more or less with the modern state of Andhra Pradesh. There is one deviation from my use of the Indian names, and that is in the trading port that I call Kantakossylla, the name given to the port city at the mouth of the modern Krishna River. The reason I used the Greek name is that the specific site of what was an important trading port to the Andhra is unknown, probably due to the shifting nature of rivers in general, and it's likely that the ancient port is several miles inland from the modern mouth due to the inevitable buildup of silt. There was a Satakarni, two actually, the latter of whose reign coincides with the time period of what is now 40 and 39 BCE, although his queen is fictional.

Something else readers my notice is that I'm very vague on both religious and social customs, and that's by design for a really simple reason: I don't know very much beyond very basic information, and frankly, I don't think that would have an impact on the story, at least as far as Hinduism, and the thirty-three Vedic deities that would likely simply be added to the already crowded Roman pantheon, who always adopted every religion they ran across...save one, of course. The caste system would have had more of an impact on a Roman army, particularly when it came to recruitment and filling the ranks because, as anyone who read *Caesar Triumphant* first knows, by the time they reach the Isle of Wa, there aren't many Romans left. Like Hinduism, the caste system as practiced by Indians since approximately 1500 BCE is far more complex than the Roman hierarchical system, where you basically had the great unwashed of the Urban Tribes, the Equestrian Order, and the Plebeian/Patrician Order, although by this point in Roman history, the two are hopelessly intertwined. Again, I acknowledge that I'm grossly oversimplifying this crucial aspect of social development in Indian society, and for that I beg forgiveness.

The Gangaridae, as they were called by the Greeks, Megasthenes among them, were the Prasii, an ancient, very powerful kingdom whose holdings essentially extended for most of the length of the Ganges, of which the fabled city of Palibothra, which is modern day Patna, was the capital. The description of the size of Palibothra, along with its magnificent wealth comes from Arrian's *Indica*, who was quoting Megasthenes, the original work having been lost. Megasthenes actually lived in Palibothra for a time, which is why I used his description. As far as its wealth, it served as a gateway for the Silk Road into India from modern China, as well as having large deposits of gold within its borders. As far as Caesar's error in knowing the location of the city that has become a symbol to his army is based on just how little one part of the world knew about another part back then. One only has to look at the map in Ptolemy's *Geography* to see that it was largely based on secondhand information that may or may not have been accurate.

Finally, the elephant in the room (see what I did there?): my reliance on the use of naphtha as one of Caesar's superweapons. As part of my process in imagining the unimaginably demanding task that would stem from leading an army of fifty thousand men of the Legions, the cavalry, the auxiliaries, and the massive number of slaves that would be required, I spend a great deal of my time thinking, "If I was Caesar, what would I do?" And, in the case of the best way to combat what was the reigning superweapon of the kingdoms of India, I feel confident that the naturally occurring substance that is a crucial ingredient in napalm would be something that Caesar and his army would be quick to use. However, as I've done more research, I can't find any record of this naturally occurring substance beyond the modern-day Middle East and Iran/Iraq, at least in that form, specifically where Caesar is about to lead his army. So, this will be a finite supply that won't be featuring as heavily in their future clashes; the fact that of the foes that will be facing Caesar and his Legions, only one of them will still be using elephants I would simply ascribe to Caesar's Luck.

Table of Contents

Prologue 1
Chapter One 25
Chapter Two 69
Chapter Three 126
Chapter Four 169
Chapter Five 213
Chapter Six 263
Chapter Seven 320
Chapter Eight 369

Prologue

Publius Ventidius was in a quandary, and he had no idea how to go about addressing the problem. He knew the queen was in mourning, but she had refused to see him, or any Roman for that matter, for more than three months. Knowing nothing about the customs of these people put Ventidius at a disadvantage, yet with every passing day, his suspicion that this was a ploy on her part grew. Nevertheless, neither was he willing to force his way into the palace. Things had been peaceful in Bharuch, although it had been tense in the days immediately after the death of King Abhiraka, and more importantly, the sons of so many families in the city who had fallen with him. Balancing this, however, was the recognition by the people that, even more than themselves, the Romans had been responsible for saving the city from suffering even more damage than it had during Abhiraka's failed attempt to retake the city by devoting more men to fighting the fires than Abhiraka and his force. And, somewhat oddly, the fact that the damage had been initiated by their own king meant that, while there were some hard feelings towards the Romans, they were muted. Somewhat unusually, and contrary to his own inclination, Ventidius had ordered the men of the three Legions to turn a blind eye to the kinds of small acts of defiance that, under normal circumstances, would have exacted some sort of punishment, and gradually, a sense of normality returned to the city.

Still, there were issues that had to be discussed, and the

Queen of Bharuch was the only person with the knowledge to answer certain questions, and it was always easier to run things when the nominal leader of a conquered city went along, and that was even before Caesar had sent his message that contained the details of his plan, and his dilemma about Bharuch. Finally one day, he decided that he wasn't going to wait any longer, although for this meeting, he actually chose to wear not his uniform, but a toga, hoping that it would impress upon the queen the importance of his visit. While it was certainly cut to the same specifications of the garment that was unique to Rome, he had realized fairly quickly the impracticality of the heavy wool in this climate, yet he didn't like the manner in which a version made of cotton draped on his frame. Finally, he had succumbed to the allure of silk, telling himself that it wasn't for vanity but practicality. The fabric wasn't unknown, certainly, and even before joining himself to Caesar, he had been able to afford it, but silk was for narcissi, actors, and the fashionable set. Regardless, he thought he cut a fine figure in his new toga as he walked up the street, telling himself that his reason for eschewing his bodyguard had nothing to do with the inevitable gossip that would result from seeing the Praetor thus attired. He was especially thankful because he was sweating even more profusely than the weather called for, although he would never admit that he was nervous, but the last time he had spoken directly to the queen had been the day of her husband's death. Since then, the Lady Amodini had been the only member of the queen's court who had had any congress with Ventidius, or anyone representing Rome. The last time he had laid eyes on Amodini, however, she was obviously pregnant, but in the way of most men, it never occurred to him that there might be a connection between this and the fact that she could at least communicate in Latin. Ventidius, with some justification, had assumed that the young lady's husband had been one of Abhiraka's junior officers, although he also had assumed that he must have fallen with Abhiraka, or perhaps had escaped to join the remnant of the Bharuch elephant corps since there was no body for her to claim like her queen and Lady Eurycleia. As he ascended the steps, the door was opened by the mute attendant, informing the Praetor that he had been seen approaching from the second floor by one of the ladies or the queen herself.

"I must speak with Queen Hyppolita immediately," he informed the man in Greek, knowing that he understood that tongue, and that someone was standing out of sight next to the stairs up above listening anyway.

The attendant bowed, as he always did, then hurried up the steps, leaving Ventidius to marvel once again at how quickly the silk that had been soaked in his sweat dried out, and he began thinking about the idea of suggesting to Caesar that they make another switch for the men's tunics, from cotton to silk. He knew that it was stronger than it looked, and with a thicker weave...

"I am sorry, Publius Ventidius," he turned to see the Lady Amodini standing at the top of the stairs, "but Queen Hyppolita is unable to receive you today."

While he had expected this, he still felt a flare of irritation, which he kept under control as he replied, "I am afraid, Lady Amodini, that this time I must insist. There are decisions that only she can make, and they have been put off for too long, I am sad to say. So," he tried to sound firm without being harsh, "please tell your queen that I will be coming upstairs after I count to fifty."

"But..." Even with a veil and head covering, he heard the note of what might have been panic in the young woman's voice, "...you cannot, Publius Ventidius! She is not...well," she finished.

Now Ventidius was alarmed, knowing how Caesar was likely to react if the woman was inconsiderate enough to die.

"Is she ill?" he asked. "Because we have several physicians attached to our forces here who are quite experienced."

"No." She shook her head. "Queen Hyppolita is not ill. She is..." Clearly struggling, both because of the situation and her limited Latin, she just repeated, "...not well."

Taking a breath, Ventidius stood there, fuming but uncertain what to do. Finally, with a muttered curse, he began ascending the stairs, prompting a startled sound from Amodini that wasn't quite a scream, yet was loud enough that he heard feminine cries of alarm in answer from the second floor. He didn't stop, however, until he reached the step below Amodini, putting them eye to eye as a part of him realized that this was the closest he had been to any of these women, and if he looked hard, he could see their eyes through the fine mesh. And what he saw there didn't make him feel better; in fact, it made him think of his own daughter, dead many years now, but he was a Roman and he was under orders.

"Lady Amodini," he spoke gently, for him at least, "I mean your queen no harm, I give you my word. But there are things she needs to know so that she can make a decision that only she can make."

For the first time, Ventidius heard something besides anxiety, certain that there was a hint of anger in the young woman's tone as she challenged, "Since when has Rome allowed Bharuch to decide anything, Publius Ventidius?"

Biting back the retort that came to mind, Ventidius maintained the same tone as he answered calmly, "Since this moment, Lady Amodini. Caesar has sent very clear instructions, and just like you must obey your queen, I must obey Caesar."

Suddenly, he reached out to place his hands on both her shoulders and, while he was gentle with her, he firmly moved her out of his path, which, he was relieved to see, she didn't fight. With her out of the way, Ventidius walked the few paces from the head of the stairs down the short hallway that led to the audience room. When he opened the door, he expected shrieks of outrage, or alarm, yet he was greeted with a silence, despite the fact that the women were all present. And, he saw, all veiled, including the queen, who was actually reclining on the Bharuch version of a couch, the first time he had ever seen her do as much, stirring an uneasy feeling.

There was nothing in her voice to indicate she was feeling unwell, the tone as cool as always as she said, "I see that my wishes mean nothing to you, Praetor Ventidius." She hesitated, and he actually saw the fabric of her veil billow out as she let out a breath, then continued, "But, since you are here, please state your purpose for seeing me."

He thought briefly of insisting that the other women leave the room, then decided against it, not wanting another fuss. Behind him, he sensed more than saw that Amodini had entered

Caesar Ascending – The Ganges

the room, and she said something to Hyppolita in their native tongue, but Hyppolita shook her head.

"She is apologizing for being unable to stop you, Publius Ventidius, but I assured her that when Rome wants something, they cannot be stopped. This is a simple truth, is it not?"

"It is," he agreed, seeing no point in denying the reality of the matter. Besides, it gave him an opportunity. "Which is why I am here, Your Highness."

Then he went on to explain, in detail, what Caesar was offering her, as the sole ruler of Bharuch.

When he finished, there was a long silence, then Hyppolita said at last, "I owe you an apology, Publius Ventidius. You were telling the truth, and I am sorry for doubting you. I do indeed have much to think about. May I have some time?" Ventidius opened his mouth, about to demand that she provide a firm date, and if she didn't, he was prepared to tell her a week was the most he would allow, but she added, "Would three days' time be sufficient?"

Because of her veil, Ventidius was unable to see Hyppolita's amused expression at his surprise, but he was quick to agree, "Yes, Your Highness, that would be perfectly acceptable." He bowed. "I will return in three days' time."

Turning about, he hurried out of the room, and despite his age, he had to force himself not to act like an excited schoolboy, but his eagerness to return to the *Praetorium* was only partially based in the easy victory; he was now certain that there were two pregnant women in Hyppolita's court, something that he was sure Caesar would want to know.

Nobody was more surprised than Hyppolita at the way in which her ladies accepted the fact that she was pregnant, but it wasn't until a few weeks later after she couldn't hide it any longer that she learned why.

"It was the Lady Eurycleia, Your Highness," Amodini whispered to her one evening when the other women were occupied. "She told the ladies that she saw you and King Abhiraka..." she didn't use the term, but there was no need, "...the night that he came back to the palace and you were alone."

5

It was a fabrication, of course; yes, she and Abhiraka had been alone, but they hadn't had enough time to have coupled, and she wondered why Eurycleia was willing to lie for her. As time passed, and Eurycleia never mentioned it, Hyppolita's regard and trust in Ranjeet's widow grew, accepting that she was doing her part to protect their queen. That didn't solve the larger problem, and it was something that Hyppolita agonized over every waking moment, while it tormented her nights as well. Oddly, she didn't feel ashamed of lying with Titus Pullus, but even more oddly, it never occurred to her to take steps to rid herself of this unborn child; her concerns were purely practical. If it was a boy, she wondered, would he be as large as Titus Pullus was? This thought alone gave her pause; although she had never struggled beyond what was considered normal during her three births, none of her children had been anywhere near as large, and it was the size of her unborn child that she worried would betray her more than anything else. Yes, Abhiraka had been darker than Pullus, but the Roman had hair that was almost black, along with the olive complexion that wasn't just a characteristic of Romans born in places like Pullus' home of Hispania. As she had proudly informed Caesar and the man that she had thought was merely a huge brute on the day the city fell, she was descended from the Macedonians who fought for Alexander, so she wasn't overly concerned with the babe's coloring. The fact that she had a companion who was, if she was any judge, a month further along than she was had proven to be quite enjoyable, and the bond between her and Amodini had grown ever stronger, although in the recesses of her mind, she understood that they were united by more than pregnancy, but the fact that they had both fallen in love with an enemy. She would find herself weeping at odd moments, not unusual for pregnant women, but what she could only confess to Amodini was that, despite her attempts to block him from her mind, she worried about Titus Pullus, something with which Amodini could identify. One day, about five months after Caesar and the army had departed, by chance, she learned from the merchant who delivered the weekly supplies, albeit indirectly, that Caesar had invaded Pandya, that there had been a furious struggle, and many men on both sides had fallen. She couldn't keep anything down for the next two days, and she actually considered calling for Ventidius to ask him to inquire about the Primus Pilus of the 10th Legion. She almost convinced herself that she could disguise her concern simply because of their connection as the only Roman she interacted with, but she discarded it. Ironically, it was Amodini who provided solace to the queen.

"Do you know what Gaius told me about his uncle one time?" Amodini asked, and naturally, Hyppolita nodded eagerly. "That Titus Pullus can't be killed, because he was blessed by one of their gods." Hyppolita, more educated and worldly than Amodini, didn't dispute this openly, but Amodini saw her queen wasn't convinced, and she insisted, "No! It is true, Your Highness! I swear it! Gaius told me that he has seen it with his own eyes! When his uncle and the men he leads are in grave danger, that their god of war gives him the power of Herakles himself! That he becomes Herakles, until he has slain all of his enemies!"

The demigod Herakles was perhaps the most recognized name in the known world, his fame reaching even to Bharuch, although, like everyone in the East of Greek or Macedonian heritage, Hyppolita had been raised on tales of his heroic deeds. However, Amodini had been born and raised in Bharuch, yet she knew about him as well, and Hyppolita, certain that Amodini would never knowingly lie to her queen, had accepted this. It was the next week, when the merchant returned, that Hyppolita learned even more, and while it made her happy, it also made matters infinitely more complicated.

"The Pandyan King Nedunj is now an ally with Rome, just as we are," the man had told her, on his knees and with his head bowed, after being brought to Hyppolita by her mute attendant, taking advantage of the laxity of her omnipresent Roman guards. "They are going to be fighting alongside the Romans!"

Hyppolita's first thought was "Fighting who?" but she managed to keep this in the back of her mind. She did feel some satisfaction in intuiting that Gaius Julius Caesar would never be satisfied, that even after he had surpassed Alexander, which Titus had confided to her was his general's ultimate ambition, it didn't make her feel any better about the prospects for the father of her child, despite the fact that he would never know.

As Pullus had predicted, she had accepted Caesar's offer of Friend and Ally status, promising that a Roman presence would always be welcomed in Bharuch, in exchange for a pledge from Rome, through Caesar, of course, to defend Bharuch in the event that they were attacked by a hostile kingdom. The fact that two of the three kingdoms who would have been most likely to do that were now also Friend and Ally of Rome didn't make it any less valuable, and while the huge and powerful Andhra kingdom that lay to the east just beyond the headwaters of the Narmada River, and ruled by an ambitious king named Satakarni, the second of his name, for some reason, she wasn't as concerned. It wasn't something that she knew on a conscious level, and yet, like so many other leaders with whom he came in contact, Hyppolita had determined that, as long as Caesar lived, he was simply unconquerable, and she believed Titus when her lover said that he wouldn't be satisfied until he reached the Ganges, which meant that this Satakarni would have problems of his own, since Andhra lay between the Pandya and the Ganges, which she knew were ruled by the people of the Gangaridae. And, she was honest with herself to acknowledge that the fact that the father of her unborn child was such a large part of Roman invincibility not only made her proud, she deemed that it boded well for the child. Sometimes, when she indulged herself, she would spend her time reminiscing about their time together, yet she couldn't put her finger on the precise moment when she had recognized something, that if it weren't for a quirk of fate that saw him born as a member of the peasant class she had learned the Romans called the Head Count, Titus Pullus had the makings of not just a good king, but a great one. Certainly, his size and strength gave him an advantage, and sometimes Hyppolita would feel ashamed that she had assumed that this was the only reason for Pullus' prowess on the battlefield, but with time, she had learned quite differently, that there was a quick mind encased in this giant, along with the kind of burning ambition and drive that she had learned long before was a crucial characteristic for a great king. A less pleasant thought, one that she tried to keep in the recesses of her thoughts, was how easily Titus Pullus could have dispatched her dead husband, who was considered by his people, and by the rulers of the surrounding kingdoms, as a superb warrior in his own right. Poor Abhiraka, she thought, more than once, he was fortunate in his death that he didn't face Pullus. Of all the thoughts she tried to avoid, there was another one that was even more intriguing, and troubling; if she bore a son, and the fiction that he was Abhiraka's survived intact to allow him to grow to manhood, could the offspring of Titus Pullus be the man to help her other son, the crown prince Bhumaka, regain Bharuch's independence from Rome?

By the time Ventidius' missive reached Caesar, the relocation to Karoura had occurred, although they hadn't reached the point where he felt comfortable prevailing upon Nedunj to provide the men for the *dilectus* that was required to fill the depleted ranks. Certainly, it was a significant undertaking, but the Romans now had the experience acquired in integrating men from other nations into their ranks with the Parthians, although the officers were aware there would be unique challenges with the Pandyans. At this moment, Caesar had the men busy constructing a permanent camp outside the walls of Karoura, although this was very different in style from those that had been built at Bharuch, where the architecture and building style was more heavily influenced by the Greeks. Karoura was located at the base of low mountains that bisected the southern part of India from north to south, which Nedunj had informed Caesar served as a natural boundary and defense from the kingdoms to the east. Caesar hadn't pressed the young king, but he had laid several hints that fulfilling his father's ambition of controlling the entirety of the lower quarter of the vast landmass of southern India wasn't out of the realm of possibility. There would be time for that in the coming months; first, he and his officers worked diligently to convince the Pandyans in Karoura, and Muziris that they could expect the same treatment that the subjects of Bharuch and Pattala had received. Naturally, the sudden influx of the foreign soldiers produced a strain, particularly on the purveyors of vice, which the Romans were learning, to their disappointment, weren't nearly as numerous in southern India as they had been in the northern part of the country. Very quickly, Caesar was faced with the challenge this created, but as usual, he reacted quickly, if a little unusually.

"You want to import prostitutes?"

Nedunj was, understandably, startled, and obviously unsettled by Caesar's proposal, but the Roman was encouraged that the young king didn't immediately reject the idea.

"Not just prostitutes, Your Highness," Caesar answered. "I am also talking about merchants who specialize in...beverages, of a specific type."

"Ah," Nedunj at least understood this part. "You mean that you want to supply your men with *sura*."

"Yes, Your Highness," Caesar agreed, somewhat relieved that this didn't seem to be a surprise to Nedunj. "It's just that, when we allow our men to enter Karoura, they've discovered that those two...commodities are hard to come by. And," now Caesar hesitated, because this was a sensitive topic, "according to my Primi Pili, when their men reported that you do have prostitutes, for some reason, they refused to have anything to do with my men." His mouth twitched as he tried to fight a grin, even with the potential seriousness of the subject. "In fact, some of my Centurions took it upon themselves to investigate to determine if these women were only discriminating because these are men of the ranks, but it appears that they refused my officers as well."

Even before Caesar had finished, Nedunj knew what the Roman was referring to, and he realized that the challenges with this new alliance ran even more deeply than he had imagined. We're not only combining our armies, but our culture, he thought, which meant that he chose his words carefully.

"Those women you are referring to are called *Devadasi*, Caesar. And," he allowed, "while they are technically prostitutes, they are actually attached to the temple of one of our deities, and they can only...serve men who worship that deity."

What Nedunj had no way of knowing was that this wasn't as uncommon as he thought; there were cities in the East who followed the same practice, but Caesar suspected there was more to it than that, and he decided to broach what could be an

Caesar Ascending – The Ganges

explosive topic indirectly.

"You may not be aware, Your Highness, but we Romans are known for our openness to accepting, and following, different religions that we encounter, so over time, it's very likely that my men will find one of these deities to appeal to them. Will they be allowed to join one of these temples?"

"Yes," Nedunj answered cautiously, uncertain but suspecting that Caesar might have an idea that it was in fact more complicated. "But there is…more to it than that, I am afraid, Caesar."

"Such as their class," Caesar replied, then thought to add, "or what you refer to as their…caste, I believe is the word?"

"Yes, Caesar." Nedunj shook his head, relieved that Caesar had discerned the issue. "I am afraid that not even your Centurions would be considered…" he had almost used the word "worthy" but substituted "…eligible to be served by the *Devadasi*, even if they did join a temple."

Nedunj's relief lasted only long enough for Caesar to say coldly, "Then that is indeed a problem, Your Highness. None of my men, no matter their rank, will take kindly to the idea that they aren't considered worthy of these women's attention, especially when there is money involved." He paused for a fraction of time, then in a slightly softer tone, said, "Which is why I think you should consider my proposal."

Nedunj was feeling trapped, and he protested, "Caesar, I am afraid that my subjects do not approve of prostitution if it is strictly for monetary gains, without any religious purpose. Bringing women like that into either of my cities will be very troublesome, I can assure you."

"Then we won't bring them into your city," Caesar replied immediately, and surprisingly for him, since he had just thought of it, impulsively.

"How can you do that?" Nedunj asked, truly mystified.

However, despite Caesar acting spontaneously, as always, in the span of this exchange, he had already thought it through, so that by the time he was finished explaining, Nedunj's relief was plain to see.

"That," he agreed, "will work."

As was his habit, before Caesar actually sat down behind

his desk in the *praetorium* tent as he waited for the permanent structure to be finished, Caesar had already begun issuing orders to bring his idea to fruition.

"You mean we're going to have our very own town?" Balbus asked Diocles skeptically.

"In a manner of speaking," Diocles answered the Centurion, although Pullus, Scribonius, and Porcinus were every bit as interested.

They were dining in Pullus' quarters, although two sides of the tent had been rolled up to allow the light but cooling breeze that came from the nearby heights to pass through. It was yet another adjustment that the Romans had learned, from the Pandyans in this case, and while he didn't like the feeling of less privacy, men had learned that they lingered nearby at their peril. And, if something important needed to be discussed, the sides were rolled down, but while this was important, Pullus didn't feel the need for that level of privacy.

"What does that mean, 'in a manner of speaking'?" Balbus scoffed. "That's something that a shifty Greek would say!"

"I *am* a 'shifty Greek'," Diocles answered with a cheerful smile, knowing this was always the best way to get under Balbus' skin.

Scribonius interjected, "It's going to be like the shantytowns we had in Gaul, Quintus, that's what it means."

The look of dawning recognition, and chagrin, on Balbus' face elicited a chuckle from Pullus, causing his scarred friend to protest, "Why didn't he just say that? If he had said it would be a shantytown, I would have known right away!"

That had been Caesar's solution, which Nedunj had immediately seen as a way to preserve the peace and stability between his subjects and their new allies. There had been some incidents in Karoura, and while he hadn't heard from Maran, who he had named as the Lord of Muziris to replace the dead Subramanian, the young king assumed that similar events had occurred. The fact that Caesar—after touring Karoura, the Roman had seen that there simply wasn't enough room inside the walls—had kept his men busy building their permanent camp had helped matters. Now, this proposed small town, placed on the opposite side of the camp from the city, seemed an elegant solution to the problem.

With that settled, Scribonius decided to broach another subject, one that he had been wanting to bring up but had been putting off, and he tried to sound casual as he asked, "Any word from Bharuch?" When Pullus' head came up sharply, he hurried to add, "About whether we're keeping three Legions there? And is Ventidius going to continue as Praetor?"

Pullus was certain that there was more to Scribonius' question, but it was also valid, so he bit back a retort and answered, "The Queen has agreed to accept Friend and Ally status, but Ventidius is going to stay put with one Legion for the time being, and the other two will be joining us."

Scribonius considered this, then asked, "I wonder which two are coming?"

"I think the 5th is the most obvious choice," Balbus offered, his temporary sulk over, and the others agreed.

"The 15th?" Porcinus suggested.

This was possible, but Pullus didn't think it likely, which he explained, "The 15th has been with us from the beginning, but they haven't seen nearly as much action. In fact," he mused, "I wouldn't be surprised if, before it's all said and done, Caesar sends one of our Legions that have seen the most action back to Bharuch. Even," he finished with a shrug, "all the way back to Parthia."

Before either Balbus or Scribonius could respond, Porcinus spoke up, saying hopefully, "Maybe it will be us!"

The three Centurions stared at him for a moment, then simultaneously burst out into a roar of laughter, while Porcinus turned a deep shade of red, realizing how ridiculous an idea it was. It was only later, as Pullus was preparing to retire that he thought of that moment, remembering the look of pain in his nephew's eyes, knowing exactly what it was about, because a part of him felt the same way.

Sextus Scribonius could count the number of times he had been summoned into Caesar's presence, alone, on one hand, but every time he had, the topic had been about Pullus, and this time was no different. However, not even he could imagine what he was about to learn from their general, who began in a somewhat unusual manner.

"Before I say anything, I need you to swear on the eagle standard of the 10th that, if I deem it necessary, you will never breathe a word of this conversation to Pullus."

Scribonius was understandably nervous, but he wasn't intimidated by Caesar; part of this stemmed from the fact that he was as much of a veteran as Pullus, having been comrades in the same tent section in the 10th, which had been raised by Caesar when he was Praetor of Hispania. Also, Scribonius wasn't awed by Caesar's intellect, and while Pullus never brought it up, the truth was that he would have put his unassuming friend in the same class as their general when it came to matters of the intellect.

Regardless, after a brief moment, he finally nodded in agreement as he said, "I swear on the eagle that I will only bring this up if you deem it to be the right thing to do, Caesar."

Satisfied, Caesar wasted no time, nor did he mince words.

"Queen Hyppolita is with child, and I'm almost certain that Pullus is the father."

Scribonius felt his jaw drop, but his mind, which worked as quickly as Caesar's, immediately determined that one of the reasons Caesar had been so blunt was to elicit a reaction that would indicate whether or not Scribonius was aware of his friend's relationship. *Which means*, he thought, *he's not as certain as he says he is.*

Rather than replying directly, he asked, "How did you come by this information, Caesar?"

Now it was Caesar's turn to think, and if Scribonius were to know the truth, he would have been surprised to learn that Caesar not only recognized Scribonius' intellect, he enjoyed being challenged by someone who thought as quickly as he did, but Caesar saw no reason not to be honest, and explained about the letter from Ventidius and his observation.

Then, in an afterthought, Caesar mentioned, "And, it appears that the queen isn't the only one. The Lady…" for this, he did have to consult the scroll from Ventidius, "…Amodini is pregnant as well."

It took a massive effort on Scribonius' part not to respond

Caesar Ascending – The Ganges

to this piece of news, but he managed to maintain a neutral expression, judging by Caesar's lack of reaction.

Realizing that it was his turn to speak, Scribonius began by asking, "What do you know about the Primus Pilus' background, sir?"

Caesar thought for a moment, then answered, "I know he came from Baetica. And," he grinned at Scribonius, "I know he lied about his age to join at sixteen instead of seventeen with Domitius." The mention of Pullus' best friend, and one of the men Caesar still considered responsible for what happened at Pharsalus erased the grin as if it had never been there. "And," he finished, "I know that he wasn't particularly close with his father."

"That," Scribonius said dryly, "is an understatement. But, there's a reason for that. Titus' father never forgave him for what he believed Titus did to his mother."

"Oh?" Caesar's eyebrow lifted, and he asked cautiously, "Do I want to know about this?"

"I think it's important if I'm correct in what I believe you're asking, whether Pullus should know about the queen being pregnant."

As Scribonius expected, this elicited a nod from Caesar, who replied, "You're exactly right, Scribonius, that's my dilemma. So," he folded his arms, "tell me what this has to do with Pullus' mother."

"Because he killed her," Scribonius answered quietly. "On the day he was born, because of his size, Pullus' mother didn't survive. And his father never forgave him for it."

Caesar exhaled in a long breath, leaning back in his chair as he murmured, "Thank you, Scribonius." Then, his brow furrowed as he remembered, "But Pullus had children with his woman…what was her name?"

"Gisela," Scribonius answered, the name evoking the memory of not just the girl with hair the color of burnished copper, but of Calienus, her first lover and their Sergeant who had died at Gergovia, and Scribonius added, "but she was a Gaul."

"Who are sturdier than other women." Caesar nodded. "Yes, I remember seeing her now. She was quite a beauty, but

15

she also had hips that would accommodate a child the size Pullus obviously was." Sighing, he seemed truly sad. "But that's not how Hyppolita is built. Even with those loose robes she wore, you could see that. So," he concluded, "there's a possibility she may not survive this birth. Which means, we don't tell Pullus about this." Making a point to look Scribonius in the eye, his voice was quiet, but his meaning was clear. "Do you understand, Scribonius? Pullus must never know."

The fact that Scribonius agreed, to a degree, helped him assure Caesar he understood very well, but then he pointed out, "What about if she survives the birth? Doesn't he have a right to know?"

"Does he have a right?" Caesar echoed. "Perhaps, but what purpose would that serve? And," he pointed out, "now that Queen Hyppolita has agreed to serve as regent as a Friend and Ally client kingdom until her oldest son comes of age, if it was learned that she had been unchaste, that would jeopardize not only our relationship, but it would put her life in danger. And," he added, superfluously, "the life of the child as well."

Scribonius had reached that conclusion immediately after he posed the question, so he assured Caesar that Pullus would never know the truth. Satisfied, Caesar dismissed him, exchanging a salute, and Scribonius left the *praetorium* with every intention of upholding his promise about Pullus. However, Caesar had said nothing about informing Gregarius Gaius Porcinus that he was about to be a father.

As Caesar had predicted, the winter of the fourth year of the campaign was a busy one, for almost every man in the Legions, but for the men in Muziris, there was the added element of learning how to fight in concert with armored elephants. As Balbus had predicted, the 5th was the first Legion to be sent from Bharuch, where they were tasked with helping their comrades to become accustomed to being in the proximity of beasts that, just months before, they had been concerned would stomp them into jellied meat. The shipbuilding offered challenges of a different dimension, especially given they were designed for only a handful of passengers, namely two elephants, their handlers, crews, and their equipment and armor.

Caesar Ascending – The Ganges

This required vessels broader in the beam, and with a shallower keel, which made them stable only in calm waters; the fact that Caesar had ordered shipping built for them in the first place led to such rampant speculation, and the wagering that stemmed from it, that this became the most popular topic of discussion between the men, and not just among the Romans. Only later would it become apparent that the subject of elephants, ships made for elephants, and why Caesar would want ships for the fifty elephants that would now be part of Caesar's army helped break down the barrier between Pandyan and Roman. Much of this was due to a relatively small group of noncombatants, those like Barhinder Gotra, their numbers growing from one per Legion to one per Cohort, then finally one per Century, that made these first attempts to communicate possible. It also served as a valuable lesson; there wasn't a paucity of those able to communicate in Greek and either Sanskrit or Tamil, while only a few men could speak in all three, but there weren't many men willing to volunteer.

It wasn't until Achaemenes, during one of his forays out into Karoura, prowling through the merchant quarter, struck up a conversation with a man who informed him, "These Romans do not pay enough to make it worth the risk."

Intrigued, Achaemenes asked, "What do you think it would take?"

The man didn't hesitate, naming a sum that, in Achaemenes' opinion, was outrageous, three times what the Romans were offering. Still, he didn't think it would hurt to inform Caesar, and before Achaemenes could blink after relaying the news, Caesar had agreed. Within a week, Achaemenes and Barhinder, who had been unofficially named Achaemenes' deputy in this endeavor, were actually able to become much more discriminating in choosing translators. In fact, some of the first men who had been hired were summarily dismissed because their command of Greek had consisted of a few dozen words and simple phrases, and they now had men who were far more fluent. However, perhaps of all the things that occurred during this winter that would have far-reaching implications was the solving of the mystery of why Pandyan arrows seemed to penetrate more deeply, and it had nothing to do with their bows.

"They've learned how to heat the iron ore to higher temperatures than even the Gauls," Caesar informed his officers during a meeting that he had called to answer this very question, which had been one of the topics of conversation as well. "It makes the iron less brittle, but also stronger and able to hold an edge better."

"Any idea how they do that?" Pollio asked, but Caesar could only offer a grimace as he shook his head.

"This isn't something that King Nedunj is willing to divulge, and apparently, he's sent a warning out to all of the smiths in both cities that any of them who show us that technique will be executed," Caesar paused, then finished grimly, "along with their families."

"He can't do that!" Hirtius snapped. "Now that he's a Friend and Ally, he's required to share that kind of information with us!"

While this was technically true, Caesar took a longer view, and he actually understood why the young Pandyan king was loath to divulge anything of such immense strategic value in a relationship that was barely months old at this point. Besides, he had thought of another way to garner this information, and in fact, had already begun the process of gathering it.

"Actually, Aulus," Caesar answered, pretending to be rueful, "the agreement that we struck with Nedunj is somewhat...different than what Rome usually negotiates with a client state. But," he hurried on, not wanting to go down this particular road, "I've thought of another way that we can gain this information." Despite knowing that it was unwise to divulge the method, Caesar was like most men in the desire to impress his counterparts, but this was by a matter of degree, and as in everything, Caesar went beyond what was normal, so he gave his officers a knowing smile, "However, what Nedunj's decree covers is every smith and metalworker here in Karoura and in Muziris...not in the smaller towns." Waiting just long enough to see that his officers grasped his meaning, he finished, "I've already sent out some of the metalworking *immunes* into the kingdom, along with translators...and protection. And gold."

Caesar Ascending – The Ganges

As he had hoped, this lightened the mood considerably, and he briefly considered broaching the topic that he had been putting off; what came next for Caesar's army. While he did come closer to doing so this time, he once again decided that the time wasn't right, and he ended the meeting shortly afterward, ignoring the inquiring look from the one man in the room who actually knew what lay ahead, but he refused to meet Pullus' eye as the Primi Pili filed out of his office.

It was in the Roman month of Februarius that the Lady Amodini gave birth, after a long but not inordinately difficult labor, to a healthy baby girl, who Gaius Porcinus would be fated to never see. And, by her side through the whole birth was Hyppolita, wiping the sweat from her face, giving her sips of water and words of encouragement, not as a queen but as a woman and mother who had already experienced the most momentous event in a woman's life. Then, almost exactly a month later, with as much secrecy as possible, it was the Lady Amodini's turn to be at her Queen's side, doing the same for Hyppolita. However, just as the last months of her pregnancy had been, Hyppolita's labor was not only long, it was extremely difficult, so much so that the Lady Eurycleia actually considered sending word to the Roman Praetor that they did, after all, need the help of one of the physicians Ventidius had offered a few months earlier. It was Hyppolita herself, so soaked in her perspiration that she could have just emerged from a pool, in between her panting groans of pain, and with a fair amount of fear, who forbade her lady from it, making Eurycleia swear that under no circumstances would she do so, no matter what happened. And, it was very nearly the last order she ever issued as a queen because, with the last bit of energy she could muster and with a scream that chilled her attendants, she finally expelled the child who had been growing inside her body, lapsing immediately into a state of unconsciousness, out even before she heard the first squalling cry from a tiny but powerful set of lungs, the infant covered in more than just the fluid that had sustained it, but its mother's blood. For the next third of a Roman watch, the Ladies Eurycleia, Amodini, and Darshwana worked feverishly to stanch the flow of blood, finally able to do so with the help of a tincture made from the bark of the root of the cotton plant, one of Bharuch's most valuable exports. Despite their success, Hyppolita didn't regain consciousness, although this wasn't unexpected. When she remained in this state for the next day, and the day after, deathly pale and running a high fever, Amodini was pressed into service as a wet nurse for both infants, while Eurycleia, who had now assumed the role of *de facto* leader of the queen's ladies, agonized over what to do. As many differences as there were between Rome and Bharuch, there were similarities, and one of those was that physicians rarely had anything to do with matters of childbirth or the complications stemming from it, which was what persuaded Eurycleia to obey her queen's command, not out of loyalty, but out of the recognition there was probably not much they could offer that they hadn't already tried. On the third day, she summoned the ladies to meet with her in the audience room with the intention of setting their expectations, certain that their queen would never regain consciousness, and to remind them of the plan that Hyppolita had concocted regarding this child who, through no fault of its own, could prove to be so problematic.

"Lady Darshwana, have you made contact with your cousin and his wife?" Eurycleia asked. When Darshwana indicated that she had, using the merchant, despite knowing this was what the queen wanted, it still took an effort for Eurycleia to tell her, "I believe it is time to send for them to come take the child."

"But the Queen has not even seen it!" Amodini objected, and she wasn't alone, the rest of the women adding their agreement in one way or another.

"I know," Eurycleia agreed. She sighed, then said sadly, "But perhaps that is for the best. Better that she never lay eyes on the babe. Besides," she hated herself for doing so, but she reminded the others, "I do not believe that our Queen will ever wake up."

It was something that they had all discussed, in whispers, but hearing it said aloud had an impact that was so visceral that, within a couple heartbeats, every woman present was venting her grief, some sobbing, others emitting a low moan, united in their sorrow at the very idea of losing this woman who was not just their queen, but in some ways, their reason for existence. While Eurycleia was similarly affected, she also knew that some of this display was based in the fear of the unknown, because it was one that she shared; if she was not one of the queen's ladies, what was she, and what would become of her? Like Hyppolita, she was a widow, but unlike the queen, Eurycleia, while noble, didn't come from wealth, and neither had Ranjeet; her late husband had won his position through his steadfast loyalty to Hyppolita's husband and his sheer competence. Regardless of this reality, and somewhat to her own surprise, Eurycleia realized that her grief was based more because of the regard that she held Hyppolita in, which hadn't always been the case. For years, she had been jealous of the queen, certain that Hyppolita's acts of charity and her concern for the subjects of her husband was all a show, but the fall of their city and kingdom had stripped Eurycleia of that view, and she realized that she had been unfair. Now, she was as bereft as her fellow attendants, which was why neither she nor her ladies heard the faint cry from the queen's bedroom.

It was actually Amodini who suddenly rose, listening intently before saying, "Quiet! I think one of the babes is crying!"

The room fell silent, but when the sound came again, they all joined Amodini, leaping to their feet to go rushing back into the queen's room to find her, still supine but clearly awake.

And, after a few sips of water, she was able to whisper, "Where is my child? Is it...?"

Her eyes were normally expressive, but her drawn features accentuated the fear Eurycleia saw in them, and she hurried to assure Hyppolita, "The child is alive, and healthy, Your Highness."

"Bring it to me," Hyppolita commanded, with a trace of the old imperiousness she could use when needed, but Eurycleia hesitated, although it was Amodini, having taken the stool next to Hyppolita's head, who spoke up.

"Your Highness, do you really think that is a good idea? Given what you decided?"

"I know what I decided, Amodini," Hyppolita's voice was

a hoarse whisper. "But I still want to see this child." She gave the ladies a wan smile. "After all the trouble it caused me, I would like to see who did it."

Amodini rose, smiling at her queen's attempt at humor, but made no effort to hide her reluctance as she walked over to the crib where her daughter and Hyppolita's child lay, but when she picked up the swaddled babe, Hyppolita called out sharply, "Not your daughter, Amodini! I can tell by the size that's her! Do not try and fool me!"

For the first time, there were some smiles from the other ladies, as Amodini continued carrying the bundle back to the bed, while Eurycleia explained, "That isn't Amodini's babe, Your Highness. She's not this large yet. This," she swallowed the sudden lump that was the mass of feelings that were welling inside her, "is your son, Your Highness."

Amodini had reached Hyppolita's bed and was bending down to place the infant who, as Eurycleia said, was even larger than his older crib mate, into the queen's arms, and within a matter of a couple of heartbeats, Eurycleia knew that Darshwana's message would never be sent. Staring down into eyes that, as with most newborns, were almost black, just as Eurycleia suspected, Hyppolita discarded any plan to send this child away to be raised in anonymous comfort. In her heart, she knew that she would never see Titus Pullus again, and it was that thought that formed her decision, although she would never speak of it. She knew that there would be talk; even if she had lain with Pullus and her husband within days of each other, just the size of this infant would have raised questions, but in this moment, she didn't care. They, after all, were living in a new world, one dominated by Julius Caesar, a man who she had barely heard of before he strode up the steps of her palace; so, who knew what the future held? Who knows? she thought, her lips curving up into a smile at the very idea; what if Titus Pullus' son becomes a king in his own name? When she finally looked up, she saw her ladies, all of them affected, but in their faces, she saw their loyalty, and their unspoken promise to protect and help their queen, and her son. That, she decided, would be enough.

Caesar Ascending – The Ganges

It was the Kalends of April when, at the end of the monthly report Aulus Ventidius sent, after detailing the current situation in Bharuch, the state of the two Legions still there, and the news that the badly burned former bodyguard of the late King Abhiraka, whose name they had learned was Bolon, had managed to escape from confinement and was now being hunted, was something that Caesar could see by the ink had been written later.

"Caesar, I will close with something that I learned today, just as I was about to send this dispatch. I have managed to bribe the one merchant who supplies the queen and her household, and he has been providing me with information for the last three months. He reported to me today that Queen Hyppolita has had her child, a boy, but he did not know exactly when, which seems to be secret, although he was told the babe came early. According to him, he was told that the night Abhiraka attempted to retake the city, he was alone with the queen for a long enough period of time for them to have sexual congress. This seemed plausible and was the accepted story…until today. Somehow, I do not know how, he managed to catch a glimpse of the babe. Caesar, he says that this babe is far too large to have been born early, and it is large, even if it had been born yesterday. I believe that your suspicions are correct, that this child is the son of Titus Pullus; it is of course up to you whether you tell him or not, but as of this moment, I do not know what Queen Hyppolita plans to do with the child."

Caesar felt torn, which surprised him somewhat; yes, he was satisfied that his instinct had been correct, but he couldn't deny that he also felt badly for his Primus Pilus, who would never know that he had a son to replace the one he had lost to the plague in Brundisium while Pullus and the Equestrians were fighting for him in Africa. In fact, for a brief flicker of a moment, he considered informing Pullus, and even opened his mouth to call Apollodorus and tell him to summon the Primus Pilus. Then, the rational part of his mind, which, more with him than any other man alive, always had a firm grasp of his actions, asked: to what end? Caesar would need Pullus at his best for what was coming, the plans for which he had already decided to unveil the next day that would immediately launch his army into a frenzy of activity. If he wanted to reach the Ganges and take Palibothra, he would need every man, of all ranks, but he would need Titus Pullus and his Equestrians more than any other Legion. Pullus will already be devastated when I tell him that I'm sending the 3rd back to Parthia to take the place of the 14th, he thought grimly, knowing how close Pullus and Spurius were, and it was a decision that he had wrestled with, so adding this piece of news to that? Shaking his head, he closed his mouth, rolled up the scroll, and put it in one of the holes in the rack behind him, and while it did occur to him that he might want to destroy it, he didn't. Tomorrow, it would begin; tomorrow, he and his army would take the first steps towards placing Caesar, and Rome, above the world's greatest conqueror. After this year, the fifth of this adventure, nobody would be able to say that Caesar's name didn't belong above that of Alexander. And then? He thought, Who knows? There was still so much of the world to see, but first, Caesar's name would ascend Alexander's, and after that, the future was full of possibilities.

Chapter One

"I hate to admit it, but I think Caesar's integrating of the elephants worked out much better than I would have thought."

Titus Pullus glanced up from his meal at his dinner guest, the Primus Pilus of the 28th Legion, Gnaeus Cartufenus, giving him a grin as he gently teased his counterpart, "Are you saying that you ever had any doubt in Caesar, Gnaeus?"

If Pullus had intended to make Cartufenus uncomfortable, he failed miserably, as Cartufenus shot back, "Are you saying you didn't, Titus?"

It was the kind of thing that could have been viewed as a challenge, particularly to the giant Primus Pilus of the 10th Legion, but Pullus laughed as he admitted cheerfully, "Of *course* I did! I thought he'd gone mad for suggesting it!"

The meal was being served in Pullus' quarters in the camp that had been erected outside the walls of Karoura, which had required the construction of huts that stood up to the torrential rainfall that was even more prolific here at the southern tip of India than in Bharuch. As always, Pullus' other guests were his closest friends, Quintus Balbus, his Primus Pilus Posterior, and Sextus Scribonius, his Secundus Pilus Prior and one of only three men still in the 10th Legion who had once shared a tent together as lowly *Tirones* when a little-known Praetor named Gaius Julius Caesar had called a *dilectus* for a Legion in their home of province of Hispania. Cartufenus' presence in Karoura was due to his being summoned from Muziris, along with the Primi Pili of the 5th, 6th, 8th, and 30th Legions. It was now early

April, and the previous five months had been quite busy for all of them, albeit in different ways.

"What about you?" Cartufenus asked after swallowing his mouthful of rice. "How have things gone with those Pandyan replacements?"

Pullus didn't answer, glancing over at Scribonius in a silent signal, and he was the one who answered with a shrug, "They're willing enough, and there's the language issue, of course, but Barhinder has taken care of that for the most part. The biggest problem is getting them accustomed to their *hamatae*."

"I heard about that." Cartufenus nodded. "So, are they going to be ready for…?"

He did not finish, which caused Pullus and Scribonius to exchange an amused glance.

"I was wondering when you were going to bring that up," Pullus said, though without rancor. "I knew the moment you invited yourself to eat with me that you'd be fishing. But," the large Primus Pilus mused, "the question is: did the others put you up to it?"

Cartufenus flushed, but he didn't bother to deny the truth, and he actually admitted to it as cheerfully as Pullus had to his challenge, "Even if they hadn't, I would have come knocking."

The others chuckled, but Pullus was in something of a quandary about how to answer. It was true that they would all be learning what, through Diocles and his friendship with Caesar's most trusted secretary Apollodorus, Pullus already knew Caesar had planned for the morning; nevertheless, he was still reluctant to share it with his fellow Primus Pilus. Then, another thought intruded in his consciousness, the recollection that what Caesar had planned had actually originated with Pullus himself, although it had been at the urging of Scribonius that Pullus had approached their general with what was, by any measure, a sweeping, audacious plan.

Putting his spoon down, Pullus took a breath, then glancing over at his friends, he began, "We're going to be moving soon. My guess will be that it will be within the next two weeks."

If Pullus expected Cartufenus to be grateful, what he received instead was a dismissive snort. "I gathered that much, Titus. That's the only reason Caesar would be calling us to come upriver from Muziris. The question is…which direction? Are we going back to Bharuch to launch our campaign on Palibothra?"

"No," Pullus replied immediately. "We're heading south. Or," he amended, "at least at first."

"South?" Cartufenus frowned, not understanding. "That's the opposite direction from Palibothra." Suddenly, his expression transformed as he exclaimed, "We're going to take Taprobane?"

"Yes," Pullus confirmed, then before Cartufenus could say anything, he added, "to begin with."

Cartufenus' face changed yet again, the confusion returning as he demanded, "What do you mean 'to begin with'?"

Instead of replying directly to his counterpart, Pullus turned to address Diocles.

"Will you bring us the map?"

The Greek got up immediately, hurrying out of the private quarters into the Legion office, leaving the others to return to finishing their meal, which on this occasion was what had become the traditional fare of rice, but heavily spiced with some of the hotter peppers that were abundant in this part of the world, meaning that the sweat beading their foreheads wasn't from the heat outside. Diocles returned quickly, and with the meal consumed, he cleared away the four men's bowls to enable Pullus to unroll the map, the sight of which elicited a gasp from Cartufenus.

"Where did you get this?" he asked in wonder. "Did Caesar give it to you?"

"Not exactly," Pullus allowed, shooting an amused glance at Diocles, who returned the look with a grin of his own. "Let's just say that I have little birds. But," he turned his attention to the map, "as you can see, this isn't just the western coast of India and the area up around Pattala and Bharuch. We've all seen those maps. This," his finger traced the rounded tip of the southernmost part of this strange country of India before moving up the jagged line that represented the eastern coast, "is the rest of India, all the way up to the mouth of the Ganges." He paused to let Cartufenus examine the map, the Primus Pilus giving a nod that signaled Pullus to continue, "As you can see, India is much wider the farther north you go. And," his finger moved to a spot near the top of the map on the left side, placing it on a dot that was perhaps an inch to the right of the line demarking the eastern coast, "here's Bharuch." While Cartufenus didn't notice the change in Pullus' voice, the other three men present did, exchanging surreptitious glances with each other, each of them knowing that whenever their friend and Primus Pilus mentioned the name of that city, it caused him some form of pain, all of them knowing why. Unaware of any of this, Pullus was frowning down at the map as he continued, "So, while going back to Bharuch to march on Palibothra from the southwest does put us closer in terms of the number of miles, as you can see, given how broad India is in the north, it's still almost a thousand miles, and Hirtius only took our cavalry a hundred miles to the east of Bharuch while we were there."

He stopped and watched as Cartufenus studied the map, but Pullus' counterpart wasn't entirely convinced, asking, "And how much farther would it be if we sail up the eastern coast?"

"That," Pullus admitted, "I don't think anyone knows with any certainty, but it's three hundred miles from Muziris to Taprobane. Then, from Taprobane to the mouth of the Ganges?" For this, he looked over at Diocles, who supplied, "Caesar's estimate is a bit more than a thousand miles."

Cartufenus absorbed this, then asked the question that Pullus had been dreading, "How far is this Palibothra from the mouth of the Ganges?"

While he didn't relish the idea of answering, neither did he hesitate.

"Nobody knows. Or," Pullus amended, "if Caesar does know, he's being very tight-lipped about it."

"Maybe he'll tell us tomorrow," Cartufenus suggested.

"Honestly," Diocles spoke up, "I don't think he knows either, Primus Pilus. Not yet, at least."

"I think that he's counting on the idea that someone at the Greek trading colony on Taprobane will know," Scribonius commented, then asked Diocles, "What's its name?"

"Palaesimundum," Diocles supplied.

"Well," Cartufenus raised his cup, which contained water

Caesar Ascending – The Ganges

this night instead of the *sura* that had become the favored beverage of the men of all ranks in Caesar's army, "here's to finding out what tomorrow brings."

There were still days where young King Nedunj of the Pandya awoke in a state of disbelief at all the changes to his life that had been wrought in the previous several months; even so, his conviction that he had not only made the right decision, but really the only decision to save his kingdom grew every day that he watched Caesar and his Legions in operation. It had begun with the construction of their winter camp, followed quickly by the construction of what he had learned the men of the Legions referred to as a shantytown that, as Caesar had informed him, was a common feature around any Roman camp that was semi-permanent in nature. This compromise had worked out better than Nedunj had thought possible; however, there was one development that he had watched with some dismay, and it had caused him some issues among his own subjects. While it was true that none of the *Devadashi* had left their respective temples, a distressing number of Pandyan women had decided to move into the new shantytown to sell their bodies. Some of these women doing as much was understandable, and the fact that a large number of them came from Muziris was a direct reflection of the horrific losses the young King's army had suffered when Caesar and his army of hardened, battle-tested Legions came wading ashore. These women, most of them with children to feed, and without enough eligible men to step into the void, had heard about this arrangement and had made the trip upriver, choosing to seek newer opportunities rather than compete in the shantytown outside the city on the coast. It was, Nedunj had understood immediately, an unfortunate situation, but nothing in their society was built with the idea of supporting a sudden surplus of young widows, at least in these numbers. Yes, there had been wars before—his father Puddapandyan had been voracious in the early years of his reign in his wars of acquisition—but none of the bloodletting had ever been on such a massive scale before. From their first meeting on the beach outside the walls of Muziris, Caesar had been extremely complimentary about not just the valor of his men, but the strategy the young King, who had thought he was still the Crown Prince and under enormous pressure not to allow the second most important city in the Pandyan kingdom to fall, had employed against Caesar's Legions. Regardless, the fact that this had been echoed by several of Caesar's most senior officers only partially lessened the sting of defeat. And, just as he had been warned by Caesar, who, despite a naturally adversarial relationship, he was growing to trust more and more, the signs that these women were finding new protectors among the Romans were becoming unmistakable, as some of the earliest arrivals to Karoura now found themselves claimed as the woman of a man who, if the truth was known, might have been the slayers of their husbands. He would never dream of asking, but Nedunj was almost consumed with curiosity about whether or not the women and men who had come together as a couple had ever discussed such things. What he couldn't deny was that the business in the shantytown for all manner of vice and relaxation was brisk, and those merchants of Karoura who were willing to risk the censure of their fellow citizens by either investing or opening one of the businesses there were reaping huge profits. As part of the alliance with Caesar, Nedunj had agreed to relinquish the contents of the treasury of Bharuch that the widow of King Abhiraka, Queen Hyppolita, had sent along with the crown prince Bhumaka, and his wife Aarunya's younger sister Anuja, something that had not set well with the young monarch. He knew that Caesar had used a significant part of Bharuch's treasury to pay every man in his army a bonus that, when he learned the amounts, staggered him; the sum was five thousand *drachmae* for every man in the ranks, with the scale sliding upward for each higher rank, culminating in the amount of thirty thousand *drachmae* for what he had learned were the Primi Pili of each of Caesar's Legions. While nothing had ever been said, and despite his best attempts to find out, Nedunj was as certain as he could be without evidence that, of the highest-ranking Centurions, the huge Primus Pilus of the 10th Legion had received even more. His belief was simple, and based in his observation that, of all of these officers, Caesar relied on, and in Nedunj's eyes, deferred to Titus Pullus more than even those men bearing the rank of Legate, like Aulus

Hirtius, Asinius Pollio, and Gaius Volusenus, and certainly those men nearer to Nedunj's age, the Tribunes. Caesar's lack of formality with the lower orders, and his reliance on the counsel of men like Pullus, had been just one of the many things that young King Nedunj had to adjust to with his new ally. And now, this ally was preparing to do two things, both of which, as far as Nedunj was concerned, were positive things for the Pandyan kingdom. In something of a rarity, King Nedunj was aware that he actually knew more of Caesar's plans than even Pullus, and he would be attending the meeting to be held the next morning as Caesar unveiled what lay in the future for his massive army that was becoming even more diverse in its composition now that the king had supplied the agreed upon numbers of replacements who would be trained to fight as Romans. This had been the one area where Nedunj had received the most resistance from the men who now made up the highest rank of Pandyan aristocracy. The fact that, with the exception of Maran, who Nedunj had appointed as Lord of Muziris to replace the arrogant Lord Subramanian, Nedunj having dispatched the arrogant older lord who was friends and contemporaries with his father with his own hand, the new highest ranking members were all around his age was no accident, and Maran was only in his mid-thirties. And, given that it was Maran who displayed his trustworthiness in a fashion that left absolutely no doubt where his loyalties lay with his decapitating Alangudi in front of Nedunj, who, up until Alangudi had decided to make a move to seize the throne for himself in the wake of the death of Nedunj's father Puddapandyan, was Nedunj's closest friend and most trusted councilor, Nedunj felt confident in his trust of the older Pandyan noble. In the intervening months since that dramatic event that took place outside what had been the temporary camp erected by Caesar outside the walls of Muziris, Nedunj had come to appreciate Maran's counsel, so much so that when Caesar had asked Nedunj to attend the meeting to be held the next day with his officers, the king had insisted that Maran come from Muziris to be with him. Now, that meeting was not far away.

While the Primi Pili greeted each other with varying levels of warmth, Pullus was the Primus Pilus most affected, not by who was present, but who was not. Caesar's decision to send the 3rd Legion all the way back to Susa had been met with stiff resistance, and not just from Pullus, but on this, the Dictator for Life refused to bend with Pullus and with his Legates, all of whom objected.

"Next to the 10th, they've suffered more casualties than any other," Caesar had explained, in private, to Pullus. "And while I could leave one of the other Legions behind in Parthia, I trust the 3rd the most."

Ironically, this argument had more impact on Pullus than anything else Caesar could have said, because he immediately recognized that his general was talking less about the Legion than the man who commanded them. Of the Primi Pili, it was no secret that Sextus Spurius was Pullus' closest friend, and the two were usually of a like mind, along with Gnaeus Balbinus, the Primus Pilus of the 12th, although the 12th was staying with Caesar just like the 10th. It did not lessen the sting, but Pullus could not disagree with Caesar's characterization, remembering that it had been the 3rd who had first been confronted with the terrible weapon of naphtha as used by the Parthians during the Roman assault of Seleucia. That was a day forever etched in the memories of all the men who had been witness to the gruesome effects of this naturally occurring substance, which hadn't been lessened by the Romans' adoption of this weapon to great effect. In overall terms, this was just one of several movements that were taking place while one part of Caesar's army had been working on integrating new Pandyan *Tirones* here in Karoura, the other had been in Muziris, tasked with both repairing the ships of Caesar's massive fleet that had been damaged and building new transports, of a very specific design, and learning to operate with the reason new transports were needed in the form of armored elephants. The 3rd had been sent back to Susa, while the 14th had been summoned from Ecbatana, and although Caesar had never said as much, Pullus knew that the reason for the switch had less to do with the losses suffered by the 3rd and more to do with Caesar's concern that his nephew, and

Caesar Ascending – The Ganges

presumptive heir Gaius Octavius, might begin to entertain ideas about which Caesar wouldn't approve. In Spurius, Caesar had exactly the kind of hardened, experienced, and most importantly, trusted Primus Pilus who would stand up to Octavius should it be required. Bringing the 14th from Susa had removed the possibility that during the harsh winter campaign that Octavius had conducted against Ecbatana, the last stronghold of the once mighty Parthian Empire, if its Primus Pilus Gnaeus Figulus had sworn his loyalty not to Caesar, but to the young Octavius, it wouldn't matter. The 14th hadn't come all the way to Muziris, nor Karoura; their orders had been to remain in Bharuch, Caesar having made a provisional decision that, while he would not leave Aulus Ventidius, his oldest Legate, there as *Praetor*, his trust in Queen Hyppolita remaining faithful to the vow expected of her as a Friend and Ally of Rome only went so far. While he never spoke of it to Caesar, this was a contentious issue for Pullus, but since it was for reasons that had nothing to do with politics or military matters, he had remained silent, for which Caesar was thankful, although just as Pullus didn't bring up the subject of the Queen of Bharuch with him, Caesar never mentioned Hyppolita to Pullus. And of the two, it could be argued that it was Caesar who held the most explosive secret, that Titus Pullus had a son, born of Hyppolita in what was in essence one night of passion from a relationship that had slowly built over time, when the giant Roman had been the queen's protector and guard. In fact, Pullus would have been flabbergasted to know that, of all the hundreds of decisions, large and small, that Caesar wrestled with on a daily basis, his decision to withhold from his Primus Pilus the information that he had learned through a dispatch from Ventidius in the early days of the occupation of Pandya weighed the most heavily on his conscience. None of which was in evidence when Pullus, the other Primi Pili, and the senior Tribunes filed into the meeting room of the *Praetorium*, which had just recently been completed. As was his habit, Caesar had selected the room that served as both a meeting spot and the senior officers' mess, but it was in the former capacity that saw chairs lined up in neat rows, facing the wall opposite the one large, open window that gave a view of the mountains beyond the walls, the city of Karoura located at the base of them. Hanging from that wall where, if Pullus had to guess, there would have been some sort of tapestry, was the large map that he had only caught glimpses of during his visits. Not that it mattered; he was certain that when Caesar removed the cloth hanging down over the map at the moment was pulled back, the information Diocles had gleaned from Apollodorus would be sufficient that there would be no real surprises. Also, in another habit of his, one that Pullus and the others found irritating in the extreme, Caesar chose to let them wait for a significant amount of time before striding into the room, followed by Nedunj and Lord Maran, Pollio, Hirtius, Volusenus, and Nero, Ventidius still in transit from Bharuch. The Centurions and Tribunes all came to their feet to the position of *intente*, but as always, Caesar didn't stand on ceremony, waving them to their seats, then waiting for the four men who had entered with them to take their spots on the front row.

"I know," Caesar began with a smile that was equal parts disgust and amusement, "that you all know much of this thanks to your little birds who work in the *Praetorium*. However," he turned, and in one motion, pulled the cloth away from the map, "hopefully, I have some surprises in store."

His dramatic act elicited precisely the reaction he was hoping for, a chorus of gasps and exclamations, and while Pullus was one of them, he also offered Caesar a rueful silent salute at managing to keep what was revealed by the map a secret. Essentially, what he and the other Primi Pili were looking at was a detailed plan for the upcoming campaign in what would be the fifth year of what every man in Caesar's army now knew, and most importantly accepted, was far more ambitious than the originally stated objective of avenging the loss of Marcus Crassus and the seven Legion standards to the Parthian Empire. An empire that was now in effect the two newest Roman provinces, Parthia Superior and Parthia Inferior, run by Caesar's two nephews, Quintus Pedius in Merv and Octavius in Susa. The fact that the army was now more than two thousand five hundred miles from Parthia was the most potent sign that Caesar's ambitions were far grander than any man who had loaded on the transports in Brundisium in the days after the Ides of March had suspected; now, the only real argument among themselves was which of them realized it first. And, with Caesar's unveiling of this map, the senior officers now saw what some of them hoped would be the culmination of this endeavor, although at least one of them, in Pullus and thanks to Scribonius, had his doubts.

Caesar waited until the small uproar died down before, picking up a slender rod that served as his pointer and pointing to the spot on the map that marked Muziris as he began, "As you can see, I've created a series of symbols that I'm sure you can all see now represent each Legion that's currently encamped there." Pausing just long enough to see heads nodding, he moved the pointer slightly to the right and a bit above, "Just as I've done with the Legions here in Karoura."

"We can see that, Caesar," Gnaeus Clustuminus, the Primus Pilus of the 8th Legion, interrupted, "but what are those arrows and what do they mean?"

Because of Pullus' feelings towards his counterpart, he was forced to drop his head so that he wouldn't betray his amusement at what was coming, and he was rewarded by Caesar snapping, "If you hadn't interrupted, you'd know already, Clustuminus!" There were snickers at this, which Caesar allowed in what all present knew was a further rebuke to Clustuminus, who was wise enough to accept it. Once it quieted, Caesar returned his attention to the map as he explained, "These arrows represent the movements of this army in what will be the first part of this year's campaign." He moved the pointer to the arrow that represented the western coast until the line reached the southernmost tip of India, whereupon the line curved around, terminating at the island of Taprobane. "Under the command of Asinius Pollio, the 5th, 6th, 8th, 28th, and 30th Legions will travel by coastal waters to the island, hopefully bringing the fifty elephants that the Muziris Legions have been training with, then sail upriver and land at Palaesimundum, the Greek trading colony, construct a semi-permanent camp that can house at least ten Cohorts." For the first time, Caesar turned and indicated Nedunj as he said, "Once we've done that, Taprobane will become part of the Pandyan kingdom, who will remain a trusted Friend and Ally of Rome."

"To what end, Caesar?"

This time, Caesar didn't admonish the man who interrupted, which, between Caesar's lack of reaction and the identity of the man who posed the question alerted Pullus and the others that this was prearranged, another annoying habit of their general.

"Taprobane is going to serve the same purpose as Caesarea, Harmozeia, Barbaricum, Bharuch, and Muziris, Hirtius," Caesar explained. "It will serve as the most forward supply base for the army and will be as the last transshipping point for all of our supplies. Minus, of course those supplies that will be needed for our garrisons in Bharuch and elsewhere."

"I wonder for what," Balbinus, who was sitting next to Pullus muttered.

"Now, I'm sure that you all are wondering why we're making these preparations." Caesar's face didn't register anything that would suggest he had overheard Balbinus, but Pullus was certain that he had, as was Balbinus, who visibly reddened. Turning back to the map, Caesar continued, "But before I get to that, I'm going to talk about what will be happening with the Legions in Karoura. The 10th, 12th, 21st, 22nd, and 25th who are here in Karoura will be marching with myself in command once Legate Ventidius arrives with the 15th, and," he turned to offer a nod to the young monarch, "with King Nedunj as my second in command overall, and the commander of the Pandyan complement that will be marching with us that consists of five thousand infantry, five hundred regular cavalry, and one hundred armored elephants. Our task is simple in its goal." Moving the pointer to the east of Karoura and the inverted V's that the Romans used to denote mountains, he went on, "We're going to be marching to the city of Madoura (Madurai), which is in a disputed area of the border between Chola and Pandya, and it has been under Cholan control for a decade, with several raids and attacks originating from the city by their forces. And, since Pandya is now a Friend and Ally of Rome, we're going to help King Nedunj secure the eastern border of his kingdom from the threat posed by this enemy. Depending on how King Karikala responds to our proposal, we will either pass it by or take it and return it to Pandyan control."

Caesar Ascending – The Ganges

This part of the campaign was obvious by the symbols, small rectangles with the numbers of the Legions contained within each one, and the arrow that pointed to a dot that, while Pullus could see there was writing on the map, was too far away to read, although he assumed it was the name Madoura.

That wasn't what prompted Pullus to raise his hand to ask, "What are those other arrows for, Caesar?"

Nobody would ever know whether Caesar's completely different reaction to essentially the same kind of interruption by Clustuminus was due to Caesar's dislike of Clustuminus, or his favor for Pullus, but instead of chastising the Primus Pilus, Caesar offered him an approving nod.

"I'm happy to see that one of you is paying attention," he said, prompting a glare at Pullus' back by Clustuminus. "But to answer your question, Pullus, those are two possible actions that I won't decide on until after we march to Madoura. If," he pointed to the arrow that moved directly from the west to the eastern coast of India, the end of which terminated directly across the narrow channel between the island and India, "things go as we expect and King Karikala accepts my offer of payment, we'll take a rest day at Madoura, then we will march to the coast, where we'll be met by the fleet carrying the other Legions who, presumably, will have accomplished their own mission of erecting a permanent camp at Palaesimundum and improving the docks to make it more capable of sustaining us in the manner of Caesarea and the other waypoints. Once this linkage has been accomplished, we will continue with the next part of the campaign. But," suddenly, he turned to Nedunj, "I'm going to ask the King to explain what we might have to do once we join the two parts of the army."

Nedunj had clearly been expecting this, standing immediately and taking the pointer.

Addressing the officers in Greek, which, while heavily accented, was clearly understandable, he began, "There is one potential…complication. Before my father's death, he had been working in secret to destroy the alliance the Chola (Kariaiyar) have had with the tribe to their north, the Andhra, that has been in place since long before I was born. Just before he left with King Abhiraka to…" suddenly, his voice trailed off, unsure how to describe the fact that Puddapandyan had marched north with Abhiraka with the express goal of destroying the very officers seated before him, along with the men they commanded. Finally, he simply decided to move on, "...we received a courier from the King of the Andhra, a man named Satakarni, who recently succeeded his father, also named Satakarni, signaling that he was not opposed to the proposal put forward by my father. Then," Nedunj held both hands out from his sides, palms upward, in one of the few gestures that the Romans had learned they shared with the Pandyans, and according to Barhinder, all of those with whom the Tamil tongue was native, which emphasized his words, "my father was killed, I am now King, and I do not know whether the Andhra king will honor this agreement."

"If he does not," Caesar interjected, "then we will act accordingly."

Nedunj took this as his cue to move the pointer to a spot above and slightly to the right of the dot designating Madoura, moving the tip along the line that had been drawn on the map that stopped at another dot.

"This is Uraiyur," he explained. "This is the capital of the Chola kingdom." Turning to address his audience, he said, "I have spent a great deal of time there when I was a hostage, after Karikala's son Divakar, the crown prince of the Chola, spent time here in Karoura. I know the city well, if it is necessary to take the city."

The manner in which Nedunj was behaving, Pullus had the strong impression that the young king viewed the taking of Uraiyur as a foregone conclusion, an impression that was instantly confirmed when Nedunj moved his pointer to another dot farther north on the map.

"This is the Andhra capital of Garthapuri. It is situated on the southern bank of the Cabirus (Krishna) River. I have never seen the city myself," he turned to face the other officers to stress this, "but I have it on reliable authority that it is well-fortified, much like here."

Nedunj turned back to Caesar, handing him the pointer as the general picked back up, "If it turns out to be necessary to march on Uraiyur, then once we take the city, we're going to

Caesar Ascending – The Ganges

decide whether or not to march back south to the spot where we know that we can land the fleet to load up the Legions with me, or if possible, scout for a similarly suitable area further north and directly east of Uraiyur."

"And, what? These Chola bastards are going to let us march through their kingdom to get to this Garthaporro place?"

Pullus was certain just by Caesar's reaction that this wasn't a preplanned question, but while he glared at Vibius Batius, the Primus Pilus of the 5th and the oldest man in that post, he didn't hesitate to answer.

"That," he said icily, "depends on whether or not their king decides to accept my proposal for a very generous payment to allow us safe passage. Given the amount of gold I'm offering, I believe that he will accept it."

"Then what?" Batius asked flatly, arms crossed.

Then, we sail to," at this, Caesar turned back to the map, and in one motion, swept the pointer up to the top of the map, "the mouth of the Ganges."

Just as Pullus knew by Caesar's reaction that neither of Batius' questions were prearranged; he also knew that every single Primus Pilus had been forewarned that this would be the ultimate objective, yet even so, there was a stunned silence that lasted so long that he began wondering if perhaps he was mistaken.

"How far is it from here to Taprobane?" This question came from Felix of the 6th, one of the Legions still in Muziris.

"Three hundred miles by water."

This hadn't come from Caesar, and all eyes went to Cartufenus, who had been the one to speak up.

"And, how do you know this, Cartufenus?" Caesar asked mildly, but neither Cartufenus nor the others were fooled, knowing that Caesar did want to know.

"Fortunate guess, Caesar," Cartufenus said cheerfully, and while he was relieved, Pullus knew to stifle his smile.

"You need to spend some time in the shantytown then, Cartufenus," Caesar shot back acidly. "You're certain to come up Venus with every roll if Fortuna is blessing you that much." Then, in an unmistakable message, Caesar glared at Pullus, although he only said, "But, you are correct. Normally, this would be a bit more than a three-day voyage, but given the new transports for the elephants, I am calculating that it will be five days, as long as the weather holds. And, those Legions who will be involved will never be out of sight of land."

"And how far is it from Taprobane to the mouth of the Ganges?" Balbinus asked quietly.

"By our best estimate," Caesar answered without hesitation, "more than a thousand."

Pullus, offering silent thanks to Diocles who had helped him calculate the voyage time under the best of circumstances, spoke up.

"If everything goes well, that voyage will take a bit more than a month. And," he continued, "let's say that it takes at least a month for our part of the army to march through this Cholan territory," he had to squint to read it, "but if the Cholan king turns down your offer and we have to stop in Madoura to attack it, add another one to two weeks from the moment we arrive and perform a survey then come up with a plan for taking the city, executing it, then rest and reorganize. From there, depending on the kind of resistance we might face, it might take a week or more to march on Uraiyur. For the sake of argument, let's say it takes another two weeks to take Uraiyur. If that's the case, it puts us into Quintilis at the earliest to reach the mouth of the Ganges." He hesitated then, because he understood he was running a risk of angering Caesar, but he still asked, "Have you determined how far from the mouth of the Ganges Palibothra is?"

"No, Pullus." Caesar's tone was abrupt, sending the clear message that he didn't appreciate this question, no matter from whom it came. "We haven't determined that yet. But," he added in a clear reproof, "your assessment of how long it will take is based on the idea that we're not going to effect a landing anywhere along that thousand miles." Turning his attention back to the larger group, he warned them, "Remember that we know very little of the eastern part of India, so we can't discount the possibility that there's a kingdom that's powerful enough, and with a strong enough navy to block our passage. Which is why," he turned and indicated Aulus Hirtius, "Hirtius will be paralleling us with the entire cavalry along the coast after the

Caesar Ascending – The Ganges

army is reunited and as we sail northward." There was a rustling murmur among the officers, and Caesar waited before he said, "I have also decided that they're not to penetrate more than twenty miles from the coast, and that they're not to initiate any kind of contact with any natives they come into contact with, only doing what's necessary to defend themselves if they're attacked. And in the event that their passage is blocked, either by mountains or hostile cities and it would mean they have to go more than twenty miles inland, instead, they're going to board the ships that are reserved for the cavalry that will be sailing with us." Pausing again to allow this to be digested, he stressed what he knew would be the most important thing to the men of the ranks. "And, just as we did on our voyage here, we'll land every few days so the men can spend a night ashore in camp."

Pullus wasn't alone in not caring for Caesar, who was usually very precise in such things, using the term "few" instead of a specific number, but none of them were willing to broach the subject now. This, he thought, is something that we'll have to settle after we take care of this business with the Chola, and he suspected strongly, the Andhra, although his sense was that it was the Chola who were the main cause of concern for the young Pandyan king. It was true he didn't know Nedunj all that well, but what he did know was that, despite his youth, he was shrewd...and he was ambitious, so it made sense that, as long as he had the strength of six Roman Legions to bolster the relatively small force of Pandyans that would be marching with them, he would take the opportunity presented to him. Which meant that even if this King Karikala agreed to allow safe payment in exchange for a peaceful transit, Nedunj would probably do whatever he could to undermine the agreement, or more likely in Pullus' thinking, claim that he had uncovered some sort of treachery by the Chola king that would provide the pretext to attack. Frankly, this didn't worry Pullus overmuch, because he was equally certain that, if this was the case, Caesar would require Nedunj to do the brunt of the fighting with his Pandyans, deeming it an internal matter between these two rival kingdoms who had been enemies long before Rome arrived. And, he allowed, it would be a relatively safe way to blood the newest *Tirones* in his own ranks, their Pandyan countrymen who had taken the opportunity offered by Rome to march with them, receiving what was determined to be almost twice the yearly pay of what a man could expect to make carrying a spear and wicker shield for Pandya. Granted, the Pandyans only kept a small full-time military that was, more than anything, a royal bodyguard that served as a sort of status symbol among the tribes of the southern part of India, save for the elephants, which had been trained and bred for war and were used for nothing else, he wasn't excessively concerned about Nedunj objecting to his subjects accepting Roman silver. This was especially true once he and the other Primi Pili learned that the men Nedunj was clearly willing to allow to enlist belonged to what the Romans had learned was a caste that was roughly equivalent to their own Head Count, although thanks to Nedunj's queen, Pullus had learned from Aarunya that it was far more complicated than that, that there were further subdivisions within a caste that were strictly observed. Realizing his mind had been wandering, Pullus jerked his attention back just in time to hear what was, in the immediate sense, the most important information.

"My part of the army will be departing a week from today," Caesar announced. "Legate Pollio and the fleet will be departing two days later to give them time for the loading process." Putting down the pointer, Caesar signaled that the meeting was over by saying, "You officers who will be departing with the fleet are free to return to Muziris now. There's a barge waiting that will carry you downstream. Before you do, talk to Apollodorus. He has your individual orders, and your loading order. That is all."

Then, again as was his habit, Caesar wasted no more time, turning and exiting the room, leaving the Primi Pili to talk among themselves, Pullus among them. He was only partly paying attention to Balbinus as his fellow Primus Pilus complained that a week wasn't enough time, although even in his distraction, Pullus could tell that Balbinus was doing this more out of habit. What was foremost in his mind was realizing that he would have to pay that visit to someone, and it was one that he dreaded. However, he'd given his word; most importantly, it was to whom he had given it that meant that he actually didn't return to camp to alert his Centurions first. Instead, he walked the short distance from the new *Praetorium* to the residence inside the city walls, entering through the eastern gate, and while it was not nearly as large as the royal palace, Pullus had learned that it had belonged to the dead Lord Alangudi. It was far too large for the children, at least if one didn't count the slaves, along with the men of Pullus' Legion who were the only ones allowed access to the pair. Ostensibly, his men were guards, but fairly quickly, it turned out that they were much more than that, more often serving as playmates. That Pullus was the sole arbiter of who stood watch, and he only used men he knew had children of their own, was one of those things that his Centurions knew better than to question, and even Caesar wisely ignored, although he was aware. This had surprised Pullus, although he didn't ask why, and even if he had, Caesar wouldn't have told him, that he understood the connection and obligation Pullus would feel towards what the Primus Pilus didn't know were the half-siblings of his infant son back in Bharuch, because of a promise that Pullus had made to Queen Hyppolita. On this day, the Legionary standing outside the front entrance was from the First Century of his Third Cohort, and one of the relatively few remaining of the original *dilectus*, although Tiberius Caelius had never risen above the rank of Gregarius.

Pullus returned his salute, then asked Caelius, "Where's Pallus?"

Caelius grinned, showing his veteran status by the number of missing teeth, which to this point Pullus had managed to avoid. "He's inside, Primus Pilus. Playing ball with the boy and trying not to get beaten like a drum!"

Pullus laughed, having suspected this was the case, and if he felt a bit smug about his inspiration in using men with children of their own to watch over his charges, he felt he could be excused. Walking into the vestibule, he heard the sound of children's laughter, and as it always did, it elicited a number of emotions in him, although one would never have been able to tell by his demeanor. The fact that both of these children were about the same age as his own son and daughter would have been, had they survived, was a source of pain of which only Diocles was aware. Despite this reality, this was always one of the best parts of his daily routine, except this time, he was aware that there might be childish tears, and he paused for a moment before he stepped into the large room that, at the imperious demand of both inhabitants, had been cleared of furniture to enable what was in effect a large play area. Gregarius Pallus was standing a few feet from the doorway, but he had his back turned to Pullus, and when the other occupant in the room saw Pallus' Primus Pilus, Pullus winked at him in a silent signal that was immediately understood.

Making a show of moving silently, Pullus stopped immediately behind Pallus, then growled, "Why aren't you at your post, Gregarius?"

The manner in which Pallus jumped was humorous enough, but his startled yelp made the boy burst out laughing as Pallus whirled around, mouth open, although he shut it quickly enough.

Interpreting Pullus' expression correctly and understanding this was being done for the fun of it, he rapped out, "Because I was upholding the honor of the 10th, Primus Pilus! I was challenged by young Master Bhumaka to a game of bounceball and he cast great aspersions on the 10th!"

Pullus looked over at the boy in mock indignation, while the boy, who had just turned eleven, beamed back at him.

"Is this true?" Pullus demanded, folding his arms and giving the boy a mock scowl. "Are you saying things about my Legion?"

Pullus was speaking in Greek, but while it had not been a goal, he had been impressed by how quickly both Bhumaka and his younger sister Anuja had managed to pick up Latin, although Pullus had been forced to admonish some of his men about the choice of words they were instructing them in, particularly Bhumaka.

Consequently, he was not altogether surprised when Bhumaka answered in Latin, "I was not! I was only talking about Pallus! He throws like a girl!"

Despite his best effort, Pullus couldn't maintain his demeanor, and he burst out laughing, turning to look at Pallus, who was the only one not laughing, although he was fighting a smile. Before the Gregarius could say anything, Pullus dismissed him with a nod, offering a wink as he did so, then turned back to Bhumaka.

"Where's your sister? I heard her laughing."

"We are in here, Centurion Pullus."

He didn't know why he should be, but he was surprised to hear the voice of the Queen of Pandya, Aarunya. Bhumaka led him into the next room, which was furnished with couches in the Pandyan style, while two slaves provided a breeze with large fans, where he found the young Queen and her little sister. While Aarunya was wearing a silk gown, it was cut in the Pandyan style, which unlike Bharuch, didn't require either a head covering or a veil, and the material was more revealing than those worn by the people of northern India who had been so heavily influenced by the Macedonian conqueror and his generals. However, it was how she was sitting cross-legged on the floor facing Anuja as they were teasing a kitten with a feather tied to a thread that had taken Pullus some time to get accustomed to, since the young Queen was at least as frequent a visitor as he was, but he had learned this informal air was part of her nature.

Rising to her feet, she returned Pullus' bow, something that he felt a bit ridiculous doing, but his personal feelings for Nedunj's Queen, who wasn't even nineteen yet, made it easier and beginning with, "Your Highness," he then turned, and with a mock gravity, made the same bow to Anuja, "Princess Anuja." It had become something of a game, but it was also one Pullus had determined was a matter of some seriousness for Anuja, as she practiced the skills expected of her as a member of a royal house. And, given how this unlikely relationship had started, Pullus was only too happy to indulge these children of Hyppolita. Pointing to the kitten, he asked, "Is this a new member of your household?"

"Yes," the younger girl replied in Greek, nodding happily as she looked at her big sister with shining eyes. "Aarunya brought her just today!"

"A she?" Pullus looked over at Bhumaka and said, "You're even more outnumbered by women than you were, Prince

Bhumaka."

Pullus could not help laughing at the face the boy made as he said glumly, "I know. If it was not for Pallus, Caelius, and the others, I'd have nobody to play with." He lifted his head to look up at Pullus as he added accusingly, "And you have not played with me for more than a week, Centurion!"

Although he was mostly amused, Pullus also wasn't normally willing to tolerate the use of the kind of imperious tone that, through no fault of his own, Bhumaka had been allowed to employ to all but his parents; there was only so far a Primus Pilus of Rome would bend for anyone from a kingdom conquered by Caesar, even royalty. However, he was acutely aware of the reason he was there.

"I do apologize, young Prince. And, while I can't do it right now, what if I promise to come back just after dark, and I'll help you with what we've been working on?"

He was relieved to see that Bhumaka eagerly agreed to this, but he also knew that he was only postponing the inevitable. I'm taking the coward's way out, routed by an eleven-year-old, he grumbled to himself, but he still left the room.

When he did so, to his surprise, the young Queen said, "May I walk out with you, Centurion? I must return to the palace, and it is on your way."

This was not exactly true, and in fact, it was out of his way, but Pullus knew better than to argue the point, so he managed as gracefully as possible to assure her he was delighted.

She waited until they passed Caelius and Pallus, who for their part were confused about how to behave and whether they should salute their Primus Pilus, or bow to this foreign queen, ally as she may have been. Pullus instantly saw this was not lost on her as she gave him an amused glance when they decided to salute him.

"I think, Centurion," she said teasingly, and in a manner so reminiscent of Aarunya's mother that it caused Pullus' heart to feel as if it had missed a beat, "they made the wise choice in saluting you."

"You're right," he agreed quickly, in the hope that nothing in his demeanor betrayed him, and he was smiling down at her. "I would have striped them good later."

Caesar Ascending – The Ganges

She laughed at this, but it was the kind of polite laugh that, Pullus supposed, queens must learn.

Nevertheless, in another echo of her mother, Aarunya got immediately to the point, "My husband told me that you will be leaving soon. Is that why you stopped by?"

There was no point in denying it, and Pullus didn't try, replying simply, "Yes, Your Highness. I'm not going to have time after today, but I just didn't want to suddenly disappear."

"You really care about my brother and sister, do you not, Centurion?"

It was unexpected, certainly, but he tried to sound offhand when he replied, without looking at her, "You know that it was my Legion who...was with your mother after your father came here to Pandya. And," he shrugged, "she asked me to keep an eye on them."

"My mother speaks very highly of you, Centurion," Aarunya said soberly. They were walking down the street, the pair of Pandyan guards of the royal bodyguard, some of the few who actually wore mail armor, trailing several paces behind. Since he wasn't looking down at her, he was alerted by a slight change in her tone as she said with a casualness that he didn't believe, "In fact, I received a letter from her just yesterday."

It took effort, but Pullus managed not to come to a stop, but he couldn't catch himself from looking down at her in surprise.

"Oh? And what did she say?" He did his best to sound as if he was just being polite. "Is she well?"

He was surprised when, instead of replying, Aarunya laughed, and at his inquiring glance, she informed him, "She asked the same thing about you, Centurion. She wanted to know if you were well."

"Oh," he said, not really knowing what else to offer.

Aarunya kept gazing up at him as they walked, and he didn't need to look at her to feel the intensity of her gaze as she studied him. Out of the corner of his vision, he saw her open her mouth, but he was completely unprepared to hear what came next.

"You are in love with my mother, are you not, Centurion?" This shocked Pullus to his core, yet it was a shade compared to what came next, even before he could offer any kind of response, as Aarunya sighed, "Because I suspect that my mother has...feelings for you, Centurion. Feelings that are more than just the respect and regard she says she holds for your honorable treatment of her during her captivity."

She stopped then, and Pullus recognized he had to say something, but all he could manage was, "I...I respect your mother a great deal. And," he allowed, "for the most part, I enjoyed our time together. Given the circumstances, of course," he added hastily. Under her steady upward gaze, he couldn't fight the feeling of being entrapped somehow, yet nothing in his experience with this young woman led him to believe she was using some sort of guile to get him to admit to something that she could use against him. Finally, he continued, "And I know that she loved your father, the King. And," in this, he was not only confident, he was forced to ignore the stab of disquiet it caused him for this lie, "she was faithful to him and his cause to the very end of his life."

"Was she?"

Aarunya had come to a stop again, except this time, she had maneuvered herself so that she was essentially blocking Pullus' path, close enough that she had to crane her neck, yet her gaze never wavered from his face as she repeated, "Was she faithful to my father, Centurion?"

"Absolutely." Pullus hoped that his lack of hesitation would convince her, but she didn't budge.

Her tone turned thoughtful, however, as she seemingly mused aloud, "As I have grown older, I have realized some things, Centurion Pullus, and one of them is that it is possible to love more than one person. And," she suddenly began blinking back tears, "I cannot imagine how lonely it must have been for my mother with all of her children here in Pandya." Shockingly, she reached out and placed a hand on his chest, and the touch startled Pullus, although it went more deeply than that. "We will never speak of this again, Centurion, but I wanted to thank you for the comfort...and the love you have shown, not just to my mother, but to her children."

Am I going to start fucking crying? Right here? This was the thought that shoved everything else out from Pullus' mind,

Caesar Ascending – The Ganges

so that it took all he could do to mumble something that he hoped would satisfy her. Then, on her tiptoes, she still had to pull his head down to kiss him on the cheek.

"I will make an offering to the gods of the Pandya, of course, but I was wondering, Centurion, is there one of your gods you wish me to make an offering for your safety? After all," she reminded him, and her tone had returned to a more teasing tone, "your safety will help keep my King husband safe as well."

Pullus did smile, both from the bantering tone and the relief he felt that this unexpected ordeal appeared over, but he actually considered the question before he answered with a shrug, "Mars, of course. It's our god of war. But personally, I also like to hedge my bets with offerings to Fortuna."

"Fortuna?" She frowned as she tried to recall what she knew from the thousands of deities that were an everyday part of their world that was so much more intertwined now with the arrival of Caesar. Her expression cleared, "Ah. She is your goddess of…prosperity?"

"Close enough." He laughed. Sensing it was the appropriate time to depart, he gave her a bow that, if not perfectly performed, was honestly given. "I appreciate your prayers, Your Highness. And, I'm happy to hear that your mother is well." He paused, then thought, Why not? She clearly knows something happened, which was how he heard himself say to Aarunya, "And the next time you communicate with your mother, please tell her she's in my thoughts."

Before she could say anything in response, he turned about and walked away; marched away would be more accurate, Aarunya thought with a mixture of amusement, and some regret. She had been *so* close to imparting a piece of information that, while it hadn't come from her mother, was from a source she trusted. This was what prompted her to call out to him, and for a moment, she thought he would pretend not to hear, but he did stop, turning reluctantly.

"I almost forgot, Centurion," she had to raise her voice a bit more than she cared to, but it didn't stop her from informing him, "my mother also told me that the babe of Lady Amodini is healthy and well. I suspect that this might please someone you

49

know."

This, Pullus immediately understood, was nothing short of the truth, and it was with a combination of relief and gratitude that he assured her, "I'll let that someone know, Your Highness. Thank you."

After he resumed walking away, Aarunya stood there, yet she knew that she couldn't bring herself to do it. It was, after all, not even secondhand information, yet somehow she knew it was true. And, while she trusted Titus Pullus, he was still a Roman, and his loyalty to Caesar was well known. Given what she knew of these people, she could easily imagine that the huge Centurion would feel duty bound to report the possibility that he had fathered a child, born of another Queen like herself, and her mother in the bargain. The complications that could arise from that, and the danger it would put her mother in, those were uppermost in Aarunya's mind, and was the source of the confliction of emotions that had been swirling through her ever since the merchant, whose name she knew only because her mother had mentioned it in one of her own missives, had told her that there were two infants in the royal palace of Bharuch, and not just one. She did find it odd, when she thought about it, that she didn't blame either her mother or the Roman responsible, but she had ascribed this to the turmoil and massive upheaval to all of their lives that had arrived with a fleet of Roman ships, led by a man that, even in her somewhat limited contact with him, she understood was as singular a person as the Macedonian Alexander, and if her husband was to be believed, was probably Alexander's superior. It never occurred to her that Caesar already knew of her burden, and it was destined to remain that way for the rest of their respective days.

Pullus paused only long enough to stop at the quarters of the Fifth Section, First Century of his Second Cohort to relay to the newly promoted Sergeant Gaius Porcinus the news that Aarunya had imparted to him, although he did make sure to have Porcinus come outside to tell him.

"And wipe that stupid grin off your face before you go back in, Gaius." Pullus' voice was a growl, but he was smiling as broadly as his nephew. "You don't want those bastards in there knowing your business."

"Yes, Primus Pilus," Porcinus drew himself up, still grinning. "I understand and will obey." Then, as Pullus had expected, the grin faded as the full import of what should have been a wonderful piece of news began to mesh with the knowledge of what lay in his immediate future. Sighing, he said, "And, we're about to leave. Only the gods know where we'll be a few months from now."

It was, as Pullus well knew, the simple truth, but while he sympathized with his nephew, in his mind, this was the kind of thing best stuck away in some cupboard in the brain and only taken out on rare occasions.

He didn't say anything about this, simply nodding and telling Porcinus, "You're going to be hearing from Scribonius shortly. But," he grinned again, "if I were you, I'd go put a boot in your boys' asses now and get a jump on everyone else. And," he reminded Porcinus, "you don't…"

"I don't let them know it came from you, but I let them *think* it came from you," Porcinus nodded in acknowledgment of the one thing that his uncle had drilled into him from his first days as a *Tirone*.

It was a delicate balancing act; certainly, being the nephew of the Primus Pilus of the 10th Legion had some advantages, but it was a *gladius* that cut both ways, because there would be men who would view that fact with jealousy, looking for any sign that Porcinus was being given preferential treatment. Given that Gaius Porcinus was, by his very nature, one of the most likeable men, not just in his Century and Cohort, but the entire Legion, had certainly helped, yet even more than that, Pullus had gone out of his way to be more than fair with Porcinus. If this meant that, especially early on, Porcinus got more of the *cac* duties than other *Tirones*, it had paid dividends so that, when Scribonius, on his own, had promoted Porcinus into the post after the reorganization outside Bharuch, there was little comment made, and what there was could have been characterized as the normal grumbling of men who felt they were better qualified, which was a common occurrence.

With this duty done, Pullus had entered the Legion office and, within a matter of a hundred heartbeats, the routine that the men of the 10th had settled into was shattered and suddenly replaced by a new one. Fortunately, it was another to which they were accustomed, one of almost constant motion that, to an outside observer would appear as if it was nothing more than men being sent, usually on a run or at least quick trot, in random directions performing some unspecified task that seemed to have no purpose, but would always end in the same result. At the specified time, on the specified day, the men of the 10th Legion would be ready to march, either aboard ships or on foot, to whatever point Caesar directed. The fact that this was true with every Legion meant that the huge camp outside of Karoura resembled something akin to one of the huge ant mounds that were yet another feature of this strange land, after it had been kicked over. With a Legion, and officers, as experienced as the 10th, Pullus' main job was to be seen, clutching his *vitus* behind his back, always with a frown, and while he did not use it often, when he did, it was to maximum effect, something that every single man had learned, down to the newest Pandyan *Tiros*. In his meeting with the Pili Priores, Pullus had spent a substantial portion of his time stressing to his Pili Priores of the third line, the 8th, 9th, and 10th, that the new additions should be spared the *vitus*. He did feel a bit foolish in doing so, especially when it came to the Octus Pilus Prior, his former tutor Quintus Ausonius, although he was universally known as Cyclops, and the oldest Centurion in the 10th, but while his main target was the Decimus Pilus Prior Gnaeus Nasica, he didn't think it wise to single him out.

"They're already worn down as it is," was how he had put it. "Adjusting to the *hamatae*, all the new commands and training, the strangeness of it all means that we're not going to be doing any good striping them if they're walking around confused by all that's happening." It was to Scribonius he directed a smile while summoning a name from their past. "At least there's no Doughboy to bother us."

As he hoped, this made Scribonius erupt in laughter, and he wasn't alone, since every Pilus Prior, with the exception of Cyclops, had been part of the original *dilectus* of the 10th, and they all knew about the man who was still the most inept Tribune with whom they had ever been inflicted.

Caesar Ascending – The Ganges

Dismissing his officers, Pullus spent the rest of the day doing his bit, but when he saw the bottom of the sun touching the horizon, he knew he couldn't delay it any longer, especially having learned how much more quickly the sun vanished in this part of the world. It had been just one of the many disconcerting things that not just Pullus, but every Roman in Caesar's vast army had been confronted with as they journeyed south. They had become, if not accustomed, at least inured to the heat and the humidity, thanks in a large part to the switch to cotton tunics, and much to the surprise of Pullus, the change of diet that had been suggested by the Queen of Bharuch. The fact that the sun didn't rise but just appeared, and didn't set, but simply vanished, was something that he was still struggling with, so he found himself hurrying out of the camp, heading towards his promised appointment with an impatient eleven-year-old boy, and he was surprised at the feelings he was experiencing as he realized that he would truly miss Bhumaka and Anuja. Hard on the heels of that was the memory of his last conversation with Aarunya, and he did wonder if they would find themselves in a situation where they could continue their conversation in some privacy, because while he couldn't say why, he was certain she had wanted to say something else. In fact, he was preparing himself to see that she was back at the residence, but she wasn't. Pallus and Caelius had been relieved by new men, this time from the same Century, and Pullus stopped with them to relay their new orders, ignoring their expressions of consternation at the thought that they would be forced to catch up to their comrades, inevitably at the expense of their sleeping time, which would be in precious short supply for the next few days. It wasn't that Pullus was unsympathetic, but it was part and parcel of a life under the standard, and when it came to lost sleep, Titus Pullus in his role of Primus Pilus had lost more sleep than any other man in his Legion.

"Prince Bhumaka," he called out after he entered. "Here I am, just as promised."

The large open room was illuminated by oil lamps, which Pullus and his fellow Romans hadn't thought unusual; it was only after some time spent in the southernmost regions where the Greek influence wasn't so heavily felt that these lamps were almost exclusively used by wealthy or royal Pandyans. He was about to open his mouth to repeat his call when he heard the patter of footsteps, but his ears told him that, contrary to his normal habit of bursting into the room at a full run, Bhumaka seemed in no hurry. It was when he appeared in the doorway, and the light of the lamp across from him on the opposite wall picked up the reflection of the track of tears that told Pullus the story. Pluto's cock, he groaned to himself, someone told him.

"You are leaving."

It was a statement of fact, not a question, Pullus understood, but it was the sight of the boy's chin quivering that struck him hardest, and for the first time, he realized that Hyppolita's son viewed him as more than just an overgrown playmate.

In appreciation of this, Pullus crossed the room and knelt down so that he could look the boy in the eye as he replied simply, "Yes, Prince Bhumaka. I'm leaving. The army is marching soon, and I'm afraid this will be our last time together."

"For how long?"

Pullus knew that Bhumaka was trying his best to be the young prince he was, and that he shouldn't indulge in such childish things as tears, but he still was only eleven years old. And, Pullus suddenly realized, he had experienced more turmoil and heartache in the previous year than most children his age. Bhumaka had been inconsolable for a month when he learned of the death of his father in his failed attempt to take Bharuch and had understandably been hostile to any Roman. But, in the manner of children, over time, his curiosity had overcome his anger, so that now here he was, crying because one of the men who conquered his father's kingdom was leaving. It was, Pullus reflected, a truly strange world sometimes.

Aloud, he answered honestly, "I don't know, Bhumaka. But," despite his resolve, he hesitated, bracing himself for an outpouring of childish anguish, "it's possible that we might not come back to Karoura." The widening of the boy's eyes gave him enough of a warning for him to add, "But that doesn't mean that we won't see each other again! Who knows?" He shrugged his huge shoulders. "Maybe King Nedunj will miss your sister so much that he summons her to come to him, and I don't see her leaving you two behind."

He did feel a bit guilty at the rapidly dawning hope on the boy's face, but he told himself it was certainly *possible* that this might happen. It was a dangerous thought, but not just for Bhumaka, because following immediately behind this thought was one that Pullus had refused to entertain, the idea that Caesar might return the army to Bharuch once he had achieved his goal of besting Alexander in reaching the Ganges and conquering Palibothra. In his bones, he didn't think this was much of a possibility, although most of this came from Scribonius, who was absolutely certain in his conviction that even this wouldn't be enough for Caesar.

At this moment, however, what was important was that this cheered Bhumaka, who wiped his face on his sleeve, then asked eagerly, "What do you want to show me this time, Centurion?"

"Well, I was thinking about that," Pullus replied. "And I was wondering if you would settle for a story instead?"

"A story?" Bhumaka echoed, and Pullus hid his smile at the sight of the tugging emotions, playing across the boy's face. "What kind of story?"

"A story about my first battle," Pullus answered. And, as he expected, this was something to which the boy instantly agreed, another reminder to Pullus of the bloodthirstiness of little boys who dream of being warriors. Well, let's see how you feel about it after I tell you, he thought with amusement, although aloud, he said, "Let's go sit down, shall we?"

Moving towards the nearest couch, Pullus was completely unprepared for Bhumaka to command, "Wait! I will be right back!"

Before the Centurion could stop him, the boy scampered away, but before he had the chance to grumble about the delay, Bhumaka reappeared, and it was the fact that he was leading his sister by the hand that caused Pullus to consider making a hasty retreat. That they were both nestled against him before he made his decision essentially sealed his fate.

"The Centurion is going to tell us about his very first battle," Bhumaka informed Anuja, with all the authority of an older brother. "So you must promise not to interrupt!"

"I do *not* interrupt!" Anuja protested.

"Yes you do! You do it all the time! When Aarunya is telling us a story, you..."

"I'm not going to tell either of you if you keep on like this," Pullus spoke up sternly, which had the desired effect. Then, it was his time to talk, and he wondered, How do I do this? Before he gave it any more thought, he began, "I wasn't that much older than you, Prince Bhumaka. I was only sixteen."

"That is only five years from now!" Bhumaka exclaimed, then his expression changed immediately as he realized that he had interrupted.

"That's right," Pullus allowed, then admonished the boy, "but that's the last time you can interrupt. Agreed?" The boy nodded, and Pullus resumed, "As I was saying, I was very young. But I was *very* confident. I had always done the best in training. And," he indicated himself, "I was always bigger and stronger than everyone else."

Very quickly, not only the children but Pullus were absorbed in his story, as he relived that day, when they assaulted a town in Hispania, a town whose name he never knew. Pullus had no intention of relating the horrors that he experienced for what would be the first of literally hundreds of times; instead, he talked about the humorous moments, starting with the Tribune that he had been reminded of earlier in the day, rewarded by childish giggles as he imitated Doughboy's high-pitched voice. Very deliberately, he didn't linger on their approach in *testudo*, his first such experience under missile assault from Lusitani slingers, when he saw his first comrade slain, nor did he talk about the sight of his first Optio, Aulus Vinicius, covered in boiling pitch, still ascending the ladder while dead on his feet. Instead, he talked about how, in his eagerness and haste to prove his valor, he had actually vaulted over the parapet, something that he was now known for doing.

"Although," he said with a laugh, "I did forget just one thing."

He stopped then, teasing the children until, unable to stand the tension, Bhumaka demanded, "What was it? What did you forget, Centurion?"

"I forgot to draw my sword!"

Whether it was from the manner in which he said it, or the image it created in the boy's mind, Bhumaka began howling with laughter, although with Anuja, while she was laughing, Pullus' sense was that she was doing it more because her big brother was.

"How could you forget to draw your sword?"

"I asked myself the same thing," Pullus allowed, making a face as he did so that kept the laughter going.

"How did you not get hurt?"

"Because, Princess Anuja, sometimes our gods look after big, overgrown fools like me," he replied with a grin.

Suddenly, the rest of that day and all that had transpired came rushing back, the sacking of a town by Rome's Legions, and there was nothing he could think of to put any of that in a humorous light. Instead, he concentrated on some of the other lighter moments from what would be his first campaign, including how one of his original tentmates, Spurius Didius, earned the nickname he would bear for the rest of his time under the standard, Achilles. For this, however, Pullus roused himself from the couch so that he could recreate the reenactment first performed by one of the Mallius brothers, who had seen what happened to Didius when he had dropped down from the parapet of a Gallaeci town and driven a nail into his foot in the process. Now, both children were equally amused, clutching their stomachs at a sight that, if his men, and even his friends had seen, would have been fodder for talk around the fires for days, their giant Primus Pilus hopping on one leg while holding his foot in both hands and howling in mock pain before, with a great and thunderous crash, falling onto the floor to writhe in mock agony.

As Pullus got up off the floor and dropped onto the couch, making a great show of panting from the exertion of his performance, Anuja asked timidly, "Who is Achilles, Centurion?"

Before Pullus could respond, Bhumaka answered, with all the scorn of an older sibling, "Everyone knows who Achilles is! He is one of the greatest heroes of all time! What a silly question!"

This, Pullus knew, was certainly true in his part of the world, and it served as a reminder that, despite their location in the Pandyan kingdom, these children had just as much Macedonian Greek blood running through their veins as any other. Bharuch, both the city and the kingdom, had been modeled along lines instantly recognizable to Romans in more ways than one.

Still, he gently admonished the prince, "There's no such thing as a silly question, young Prince. It's the person who pretends to know something when they don't who's silly. Asking questions is the only way to learn."

He saw that his words had hit home, as without prompting, Bhumaka turned to Anuja and said softly, "I am sorry, sister. The Centurion is right." He brightened, then asked, "I know the story. I learned it from Father. Would you like me to tell it to you?"

She nodded eagerly, and Pullus took this opportunity, gently disengaging the pair of tiny arms from around his own huge ones, to stand up.

"And now, I have to go, Your Highnesses," he said, yet while he expected the tears, it still caused a sharp pang that threatened his own composure, although he was aware that it wasn't due solely to these two children, but the memory of another pair, a brother and sister who had been snatched from him too soon. Looking down at them, the siblings now holding each other's hands as they stared up with shining eyes, he could only manage, "It has been my honor, and my great pleasure watching over you, Prince Bhumaka and Princess Anuja. I hope that we will meet again, but until we do, please know that I will be offering prayers to keep you safe."

Bhumaka stood, and while there were tears, Pullus could see the solemnity that he knew would be expected of him as a monarch at some point in the future as he replied, "As will we, Centurion. I know that we…" he paused, trying to find the right words, "…have been enemies. But when I think of you…" the boy's lip began to quiver, threatening Pullus' composure even more, "…I cannot think of you as one. I will never forget you, Centurion Pullus," Prince Bhumaka promised solemnly.

"Nor I you. Or," Pullus gave Anuja another bow, "your

sisters."

Before Bhumaka could say anything else, Pullus spun about and left the room, trying to shut out the sound of childish sobs as he closed the door to leave the residence. He took his time returning to the camp, so that by the time he walked through the gates, nobody would notice that he was anything other than Titus Pullus, Primus Pilus of the 10th.

When Caesar's army departed Karoura, it was a mixture of the familiar and the strange. The Legions were aligned in marching columns five men across, the Legion eagles polished, the Cohort and Century standards gleaming, and the sun glinted off the helmets of what was the might of Rome. It was a sight that most of these men had seen and participated in before, and it was customary that on their departure, Caesar would require them to wear their entire uniform, plumes freshly blacked, their shields painted, and their *hamatae* oiled. And never once had it failed to stir the heart of Titus Pullus, but it wasn't always a given that the crowds that would be inevitably drawn to this spectacle were unhappy to see them go. This time was different, however, but it was because of the new element that meant the people of Karoura, particularly the women, were behaving in much the same manner as Hyppolita's children had with Pullus. It had been a matter of debate, turning somewhat acrimonious, but for this ceremonial departure, the newest addition to Caesar's army led the way, and while none of the Romans relished the inevitable mess that came from being second, it was nonetheless a moment none of them would forget as they were led by one hundred armored elephants, with King Nedunj leading a double column of animals, all of them wearing their full armor, bearing the platforms that the Romans had learned were called *houda* by the Pandya, while the men who rode them in the special saddle were called *mahouts*. The Pandyan *houdae* carried four men, made possible by the size of the *houda* that was a bit larger than the ones used by Bharuch, allowing for three archers and one spearman. Even now, after the introduction of the Roman *hamatae*, their armor consisted of stiffened linen vests with rectangular pieces of leather sewn on, and turbans with leather wrapped inside the folds. As might be expected, the elephant bearing King Nedunj was the largest by far, but it was an animal with which Nedunj had only recently begun to form a bond. It was a bull, his name Darpashata, and aside from his children and widow, was the last link to King Abhiraka, first of his name, the dead King of Bharuch. Darpashata, and the last twenty elephants of the Kingdom of Bharuch had arrived in Pandyan territory a month after Lord Maran had led the Pandyan army home after the murder of Puddapandyan by Abhiraka. Led there by Damisippos, the last surviving officer of the elephant corps of Bharuch, he had only very grudgingly relinquished the animal to Nedunj's care, and then it had only been at the insistence of Abhiraka's oldest child and Queen of Pandya. The fact that it meant that she had been deprived of the King's company as he sought to forge a bond with this magnificent but, as with all elephants, temperamental animal was, in her own small way, a sacrifice she was willing to make to honor her father.

Now, the huge bull elephant was at the head of a double column as they left through the eastern gate of Karoura, the mountains that served as both protection and barrier to the kingdoms to the east rising above them. Their route followed what the Pandyans called the Periyar River, while the Romans still referred to it by its Greek name Pseudostoma, and there was a brief pause once the entire mile-long column had cleared the city walls, signaled by a pair of horns, which was unusual. One was familiar to Pullus and the rest of Caesar's army, the low, rolling note of the *Corniceni* who relayed the order to stop, and those Legions nearer to the end of the column than the front only heard that one. But, since Pullus and his 10th had, as custom dictated, been the vanguard Legion, he and his men were treated to a much different sound that they were still getting accustomed to, the horns used by the Pandya that were specifically for the elephants and their *mahouts*. Nevertheless, Pullus didn't hesitate, nor did his Centurions.

"All right, you bastards! Helmets and armor off and shields back under cover and slung!"

Since this was expected, the men responded immediately, but once Pullus saw that his Optio Lutatius had matters in hand, he walked a short distance away to look with curiosity towards

Caesar Ascending – The Ganges

the front of the column. Caesar, his generals, and his small army of staff, all of them mounted, had moved immediately to the front once the ceremonial aspect of the march was over, but what Pullus was watching was whether the elephants would be allowed to do essentially the same thing by shedding their armor. He doubted it, simply because they had by this point experienced the process involved in making these huge beasts ready for war and how time-consuming it was, and he saw very quickly he was correct. The march resumed, the men more comfortable in their cotton tunics, but like them, Pullus still hadn't fully adjusted to the brutally hot and humid conditions. If he was forced to sum up his attitude, it would be one of resignation, that this was simply how it was going to be for the foreseeable future. Otherwise, the sun beating down on them was relentless in its heat, but the pace was, for Romans, almost leisurely, the huge animals leading the way on this day lumbering along at their own speed that had taken some getting used to, not just by the men, but Caesar. If there was one constant about the Dictator for Life throughout the years Pullus had marched for him, it was that he prized rapidity of movement above almost everything else, and during the integration of Nedunj's army, there had been clashes between the two about the relative pace that would become the standard for a march. Pullus viewed the result of this with mixed emotions; naturally, he supported his general, but he couldn't help feeling a bit of satisfaction when the young King of Pandya had proven to be every bit as strong-willed, at least in this one area. It would have been one thing if Nedunj fought with Caesar on everything else, but that hadn't been the case; if anything, the young monarch had been an eager and willing student to Caesar's teacher. However, on the subject of his elephants, not only had Nedunj proven implacable, but his argument had, once Pullus heard it, from Diocles through Apollodorus, forced Caesar to acknowledge that, in this, Nedunj was the authority.

    Pullus took particular delight in hearing that Nedunj had pointed out to Caesar, "I have been around these animals every day of my life. I have lived here in this climate for the same amount of time. As I understand it, your experience with elephants is not as...extensive?" Hearing Diocles recount it, even if it was thirdhand, Pullus found himself roaring with laughter at the description of Caesar's consternation.

"I wonder what was worse for him?" Pullus mused. "Knowing that Nedunj is right? Or the fact that Nedunj is a pup?"

The consequence was that, at least for the foreseeable future, the days of covering more than twenty-five miles a day were over, but fairly quickly, the men of the ranks were every bit as grateful for the king's intransigence as his animals.

"This isn't Gaul, or Hispania. It's not even Parthia. It's worse."

This was a common refrain heard throughout the ranks of every Legion, and while he would never say it aloud, Pullus agreed, and he knew that his own Centurions, along with the other Primi Pili and their Centurions agreed. Another thing he would never say, but Diocles, Scribonius, and Balbus knew was that Pullus was missing his friend Spurius because, while the other three men were his closest friends, there were still some things that Pullus could only share with men of the same rank. He and the Primus Pilus of the 12th had a cordial relationship, certainly, but it wasn't as close as Pullus had been with Spurius. In fact, if Pullus had been asked, he would have counted Torquatus, the Primus Pilus of the 25th as a closer friend, owing to their connection to the 10th. Torquatus had been one of the veterans from Pompeius' 1st Legion that were salted into the newly formed 10th, and he once had held the posting of both Balbus as Primus Pilus Posterior, and of Pullus himself. It had been his misfortune to be the Primus Pilus of the 10th at Pharsalus, the day that had shattered the friendship between Vibius Domitius, who had chosen to side with those men who mutinied, and his childhood friend and Secundus Pilus Prior Titus Pullus. Nobody, not even Caesar once his anger had cooled, faulted Torquatus for what happened at Pharsalus; it was common consensus among the Centurionate that not even the great immortal Crastinus, who had returned as Evocatus and fallen at Pharsalus, could have quelled the uprising of the 10th that day. Unfortunately, it had been Torquatus' further misfortune to have been stuck with the 10th on the Campus Martius outside Rome for the time when Caesar, along with

Caesar Ascending – The Ganges

Pullus, had first spent seven months in Alexandria under siege, followed by a brief campaign against the Pontics at Zela. During that interval, the restless soldiers, not just of the 10th, had gone on a small rampage, roaming the area outside Rome and even into Campania, falling on the villas and estates of their wealthier fellow citizens, looting and burning. When those Legions had been summoned to meet with Caesar in Africa, Torquatus had been replaced, and Pullus had been in the post ever since, but it was through Pullus' personal intercession and insistence that Torquatus didn't deserve to be shamed that found him named the Primus Pilus of the then-newly formed 25th. It was something that Pullus never brought up with Torquatus, but if Torquatus hadn't known outright, he strongly suspected this to be the case. The result was that, on those occasions when Pullus felt he could only confide in another man wearing the white transverse crest, it was now as often to Torquatus as Balbinus that he turned. Next to Torquatus, Pullus had the closest relationship with Cartufenus, by virtue of their time spent together in Alexandria, when Pullus, as the *de facto* Primus Pilus of the two Cohorts of the 6th, had shared the cramped conditions of the royal enclosure with the 28th. Together, they had faced a potential mutiny of Cartufenus' men when Ganymede, the former tutor of Cleopatra's sister Arsinoe who had assumed command of the Egyptian forces, had flooded the streets of Alexandria with seawater from the Great Harbor, threatening the Roman water supply. It was a short-lived uprising, solved when Caesar simply ordered that wells be dug throughout the Roman position, knowing that the low water table under the second largest city in the known world required his men to dig only a few feet deep before striking potable water, bringing the crisis to an end. Pullus' behavior, and his willingness to work with Cartufenus during this trying time, had forged a bond between the two.

None of which mattered in the moment, just the sounding of the signal that marked the end of the first day, prompting the various parts of this polyglot army to begin the process of making camp. This, as Pullus watched with a mixture of disgust and amusement, was still a work in progress, and it was certainly a challenging prospect to divide the labor of constructing a massive camp that would measure almost three-quarters a mile along each side, with a small channel dug to provide water from the Periyar. Early on, there had been real resistance by a substantial number of Pandyans who remained under the command of King Nedunj to perform this kind of work, which Pullus had learned was because of what the Pandyans called their caste system. As Pullus had learned from Aarunya, while similar in some ways to the Roman class system, it was far more rigid, and there were a dizzying number of sub-castes and rules that he was certain that, if he had another year to learn, he wouldn't be able to decipher. Regardless, it became very clear early on that the Legions wouldn't accept being the only source of labor for the entire army, although in this, Pullus placed some of the blame on Caesar's shoulders.

"We've always had separate camps before," had been Balbus' complaint. "Why does Caesar want to change it now?"

On balance, it was a good question, but since Pullus implicitly trusted Balbus and knew that his second in command wouldn't tell anyone other than Scribonius, who, Pullus was acutely aware, had been the first to divine their general's true ambitions, he answered readily enough.

"Because he plans on using elephants for more than a campaign season." He regarded Balbus with some amusement, interpreting the expression on his friend's scarred visage correctly, adding, "This shouldn't be a surprise to you, Quintus. Sextus and I have been talking about what's coming for months. You didn't think we were stopping with Palibothra, did you?"

Because of the severed nerves that came with the gruesome scar tissue, only someone close to him like Pullus would be able to tell that Balbus was embarrassed to admit, "You know I don't listen while you two are nattering on. But," he allowed with his version of a grin, "now that you mention it, I do seem to recall hearing something like that."

Rather than press his point, which Pullus would normally do in a subtle but unmistakable message that he had vanquished his friend, he said with a hint of concern, "I just hope we get this untangled before we get anywhere near these Chola bastards, because if we're still doing things the way we did them today, it would be a perfect time to attack us in case their king

Caesar Ascending – The Ganges

decides he'd rather kill us rather than take money from Caesar."

This, ultimately, was what concerned Pullus more than the larger meaning of consolidating camps. He had learned long before this moment how to worry about those things where he had an opportunity to impact matters, while leaving larger issues beyond his control to Caesar. Not that it was easy, but he had found it particularly helpful, hence his focus on what practical changes could be made in the seemingly mundane process of making camp.

It was that night that Diocles, returning from submitting the daily report required by Caesar, entered Pullus' private quarters, with an expression that immediately caused Pullus to swing his legs off his cot and dropping the scroll that he had been reading.

"What is it? What's happened?"

Rather than answer directly, Diocles suggested, "I think it might be a good idea for you to send me to fetch Master Sextus, at the very least, and probably Master Quintus."

Normally, Pullus would have impatiently ordered the Greek to spit it out, but his expression was such that he only nodded dumbly, leaving him to sit on the edge of his cot, trying to conjure up the reasons that might be the cause for the normally calm Diocles to look so shaken. Nothing he could think of gave him any comfort whatsoever, but fortunately, the Greek returned quickly, with both of Pullus' closest friends with him.

Understanding that further delay would only exacerbate the tension, Diocles began, "First, I must ask you to swear on the eagle of the 10th that you won't divulge a word of what I'm about to tell you."

Scribonius and Balbus exchanged an alarmed glance because, despite their seemingly contentious relationship with each other, they were both more attuned with each other than appearances would suggest, and both men knew that Diocles wouldn't make this kind of request unless it was not only important, but potentially dangerous information. They both readily agreed, but then they *were* shocked when Diocles looked at Pullus.

"Master, forgive me, but I must ask you to do the same." More startled than angry, Pullus quickly did so, whereupon the Greek said, "First, I want to stress that this is *not* coming from Apollodorus, or any of the other slaves and clerks in the *praetorium*. It was something I overheard when I was standing next to Caesar's office, waiting to submit our report." Frowning, he said thoughtfully, "While I'm thinking about it, I'd suggest that we need to keep our voices lower than we're used to, now that we've changed our tent construction from leather to canvas. It's much thinner, and I'm certain that's the only reason I overheard Caesar and King Nedunj talking." He took a breath before continuing, "Neither of them want King Karikala to agree to the payment for safe passage, because they need a pretext to carry out the terms of their own agreement."

When he paused, Pullus asked, "Which is?"

"While I don't know who suggested it first, Nedunj or Caesar, what matters is that Nedunj intends to conquer and annex Chola, using his status as Friend and Ally of Rome to ask for assistance."

"Which Caesar will give."

It was less the words than the thoughtful tone of Scribonius' voice that prompted Pullus to turn to him and nod in an indication for Scribonius to continue, asking, "What makes you say that?"

If Diocles was irritated by the interruption, he hid it well, and Scribonius did offer an apologetic glance as he replied, "Because it makes sense, for both Nedunj and for Caesar. Removing Chola as a potential enemy who will be effectively in our rear as we sail north is something we've talked about before."

This was true; it had been a common topic of conversation, but the prevailing sentiment had been, knowing Caesar and his liberal use of gold and silver when it would achieve his aims just as well as using iron and the blood of his men, that Karikala would be a fool to refuse.

"There's something else," Diocles interjected, and now Pullus was certain he did detect a note of, if not smugness, then satisfaction as he explained, "and it concerns the real reason that Legate Pollio is delaying his departure." Perhaps he was exacting a bit of revenge by pausing dramatically, but before Pullus or the other two men could say anything, he went on, "It's because Taprobane isn't controlled by the Greeks. It belongs to Chola."

The response was a combination of a hiss of indrawn breath and gasps from Pullus and Balbus, but it was the scarred Centurion who beat his friends, "*Gerrae*! That can't be right, or Caesar would have told us!"

"Would he?"

Pullus looked over at Scribonius, who had posed the question, albeit quietly.

Understanding, Scribonius began frowning as he explained, "I had always wondered why Pollio would need such a large army for what was nothing more than a construction project. It always seemed excessive to me, but this why, and it's also why Caesar needs the Chola to initiate hostilities. I'm sure that Pollio has been given orders to wait so that we've already started them before he sails. Remember, it won't take a week for them to reach Taprobane. Although," he allowed, "I suppose it's possible that Pollio could set sail early, then be waiting off of Taprobane for a message from Caesar. But," he shook his head, "that seems risky. There's a lot of ship traffic going back and forth, both to the western coast and to the eastern, and it would alert this Karikala that we have no intention of a peaceful passage."

"Did you overhear why they're so sure that Karikala will do what they want him to do?" Pullus asked.

"Not directly," Diocles admitted, "but I think I have an idea. It involves the Chola Crown Prince Divakar, Karikala's son. I heard Nedunj mention that his reason for being certain is that he knows Divakar well. They both spent time in the other's court back during a period when Puddapandyan and Karikala were actually negotiating a peaceful settlement of their latest dispute. From what I gathered, Nedunj is confident that Divakar will never accept this agreement, and he will do what he can to stop it from happening."

They fell silent then, Pullus breaking it by asking them all, "What do we do?"

"There's nothing we can do," Scribonius replied

immediately, then he pointed at Pullus to admonish, "and you can't spread this to the other Primi Pili either, because I can guarantee that it will get to Clustuminus, and he'll run to Caesar and tell him that you're causing trouble."

"But they need to be aware of this so they can be prepared!" Pullus protested, but before Scribonius could argue, he grumbled, "But you're right. That *mentula* would love to stick it in me. He hates me."

"Well," Balbus said with his version of a grin, "you did knock him out with one punch."

This brought laughing agreement from Pullus, but Scribonius and Diocles could only muster smiles, both of them equally troubled at this development. What was the most maddening, however, was that there was nothing they could do about it.

Chapter Two

Fortunately, there was no Chola attack that day, or the next, or the one after that, although the scouts returned with their first sighting of a party of mounted, armed men observing them from the slope of the ridge that paralleled the Periyar on the third day. By the time Pullus and the 10th arrived at the spot as the massive column plodded past, there was no sign of anyone, but he and the other Primi Pili took the opportunity to order the men to don their *hamata* at the next rest stop, although they relented and allowed them to keep their helmets strapped to their chests. Over the course of the march, which was becoming increasingly difficult because of the terrain, now that he was aware of their two leaders' intent, Pullus had sent Barhinder out among their Pandyan allies marching for King Nedunj, trying to learn as much about the Chola as a fighting force as possible, without divulging to the youth why he was so interested. Based on what Barhinder learned, Pullus had made sure to inform his fellow Primi Pili, again without saying why, although he wasn't surprised to learn that most of them had at least attempted the same thing, and it made him wonder if perhaps one of their little mice in the *praetorium* had heard the same thing, just in a different manner than Diocles. Of more immediate concern was the knowledge that the next day's march, two days outside of Madoura, would be through that narrow pass that was the practical border between the Pandyan kingdom and that claimed by the Chola.

At the nightly meeting, Caesar let Nedunj inform the other

officers, "This pass has been used for ambush before, both by the Chola and with us for generations, and my father once lured their army to pursue our troops. When they entered the pass, our men fell on them from the slopes above and we slaughtered them."

"'We?'" Balbinus whispered. "You know he wasn't there. He's a pup!"

"It's the prerogative of royalty," Pullus whispered back, then nudged his friend in the ribs, "Now be quiet. You might learn something."

If Nedunj had heard, he gave no sign, continuing, "The most dangerous stretch is the last mile of the pass on the Chola side because the slope is a bit more gradual, so it will be easier for them to keep their animals under control as they attack. Just before that, it is not only very steep, it is the narrowest part of the road."

Pullus managed to avoid groaning aloud, and he wasn't alone, his fellow Centurions similarly dismayed. A glance over at Caesar told Pullus that their general had been forewarned, but it was very easy for Pullus to imagine just how tense negotiating the pass would be.

"How long is the pass itself?"

Nedunj had to think for a moment before he answered cautiously, "Between three and four of your miles."

He looked to Caesar, who nodded confirmation, which also seemed to be a silent signal for the Dictator to take control of the meeting.

Before he could begin, however, Crispus of the 22nd raised his hand to ask, "Who will be in the vanguard tomorrow, Caesar?"

While Pullus thought he saw a flicker of irritation on their general's face, Caesar did not hesitate in answering.

"I haven't decided yet, Crispus, but I assure you that I'll be sending your marching orders tonight."

It was still something that a newly crowned king was adapting to, that when Caesar used words like "discuss," he meant it. For someone who was a member of royalty their entire life, this was completely unheard of, at least to the level that Caesar practiced. Certainly, his father Puddapandyan had allowed his highest-ranking nobles, like the dead former Lord of Muziris, Subramanian, to express their thoughts, but Nedunj could never recall any circumstance where his father availed himself of the opinion of what was essentially the rank and file men of his army, even if they were officers. But, while he was unaccustomed to it, Nedunj had almost immediately seen the wisdom of these moments, as Caesar relied on the collective knowledge represented in this room, well more than a century of experience in military matters. This, however, wasn't the part he was still trying to grasp, it was the extraordinary amount of latitude Caesar offered these men to continue arguing their individual point of view. Although he was relatively new to this, he had quickly determined that there were Centurions who Caesar relied on more than others, but it didn't surprise him that the one with the most latitude was the largest man in the room. Of the many qualities that the young King of Pandya possessed and which Caesar respected, it was his ability to be honest with himself in acknowledging mistakes made in the past that the Roman general rated highest, and Nedunj had learned fairly quickly that his perception of Titus Pullus as a heavily muscled brute whose only redeeming quality was his ferocity in battle had been in error. What would have astonished and worried Caesar was that, despite what the Roman thought, more people at least suspected there was a deeper connection between Pullus and Queen Hyppolita than the fact that he had been her protector during the occupation of Bharuch after the city fell. It was something that Nedunj had learned very recently; in fact, it was the night before the army's departure that his wife confided in him her suspicion that her mother and the Centurion had been lovers. Fortunately, this was all Nedunj knew; Aarunya couldn't bring herself to divulge the other part, that there were in fact two infants inside the palace that had been her childhood home. She hadn't had any qualms about informing her husband about the Lady Amodini, and while Nedunj had been shocked, it was less that it had happened than the fact that it was with a man who would have been considered from an inferior caste in Pandyan society, in the form of Gaius Porcinus. Nedunj had toyed with the idea of informing Caesar about Aarunya's revelation, but his sense of honor wouldn't allow it since she had made him swear an oath not to, so the two men would be blissfully unaware that either of them had any knowledge of what could prove to be a highly explosive secret.

"Does that meet with your approval, Your Highness?"

Nedunj started in his chair, embarrassed as he realized he hadn't been paying attention, but it wasn't entirely to cover this that he responded, "Yes, Caesar. That makes sense."

The Roman didn't say anything, but Nedunj could see Caesar wasn't fooled, simply giving a nod as he addressed the rest of the men. "Now that this is settled, that will be all. We break camp at the normal time, in the marching order we've just discussed."

When the Centurions got up to leave, Nedunj stayed behind, although it was only partially to find out from Caesar who would be in the vanguard, although he suspected he knew the answer.

Once they were alone, save for Apollodorus, whose presence Nedunj had long before learned to accept, Nedunj asked, "Is it safe for me to assume that you will have Pullus and his Legion in the vanguard tomorrow, Caesar?"

"Safe?" Caesar raised an eyebrow, but it was the quirk of his mouth that Nedunj had learned meant that the Roman was amused. "I don't know that it's safe to assume anything, Your Highness." He hesitated, then said, now smiling fully, "But yes, your assumption is correct. Given how matters should unfold tomorrow, I want my most experienced Legion in the right spot." The smile vanished, and there was an added coolness in Caesar's voice. "I just hope that your confidence about how Divakar will behave is well placed, Your Highness. And," he pointed out, "we also don't know with any degree of certainty that he's leading the force that your scouts have reported seeing."

"It's their Southern Army," Nedunj replied with a confidence that he felt was justified, yet still wasn't as solid as he would have liked. "And King Karikala only allows direct family members command their armies. The Army of the North is led by Kavirathan, Karikala's younger brother. And," he finished with a shrug, "Divakar is the only other male relative of age."

"That's only part of it," Caesar warned. "As you admitted yourself, it's been quite some time since you spent time with Divakar. He may have matured over the years."

This caused Nedunj to laugh, and he was much more confident in assuring Caesar, "I do not believe that will be a problem, Caesar. While it is true I have not seen him with my own eyes, his behavior is hardly a secret. If anything, he has become emboldened by being named Crown Prince. There were rumors that Karikala favored his younger brother Kumaran. No," he nodded his head, something that Caesar and his fellow Romans had become accustomed to, that Pandyan head gestures were essentially opposite of their own, "while there are things that are unanswered, I am certain that when Divakar sees that we are marching with you, he will be unable to control himself."

For that was the crucial component in their plot to provoke Chola, and was something that Caesar had deliberately withheld from his officers; during their negotiations, Caesar had assured the Chola king that the Pandyan army wouldn't be accompanying them and would remain within their own borders. They would be at the rear of the Roman column, which being more than a mile long, meant that Caesar and Nedunj were toeing a very fine line, since the narrowest, highest point of the pass marked the actual border, which would mean that the Pandyan contingent would technically be within Pandyan lands in the event that Nedunj's prediction about Divakar's actions proved accurate. In fact, they hadn't even discussed the alternative by common, but silent, consent; it would all depend on Divakar.

"Why us? Why not the 12th?"

The fact that Pullus silently agreed with Balbus' complaint didn't make things easier, but Pullus was too experienced and knew this wasn't the time to signal that agreement to his Centurions, so his answer was terse.

"Because Caesar ordered us to be the vanguard, that's why."

"It's possible that they'll wait for us to pass in order to try and get to the elephants," Scribonius pointed out.

"But they're going to be just ahead of the baggage train,"

Nigidius, the Quartus Pilus Prior, spoke up. "That seems like a big risk for them to wait that long and hope we won't spot them."

"But they won't know that's where the elephants will be," Scribonius countered, but whereas with someone else, Nigidius might have taken this as argumentative, his response was a thoughtful nod.

It is, Pullus thought ruefully, the one skill of his that I admire the most but can't seem to emulate, the ability to say something potentially inflammatory but do it in a way that doesn't arouse the ire of others. Following hard on that was another thought, and it caused Pullus to hold up a hand in a silent signal, the quiet talk immediately stopping as his Centurions waited for him to speak.

"That," Pullus had a habit of speaking slowly when he was still in the process of forming his thoughts, and he frowned down at his boots, "is actually something we need to consider." When he saw that they weren't following, he explained, "I mean, the idea that even if they let us pass, they might either lose patience waiting for their real target, or one of the bastards will move, or sneeze and give their position away. And we'll already be through the pass. So," he spread his hands out, "if that happens, what do we do? We'll have a force of angry elephants in between us and the rest of the army."

It was an almost exact copy of the meeting Caesar had held about a third of a watch earlier, and it was a characteristic of all of Caesar's Primi Pili, although there were differences in the degree to which Primi Pili allowed their subordinates to air their opinion. None of them, for example, were surprised that Aulus Batius was the least among them in giving his Centurions the ability to speak freely, but even this would have been unheard of in the armies of Pandya, Bharuch, Pattala, Parthia or, though they didn't know it, Chola. Not lost on any of them was the fact that the one thing these kingdoms had in common was that they were all now under Roman control to one degree or another, while only Pullus, Scribonius, and Balbus were aware that this was the likely actual goal for Chola. By the time Pullus called an end to the meeting, he and his Centurions had hammered out three possible actions that he and the 10th might take, depending on the circumstances. While the Centurions held their own meetings with their Cohort's officers, then had their evening meal, Pullus had gone back to the *praetorium*, leaving Diocles grumbling about the need to reheat the soldier's porridge, of which rice was now the staple, not that this was an uncommon occurrence.

As was usual, Caesar immediately had Pullus brought to him, then listened carefully as the Primus Pilus offered his general what he and his Centurions had devised, as always taking pains to minimize his own input and emphasizing the contributions of his Pili Priores. Caesar listened, nodding thoughtfully at times, frowning and offering a suggestion at others, but ultimately satisfied that his most experienced Legion was prepared for whatever might come the next day. Caesar, being unaware of Pullus' knowledge of his real intentions, said in a deliberately offhand manner that it probably wouldn't be needed. Indeed, if they had both been asked publicly but separately, Pullus and Caesar would have had essentially the same answer; it would be the height of folly for the Chola to try and inflict damage now instead of waiting for the Roman arrival at the fortified city of Madoura. That Pullus knew this was exactly what Caesar was counting on was a fact about which the general would be unaware...for the time being.

In his appearance and style of dress, the Roman members of Caesar's increasingly polyglot army would have been unable to distinguish Divakar from Nedunj or any other Pandyan, but even with the similarities, Divakar considered himself a Chola, and these upstart Pandyans were the mortal enemy of his people. However, despite being almost identical in age, Crown Prince Divakar couldn't have been more different than his counterpart Nedunj; if anything, in his character, Divakar more closely resembled Marcus Aemilius Lepidus, a man whose belief in his own superiority was based in his bloodline and nothing else, and whose ill-founded confidence in that superiority ended in a bloody and spectacular fashion with his decapitation on the paving stones of Merv. Nevertheless, when his father, King Karikala, named for the mythical founder of his people, decided to greet the Romans before they reached his capital of Uraiyur by waiting in Madoura, just as Nedunj had predicted, he had kept his oldest son as the commander of the Southern Army, despite his misgivings. The king wasn't blind to his son's faults, but like many fathers, he was either unable or unwilling to assess the degree of his son's character flaws, and more than one of Karikala's councilors had learned the hard way the danger of trying to force their king to view his son more objectively.

Now, Divakar was leading fully half of the entire armed force the Chola were capable of fielding in the form of the Southern Army, including one hundred armored elephants, although the Chola favored a crew of four men composed of all archers who were specially trained to loose their missiles even more rapidly than normal for the kingdoms of southern India and more akin to the manner of the horse archers of Parthia, who favored volume of fire over accuracy. The composition of the infantry was almost identical to that of Pandya; spearmen carrying shields of wicker covered in hardened leather, with vests made of stiffened linen with rectangular pieces of leather sewn on, and turbans with leather in the wrapping to provide some protection. Where the Chola differed from the Pandya was in their use of cavalry that relied more on lancers than mounted archers, and it was these lancers that Divakar intended to use to run down the shattered remnants of the Romans in the ambush he had planned, in exactly the spot that Nedunj had predicted. As a precaution, King Karikala had sent two of his most experienced noblemen along with the Crown Prince, and both of them had spent most of their march from Madoura trying to dissuade Divakar from his plan.

"That spot has been used by both sides more than once, Lord Prince. It's very likely that the Pandyan king informed this Roman Caesar that this will be a likely spot for an ambush, so they're going to be prepared."

This came from Lord Senganan, who under different circumstances might have been commanding this force by virtue of his experience, but Divakar retorted, "The reason that it's been used is because it's the best place for an ambush." He turned to look across at the older man, riding the elephant next to the prince's, asking in a challenging manner, "Do you deny that?"

"No, Your Highness," he replied patiently, but he wasn't ready to concede. "But neither can you deny that the very reason you just gave is the reason why we shouldn't use it, because our enemy knows that as well as we do, and even then your father has ordered that we only respond if these Romans provoke us."

Even as he said the words, Senganan understood they would have no effect, but he felt compelled to at least make the attempt, and for a bare moment, he thought he might have gotten through to the crown prince. Divakar didn't immediately reply, choosing instead to stare straight ahead with a frown, the silence drawing out to the point that Senganan felt a flicker of hope, but it was dispelled in the amount of time it took for the prince to give an emphatic bob of his head, which, as the Romans had discovered, carried the exact opposite meaning.

"No," he broke the silence, "I've made up my mind. These Romans can't be allowed to set foot in our kingdom unopposed." He turned back to Senganan to say, "My father is a good man, and he is a great king, but he's wrong to allow this." It would be a moment Senganan would replay in his mind many times, because he said nothing, understanding that it was unrealistic to expect Divakar to betray his true nature, something that his father should have understood himself. When Senganan was the man to break his gaze first, the prince smiled, reveling in this small victory before returning to more immediate matters. "We'll place our lancers at the top of the northern slope where the trees are the thickest. They'll allow the leading element of their army to pass through before they begin their charge. Our infantry will be waiting on the opposite side for the moment the dogs break and try to escape by climbing the southern slope, where we'll have the advantage of being uphill."

On its surface, even Senganan couldn't argue that it wasn't a sound plan, but it was also a plan that assumed far too many things, and while he had resigned himself to the idea that the prince would go through with his conception, he still felt compelled to ask, "And what if they're not marching wearing their armor and clearly prepared for a fight?"

"Even if they're not, we proceed as planned, allowing them

to pass through and begin the descent on our side, where I'll be waiting with our elephants, and we'll rain death down on their heads! They'll pay for their effrontery in thinking that the Chola can be bought off by gold and silver!"

It was the boasting of a young man who had never tasted true battle against an evenly matched enemy before, Senganan thought sadly, but it was the heretofore silent second Chola nobleman who spoke for the first time.

"Your Highness, what about the reports we've heard about this demon fire the Romans brought with them?"

"Do you really believe that nonsense, Lord Ajay?" Divakar scoffed. "That they have some sort of magic substance that can incinerate an animal the size of an elephant like this?" He snapped his fingers as he said this. "No," he nodded emphatically, "that's a fiction created by those Pandyan dogs to explain their cowardice in submitting to these invaders!"

Ajay was a few years younger than Senganan, but like his older counterpart, he was a veteran of battles between Chola and Pandya, and while he couldn't deny that what Divakar was saying hadn't been making the rounds of the army and back in Uraiyur, he was finding that it was much easier to believe that was the truth when he was behind the city walls. Out here, with the mountains looming ahead of them, and within a day of battle, he was no longer so quick to dismiss the idea that there was truth buried there somewhere. Like every loyal Chola, Ajay believed that the Pandyans were faithless dogs, but unlike Divakar, he and Senganan had faced them in battle, and there was nothing cowardly about them, which in turn meant that these Romans had to be very formidable indeed to force their king, even as young as he was, to reach an accommodation. Because of his position on the prince's side opposite of Senganan, Ajay couldn't risk throwing his counterpart a beseeching glance in a silent plea for help, but he could tell by the other nobleman's expression that he harbored similar doubts that these reports of some sort of pernicious, fiery substance were completely fabricated by their enemy.

Taking their silence as assent, Divakar pronounced, "Good. It's decided. Now," he smiled at each of them in turn, reminded of what his father, King Karikala had drilled into him about the importance of at least appearing to value subordinates, "with Lord Senganan leading the lancers, and you, Lord Ajay, leading our infantry, I just hope you leave some of the dogs for me so that I can get my sword wet!"

The lack of enthusiasm displayed by the other two men Divakar either missed or chose to ignore; frankly, his mind had already begun racing ahead to his triumphant return to the capital, bearing the heads of his vanquished enemies, especially that pale barbarian named Caesar who had so disrupted their world.

The combined army reached the beginning of the pass fairly early in the morning, but Caesar ordered a halt nonetheless.

"Have your men quench their thirst now," he ordered his Primi Pili, allowing Nedunj to give his own instructions. "The next two miles are supposed to be very steep, and I don't want to be forced to stop while any part of the army is still in the pass." Satisfied by the reaction from his commanders, Caesar addressed Pullus, "Primus Pilus, your men are ready?"

It was a superfluous question, but to Pullus, it was also a sign of his general's nerves, because he never would have asked under less stressful circumstances, so all Pullus did was reply crisply, "They are, Caesar."

Glancing at the young king, Nedunj signaled to Caesar that he had issued his own instructions, whereupon Caesar said, "Return to your Legions. Once the men have drunk their fill, I'll be sounding the command to resume after a count of two hundred."

Given that Caesar normally only counted to a hundred was another sign of the potential strife that lay ahead, but Pullus was nonetheless thankful that he could walk back to the head of the column and still have time to stop at each Pilus Prior as part of his own last moment check. Pullus was also aware that Caesar's order had two purposes; not only would his men's thirst be sated, it would empty one of the two canteens that had become the standard part of the load carried by the Legions here in this hot, humid land. Parthia had, of course, been challenging when it came to water, but there the danger had been with men being unaware how much water they were losing through sweat because it evaporated immediately. Here in India, it was literally the opposite; men were unaware how much water they were losing because they were always wet from their sweat that never seemed to evaporate. Like so much of the knowledge being accrued by Caesar and his Centurions, the recognition that, if anything, men required *more* water here had been won at a high cost. For the first few months of their time south of Bharuch, at any given moment, a full ten percent of each Legion had men on the sick list, unable to perform their duties because they had been prostrated by the heat and humidity. Now, they were about to embark on what would be the most strenuous march they had participated in since their arrival in India, negotiating the mountains the Pandyans called the Ghat, which towered above them several thousand feet. By the time Pullus arrived at his Cohort, he barely had time to guzzle down the water skin Balbus had kept for him, which he only did after ensuring that his second in command had done the same.

"You probably need two skins because of all the *sura* you guzzle," Pullus had commented wryly. "I can smell it coming out of your skin."

"*Gerrae!*" Balbus retorted; then, he took a sniff of himself, and Pullus didn't miss the look of chagrin on his friend's features, but Balbus wasn't the type to concede easily, and he insisted, "It keeps the bugs away! That's really the only reason I drink so much."

He barely got the words out before he burst out into his version of a laugh, while Pullus joined in as he gave his friend a shove.

"I knew you wouldn't be able to keep a straight face trying that *cac*." He shook his head, but any other attempt at conversation was cut off by the sound of the *Cornu* from behind them, and Pullus immediately bellowed, "All right, boys, let's get moving!" As the men hoisted their *furcae*, he reminded them, "Remember, it's supposed to be steep, so I don't want to hear any of you bastards talking! Shields are already uncovered, so put your helmets on, and you know what that means! Eyes open, mouths shut!" Then, with a nod to Valerius, his *Cornicen*, at the signal, the 10th resumed the march.

Before they had covered the first mile, Pullus and his Centurions were faced with a dilemma that none of them had encountered before, even in the early days of the Parthian campaign.

"I've got more stragglers than I've ever had before," was how Balbus put it, while Pullus could only commiserate, since his First Century was in similarly dire straits.

For once, there had been no exaggeration about the severity of the grade, but it was the footing that made it even more difficult, because while Nedunj had characterized it as a road, it was starkly reminiscent of the mountains inhabited by the Elymais in Parthia. The difference was that nothing they had covered in Parthia had been this steep and unrelenting, and what immediately faced Pullus was, to his eye, at least another mile of more of the same. In fact, there were spots where he was certain he could simply lean forward a bit and touch the roadbed with his outstretched hand.

"Titus, we're going to have to stop," Balbus panted. "I mean, before we get to that spot, or we might only have half the Legion."

Pullus knew perfectly well what Balbus meant, and in his heart, he agreed. Whether Caesar would agree was what mattered, yet as desperate as he was for some guidance from their general, for one of the few times in his life, Pullus was unwilling to leave his post and move back down the column since it would mean he would have to traverse the same ground twice. And, he would only admit to himself, he was almost certain he wouldn't have the energy to do even that; the secret idea that they might be going into a battle within the next watch was even worse. He was well within his rights to pick a man to act as a runner, but he didn't even consider doing so, meaning that he was left with just the hope that Caesar would make his way up the column himself, or send someone like Pollio or Hirtius in his place. Until then, there was no other alternative but to keep going and pray to the gods that he had a chance to get his men back together before they had to face whatever was waiting for them.

Behind the First Cohort, in the First Century of the Second Cohort, Gaius Porcinus was struggling just like his comrades, but he also carried the extra burden that came from being responsible for more than just himself for the first time, at least when doing so was such a challenge. Somehow, he was managing to put one foot in front of the other, but he also kept watch on the rank of men to his left and immediately behind him, the men of his tent section, who were almost touching shoulders because of the narrowness, and which was already missing two members. One hadn't been a surprise; Placidius was the oldest man in the section now that Vulso was gone, killed in the fight for Bharuch, but Rabinius was one of the strongest men in not just his section, but in the Century. However, he had also been stricken with a fever over the winter, which had obviously weakened him, but there was nothing Porcinus could do about it in this moment.

"Porcinus, do you think your uncle will sound a halt soon?"

Normally, Porcinus would have bristled at anyone who emphasized his familial connection to the Primus Pilus, but not only was he too tired to do so, he also fervently hoped that his uncle would do that very thing.

Consequently, he managed to gasp, "Gods, I hope so, Libo."

This part of the pass was not only steep, but the slopes on either side of the rough track in this section were devoid of trees, at least of a size to provide any shade, but to Porcinus, it appeared as if this was about to change, seeing a line of verdant green spreading up the incline on either side of a height that suggested that they were reaching a forested part of the pass. Maybe we'll get some shade at least, he thought miserably, forced to shake his head back and forth like a dog as he tried to fling the sweat from his face. Like every other ranker, his hands were full, but it was even more awkward than normal because, in his right hand, instead of two javelins, there was a javelin and a heavier siege spear, the larger shaft of the latter making it more awkward than that to which he was accustomed. This was a change, certainly, but Porcinus was every bit in the dark as to why his uncle had ordered this change as his comrades, although he assumed it was a precaution against elephants,

Caesar Ascending – The Ganges

which he privately believed was a waste of time, though he would never say as much. He was wrong, however; the heavier spear wasn't for the prospect of armored elephants, but for the prospect of normal cavalry. What hung from his *baltea*, in a mesh bag that was stuffed with straw to protect the single small jar barely larger than his fist, *that* was what he and his comrades were counting on, which his uncle had decreed at the beginning of the day's march. Early on, and up until they reached the pass, Porcinus had been acutely aware, and was made quite uncomfortable by the weight of contents of the bag as it bounced gently against his hip. Now, however, he barely noticed it, although even as he knew it offered the best chance between seeing another sunrise or being stomped into jellied meat, or as had happened to Vulso, being transfixed by a huge tusk, he would have happily discarded it because of the weight, which had seemed negligible at the beginning of the day. What, he thought with some bitterness, good will it do to have this naphtha if I'm too exhausted to throw it? It was a demoralizing thought, which he tried to shove back into the recess of his mind as he focused on one foot, then the other, over and over as he and his comrades struggled up the pass.

Caesar almost immediately recognized that his army was potentially in trouble, particularly the 10th, and to a lesser degree, the 12th, which was the second Legion in the column. While he certainly didn't know the names of every single man in every one of his Legions, his astonishing memory did enable him to recognize men to the extent that he knew to which Legion and, at the very least, which Cohort they belonged, and he had been shocked when, barely a mile into the pass, he began recognizing men who were either stumbling forward at a much slower pace, or had come to a complete stop to stand, panting and dripping with sweat. This was bad enough, but there was a scant amount of spare space on either side of the track for these men to rest, though some of them leaned back against the slope, but more commonly, they were sprawled out, their faces turned up to the broiling sun, mouths open as they sucked in as much air as they could. The sight of his ablest, most experienced, and hardened veterans essentially helpless and prostrate was alarming to put it mildly, but he was also faced with a dilemma of his own. He and the other officers had been forced to dismount, their horses struggling with the gradient with a load on their backs, which precluded him from riding up the column to confer with Pullus. And, like his Primus Pilus, he was loath to send someone else in his place. Fortunately, he was not riding Toes this day; the horse was older now, and was more of a symbol than anything else, and he had selected a gray stallion for his everyday mount, but as strong as the animal was, Caesar wasn't willing to sacrifice it, at least not yet. If something occurred before they expected, then he would immediately flog his mount to death to get to the fighting, but they weren't at that point yet. Even walking, the sight before him was something he couldn't recall seeing, a column of men that seemed to be ascending straight up, as if they were climbing a broad staircase, but without the precision and alignment that marked Caesar's Legions on the march. As far as his eye could see, it was clear that his men were struggling, moving side to side more than normal, while there would be a bobble as a man lost his footing and went sliding back down, to be caught by a comrade behind him...if they were fortunate. Far too many times, the result would be a man being knocked off his feet by a stumbling comrade, causing a momentary delay in that file as the men around them, engaged in their own struggles, continued plodding upward.

"Caesar," Pollio's panting voice intruded into his thoughts, "at this rate, it doesn't look as if Pullus will have half of his Legion with him by the time he gets to the spot where we're expecting trouble."

Biting back his initial response, Caesar forced himself to acknowledge, "I am aware, Aulus. But," he had to take a couple more breaths before he resumed, "I'm not sure that stopping to regroup is a better option. We'll be motionless, and it will give the Chola time to adapt themselves."

This was true, but Pollio wasn't willing to give up, although he did have the presence of mind to phrase it as a question.

"So, which is the worse alternative? Perhaps the sight of us not moving forward will provoke their prince? If," he added in

Caesar Ascending – The Ganges

what might have been a rebuke, "he's actually leading the Chola."

That, Caesar understood, was the crux of the problem. Nevertheless, as pressing a matter as this was, it was far from the only concern for the allied army, because as badly as the Legion leading the way was faring, he knew that matters with the baggage train were even direr. Strangely enough, the only good news was that Nedunj's elephants were faring better than just about every other segment of the army. The crews had all dismounted, which was certainly a help, leaving only their *mahout* to guide their animal, but they were all carrying the *howdah* as well, yet there they were behind Caesar but now ahead of the other three Legions, moving to this spot during the last rest break, with Darpashata leading the way, ridden by Nedunj, whose dark features gleamed with sweat. It had been a fundamental error on Caesar's part, relying on the young king's description of what passed for a road in this part of the world and not scouting it personally. Although it was true that the track was as wide as Nedunj had said it was, and he had warned that it was a sharp climb, while the incline was steep on both sides, Caesar had instantly understood that being told this, and seeing it firsthand were two different things. Yes, he knew it was going to be difficult, and this was why he had his most experienced and valuable Legion leading the way, trusting Pullus to keep his head in the event that the Chola behaved as expected in the pass itself but if, as it appeared at this moment, that half of the 10th Legion was straggling, would there be enough men to fend off a determined attack, if the Chola prince launched it at the most obvious spot? Caesar was making a gamble that, whereas the normal tactic for warring armies in this part of the world was to target their foe's most potent, and valuable, asset in the armored elephants, the sight of a Roman Legion, which they had undoubtedly only viewed from afar at this point, would prove to be too tempting a target. And, he also recognized, he was relying on Nedunj's assessment that the Chola would use their elephants immediately, rather than let the less lethal and less valuable parts of the Chola army to soften their combined army up first. The real question was whether the Chola commander had the discipline to refrain from launching his surprise on the 10th because of his impatience. Shading his eyes, Caesar stared up ahead, scanning the northern slope, and he thought he could see where the road curved to the left, which Nedunj had informed him would mark the beginning of the mile of ground where the slope lessened, and the upper part of the slopes on both sides provided the necessary cover to hide an army. Where he was standing, however, was still too steep to climb without difficulty.

Suddenly, Caesar turned and snapped an order to his *Cornicen*. "Sound the halt, immediately!"

While he was not instantly obeyed, it was because his *Cornicen* had to catch his breath, but as soon as the note sounded, in a sign of their fatigue, the men immediately ahead of the command group not only stopped, but most of the men fell to their knees.

"I thought we weren't stopping!" Pollio gasped, leading his horse next to Caesar. "We're too exposed and unable to defend ourselves!"

"As you said, Asinius," Caesar answered, "if we don't, it's likely Pullus won't have half of his Legion left when he needs it most, if the Chola do as we anticipate."

The men of the 10th were thankful for the command to stop, despite the danger, although on their own initiative, the Centurions ordered the men of the outer files to remain standing, and while they were allowed to ground their packs, they were told to face outward, their shields resting against their legs, leaving Pullus to wonder why Caesar had ordered the halt. They were still what he estimated was a half-mile from the spot that posed the most danger, which he now saw was compounded by the curving of the track as it followed the contour of the ridge. There was a slight hump in the slope that ran down to the point where the track curved out of sight, and he knew this meant that their view would be blocked even when they were just within a few paces of the bend. The advance guard had been ordered to maintain visual contact with the rest of the army, and the men, like all the others who were mounted, had been forced to dismount and lead their horses up the steep incline, and he could see them roughly halfway between where he was standing and the bend, looking back in Pullus' direction.

"Keep your eyes uphill, you stupid *cunni*," Pullus growled, but knowing he was too far away to be heard, he used his *vitus* and made an emphatic gesture with it, pointing to the tops of the northern, then the southern slopes.

It was best for both parties that Pullus could not hear what was said, though he could guess, but what mattered was that they did as he indicated. With this dealt with, while he dreaded it, Pullus stepped to the side of the column and walked downhill to check with Balbus and the rest of the First Cohort. He was pleased to see that, while there were still men missing, many of those who had fallen out had not stopped with the rest of the column and were even now struggling uphill to rejoin their comrades.

Understanding this wasn't the time for the *vitus*, or as they called it, "the vinegar," Pullus used "the honey," in the form of calling to the stragglers, "Come on, boys! We're less than a half-mile away from where it flattens out, then it will be downhill from there. Just hang on until then!"

What Pullus didn't know was how long Caesar intended to allow the army to rest, so he didn't go farther than the Second Cohort, where Scribonius had taken off his helmet and was wringing his helmet liner out, which in another change, was no longer made of felt but padded cotton.

"I should probably do that," Pullus commented, but he kept his helmet on, and while he was addressing Scribonius, his eyes were on his friend's Century, which Scribonius saw.

"He's still with us," Scribonius assured him. "He's lost two men from his section, and I'm down a dozen men. Although," he turned as he put the liner and helmet back on, pointing at a pair of men who were just then trying to slip unobserved back into the First Century through the rear ranks, "those two are mine and they're back." He paused to scan his ranks, then grunted, "Actually, it looks like we've got half of them back."

"We've only got a half-mile to go before it gets easier," Pullus repeated, but Scribonius gave him a sardonic smile.

"The marching might get easier, but if Nedunj is right, we're likely to be up to our asses in those Chola bastards."

"One problem at a time, Sextus." Pullus clapped his friend

on the shoulder. "One problem at a time." Taking a breath, Pullus said unenthusiastically, "I better get back up there. I *hate* covering the same ground twice, especially when it's like this."

"You wanted to be Primus Pilus." Scribonius was anything but sympathetic. "That's what comes with it."

"Oh, go piss on your boots," Pullus grumbled.

He was moving as he said it, but any hope he might have had that the rest stop would last longer was dashed when, just as he reached the rearmost rank of his Century, the *Cornu* sounded the call that alerted the men to heft their *furcae*, then a handful of heartbeats later, the call to resume played.

As Nedunj had anticipated and assured Caesar would be the case, Divakar was growing increasingly impatient, and twice, Senganan had to persuade him not to put their plan in motion yet, rightly pointing out, "If we move now, we'll ruin any chance of surprising them at the spot where we can control our Beauties." He referred to the Chola elephants by their nickname, similar to the dead Abhiraka's use of the Harem, despite the fact that there were as many males as females.

Divakar snarled and snapped at his second in command, but Senganan was accustomed to this treatment, and while it was personally infuriating that a man that he considered to be little better than an idiot in matters of warfare should hold that kind of power over him, it was the way of their world. Consequently, he reminded himself that what mattered was the result, but he wasn't sanguine about the prospects of reining the crown prince in a third time, so he resigned himself to the idea that it would be a race between the Romans' progress and Divakar's impatience. Around them, the men who served as the crews of the *howdah* were on the ground, not wanting to burden their respective animal until it was necessary, while the cavalrymen were similarly dismounted, all of them in the shade of the thick stand of trees that screened them from view. On the opposite, southern slope, the Chola infantry were waiting, all of them well within the edge of forest on either side, which in fact was too thickly vegetated with smaller trees, shrubs, and plants to be called a forest, but not quite as dense as what the people of this land called the *jangla*, although Divakar had at least taken the precaution of sending men out of the forest and in the direction from which the Romans would be coming to ensure they couldn't be seen, which had required them to withdraw another twenty paces before not even the gleam from the brass headpieces of the armored elephants caught a stray ray of light.

The Chola infantry, similarly to the Pandyan infantry, was an afterthought, and they were actually deeper in the forest on the other slope, with their task to essentially sweep up the remnants of what the prince was certain would be a shattered foe. Despite his efforts, Senganan hadn't been able to dislodge this idea from Divakar's head, even by pointing out that the relative size of the invading Roman army meant that it was next to impossible to do anything more than inflict serious damage, let alone force a decisive battle that would end the threat, and that the king's orders had been to only engage if the Pandyans crossed the border with their Roman allies. This had been the strategy conceived by Divakar's father after his spies had sent enough reports back from their observation of the Pandyan capital to convince the Chola king that, in terms of raw numbers, these Romans were simply too numerous, especially when combined with their traditional enemy of the Pandya. And, to Karikala's credit, the king had already deduced that, numbers aside, these Roman invaders were a formidable foe that, even if they weren't allied with the Pandya, posed the greatest danger to the Chola kingdom in his lifetime. As Karikala continued to stress to Divakar, this was an army that had subdued the mighty Parthian kingdom in two years, and then in a single season had taken both Pattala and Bharuch, essentially shifting the balance of power in the northwestern part of India almost overnight, then followed it up the next year with their conquest of Pandya, a kingdom the Chola had been struggling with for decades...all to no avail.

"That's because these dogs haven't faced us yet, Father!" Divakar declared, more than once. "We have twice as many elephants than the Pandya, our men are more skilled, and more courageous than those hyenas that call themselves Pandyan!"

It was the kind of bluster that one would expect from a young man, at least if that young man wasn't the heir to a kingdom and had been groomed almost from birth to succeed his father. But, Karikala would occasionally remind himself, Divakar had always been not only a stubborn child, but like Senganan, he had observed firsthand that his eldest son didn't possess a clever bone in his body, always preferring brute force, whether it be in military matters like this moment, or in asserting his rank over his playmates when he was a child in order to win at a game. He was, Karikala knew, a bully, but on the heels of that thought, when it came to him, he would also remind himself that Divakar wasn't a coward, and had proven his courage in battle several times, earning a reputation as a formidable warrior. That it had been against a rebellion, which he had ruthlessly crushed, on his own and without Karikala's help, where he faced poorly equipped subjects in the northwestern reaches of the Chola kingdom, was a much different prospect than what faced him with this threat from the forces of Rome. In fact, it was this recognition that had enabled Senganan, along with the majority of his courtiers, to persuade Karikala to seek a diplomatic solution to the threat.

"Your Highness, look what this Caesar did, not only with the Pandya, but Bharuch," Senganan had argued. "He could have stripped both kingdoms of all of its gold, silver, and jewels, and razed their cities, but he didn't. The question is, why?"

Senganan had posed the question honestly enough, but as he hoped, Karikala was at a loss to explain why, and Senganan provided his own answer.

Once Karikala had demurred in trying to guess, Senganan went on, "I believe that Caesar has no real interest in conquering our kingdom, that he is just passing through exactly as he says."

This had baffled the king, who, just like the Pandya, expressed his rejection by nodding his head vigorously, the gesture being the opposite of what those who came from the West used, and he expressed his rejection with the question Senganan hoped, because he had wrestled with it almost from the moment their spies reported the invaders were heading in their direction.

"Why do you believe this, Lord Senganan?"

Now, Senganan offered his theory, one where he had been forced to consult the handful of scholars in the kingdom who deigned to pay attention to the world of those kingdoms to the north who had been so heavily influenced by a Macedonian king.

"I believe," he spoke quietly, but with as much conviction as he could muster, knowing his king well and that he responded best when one of his advisers sounded confident, "that what this Caesar is doing is all about trying to accomplish what the Macedonian Alexander couldn't do, and reach the sacred Ganges."

Senganan wasn't all that surprised that Karikala immediately pounced on the one fact that would seem to disprove that theory, exclaiming, "That makes no sense, Senganan. The Ganges is more than a thousand miles to the north! And," the king thought to remind Senganan, "if that was his goal, he would have kept marching east from Pattala, or even Bharuch, not continue all the way south." Sitting back in his ornately carved throne, Karikala offered his councilor the kind of smile that a tutor would offer a pupil who had gone astray in his argument on a topic. "Now, how do you explain that?"

Like courtiers of other kings who were sensitive to their own dignity and status, Senganan knew to not betray his satisfaction that his king had actually asked the question Senganan had anticipated, and for which he had hoped, because it had been the thorniest part of the problem.

"Their fleet, your Highness," Senganan replied quietly. Before Karikala could respond, he went on, "As you know, Highness, these Roman savages arrived in a massive fleet, and they rely on it not just to carry them, but to keep them supplied. If this Caesar had marched east from Pattala, his fleet could only have carried him perhaps another hundred miles up the Indus, and it's almost as far to the mouth of the Ganges from Pattala as it is from here. The same is true for the Narmada. The difference is that by taking this route, the Romans can have their fleet sailing with them for the entirety of their march."

The Chola didn't rely on written maps to the extent that Greeks and Romans did, but they did use them, and this was when Senganan unrolled the large piece of vellum that he had brought with him. While he would never know it, this map would in the future prove to be crucial in more than just clinching his argument at this moment.

Laying it on the floor in front of Karikala, Senganan pointed to the large mark that designated their own capital as he continued, "As you can see, once these Romans pass through our kingdom, they'll be within marching distance of the eastern coast."

He stopped then, waiting for his king to speak next, and he was cautiously optimistic by what he saw in Karikala's expression as he leaned forward and regarded the map with narrowed eyes, an expression that he had learned meant the king was deep in thought.

Finally, Karikala sat up and asked bluntly, "What are you proposing, Senganan?"

"That we meet these invaders with a part of our army, to show strength," Senganan explained, despite thinking that this was not only unnecessary, but could be provocative; he also understood that his king was a proud man who would only bend so far. "But once we make contact with them, we follow through with our agreement. Provided, of course," Senganan, courtier that he was, knew how important this was to stress, "that you determine that this is their true intention."

"That," Karikala allowed, "is a worthy idea, Senganan." Then, he began nodding again, "But you're forgetting the Pandya. Those hyenas have already allied themselves with these Romans. How do we know that part of their agreement to join with them isn't with the agreement that the Romans will help them conquer us, their lifelong enemy?"

It was, Senganan knew, a good question, and one that he had hoped his king wouldn't ask, because he had nothing more than another guess as an answer. However, he was too experienced in dealing with Karikala to attempt to dissemble, or to offer what was indeed a supposition as a factual response; he had seen what happened with two other Chola noblemen who had done that, and neither of them were in the land of the living.

"We don't, Highness," Senganan admitted, but he was prepared for this possibility. "But, wouldn't it be wise to at least try to discover what the terms of Pandya's capitulation might be?"

There was another long silence before, at last, Karikala shook his head in a signal that preceded his words, "Very well, Senganan. We will do as you suggest." He smiled then, but it was without humor. "We'll prepare for war, and we'll show these Romans and their pet Pandyan hyenas our might, but we'll at least listen to their explanation for this offense against my kingdom."

When Senganan left, while he was optimistic, it was with a fair amount of caution because of his intimate knowledge of his king's character. While Karikala was decisive, he was also easily influenced, and over his time serving his king, Senganan had witnessed that, more often than not, it was the man who spoke to the king last whose advice he tended to follow. I've done all I can do, he thought as he left the palace to prepare for the journey. Now, it's time to pray that Divakar doesn't talk to his father, or that if he does, he doesn't persuade Karikala to behave rashly.

Senganan's hope proved to be forlorn, but not even he anticipated just how disastrous the clash between the Chola and the Romans and their Pandyan allies would turn out to be, and there was only one man who bore the brunt of the blame. If there was a positive, it was that Divakar was no longer the heir to the throne, his younger brother Kumaran now the crown prince by default. Now, they would never know that Senganan's guess had been incorrect, that the Romans had been sincere in their desire to simply transit through the Chola kingdom as their leader Caesar sought to achieve what Alexander could not. Where Senganan erred in his assessment was based in his ignorance of one salient fact; he had chosen to flee from the scene before the Pandyans moved to the head of the column and crossed the border to take advantage of the chaos and confusion created by the incineration of Divakar and the leading element of the premature Chola attack to shatter the Southern Army. And now, a matter of a Roman watch later, too much had happened, too much blood had been shed, but while Karikala would undoubtedly grieve for his oldest son, Senganan suspected that he felt almost as much pain for the terrible fate of some of his Beauties, the deaths of which Senganan had witnessed and would be the first to relate to his king. Much like the deceased King of Bharuch, it would be a sight that Senganan would remember for the rest of his life, and if he allowed himself to dwell on it, he would give an involuntary shudder at the images that were almost literally burned into his mind. Indelibly linked with those images was another emotion, at least at first before his passion cooled, one of a visceral hatred of the Romans; more specifically, one Roman in particular, although it wasn't Caesar, who Senganan was reasonably certain that he never laid eyes on during that disastrous attempt by Divakar to earn everlasting fame and glory. This Roman had been easy to spot, even without the distinctively different colored crest of his helmet, white instead of the black and red of other Romans that Senganan had seen wearing the same kind of crest, because he was, in simple terms, a giant who stood at least a head taller than the men around him, and was clearly much broader across the shoulders and chest. By the time he returned to Madoura, trailing behind what was a bare remnant of the army that had comprised half of Chola's military might, Senganan had turned this giant Roman into a symbol for the threat that Rome posed, now that he was certain that the chance of any kind of negotiated settlement had vanished in the amount of time it took for Divakar to ignore Senganan's pleas to allow him to carry out the plan to which Divakar's father had agreed, that they only show these Romans what the might of Chola looked like.

In what would be the last words the pair ever exchanged, Divakar had scoffed, "My father has grown too old to remember who we are! But," he had drawn his sword in a dramatic flourish, "I haven't!"

Before Senganan could stop him, Divakar had snapped the order to the horn player who rode in his *howdah*, taking the place of one of the archers, who naturally obeyed immediately, blowing the long note that unleashed the fury of the Beauties, completely ignoring that the plan had called for the traditional cavalry to engage first with their shower of small javelins. Even if Senganan could have argued with the prince, he would have been drowned out by the roar of both animals and men as, just as the Bharuch king had done with the part of the Roman army led by Asinius Pollio as he advanced overland from Pattala, Divakar sprung an ambush using his most powerful weapon. Perhaps if the Chola king had been made aware of the particulars of Abhiraka's ambush of what he believed to be the bulk of the Roman army, marching south from their conquest of Pattala but would turn out to be only half of it, Karikala might have taken steps to keep Divakar under control. What made it worse, at least in Senganan's view, was that, while they hadn't known the details, by this point, the terrible weapon that had proven so devastating to Bharuch's elephants was common knowledge. Regardless, as Senganan was forced to admit to himself, hearing about what seemed to be sticky fire and its effectiveness and seeing it were two distinctly different things, and he was forced to watch what was more than just an enormous investment of resources but a source of great pride, not to just the Chola, but all of the kingdoms of India to one degree or another, literally go up in flames. If there was any positive effect, it was a personal one for Senganan, because he knew that if Divakar had survived, he would have accused Senganan of cowardice, because when the Beauties came bursting out of the forest, their passengers shouting to go with the trumpeting of the animals themselves, he hadn't moved, ordering his *mahout* Shanu to remain standing. He did allow the *mahout* to guide his animal, named Karna, to the edge of the forest to give him a better view, something that he almost immediately regretted. From his vantage point, he could see everything, both with the manner in which the Romans responded, but the Roman who seemed to be the most responsible for their quick reaction, the giant who would go on to haunt his thoughts to a degree he could never have imagined.

Pullus' first thought when he heard the sudden eruption of noise, followed less than a half-dozen heartbeats by the sight of a line of armored elephants bursting out of the thick underbrush, was to remind himself to give an offering to Fortuna for putting a fool in command of these animals.
"All right, boys!" he bellowed. "You know what to do!"
Then, he turned to his *Cornicen* but didn't even have to give the command, seeing Valerius putting the horn to his lips,

whereupon he blew the first in what would be a series of notes that not only informed the men outside the range of Pullus' voice what was expected of them, but alerted the rest of the first part of the army, including Caesar, of what was happening; most importantly, the notes sent the signal to their new allies that it was time to begin to move.

If the stupid bastards had waited a little longer, Pullus thought with grim amusement, we might have been fucked, but he was never one to question the gods whenever they seemed to favor him. Working with the speed that came from many watches of practice, albeit never with the real weapon, the pair of men in all ten sections of every Century in every Legion of Caesar's army began to move, starting by dropping their *furcae* before stepping in between the files, although they didn't move into their final position, where they would arrange themselves in a line in front of their Century. When this tactic was first developed, the thought had been to place the men with the strongest arms in the same spot in every Century, but this was quickly discarded, it being correctly pointed out that their ability to respond quickly depended on from what direction an attack by elephants would come. The result was a slight reshuffling that put the man who would be responsible for hurling the very volatile jar, and the ranker who served as his assistant, who would light the rag that he carried in a special pouch so that the oil it was soaked in didn't leak out, in the middle of every section. This way, their speed of deployment would be the same no matter what flank was attacked, and they had even trained for the event that they were surrounded, where the men of the first two sections moved to the front, the two at the rear moved in that direction, and the other six pairs aligned three pairs on each side.

Thousands of clay jars, filled with a mixture of water and sand in order to simulate the weight of the slightly heavier substance of naphtha, had been shattered, and they wouldn't have been Romans if, with Caesar's secret contribution of silver, their Centurions didn't make a game of it, rewarding men for both distance and accuracy, while encouraging wagering. As they were accustomed to hurling javelins, the lighter jars traveled almost twice as far as those missiles, depending on who was throwing it, giving them a range of about forty paces. That wasn't much, as by this time, they had all witnessed how quickly elephants in full stride could move despite their appearance, but they were confident in this weapon being so devastatingly effective that none of them seriously considered the possibility that there would be an animal whose rage overpowered their fear of fire, especially once they witnessed one of their own kind suffering what, even as much as the Romans hated the animals, all agreed was a cruel end. It was accepted wisdom that there was no species of animal in the known world who didn't fear fire, even man, and when that fire had the pernicious nature of naphtha, which not only clung to the surface it hit, but couldn't be extinguished with water, it made it a doubly devastating weapon. And now, Pullus and his men were about to put what had only been a theory into practice when the twenty men would dash out in front of the Century, arranging themselves in a line that, unfortunately, was a little closer together than the manner in which they had trained, but they were confined by the slope on either side of the track, although it wasn't nearly as severe as it had been during the steepest part of the climb, and it would allow the pair of men on either side to move a few feet up the slope.

"Wait, boys! Wait for my signal!" Pullus shouted, then risked a glance over his shoulder to see that, as expected, the twenty other men who had exchanged their pair of javelins for a single siege spear were now passing them up to the men in the front ranks.

These, they all knew, were a last resort, especially in as confined a space like this road, the maneuverability of the Legionaries, who would have normally ducked to either side of a rampaging animal and thrust their spears at the unarmored spots on their bodies as they thundered past were now severely hampered by the narrowness of the road and severity of the slope. The trick, as Pullus knew very well, was timing his command so that the process of putting the rag in the jar that the thrower was carrying, then lighting it, immediately followed by the designated man hurling it as far, and as accurately, as he could in less than a heartbeat's amount of time, had to happen when the elephants were too close to either stop or to maneuver around the explosion of flaming viscous liquid. When they had trained for this maneuver, the goal had been to create a flaming line similar to what Pullus had done during the assault on Bharuch that stretched across the path of the elephants' attack, but as all veterans know, what men can routinely do in training rarely translates to the same performance in battle. That reality was about to be put to the test, but even in the moment, Pullus was thankful for the rash behavior of whoever was leading these Chola, who, to Pullus and his comrades' eyes, looked almost identical to the Pandya in terms of their elephants and armament. The *howdahs* were perhaps a bit bigger, with taller walls, and he saw that many of the onrushing animals had four men swaying in the larger *howdah*, which presented its own challenge, because they were all archers, and the range for an archer was naturally greater than even the strongest arm, which was why he hadn't given the signal for the men to dash out in front of the formation. It was, Pullus understood, going to be a finely cut thing, and it was likely that at least one of his men would be struck by an arrow, and only if the gods were kind would it be the man who was lighting the jar and not the man hurling it, because the likelihood that it would cause the stricken man to either fumble, or even worse, drop the jar after it had been ignited was very high. The idea that it wouldn't work at all had, frankly, never occurred to Pullus, nor to any of the men who had witnessed the effects of flaming naphtha, and its reputation was such that the men who would be in most danger of being immolated didn't do more than the normal soldier's grumbling about it, all of them acutely aware of the critical nature of their duty. Helping the Roman cause was that, by not waiting until the column had reached the spot where the slope was much less severe, it meant that rather than thundering down the slope to hit Pullus and his men in the flank, whoever was commanding this effort had chosen to attack head on, and by doing so was constrained by the width of the road and the twenty paces on either side of it where the elephants could traverse, albeit canted at an angle that, hopefully, would require the men in the *howdahs* to worry more about staying in them than loosing missiles at their foes.

Seeing the men standing in their *howdah* raise their left arm while drawing their right arm back, seemingly aiming their missiles at the sky, Pullus bellowed, "*Shields up!*"

He didn't bother to check, hearing the clattering sound as men's shields collided with each other as they swept their arms up, only the pairs of men exempt from this, having left their shields in their spots. Instead, they crouched down, while Pullus, who had perfected the habit, deliberately stopped thinking, turning his gaze skyward while allowing his body to react before his mind could command it. Working to the Romans' advantage was that, no matter how experienced these archers were, precision in their aim was impossible as the beasts under them swayed back and forth or encountered something underfoot that broke their stride a bit. The result was a widely scattered volley, of which less than half of the missiles even came close to striking the rows of upraised shields, none of them striking a fleshy target. Another change that had taken place during that winter season was brought on by the recognition of the superiority of the iron that the Romans encountered during their assault on Muziris, when they saw the arrows used by the Pandyan archers penetrating their shields to a greater degree than any foe they had encountered to that time. While Nedunj had done all that he could to keep the smiths in both Muziris and the capital Karoura from divulging the secret behind their craft, it had been to no avail because Caesar had sent men out into the Pandyan countryside, and while there hadn't been time and enough iron ore to forge blades for all of the *gladii* of the Legions, the metal part of the Roman siege spears had been refitted with the improved metal. And, in recognition of the likelihood that the kingdoms through which they would be traversing possessed the same ability in creating superior iron, the Legion shields had been remade, with the wood, normally poplar, which was plentiful on the Roman side of Our Sea, replaced by teakwood, which proved to be denser than anything the Romans had encountered, yet with just enough flexibility to accommodate the curvature that made the Legionary shields unique.

While the new configuration had been tested, this was the first time that Pullus, and his men, were subjected to a volley of arrows, and what was instantly noticeable was the different sound that was made when a barbed iron tip struck the harder teakwood. It still had the same hollow quality to it, but it was a lower pitched sound; most importantly, while the arrows did penetrate, it was rarely enough for more than just the tip of the arrow to protrude all the way through the back. Afterward, the Centurions discovered there was an unexpected benefit; before they were put to the test in combat, the men had unanimously complained that the shield was heavier, perhaps not as heavy as the training shield every *Tirone* who aspired to be under a Legion standard came to know and loathe, but close to it. From that day forward, however, there was no grumbling about the extra weight, and it would become something that the Centurions would come to appreciate. At this moment, however, while Pullus did notice the different sound, it barely registered because his concentration was solely on what was happening. Because of their overeager commander, it was essentially a column of elephants of only five animals across lumbering towards them, although the one to Pullus' far left was, in fact, forced to use the slope, and it was already falling behind the other animals as it had to contend with keeping its footing. In that instant, Pullus made a decision.

"Boys, we're going to wait a bit longer before you throw your jars," he shouted from his spot behind the single line of men now arrayed in front of the rest of the Century. "We're not going to make a line of fire; we're going to light those bastards up and turn them into torches, do you understand? So wait for my command!"

Pullus' decision, made in the span of a couple of heartbeats, was the culmination of the years he had spent waging war for Rome, and for Caesar. Deciding to use the terrain to his advantage, Pullus' initial goal was to stop the attack by employing the naphtha to create a line of fire that would repel the animals and send them in a headlong, panicked retreat that could be exploited by Nedunj and his elephants, but only after the flames were extinguished, since not even the best trained animal could be forced to cross a flaming barrier. By executing the expected ambush early, in some ways, the Romans were at the same disadvantage as their foes because of the lack of maneuvering room. Yes, they could stop the Chola attack, but they would have difficulty in exploiting it because it wasn't feasible to spread their forces out to sweep the enemy from the field because the slopes were too steep. Instead, while Pullus didn't experience it as a conscious thought, he understood that, just as had happened at Bharuch, they needed to turn these rampaging elephants into weapons that could be turned on the Chola to a greater degree than just stopping them.

The animals were within a hundred paces, and Pullus bellowed, "Light the jars!"

As they had practiced, the men carrying the rags had already used their *pugiones* to cut a slit in the leather lids, and stuffed the strip of cloth, all of them measured to be the same length, into the first jar so that there was at least six inches of exposed oil-soaked cloth. This, they had learned, was the minimum length that gave the men hurling the jars the chance to fling it without the invisible but deadly fumes that inevitably leaked out through the slit their comrade had just cut being ignited.

Pullus didn't realize he was holding his breath until, over the span of perhaps two heartbeats, all ten jars, held in the palm of each man's hands, were lit, but in the eyeblink of time it took for the last jar to be ignited, he could see how rapidly the flames were leaping up the cloth of those men who it had taken only one strike of the flint to ignite instead of the two it took the final pair, and he bellowed, "*Throw 'em, boys!*"

Not surprising any of their onlooking comrades, there was no hesitation as every man flung their jar, the flight easy to track by the trail of black, greasy smoke, and, as Pullus' gaze followed the arcing, tumbling jars, he got what would be his first and only glimpse of the man who, while he didn't know the identity, he recognized had to be the commander of the Chola because he was wearing an ornately decorated helmet, with the kind of lamellar armor, with strips of iron instead of leather, standing in his *howdah*, sword thrust into the air, his bearded mouth open as he was undoubtedly bellowing whatever gods these people invoked, or some form of war cry. Then, he vanished in an explosion of flame that, despite the bright sunshine, still made him squint at the intensity, when one of the jars actually sailed over his elephant's head, and with the *mahout* lying flat in the manner Pullus and his fellow Romans had witnessed was common when attacking, it struck the wooden side of the *howdah*. More quickly than his mind could process the sight, once again, Pullus had unwittingly slain a crown prince of a kingdom, although whereas the Parthian prince Pacorus' death was more conventional, with a sword thrust through the mouth, Divakar's end was more spectacular, and undoubtedly more painful, as he transformed into a torch that only resembled a flesh and blood man because his arms were waving wildly as he writhed in an agony that always made Pullus shudder when he thought about it. Under other circumstances, Pullus wouldn't have been able to look away, but the first volley of jars had created similar scenes with every animal, despite the fact that not every jar hit its target. With a rapidity that, while expected was still astonishing to watch, what had been a thundering menace was turned into a mass of flaming agony of both men and beasts, with every one of them united in the same thought, to turn and escape the awful vengeance of a fire that wouldn't stop burning.

Almost too late, Pullus shouted, "Hold, boys! Don't light the second jar yet!"

Each man who had been chosen to throw the jars carried one, and their assistant carried another, while another ten men had a jar suspended from their *furca*, and as they had been trained, the assistants were already preparing the second jar to be thrown. The problem was that their targets, displaying the agility that had caught the Romans by surprise the first time, had behaved in a manner that, while it was the result Pullus hoped for, happened so quickly that there were immediately no elephants left within range. All that was left, beginning about thirty paces away from the single line, were burning human corpses, along with smaller fires where the globules of flaming naphtha that had landed were strewn across ground that was now scorched and blackened for the width of the track and at least fifteen paces upslope on either side. Beyond the scorched earth, burning animals were blindly colliding with their own kind who had been following behind them, the sound of animals and men in agony mingling with the bleating cry that they had learned signaled an elephant out of its mind with fear. None of

Caesar Ascending – The Ganges

the men who stood there, slack-jawed and frozen in their spots, some of them still holding their shields above their heads, would ever forget the sight of what was essentially an entire army collapsing on itself.

It was left to Pullus to recover his senses first, snapping over his shoulder, "Everyone up the slope with your packs!" To Valerius, he ordered, "Sound the pursuit. It's time for those Pandyan bastards to earn their pay."

He was barely finished when, from the rear the shout came that riders were coming, and he turned just in time to see men diving out of the way, as Gundomir and Teispes, riding side by side, led Caesar to the front. Just beyond these mounted men, Pullus could see the upper part of the elephant he knew was called Darpashata, with the young Pandyan king Nedunj standing, much in the same posture as Divakar, save waving a sword, whose fiercely burning corpse was just one of the couple dozen strewn in their path.

"I see that our tactic worked," Caesar commented as he drew up, his eyes narrowed because he was trying to understand what he was seeing.

"Better than I ever imagined, Caesar," Pullus agreed.

"I thought I ordered you to create a wall." Caesar frowned. "But all I see are burning men. Surely the naphtha hasn't burned out this quickly."

"I changed your orders," Pullus replied simply, but before Caesar could say anything, the Primus Pilus pointed up the track. "I had the men aim for the elephants because we didn't have the room to flank them because they attacked too soon."

It was another example of the relationship between the Dictator for Life and the Primus Pilus of the Equestrians, because whereas Caesar normally didn't appreciate his subordinates altering his orders without at least informing him, over the span of a matter of heartbeats, Caesar saw that Pullus had made the right decision. The Chola had been premature, and in doing so, had forced an alteration to the plan, something that, Caesar admitted to himself, happened more often than not.

Still, he wasn't effusive in his praise, saying curtly, "I understand." Then, he turned in his saddle, and lifted his hand in a signal to Nedunj.

As Pullus had ordered, the men of the 10th had collapsed down and, where possible, had scrambled up the slope on both sides to make room for the elephants, with Darpashata leading them, although Nedunj stopped to confer with Caesar. Which, as always, made the horses nervous, forcing Caesar to curb his animal.

"You can see better than we can," Caesar called up to Nedunj. "It looks like at least two of the animals Pullus' men hit have already collapsed, but I can't tell whether the Chola are still retreating."

Nedunj didn't answer immediately, shading his eyes as he scanned the track, but it was the sounds as much as what he saw that informed the Pandyan king. While it was fainter, the noise created by dozens of elephants trumpeting in a panic was still clearly audible, and Nedunj didn't waste any more time.

"If your men will use the vinegar to douse those men still burning," he told Caesar, "I'll be able to shatter these dogs before they can get reorganized. Although," he grinned, "they might run all the way back to Madoura before the *mahouts* can get them under control again."

Pullus didn't wait to be told, trotting over to where his men were now clustered together on the lower slope.

"Vespillo," he ordered the Sergeant of his First Section, "gather up everyone's vinegar skins and you and your section go put those fires out."

As they had learned by accident during the first winter in Parthia, after their initial encounter with the Parthian weapon that had proven to be so devastating, whereas a normal fire could be doused with water and extinguished, this had no effect on naphtha, and in fact, only vinegar worked.

The Sergeant and his men worked quickly, gathering up the skins that they now carried for this purpose, and trotting the short distance to the first of the corpses that, while not blazing as fiercely as they had even a hundred heartbeats earlier, still burned to a point that Nedunj knew his animals would balk at passing. It quickly became apparent that there wasn't enough vinegar to completely extinguish all of the bodies, leaving the men with the grisly task of dousing a limb or two, then using that to drag the corpses out from the middle of the road. This was one of the only times when, as Vespillo and his men began retching from both the odor of cooking flesh and just the idea of treating what had just moments earlier been a man not that different from themselves, none of their comrades mocked them for showing this kind of weakness. Even Caesar looked slightly pale, although he otherwise watched impassively, as did Nedunj. Pullus' own stomach began to roil at the sight, but in something of a contest between the two Romans, he decided that if Caesar wouldn't look away, neither would he, something that Caesar knew, and which amused him. The men of the First were talking quietly, although most of them quickly decided they had seen enough, turning their backs on Vespillo and the others, until there were only smoldering, charred corpses that barely resembled humans piled up on either side of the narrow roadway.

"King Nedunj," Caesar spoke loudly enough for him to be heard by everyone in the immediate area, "now that they have announced their intention of not honoring our agreement, you're free to pursue the Chola. The 10th will follow you in support, but once we're beyond the pass and out on open ground again, the cavalry will catch up to you."

While he had no need to do so, Nedunj nevertheless appreciated the manner in which Caesar had phrased what he knew very well was an order, and he responded in the same tone, "It will be our honor to finish what the 10th has begun, Caesar." Then, in something of a surprise, the young king turned and, while he didn't address Pullus, he did incline his head in a gesture that might have been a recognition of the 10th's role. Then, speaking in Tamil, Darpashata immediately responded, moving forward as Caesar, Gundomir, and Teispes reined their mounts in to avoid them reacting as the huge beast lumbered past. As it passed Pullus, who out of principle refused to move from his spot, challenging the elephant to go around, he saw the animal eyeing him, and while he would never say it aloud, he was certain that the huge beast was amused at this sign of defiance from another giant among his own kind. It took some time for the entire complement of elephants to pass by, and Pullus' best guess was that, from the moment he had spotted the onrushing Chola to this one, less than a sixth part of a watch had passed, prompting the thought, If this is the last thing we do today, this will be the shortest battle we ever fought. Which, Pullus thought wryly, he found disappointing.

Not only was Divakar dead, so too was the other noble who might have assumed command, Ajay being burned alive, with Senganan fleeing, but even if Ajay had survived and Senganan was present, the panic created by the elephants who had been doused in blazing naphtha that spread through what was, in essence, a herd of them, would have been impossible to stop, let alone organize to put up a defense. With Nedunj in pursuit, once they managed to maneuver around the elephants who had finally succumbed to the flames and collapsed in the road, they were greeted by a sight that, given their own relationship with their own animals, elicited at least a twinge of regret. Just as the *mahouts* of Abhiraka's Harem and those of the Pandya, every *mahout* of the Chola wore a bronze spike suspended from a heavy thong around their neck, and a hammer hanging from their belts, and once Nedunj passed the still-burning corpses of the first five animals that had been doused in naphtha, there was a trail of other fallen elephants who, having gone out of their minds from fear, had to be killed by their *mahouts* before they did more damage to their own side. As usually happened, it wasn't done without some human loss; while the men riding in the *howdahs,* either having been warned by the *mahout* about what was coming, or saw for themselves that their elephant was no longer under any semblance of control, universally leapt out of their *howdahs*, it was inevitable that some of them landed awkwardly, and, as Nedunj could see, either failed to get out of the way from one of the trailing elephants and were crushed, or in at least two cases, had been run through by a bronze-capped tusk. This wasn't unusual, but it didn't make it any less horrific to see what had once been men turned into a mass of splintered bone and gelatinous meat that was only recognizable because of the blood-soaked clothing and armor scattered around the corpses of what Nedunj counted to be twenty-seven elephants, including the first five. He hadn't ordered his own elephants to go to the run yet, but they were moving at what would have been the equivalent of a trot as the Pandyan tracked a trail that a blind man could follow.

When they reached the treeline where Divakar had been waiting, he halted Darpashata just out of bow range, waiting for the rest of the force to take advantage of the first open expanse where they could spread out to form a double line, while never taking his eyes off the undergrowth. The sounds of trumpeting elephants were more muffled but still clearly audible, along with a new sound of crashing underbrush being trampled, and he knew from experience that a panicked animal, with the kind of blind spot that elephants had, would topple over small trees in its flight, making the trail as easy to follow as one strewn with the dead. It took perhaps a count of five hundred before his animals were aligned in a manner he found acceptable, and just before he resumed his pursuit, Nedunj turned to see that the eagle of the 10th Legion was visible, its men moving at a trot but still perhaps a quarter-mile away. Consequently, when he gave the command to continue, it was back to a walk, but it wasn't solely for the purpose of allowing Pullus and his Legion to catch up, and as he anticipated, when his first line reached the edge of the forest, a flurry of missiles came streaking towards them. Just as the Romans had developed tactics for their own style of warfare, the tribes of India were no different, and as he had anticipated, the surviving archers of the fleeing animals had abandoned their elephant to form a skirmish line, using the undergrowth as cover.

Like Nedunj, his men were ready, and while he heard shouts of pain from men who were struck, a flurry of Pandyan arrows streaked back in the opposite direction. Aiding the Pandya was how the cover had been substantially reduced into smaller clumps because the retreating elephants had crushed everything in their path, giving the Pandya a natural aiming point at the clumps of underbrush still standing, knowing that there were probably enemy archers using them for cover. Naturally, the leaves and branches caused the plunging arrows to carom off their course aiming for one of the Chola archers, but there were enough missiles that cut through the foliage that it only took three volleys from the hundred archers on the fifty elephants of the front rank to break an already demoralized enemy. With this last impediment swept aside, taking advantage of the multiple trails created by the Chola animals, Nedunj had his horn player signal the call to increase speed.

Although he had never penetrated this far into the Chola kingdom personally, Nedunj had been informed by men he trusted that this forest was no more than three miles across in the direction he was heading, with the ground sloping gradually downward until there was flat, open land. His intention was to close with the fleeing Chola, first running down that portion of Chola infantry on foot who had never left their position on the southern slope, turning instead to flee when their most potent weapon was shattered, then come to grips with the remaining elephants, which by his count, had already lost more than thirty of their number of what he guessed were a hundred, basing his supposition on the knowledge that this would comprise roughly half of the entire number of Chola elephants. Before they had gone a mile deep into the forest, the archers on the elephants on the southern side of the road had killed dozens of Chola infantry, while, within Nedunj's range of vision, the archers had struck down dozens of fleeing spearmen, and he felt reasonably certain that it was the same for those of his animals that he couldn't see farther out on either flank.

As he gripped the side of the *howdah*, swaying back and forth to the rhythm of Darpashata's lumbering trot, the king occasionally glanced over his shoulder, but while the pace of an elephant trotting wasn't as quick as that of a horse, it was still faster than men could move, and he began to worry that he was outstripping the supporting Legion. By the time they had covered another mile, Nedunj heard a horn behind him, and turned to see that the conventional cavalry, both Pandyan and Roman with the Legate Hirtius at its head, was closing rapidly, using the path that Darpashata was following which was only wide enough for three riders abreast. Even with the trails forged by the larger animals, the pursuing horses were forced to weave back and forth to avoid either a tree that was too large to have been knocked over, or a thick tangle of vegetation that even the elephants had avoided, but Nedunj's concern was that Hirtius would insist on leading his troopers past Nedunj and his elephants. While there was an element of pride at work in not allowing the Romans, even bolstered by his own cavalrymen, to reach their main quarry first, it was also based in concern, knowing how cavalry was largely ineffectual in inflicting damage on armored elephants, even the Pandyan lancers, whose main role was to harry the larger beasts, and to run down infantrymen fleeing the battle, similarly to the Chola. Fortunately, as he quickly learned, Aulus Hirtius had already experienced a taste of battling these behemoths, so that when he got within a hundred paces of the second line of Nedunj's elephants at the head of his column, he slowed his command down, signaling that he was content to follow behind the Pandyans. Once Nedunj determined this, he returned his attention to the front, seeing up ahead the line of lighter green that he knew signaled they were reaching the far edge of this forest. Prudence dictated that he sounded the call to slow down, both to allow the animals to regain their wind, and to avoid running headlong out into the open only to find that the Chola had regrouped and were waiting. And, if it had been his father Puddapandyan, Nedunj had no doubt that this would have been his decision, but Nedunj was not only a young king, he also had determined that he had good instincts when it came to waging war. This had been confirmed by no less than the greatest general of their age, Caesar himself, when he had complimented the prince who, in their first meeting on the beach of Muziris and unaware he was now a king, had fought Caesar's Legions to a bloody standstill. Therefore, he made his decision quickly, and without much hesitation, which was made clear to his men when there was no horn command to slow down, although he didn't increase the pace either. As certain as he was, when he and Darpashata burst back out into the bright sunlight, he felt his body relax at the sight before him of nothing but fleeing elephants, the rearmost of them now less than a quarter mile away.

"There they are, Darpa!" Nedunj shouted, using the nickname he had given the huge elephant during their time getting to know each other. "We have them now!"

The bull elephant was puffing, his huge lungs sounding like bellows, and Nedunj knew that the animal was already winded, but just as Nedunj had been bred to be king, Darpashata, and all of the animals who bore the *howdah* and armor were bred for war, which Darpashata signaled now by raising his trunk in an eerily similar matter to a man lifting his sword. Even winded, the elephant was capable of producing a sound that made Nedunj and his comrades aboard Darpashata wince, but the bull's call was immediately answered by the rest of his kind in a similar manner. They were close enough now that Nedunj saw the Chola riding in the *howdah* of the nearest elephants whirl about at the noise, then begin frantically gesturing and, while he couldn't hear them yet, Nedunj was certain they were shouting the alarm. Nedunj briefly considered having his horn player play the call to attack, but a quick glance to either side told him there was no need; like Darpashata, every animal had seen the enemy and knew what to do. Even in the moment, Nedunj experienced a sudden insight, more specifically a memory, of when he had been young and, with childlike logic, had asked the *mahout* who was his first tutor in handling elephants how one could be certain that, when the moment came, an elephant would attack one of its own kind?

"Why do men try to kill each other?" the *mahout* had countered. Then, before young Nedunj could reply, he had explained, "While it is in our nature to make war on our own kind, we are not the only ones. Bull elephants fight each other for control of their herd, the females fight to protect their young. And," he had finished with a shrug, "we are not much different, really. We either fight to gain what we do not have but desire, or we fight to protect that which we love, and elephants are the same."

This was why, without slowing down, Darpashata took aim of an animal whose *mahout* had managed to slow and begin to turn his animal to face the oncoming threat, and Nedunj grabbed on to the side of the *howdah* with both hands while dropping into a crouch, as did the other three men, while the *mahout* had already laid himself flat in the bare instant before Darpashata's bronze armored headdress struck his foe in its left side. The impact, as might be expected, was tremendous, flinging Nedunj forward so violently that the breath was driven from his lungs when his chest slammed into the wooden wall of the *howdah*, and he was vaguely aware that his horn player went tumbling out of the basket with a shout of alarm. Darpashata had struck his foe squarely where the armored blanket, also made of bronze scales, hung below the *howdah*, but no amount of armor could have protected the other animal from the brutal force behind the collision, and even as he was slamming into the *howdah,* Nedunj heard a sound similar to several thick branches being snapped in two at one time as the animal's massive ribs gave way. Accompanying the sound, perhaps a full heartbeat later, was the sight of a gout of bright blood spraying from the trunk of the stricken elephant, but Nedunj had recovered and snatched up and immediately hurled one of the heavy javelins contained in the quiver attached to the *howdah* into the face of one of the Chola who, like him, had clung to the basket of his animal, although the Pandyan king recovered first, the throw sending the enemy warrior somersaulting out of the basket. Even if the Chola could have survived a javelin to the face, it was his fate to hit the ground a bare instant before his elephant toppled over to crush whatever life was left from him. The *mahout* of the fallen animal tried to throw himself clear but was unsuccessful, and he gave a shrill scream of pain as his legs were crushed between his elephant and the ground, while the remaining men were sent flying on the impact. One of Nedunj's archers drew and loosed in a fluid motion, pinning two of the men who were lying, stunned, to the ground, then sent an arrow into the back of the last man who had managed to scramble to his feet and was already beginning to sprint away. Darpashata's reaction was to give a shake of his massive head, while Nedunj felt the animal stagger a bit underneath him, then his trunk went back up and he gave another mighty blast, similar but slightly different than his first one, which the Pandyan king recognized as the sound of the triumphant warrior who has vanquished his foe.

For Hirtius and his cavalry, who were the only Romans present to witness combat between elephants, it was as memorable a sight as the day when his part of the army, under the overall command of Asinius Pollio, had encountered India's armored elephants for the first time. That had also been the day when, in their moment of extreme danger, Aulus Batius had come up with the weapon that they had used on this day to initiate the rout. While not quite as horrific as the sight of men and animals being burned alive, it was no less memorable seeing elephants slamming into each other, using their massive heads and their tusks as weapons, and in the process creating a noise that none of them had ever heard before. Despite his relative inexperience with the animals, Hirtius could see that the Chola elephants were in no frame of mind to put up much of a fight, which seemed to have been taken out of them with their first encounter when their fellow animals were essentially turned into moving torches.

He also observed how the elephants of Nedunj's force used their bronze-capped tusks, commenting to Decurion Silva next to him as he pointed to an example, "See that, Silva? They almost act like our Legionaries!"

On the surface, it was an odd comment, Silva thought, but he quickly saw why Hirtius had drawn the comparison as he watched one of the Pandyan elephants in the first line lower his head as it slammed into its foe, which had partially turned to face it, the attacker using the combination of bronze headdress and bony protuberance on the top of its head in much the same way a Legionary thrust his shield out at his foe, then, by whipping its head up, brought its tusks up like a Legionary would execute a thrust that came up from under his shield. In this case, the attacker was only partially successful, its head striking the shoulder of its opponent, while only one tusk drew blood, leaving a bloody gouge across the front leg as, again with an agility that was decidedly at odds with their appearance, the defending elephant made what could only be described as a hop backward. Despite it being successful in opening up some distance, it wasn't without cost, the initial impact causing the *howdah* on its back to lurch violently enough that one of the occupants lost his grip on the side, while its evasive answer then jolted that Chola up and out of the basket, the man giving a scream as he went flying into the air before plunging headfirst and striking the ground at an angle that made Silva wince, cutting the man's cry short as his neck was broken. The Pandyans atop the attacking elephant took advantage of the momentary lull as each animal recovered, with the pair of archers managing to loose their arrows an eyeblink more quickly than the four Cholas, while the lone Pandyan spearmen hurled the same kind of javelins that Nedunj had used. Three of the four missiles from the Chola missed, but an arrow struck one of the Pandyan archers in the shoulder, and he dropped out of sight down into the *howdah*, then the Pandyan elephant was already rushing forward again, its head lowered, except this time its foe was ready, and Silva was certain that he felt the ground vibrate up through his horse's legs when the two beasts collided, head to head. This time, the occupants of both *howdahs* were better prepared, and none of them left the basket involuntarily, the sound of the bronze headdresses crashing together making an unforgettable sound that, while similar to the clashing sound of iron on iron, was distinctly different.

All along the front line, similar smaller battles were taking place, although this one was better matched, and both Hirtius and Silva saw that the Chola animal was about to be isolated from its companions on either side, as the one to its left turned and tried to lumber away from its Pandyan opponent, while the one on the opposite side, with an agonized bellow, suddenly collapsed to its front knees, pitching all but the *mahout* off its back, whereupon the Pandyan elephant lifted one massive leg and brought it down onto one of the screaming Chola in the same way a human crushed an insect. Like all battles, the noise was horrific, but while there were similarities in the shouts, curses, and screams of the human combatants, there was the added element of the trumpeting calls of elephants celebrating their triumph over their foe, along with an almost human sounding groan when one of them succumbed to their wounds.

"I wish," Hirtius had to shout to be heard, "Caesar could see this."

It was less than a sixth part of a watch before Hirtius and his cavalry had anything to do, which was not much more than run down fleeing men, usually alone or in groups of twos and threes.

In the aftermath of what was by any measure a smashing victory, there would be officers, almost all of them Roman, who would question why Nedunj didn't send his elephants in pursuit of what was well less than fifty surviving animals, most of them missing some or all of their crews, including a few *mahouts*.

However, when Caesar did arrive and asked the young Pandyan, Nedunj's answer was simple.

"Because my animals were exhausted, Caesar. That is the only reason we did not pursue."

And, Caesar assured him, this was a reasonable explanation, and one that the general accepted. The truth was, in simple terms, that Caesar and his army hadn't expected such an easy, and overwhelming, victory. Certainly Caesar had expected to win, but the rashness of the dead Divakar had been a gift from the gods, the combination of the shock of seeing what, like Abhiraka, the Chola had believed to be an invincible weapon so easily destroyed, in both a grisly and memorable way, and what could only be called a foolish decision to confront Caesar's army in a manner that didn't allow them to use their numbers in an effective way had proven to be crucial. Caesar's estimation of the young Pandyan king had risen even more from this; after all, he had correctly predicted that the dead Crown Prince Divakar, whose demise at this moment was still unknown to them, would behave as rashly as he had, thereby giving Caesar and Nedunj the pretext for what came next. Not everyone was happy, as Pullus could attest, having to endure the complaining of his men at what they perceived to be an injustice.

"Those bastards in the cavalry didn't even have to draw their *gladii*," Sergeant Vespillo had complained to his Primus Pilus. "We're the ones that started this whole business by turning those fucking beasts into candles, but they're the ones who got first pickings just because they happened to be there? It's not right, Primus Pilus!"

As Pullus well knew, thanks to his Centurions, Vespillo wasn't alone in his complaining, but he also knew that the only time rankers complained about fairness was when they weren't the beneficiaries of whatever largesse was on offer. Still, he listened patiently, at least externally, although a part of him thought that perhaps putting his Legion on guard duty as the rest of the army constructed the camp might have been better. It was now afternoon, and while there was still almost a watch's worth of daylight left, which Caesar wouldn't have normally wasted, he announced that, in recognition of the extreme difficulty of the day's march, the men would be given extra time to recover by making camp early. The reality was far different; he needed the time to confer with his officers and regroup, given what he claimed was the completely unexpected result of the day. Only Pullus, and he assumed, Caesar's Legates, along with Nedunj, of course, were aware that this was a falsehood perpetrated by their general, and in collusion with the Pandyan king, something that Pullus had already decided he would take across the river with him.

"We could have pressed on," Caesar began, once the *praetorium* had been erected, "but there are matters we need to discuss now because of this unexpected development."

The assembled officers sat there, faces glistening from the heat, which was exacerbated by Caesar's order to keep the sides of the tent lowered, a convention that the Romans had adopted on their arrival in India by dividing the panels on each side so they could be raised to take advantage of a breeze, but it hadn't taken long for the men to determine that, when the sides were down, something important that would undoubtedly impact them was being discussed. Which, of course, meant that every man who worked in the *praetorium* in some capacity would be bombarded for information from rankers, and from officers below the grade of Primus Pilus, about the subject being discussed. It was a running joke that the richest men in the army were the clerks in the *praetorium*, and while it was untrue, every man under the standard would have been shocked to know that it was only by a matter of degree. Now, the Legates, Primi Pili, Nedunj, and the three Pandyans he had appointed as sub-commanders of the three arms of the allied forces sat listening as Caesar opened the discussion. Surprising none of them, it was the Pandyan king Caesar turned to first.

"Now that we've inflicted this much damage on their forces, what do you think the Chola will do next?"

Nedunj didn't answer immediately, considering the question before he replied, "It depends on whether or not their king listens to his son." With a shrug, he added, "If Prince Divakar has his way, I suspect that he would be willing to fight to the last man. Karikala is more like my father was, more cautious, and more likely to at least listen to what we have to say."

"And what *do* we have to say, Caesar?"

Instead of answering Pollio's question directly, Caesar instead indicated that Nedunj should answer, which earned him a glance that was both rueful and annoyed from the young Pandyan monarch. The truth was that, if Pollio had asked this question no more than two weeks earlier, Nedunj's answer would have been different, but it had been a subject of ongoing debate between himself and Caesar, who, as was his habit, had been persuasive in his argument. And, Nedunj only realized with hindsight, who had outmaneuvered the younger man by capitalizing on the combination of Nedunj's inexperience and eagerness to be known as the Pandyan king who had brought the mighty Chola low.

Consequently, he replied, "We will be content if Karikala agrees to a treaty that will secure our border with the Chola, he returns control of Madoura back to us as the rightful owners, and that he makes no overt offensive moves against my people, Legate Pollio."

This was a far cry from Nedunj's original demand, that Caesar help him crush the Chola threat once and for all by waging an all-out campaign against their bitterest rivals. In most ways, Nedunj was a rational thinker who naturally preferred to work out disputes in a way that limited bloodshed, but on the subject of the Chola, he had been conditioned from birth to hate the kingdom that posed the greatest threat. The idea of an alliance through marriage, for example, such as Nedunj's betrothal to the Bharuch princess Aarunya, would have been out of the question, and when Caesar had first broached the subject with his new ally, the Pandyan king had been blunt.

"I want to destroy the Chola kingdom for the rest of eternity, Caesar," he had replied flatly. "I want to ensure that my subjects' children and grandchildren never have to worry about those vermin raiding and destroying their crops and taking their livestock and raping their women."

Caesar didn't argue the point in that first conversation, but over the ensuing days, as they made final preparations to begin the campaign, he took every opportunity to point out the

Caesar Ascending – The Ganges

drawbacks and dangers inherent in the Pandyan's vision for obliterating his traditional enemy, and in doing so, gave Nedunj a unique insight into the older man's inner thoughts.

"You should be careful what you wish for, Your Highness," he had said this as the pair sat in Caesar's private quarters, which had belonged to the nobleman who had been Nedunj's closest adviser, and until he betrayed Nedunj in an attempt to seize power, friend in Alangudi. "The total destruction of an enemy can sometimes create at least as many problems as it solves."

There was something in the way that Caesar said it that alerted Nedunj, and as much as he had come to learn about Caesar, and recognized him as a singular personality in this world, he still wanted to learn as much about Caesar the man as he could; one never knew when such information might prove useful.

However, knowing that he had to tread carefully, Nedunj did his best to sound only partially interested, taking a sip from his cup before asking lightly, "Oh? How so?"

Caesar, who usually could be counted on to look directly in another man's eye when holding a conversation, instead studied his own cup, which was filled with the fruit juice concoction that he had first been offered by Nedunj when they were enemies, and which was his current choice of beverage that wasn't water.

"Several years ago," he began, still looking into his cup, "I gave orders to my Legions to punish two of the Gallic tribes during my campaign to subdue Gaul. They had violated the terms of an agreement between us, whereby they swore that, during my negotiations with their tribal elders, they wouldn't move from their current location, nor would they engage in any hostilities with my men."

He stopped then to take a sip, and despite suspecting this was his intent, Nedunj couldn't stop himself from demanding, "And?"

His belief was confirmed by the amused gleam in Caesar's eye, though it didn't last long as he explained, "What's important to know is that, at the time, I had been given information by one of the men in command of our cavalry that they had been ambushed, and he insisted that the ambush was carried out by a group of warriors from both of these tribes." Pausing, his tone took on a quality that Nedunj had never heard from Caesar before, and he wondered if it was regret, but it was the grimace that he noticed when Caesar continued, "The problem was that my cavalry at that time was almost completely composed of Gauls from a number of different tribes, and I didn't recognize just how much tribal hatred controlled everything these men said and did. It was only later that I discovered that my commander belonged to a tribe that was a traditional enemy of both these two tribes, and while there *was* an ambush, it wasn't by the Usipetes and Tencteri, but by members of his own tribe on them."

He stopped to take a sip again, while Nedunj was now listening intently, but this time, he didn't have the sense that Caesar was toying with him, but instead was reluctant to continue, which prompted Nedunj to gently press, "And, what happened, Caesar?"

"I marched my army to where the two tribes were camped along the Rhenus," Caesar's tone suddenly turned matter of fact, "and I ordered them to massacre every man, woman, and child we found there, as a punishment for breaking the terms of the agreement."

Nedunj, who had been leaning forward in intense interest, suddenly sat back, stunned into silence, and later, he decided it was as much from the manner in which Caesar described the wholesale slaughter of noncombatants as it was the thought itself.

"How...how many people were killed?" Nedunj finally managed to ask, and Caesar answered in the same detached way, "All told, we counted more than twenty thousand bodies."

Only vaguely recognizing the gasp of shock as his own, Nedunj didn't know what to say, and he sat there, staring at Caesar, who still refused to look at him as he went on, "At the time, it was believed that we had removed both tribes from existence. They were small to begin with, and before the elders were executed, they insisted that the encampment we found them at held the entire population of both tribes. That," Caesar did offer Nedunj a small smile, though it was a grim one, "turned out to be an exaggeration. In fact, both tribes exist, but they rely on Rome to protect them from the tribes around them from finishing the job." He paused again, his voice becoming softer, and more reflective. "It's the one decision during that campaign that, if I had to do it all over again, I would have done differently." Suddenly, he gave a short laugh, but Nedunj, who had heard Caesar laugh, though not often, heard no humor there. "If only because of all the trouble that it gave me back in Rome with my enemies, who tried to use it to have me stripped of my command and returned to Rome to face charges for mass murder."

This, unsurprisingly, deeply intrigued Nedunj, who knew next to nothing of Caesar and his life before he suddenly appeared off the beach of Muziris, leading a massive army. Naturally, he had heard of the Roman before that day, and he had witnessed firsthand the destructive capability of these foreign invaders, but only belatedly did the young Pandyan regret that he hadn't invested more time with Romans besides Caesar to learn more about him. Regardless of this, by the time Caesar posed the question in the *praetorium* fifty miles away from Madoura, Nedunj had been persuaded to take a different view than his original aim of conquest and subjugation.

"Should we send a delegation?" Caesar asked him, but this had been prearranged, something that Caesar did quite a bit, and he would have been surprised to know that this habit didn't surprise any of his Centurions anymore. "Or should we continue our march?"

"In my opinion," Nedunj replied, without hesitation, "we should get closer to Madoura to see how the Chola react. As I said, much depends on..."

He got no further, cut off in mid-sentence by the sound of the *Bucinator* of the Legion in charge of the first guard shift now that camp had been made, playing the call of a party approaching the *Porta Praetorium*. While this certainly created a stir, there wasn't the same level of urgency as the officers rose to their feet, because the notes played informed them that, while this was an unknown party, undoubtedly the Chola, the Centurion in command didn't believe it was an attack, which would have required a different rhythm and notes.

Nevertheless, when Caesar led the way from the *praetorium*, none of them hesitated to follow him, or match his fast pace to the earthen gate. As usual, Pullus, Balbinus, and Torquatus walked together, but they were far from alone; every Primus Pilus had a peer with whom he had a closer relationship than others, save one, and just as predictably as Pullus and the other two Centurions choosing each other's company, the Primus Pilus of the 8th, Clustuminus, walked alone.

As Balbinus had once put it, "If not even Batius wants to be around him, you know he's a miserable bastard."

None of which mattered now, but during the time it took them to cover the distance to the gate, which wasn't inconsiderable, the three Centurions learned they were of a like mind, that this could mean anything.

In one way, it had been an easy decision for Senganan to make. While he hadn't participated in the battle, or, more aptly, massacre of the Chola forces, he hadn't immediately joined the headlong flight back in the direction of Madoura, actually trying to stop it.

However, as one of the few *mahouts* who even deigned to slow his animal down had put it, "The only way I will be able to stop Arjuna here," he pointed down to his elephant, who was visibly quivering, the most potent sign that his *mahout* barely had his animal under control, "is to use this."

He had pointed down to the bronze spike hanging from his neck, but it was the elephant's behavior that convinced Senganan more than the *mahout's* words, and he had given the man a disgusted wave, noting that the *mahout* didn't hesitate in resuming their progress, joining back into the single line of animals that were moving at something more than their trot but not quite moving at their top speed. This was just before he saw the enemy cavalry move into position in front of the Pandyan elephants, and by doing so, it told Senganan that the enemy's elephants were done for the day, and while he understood that the battle was lost, he thought that they could at least inflict damage on the approaching horsemen. Standing in his *howdah*, he shouted at his retreating comrades, imploring them to regroup before changing his approach to harangue them, ending by insulting their courage, but while he received angry glares from several men atop their elephants, and a few even cursed him, most of his fellow Chola refused to acknowledge, or even look in his direction, and none of them stopped. Seeing that he would be isolated, only then did he give his own *mahout,* Shanu, the command to turn and join his fleeing compatriots, cursing each of them and their ancestors. Matching the pace set by the elephants already retreating, Senganan soon outstripped those unfortunate enough to be of the caste consigned to serve as infantry, many of whom begged the *mahouts* to stop their animals to allow them to climb up into their *howdah,* but they were universally ignored and soon were left behind.

    Since Senganan and his elephant Karna was one of the last to leave the field, it meant he was forced to witness the moment that the Roman cavalry came sweeping down to butcher the Chola infantry, but worst of all, he was still close enough to hear the screams of his countrymen as they were methodically run down and slaughtered. Senganan normally didn't particularly care about the plight of these men of the lower castes of Chola society, but he did feel he owed it to them to at least turn about in his *howdah* and watch as they were being annihilated, if only so that he could more accurately convey the scale of this defeat to Karikala. And, of course, to bring his king the news that his heir was now a charred lump of meat and lying in the middle of the pass, along with his elephant and crew. It was this thought, and all the ramifications of it that prompted Senganan to suddenly order Shanu to stop Karna's trot once he determined that the cavalry had no intention of trying to run down the Chola elephants, slowing back down to a walk as he thought things through. The Chola had certainly heard about what their peasants called the "demon fire" used by these foreign invaders, but while some of Senganan's class knew the name of the substance naphtha, none of his peers with whom he had spoken, including his king and Prince Divakar, believed it was otherworldly in origin, not that it mattered. What did matter was just how much of this substance their enemy had, and while it was certainly possible that the invaders had an extremely limited supply, it had only taken a veritable handful of what he could just make out were small pots hurled by the men on foot at the head of the enemy column to completely shatter the Chola attack. Yes, they had certainly been aided by Divakar's own foolishness in launching his assault far too soon, but Senganan reasoned, correctly, that if the men in the front of the column were armed with this terrible weapon, it stood to reason that there were more men in those neatly ordered rows who possessed it as well. Therefore, even if Divakar had waited until he could have initiated the ambush against the enemy flank, thereby bringing even more of the Chola elephants to bear, would it have changed the outcome? The answer, he was certain, was that not only would it have had the same result, but with far more than just five of their elephants being immolated, and it would have created even more of a panic among the other animals than it did, therefore it was easy for Senganan to envision that he would have returned to Madoura to report the total destruction of more than half of the total Cholan military might. As it was, while Senganan didn't know exactly how many animals had perished, either from the attack by the Pandyan elephants, or at the hands of their own *mahouts*, his guess was that less than fifty would return to Madoura. In fact, he wasn't altogether sure what Karikala would be most devastated by, the loss of his son or the loss of so many of their world's most potent weapon.

The more Senganan thought about it, the more he realized that, given that he was now the highest-ranking nobleman left with this remnant of the army, the likelihood that his king would lash out at him was extremely high. He would be bringing back the news of not only their defeat, but of Divakar's death, and it would be a fair question for Karikala to ask how it was that Senganan had survived while his son had not, nor the other senior nobleman Ajay, and the minor nobles Sanjaya and Vijaya that had comprised the high command of this effort. Because of his status as one of Karikala's senior councilors, Senganan had witnessed more than one execution ordered by the king, and indeed, he had been responsible for bringing some of the condemned to justice, which meant he had witnessed the ways in which Karikala had meted out punishment, of which being slowly crushed by an elephant was perhaps the kindest death of them all. He made his decision when the surviving remnants of the Chola army finally stopped their flight, the animals simply too exhausted to continue, and Senganan found them gathered together in a small forest, the elephants forming a series of protective circles around each other that none of the *mahouts* tried to prevent, long experience teaching them this could prove fatal to them.

When elephants were at the end of their collective tethers, much as their human counterparts, they found security and comfort with their own kind, which meant that Karna ignored Shanu's command and broke into a jolting run, his trunk raised and sounding a series of bleating calls that were answered in kind. The humans aboard the elephants were no less exhausted, but none of them clambered down from the backs of their animals, knowing the danger of dropping down into the midst of a herd of agitated beasts. Anyone with experience with elephants knew they were highly intelligent, and tales abounded of elephants who, rightly or wrongly, decided their human handlers and crewmen were responsible for the condition in which they found themselves, inevitably to the detriment of the two-legged beasts. Despite their fatigue, they were still incredibly dangerous, which meant that these men were essentially trapped in their *howdahs* and saddles, and they were careful to speak softly, nor did they move about, most of them dropping down into the *howdah* to sit there, waiting for the animals to recover enough, while the *mahouts* were universally stroking the massive head of their elephant while murmuring whatever each of them used to help calm their beast. For a short time, it appeared that only Senganan was aware of the possibility that there would be pursuit, and he stood erect as Karna settled into the outer ring of what was essentially several circles of animals, staring back in the direction from which they had come. Once or twice, he thought he saw the glint of metal, but it didn't have the golden tinge that would have been reflected off the bronze armor of other elephants, and he slowly relaxed as he determined that they weren't being pursued. It was then he made his decision, and while there was a certain level of self-preservation in it, there was another factor, and that was in his real concern for the likelihood that, should the Chola continue to resist, they would be forced to witness the further destruction of their power.

To Shanu, he ordered, "Turn Karna around, Shanu. We're going to speak to these Romans."

He wasn't surprised when Shanu balked, but when Senganan insisted, he learned that not only Shanu was reluctant, and it quickly became obvious that the three other men in the *howdah* with him were of a like mind. The fact that Murugan, one of the relatively few spear-wielding warriors among the *howdah* crews who was ostensibly there to protect Senganan, lowered the weapon so that it was not quite pointing at Senganan but was sending an unmistakable message, meant that the nobleman was forced into allowing the others to transfer to one of the animals on either side.

"I will inform King Karikala of your cowardice when I return to Madoura," Senganan warned, although he waited until the men were aboard other animals before issuing it.

In a sign of just how much matters had deteriorated, Murugan had sneered at this threat, saying confidently, "You won't be returning to Madoura, Lord Senganan. Those Roman demons will kill you and eat your flesh."

Before this day's events, Senganan would have scoffed at what he viewed as superstitious nonsense, certain that, while strange, these Romans were mortal men just like the Chola, or the Pandyan for that matter. Now, he experienced a sudden chill at Murugan's words, but he was committed, and he ignored the spearman. It was only then when he returned his attention back to Karna that he saw that Shanu hadn't moved from his saddle.

"Move, Shanu," Senganan snapped. "If you're as much of a coward as Murugan and the others, then I'll ride Karna myself."

However, Shanu, clearly unhappy, still didn't budge, instead looking up at Senganan as he said imploringly, "But what will they do to Karna, Lord Senganan? They are just as likely to use the demon fire on him as they were with Prince Divakar and his Ganesh!"

Although Senganan didn't miss the fact that the *mahout's* concern was for the animal and not for Senganan himself, he didn't fault Shanu for this, knowing the kind of relationship a *mahout*, a good one at least, had with his elephant, and he,

Caesar Ascending – The Ganges

Shanu, and Karna had been together for many years, and he knew that the *mahout* was sincere.

"Shanu," he said, not unkindly, "if that is fated to happen, it will happen, even if Karna is here, or with me, isn't that true?"

Shanu's dark features clouded as he tried to think through what, for him, was a complicated question, but he finally admitted, "Yes, Lord. I suppose that is true." This seemed to bring him to a decision, because he surprised Senganan then by saying, "Then, I will come with you, Lord. Karna will behave better with me than he would with you."

This show of devotion to his elephant brought a lump of what felt like hard iron to Senganan's throat, but he managed to reply in a voice choked with all of the emotion of that day, "And *when* we return, Shanu, I will tell our King of your courage, and you will be rewarded. I will see to that personally."

Shanu didn't respond verbally, but he did incline his turbaned head, then turned back around, but instead of using his goad, he bent down to speak softly in Karna's ear, which flapped in response. At first, the animal didn't move, but Shanu persisted, patting Karna on his massive head as he continued speaking, and while Senganan couldn't hear what the *mahout* was saying, he could hear the soothing tone. Finally, with obvious reluctance, Karna began moving backward, out of the circle of animals, some of whom raised their trunks and began chuffing at their comrade, which Senganan felt sure was their attempt to persuade Karna to stay. Instead, the elephant made a ponderous turn, and began walking back, towards the danger of an unknown but possibly horrific fate, for all three of them.

Chapter Three

It took almost a third part of a watch for Karna to retrace their steps back, the animal stopping more than once as if changing its mind, but Shanu managed to coax the elephant to resume walking each time. From his higher vantage point, Senganan finally saw what was nothing more than a darker line on the horizon that, only slowly, resolved itself into what he saw was a long dirt wall that appeared to be almost a mile long, and by the time he drew closer, holding the leafy branch of a tree that the kingdoms of southern India used as a sign of truce, he could see that it was lined with men, all of them wearing helmets.

While he knew that there would be someone who spoke Tamil, he was nevertheless surprised when he heard one of the men, he couldn't tell which, shout in his tongue, "That's far enough!"

Since it was in their tongue, Shanu didn't need to be told, stopping Karna, who signaled his anxiety with a low, rumbling groan, and Senganan wondered if it was because of the odor of these men who had slaughtered so many of his herd, or perhaps the smell of others of his kind who, by a fluke of birth, happened to be enemies.

Suddenly, he realized he hadn't thought about what he intended to say, other than in a general sense, and he hesitated, prompting the same man to demand, "What do you want, Chola?"

Even with the distance, and shouting, Senganan could hear

the loathing in the man's voice, a sentiment that he instinctively shared for what was obviously a Pandyan dog who had chosen to lick the boots of these invaders.

Somehow, he managed to keep the hatred from his voice as he answered, "I wish to speak to whoever is commanding this army."

"You mean you do not know?" the Pandyan retorted scornfully.

By this time, Senganan had identified the man among the dozen who were standing behind a wooden palisade that came up to the mid-chest of everyone but one man, and Senganan realized that that man was the giant he had seen earlier, both by his size and the white crest on his helmet, unleashing a feeling of such hate-filled but impotent rage, it caught him by surprise.

The Pandyan was young, and while he had never laid eyes on him, Senganan guessed, correctly, that this was the new king of the Chola's mortal enemy, so Senganan replied, "I know that you are Nedunj, first of his name and the new King of Pandya. But," he knew it was a bad idea, but he couldn't refrain from adding, "where is your new master? The Roman they call Caesar?"

He was rewarded by the manner in which the Pandyan king reacted, visibly stiffening, but he wasn't the man who answered.

"I," the man next to him, whose helmet bore a black crest instead of the white ones of the Romans surrounding him, and in another difference ran front to back, spoke for the first time, "am right here."

Caesar's gamble that this was a high-ranking noble of the Chola, and that, like the Pandya, would have a knowledge of Greek, had used that tongue, and he was rewarded by the manner in which the Chola reacted.

"You," Senganan switched from Tamil to heavily accented Greek, "are Caesar?"

"I am," Caesar confirmed. Before Senganan could say anything more, the Roman general demanded bluntly, "Why are you here, outside our camp? Have you come to surrender?"

Why, Senganan suddenly wondered, *had* he come? And, even if he did want to negotiate a surrender, what chances were there of Karikala accepting this as the best course? Yes, the fact that less than half of the army he had sent from Madoura would be returning would be a warning of the danger posed by these invaders, and Senganan was certain that, once the survivors were allowed to tell their tale, the scale of the disaster would be impossible to ignore, but would that be enough?

What came out of his mouth was, "I have come to talk, nothing more. I have no authority to negotiate on the behalf of my King."

Neither the Pandyan king nor Caesar responded to Senganan, and instead turned their backs, while the other men moved to cluster around the pair. It was impossible to hear, but he saw that whatever the conversation was about, it was spirited, and it seemed to be divided into two camps, with some men nodding their heads vigorously, while others were just as emphatic in shaking theirs. Just as had happened the first time the Romans had any contact with the kingdoms for whom the Tamil tongue was spoken, Senganan assumed the opposite of what was happening, that the men shaking their head were seemingly agreeing with whatever this Caesar was saying, while the others were disagreeing. The only thing he was right about was that it seemed to be evenly divided, but then, the Roman general lifted a hand, and he saw how the others immediately ceased talking, correctly seeing it as a sign of Caesar's complete authority that wouldn't have been out of place for a king.

When the men turned back to face in Senganan's direction, he got his answer not from Caesar, but from the Pandyan king, who said coldly, and in Tamil, "We will meet with you and hear what you have to say." Nedunj paused, then seemingly embarrassed, asked, "What is your name? And how do you serve your king? Or," Nedunj added, "do you serve Prince Divakar?"

"My name is Senganan, and I serve Karikala, son of Ilamcetcenni and called Karikala the Great, first of his name, and King of the Chola Dynasty." For half of a heartbeat, he considered informing them about Divakar's demise, but decided this was best withheld for the time being. However, he wasn't lying when he said, "And I am the commander of the part of our army that you just faced. A *very* small part of our army," he added, not wanting to appear as weak as he knew his kingdom was at this moment.

"Well, Lord Senganan, if you wish, you can bring your elephant into our camp," Nedunj informed him, but while he didn't need to, the Pandyan demonstrated that he was a man who was familiar with elephants by adding, "unless your animal is unwilling. He has already smelled our elephants, of course. And," for the first time, Nedunj's tone was not unfriendly, "I know that can be a good thing...or a bad one."

Recognizing the gesture, Senganan replied, "I think it would be better if I leave Karna out here. But," he tried not to sound as if he was pleading, "may I impose on you to give him water, and some feed?"

"Of course," Nedunj answered immediately. "I will have one of my *mahouts* attend to your Karna, and we will bring water and food for your own *mahout* while he waits."

Only then did Senganan give Shanu permission to order Karna to drop to his knees, allowing Senganan to climb out of the *howdah*.

As he lowered himself by stepping on Karna's huge knee, Shanu asked anxiously, "Lord, what should I do if these savages betray you?"

"You will return to Madoura," Senganan said. Then, appreciating the *mahout's* concern, he tried to sound confident as he assured Shanu, "But I don't think they will betray me, Shanu. After all," he pointed out, "they wouldn't be wasting water and feed for either of you if they intended to kill us, would they?"

Senganan was relieved to see that Shanu accepted this. Or, he thought with bitter amusement, he's a better liar than I thought. Then, he was on the ground, and with a pounding heart, he walked towards the earthen gate of his enemy's encampment, still unsure why he was doing so, and what he was going to say when he got there.

The debate on the rampart had been about whether or not to allow the Chola into the camp, with Batius leading the Primi Pili who didn't want to let an enemy to get a glimpse of anything that they might use against them later. On the other side was, among others, Pullus, but his reasoning was based more on his knowledge of how Caesar thought, which he proved when he gave his reason for allowing the Chola into the camp.

"If he sees what his king and his people are up against," he had said simply, "I think it can only help us, not hurt us."

As Pullus surmised, this was exactly what Caesar was thinking, but for reasons of his own, the general let the debate go on for longer than he otherwise would have, given the circumstances.

Once the agreement was reached, Caesar informed the Primi Pili and Legates, "While you'll accompany us with our guest to the *praetorium*, only King Nedunj and I will talk with this Lord Senganan."

He wasn't surprised when Pollio, Hirtius, and some of the Primi Pili clearly didn't like this, but he noticed that, of the others, Pullus looked more relieved than anything, reminding Caesar that, of all the dizzying array of challenges that faced a Roman army in such a foreign land, acts of diplomacy, and the subsequent negotiating required, didn't interest his huge Primus Pilus at all. Titus Pullus was, Caesar had learned, completely disinterested in such matters, particularly politics as practiced by the Romans of upper classes. What Caesar only intuited was that this lack of interest wasn't based in an inability to follow the nuances and intricacies of that world, but in Pullus' recognition that, because of his status, which, as powerful as a Primus Pilus in Caesar's army might have been, he had limited ability to influence events. In the soldier's parlance, Titus Pullus had learned, like many of his comrades, that there was no point in worrying about things that one didn't have the power to change or influence. Nedunj had summoned Sundara, the Pandyan who had served under Lord Maran, who had remained behind in Muziris, and was now the sub-commander of the Pandyan elephants, giving him the task of ensuring that the Chola elephant was cared for, which in itself wasn't a simple task.

"He probably needs to water himself down," Nedunj told Sundara, "so he'll need a whole barrel. Have Sekhar see to it," naming Darpashata's *mahout* who, even more than Nedunj, had an affinity and bond with Abhiraka's bull that the Bharuch king might have envied, given their short association.

Sundara was unhappy about being given what he saw as menial task, but he bowed nonetheless and hurried off, while the assembled officers descended the sloped rampart and stood at the *Porta Praetoria*, relying on the pair of Legionaries who stood on the outermost dirt wall that served as the gate entry to track Senganan's progress. Winding his way around the barrier, he appeared, and while he was certainly nervous, he didn't show any fear.

There was an awkward moment as he stood there, while the officers did the same, staring at each other before, finally, Nedunj took a step forward, saying formally in Tamil, "Greetings, Lord Senganan of the Chola. As you said, I am Nedunj, son of Puddapandyan and the King of Pandya, which has been named a Friend and Ally of Rome. And," he turned to indicate Caesar, "this is the Roman, Gaius Julius Caesar, Dictator for Life, who..." suddenly, Nedunj's face clouded as he tried to recall the proper wording, "...represents the People and Senate of Rome."

Caesar didn't correct Nedunj for transposing the two, but he made a made a mental note to remind the Pandyan that the name of the Senate always preceded the People.

Caesar didn't bow, but he did ever so slightly incline his head as Nedunj made the introduction, then, without saying anything himself, turned and began striding towards the *praetorium*, surprising only Senganan, while the others tried to hide their amusement at the sight of the Chola nobleman forced to hurry to catch up. For his part, Pullus actually felt a stab of sympathy, having been subjected to this treatment himself, the only consolation being that, with his longer legs, he didn't have to run to catch up like a boy chasing after his Tata.

As Caesar intended, the walk along the *Via Praetoria* to the large tent in the center of the camp was both instructive and disheartening for Senganan. More than the size of it, it was the plainly visible order and regularity, with tents of a uniform size, now made of canvas instead of leather, another modification made in recognition of the climate of India, aligned in neat rows and in a pattern that he could recognize as a grid that was daunting in itself, this level of organization completely unknown to the Chola. In front of each tent, he saw men dressed in tunics all dyed red, although the shade varied, gathered around what he saw was a charcoal fire, and he tried to ignore their stares as he followed the Roman and Pandyan. It looks, he thought dismally, like a small city, and in fact, he wondered if there were as many men within the dirt walls that stretched as far as the eye could see in every direction as there were in all of Madoura. By the time they reached the tent, the nagging belief that had prompted Senganan to turn back and return hardened into a conviction that, had he known it, was shared by the Pandyan next to him, to Parthians like Bodroges and the one-eyed Teispes, the King of Pattala and the Queen of Bharuch, Hyppolita, that these Romans represented a threat that their world had never encountered before. Most crucially, combined with what he had witnessed what was now just two Roman watches earlier, Senganan reached the conclusion that, in simple terms, this invader was unbeatable, at least by the Chola alone, although the idea of allying with the Pandya for the purpose of defeating these Romans never entered his mind, but the thought that it might be time to suggest to King Karikala to prevail on their supposed ally Andhra to combine forces did occur to him.

When they reached the large tent, Senganan noticed that none of the other men, not even the giant Roman who he had been surreptitiously, and nervously, watching out of the corner of his vision entered, only Caesar, the Pandyan, and him. The contrast from bright sunlight to the dimmer interior of this space took him several heartbeats to adjust to, but he immediately saw that it was full of men, and every one of them seemed to be moving in one direction or another, holding either what looked to him like two pieces of wood pressed together or the more familiar scroll. While none of them were shouting, there was a buzzing of conversation, but with a cadence and intonation that was completely foreign to him, although, by their coloring and complexion, he recognized some of them as likely being Greeks, like those merchants who regularly came to Uraiyur, usually from the island they called Taprobane that was under

Cholan control. Others were paler, but what intrigued Senganan were a handful of men who, he felt certain, were Pandyan judging by their coloring, although he couldn't hear them speaking. Following the Roman, when Caesar reached the far side of the main chamber, he swept aside a hanging partition that served as a door, motioning to Senganan, who tried to show no fear as he walked into what, he immediately saw, was undoubtedly the private quarters of the commander of this mighty army.

Pointing to a small table, where Senganan noticed there were three stools, Caesar's tone was that of a host, albeit one who spoke in Greek, "Would you care to sit, Lord Senganan?"

Feeling a bit more at ease now that he was operating in the world of the courtier, Senganan took the offered seat, then waited as what he assumed was a slave appeared with a pitcher and three cups on a tray, which he set on the table. The Chola was slightly surprised when, rather than the slave, it was Caesar who poured three cups, then with elaborate courtesy, offered Senganan one, which he gratefully accepted, suddenly aware of how thirsty he was. He expected water, but instead it was a fruit juice that, unknown to him until he tasted it, was something that the Chola and Pandya shared, both kingdoms having a strong affinity for the mixture. Before he could stop himself, Senganan drained the cup, which Caesar noticed and immediately refilled, offering the Chola a small smile.

"It has been," he said with what Senganan took to be a wry amusement, "a hot day."

Before Senganan could respond, there was a knocking sound from the direction of the hanging partition, the Chola having missed the piece of wood that hung next to it, while Caesar said something in Latin that, when the partition was pushed aside, Senganan deduced was permission to enter. The man who entered was young, perhaps slightly older than Nedunj, who, to this moment, hadn't said anything, but while the new arrival was darker in complexion than Caesar, he wasn't nearly as dark as Senganan, or Nedunj for that matter. He was, however, wearing the same kind of tunic that he had seen worn by the soldiers around their fires, which made Senganan wonder if Romans were more diverse than he had assumed. The mystery of the new man's identity was solved when Caesar introduced him.

"This is Achaemenes," Caesar announced. "He is a Parthian, but he speaks several languages, including Tamil." Seeing Senganan's confusion, he explained, "Achaemenes is originally from Parthia, but his father was a merchant who traded with Bharuch. Achaemenes spent time there, and learned both Sanskrit and Tamil."

This, strictly speaking, wasn't true; Achaemenes had learned to speak Sanskrit, but it had been Barhinder Gotra, who now worked as the interpreter for the Primus Pilus of the 10th Legion, who had taught him the differences between Sanskrit and Tamil, none of which mattered in the moment.

Senganan, despite knowing that it was a breach of etiquette, addressed the Parthian, asking bluntly in Tamil, "Why are you serving these Romans?"

If his intent was to rattle Achaemenes, he didn't succeed, the Parthian not hesitating to explain, "Because I have seen what Rome is capable of, and I know that they cannot be defeated." Sensing there was an opportunity, he added, "And they allowed us to keep our dignity, Lord Senganan. We can still worship our gods, and we are allowed to conduct our business as we always have. The only thing they require is that we do not cause trouble."

"So," Senganan replied bitterly, "you are slaves."

In what would turn out to be the most persuasive argument Senganan would hear during this meeting, Achaemenes countered quietly, "No more than we were under our Kings, Lord Senganan. If anything, my people of the lower classes have more freedom than they ever had under King Orodes. And," while he didn't know Achaemenes, Senganan clearly heard the bitterness, "far more than with our last king, Phraates."

Suddenly, Nedunj spoke for the first time to assure Senganan, "What Achaemenes says is true, Lord Senganan. Yes, the Romans came as invaders, but they have shown themselves to be just in their dealings with us. Far more," he added, "than what we show those people we conquer."

Taking this as an opening, Senganan asked bluntly, "Is that

why you surrendered to them, King Nedunj? Is that why you allied yourself with your conqueror?"

The only sign that Nedunj was angered was the slight tightening of his jaw, but his tone was even as he answered, "Caesar and I reached an agreement to save my people more suffering and loss, Lord Senganan. In fact," he said with a quiet, and justifiable, pride, "we had stopped the Romans on the beach at Muziris, something that nobody, not Pattala, nor Bharuch, nor the Parthians had done before." He glanced over at Caesar, suddenly worried that the Roman understood more of what he was saying than he wanted, having learned never to underestimate the man, but Caesar seemed to only be interested, not irritated or angered by what Nedunj was saying. And, he was honest enough to admit, "That being said, I also recognized that, while we *might* have repelled the Romans, it would be at such a horrible cost that we would never recover."

This was the conclusion Senganan had drawn, and despite the circumstances, he suddenly felt vindicated in that belief.

"So," he asked cautiously, "what is your status, then, King Nedunj? Are you a vassal state?"

Rather than answer immediately, Nedunj turned to Caesar, and while his Latin wasn't fluent, Nedunj was able to communicate well enough that the Roman understood what Senganan was asking. Instead of trying to relay the information through Nedunj, Caesar turned to Achaemenes, who by this point had been versed in the intricacies of the various meanings of the terms Roman used for those they had conquered.

"The Romans do not use the term 'vassal'," Achaemenes explained, "but 'client' instead." Seeing Senganan's blank stare, which the Parthian could understand, he went on, "Romans use a system they call clientage, and what that means is that, while a client owes their patron fealty, the patron also has responsibilities to the client."

"What are those responsibilities?" Senganan asked.

For the next several moments, Achaemenes explained the various duties that existed between patron and client, which was completely foreign to Senganan, recognizing that there was no such system in their world. If one kingdom conquered another, the conquered were to be used and abused as the conqueror saw fit, and there was no kind of reciprocal agreement whereby the subjugated had anything resembling rights. And, while he suspected that this Parthian might be oversimplifying the relationship, it was nevertheless intriguing to think that his king would have some sort of autonomy.

"What about taxes?" Senganan asked, once Achaemenes had finished his initial explanation.

"A client kingdom is free to set taxes at whatever level he sees fit," Achaemenes assured him. "Provided that Rome gets the payment that is agreed to beforehand."

Senganan considered this, and while he was certain that matters weren't that simple, he couldn't deny the fact that he was sitting there with a Parthian and a Pandyan, both of whom seemed to accept Rome's dominion over their respective kingdoms.

Nedunj spoke up again to inform Senganan, "As part of our agreement, Lord Senganan, we now have a new market for our peppercorns and other spices, our hardwoods, and our cotton. All of which," he pointed out, "you Chola produce as well. Yes, it is still early," he allowed, "but if the Romans uphold this agreement, my people will reap even more benefit from our trade than they ever have before, because the Han will no longer be our largest source of trade income."

This certainly was interesting to Senganan, but one of his areas of expertise was in trade, and he immediately saw a potential issue, which he pointed out.

"If what you say is true, King Nedunj, and," he hurried on, seeing the Pandyan's features darken at the insult, "I believe you are being honest, since you are already supplying these Romans with, as you point out, the same things that we produce, will that not mean there is not as much demand for them?"

Nedunj didn't reply directly to Senganan, turning instead to explain to Caesar, in Latin, Senganan's concerns. Caesar signaled Achaemenes, who had remained standing just behind the general, then, still using Latin, spoke for a span of several heartbeats of time.

When Caesar was finished, it was Achaemenes who spoke next. "Caesar assures you that there is more demand for these things than the Pandyan and the Cholan kingdoms can supply.

Caesar Ascending – The Ganges

Rome," he explained, "is just a city, that is true, Lord Senganan, but it now controls more territory than any nation on earth. And Rome's wealth is such that their upper classes can both afford, and strongly desire these items as a way to let their fellow Romans know that they can. It is," Achaemenes finished with a sardonic smile, "not that different in Parthia, if I am being honest."

"Nor is it that different in my kingdom," Senganan decided to repay the Parthian's honesty with his own, and he also smiled. Deciding to accept the Pandyan's claim for the moment, Senganan turned to look at Caesar as he asked bluntly, in Greek, "So, what do you want from the Chola, Caesar?" Suddenly, he felt a flood of heat rush to his face, and he hurriedly added, "Forgive me, Lord Caesar, but I do not know how to address you since I do not know your title."

Senganan would have cause to remember this moment, if only because in his experience no man of high status behaved in the manner in which Caesar did.

"I," the Roman said, with an enigmatic smile, "am Caesar. That is enough." The smile went away, and Caesar continued, "Now, as far as what I want, it is simply this."

For the next few moments, Caesar did all the talking, while Senganan sat silently, his mind whirling at what he was hearing, but when Caesar was finished and asked Senganan if he had any questions, the Cholan couldn't think of any, so thorough had Caesar explained his requirements.

However, he knew that he had to say something, and he heard his own voice say, "That is...acceptable, Caesar." He had to stop himself from the absurd impulse to thank the Roman for showing what, in his experience, was a remarkable level of clemency for a man who commanded a force of such overwhelming power. Finally, something occurred to him, and he asked, "But how can I convince my King that it is in our best interest to agree?"

Because his association with Caesar was so short, he was surprised when the Roman said, "I actually have had an idea about how to do that very thing."

Then, in another unusual moment, Caesar seemed to defer to Nedunj, but they again spoke in Latin, so Senganan didn't understand Caesar when he asked the Pandyan king, "Your Highness, do you think that the Cholan king would have the same reaction you did if we do a demonstration similar to what we did when Alangudi tried to seize power?"

While the Pandyan king didn't care for Caesar bringing up the nobleman who had been Nedunj's closest friend and councilor until his betrayal when he attempted to usurp the new king's throne, he forced himself to think about the Roman's question objectively.

"Yes," he finally answered, recalling the moment when he witnessed firsthand the weapon that Rome, as was their habit, not only copied from the Parthians, but had refined and improved its usage, and his understanding that, as long as they had it, his elephants were rendered largely impotent. "I think that should be enough."

Senganan's return to Madoura three days later was less than a day ahead of Caesar and his army, and the Cholan nobleman had resigned himself to the idea that, by the time Caesar arrived within sight of his Madoura's walls, Senganan would in all probability be dead. His only real hope was that King Karikala would be merciful and simply behead him and not choose another, more excruciating method. Despite his repeated assurances to the *mahout*, Shanu grew more and more fearful as they approached the city, and it didn't help that, by this time, every village and town they had to pass through to get there had been informed of the crushing defeat at the hands of foreign invaders. The fact that Senganan was lagging so far behind the remnant of the army was a cause for suspicion on the part of the villagers, and it was only because of his own status that their anger and grief was restricted to glares and muttered curses as Karna lumbered through each town. Every one of these places had lost someone, Senganan knew, since the men who served as the Chola infantry were invariably drawn from the lowest castes, which comprised the bulk of the population in both kingdoms. Complicating matters further, and another factor in the hostility on the part of these simple people, was that this entire area between the Ghat Mountains and Madoura had changed hands many times over the previous centuries, making for a complex tangle of loyalties, not that the Cholan king cared all that much, provided that they pay their taxes and pick up spear and shield when commanded.

When the walls of the city, located on the southern bank of the Vaigai River, were visible, Senganan fought the urge to order Shanu to take the road heading west that would take them to one of his private estates ten miles from the city, where his wife and children were waiting for him, to make final arrangements with his wife for what he viewed as his almost inevitable death. Judging from the *mahout's* behavior, Shanu was of a like mind, but when Senganan ordered him to continue guiding Karna north on the wide main road, he obeyed without comment. Like the Romans, the walls of the Chola controlled city were manned, although these men were of the Chola royal guard, who had been ordered to stay behind by the king, despite his son's pestering to be allowed to take them on what the crown prince had believed would be a resounding victory that would add fame and glory to Divakar, and he would quickly add, to his father's name as well. Karikala had refused, and while it seemed to have been a prudent decision, in his heart, Senganan had come to the conclusion that it wouldn't have made any difference either way. Over the course of the previous two days, starting once he had been allowed to leave the Roman camp, although they only went a short distance before stopping for the night, Senganan had had more than enough time to think, actually welcoming the solitude that came from it being just himself and his *mahout*, who had always been taciturn by nature, preferring to reserve most of his conversation with his elephant than with his human master.

There was one unfortunate consequence of not having a full crew for Karna, because two men couldn't remove the *howdah* by themselves, which meant the elephant was forced to endure it for longer than was ideal. While elephant hide was tough, it was less so along the back and spine, which meant that the equivalent of saddle sores that horses could suffer were a constant danger. The best the pair could do was loosen the straps of the girth that secured the *howdah*, while Shanu used a special salve that he rubbed into the elephant's sides, under the armored blanket. They did remove the headdress, which was carried in the *howdah*, but Karna's mood had been growing increasingly obstreperous, making it a fair question of whether or not the animal would rebel before reaching Madoura. Thankfully, for all of them, Karna's acute sense of smell alerted the bull that they were returning to what he thought of as home, in the form of the other elephants that served Chola's army, so that Shanu actually had to do his best to curb the elephant, who had broken into a trot the last half-mile to the southern gate. Despite the uncertainty surrounding his return, Senganan did feel his face crease into a smile as the elephant began making the short, staccato bleating sound that, while it could indicate either alarm or anticipation, every experienced handler could differentiate between the two, and he knew that Karna was excited to be among his own kind again. *I can only hope that I have a similar reception, my giant friend*, Senganan thought, though he didn't expect to be welcomed back with the same warmth that elephants showed each other when one of them had been away.

When they came close enough that the guards on the wall could make out his features, Senganan was relieved that the gates were opened, but there was no mistaking the hostility that was strikingly similar to the people of the villages through which they had passed, although Senganan pointedly ignored the guards. As Karna walked through the high arched gateway, Senganan noticed that the traffic on the streets was lighter, and the people who were out seemed subdued, a few even looking frightened as Karna lumbered by, which was unusual in this city so accustomed to the animals, not only those bred for war like Karna, but for the much larger number who were used in the same way as mules and oxen in other cultures. His mouth had gone completely dry by the time Shanu guided Karna across the open paved square, where what served as the royal palace whenever the king was present was located on the northern side, but the nobleman immediately saw that, rather than the customary pair of royal guards standing at the entrance, there were more than a dozen. *What's that about?* he wondered. *Is the King concerned for his safety? Has someone threatened him?* While this was certainly a valid question, not just with a Chola king, but with a monarch from any of the kingdoms of India,

Senganan quickly dismissed this as a possibility, if only because the most potent threat to Karikala was from his own son, it being a common occurrence for sons to depose their fathers, but Divakar was gone now. As Karna knelt and Senganan climbed down, a thought occurred to him, one that caused him to stand there, motionless, as his mind raced through the possibilities. Maybe none of the men who returned had had the nerve to tell Karikala that Divakar is dead, he considered, and since he hasn't returned, the king's mind has gone through the reasons for the prince's absence, and has decided it must be for a nefarious purpose. After all, it had been no secret that Divakar had begun to chafe at what he considered his father's soft rule, and Senganan had certainly heard the whisperings about the prince's ambitions. But, even if Divakar had been plotting, he had been wise enough not to approach Senganan, whose loyalty to Karikala had been unwavering since his arrival at the king's court. Determining that there was only one way to find out, Senganan squared his shoulders, took a breath, and readied himself to walk up the steps to the portico, where the bodyguards were standing, spears held vertically, watching the two men and animal.

Remembering the presence of the other two at the last moment, Senganan told Shanu quietly, "Take Karna to the royal enclosure and see to his needs. I'm sure there will be men to help you remove his *howdah* and you can check for sores. Then," he said firmly, "you see to your own, Shanu. And," he hesitated, feeling awkward because he normally didn't say such things, but he felt it was necessary, "thank you for your service, Shanu. If things don't go...well," he settled on that word, "...for me, I want you to tell the Mistress Hema that I am rewarding you for what you have done these last few days."

Shanu looked unhappy, and Senganan experienced a stab of irritation, thinking that it was because Senganan hadn't been specific in naming what that reward would be, but he quickly learned differently, and felt ashamed when Shanu said quietly, "Don't you have any message for the Mistress besides that, Lord? So that I can tell her that she was in your thoughts, if...?"

He didn't finish, but there was no need, Senganan cursing himself for his thoughtlessness, and he replied, "You are right,

Shanu. That would be unforgiveable. Tell her that her husband loves her more now than the first day I laid eyes on her at our wedding, and that I am thankful to the goddess Kamakshi that she sent her to me. And," he felt the lump forming in his throat, "have her tell our children that their father loves them, and is proud of the men and woman they will become."

"Yes, Lord, I will," Shanu assured him, but all Senganan could manage was a brief shake of the head.

He took a step to place his hand on Karna's massive shoulder, as he murmured, "Thank you for your service these last years, Lord Karna. I hope we're reunited, but if we're not, I could not have had a better champion than you."

Karna's response was to lift his trunk and wrap it around Senganan's shoulders as he made snuffling noises that those who knew elephants understood. Giving his trunk a pat, Senganan stepped away from Karna, then on legs that he hoped the guards couldn't tell were shaking because of the loose trousers he was wearing, Senganan walked to the steps and ascended them. Recognizing one of the guards, taller than average, with a short, trimmed beard and a livid white scar that ran diagonally across his face, Senganan addressed him, knowing that he was the commander of these men.

"Commander Prashant," he thought, adding the appellation might help his case, "I have returned from the south..."

"Yes, Lord," Prashant cut him off, warning Senganan that he might be in danger, "we know where you were." His tone was brisk and businesslike, but now Senganan thought he heard something else there as Prashant continued, "But the rest of the army arrived some time ago, and the King has been asking about your whereabouts, and why you were not with them."

"That," Senganan replied coldly, "is why I must see our King immediately. And," he knew it was a risk, but he thought it worthwhile, "I will be sure to tell him that I was delayed by you because you couldn't control your curiosity."

This angered the bodyguard, but Senganan saw it also made him cautious, and he guessed that Karikala might be in a dangerous mood at this moment.

"Please wait here, Lord Senganan," Prashant inclined his head. "I will go let the King know you have arrived."

Caesar Ascending – The Ganges

Now, he thought, I'll learn something about what awaits me; if the King makes me wait, then I'm almost certainly a dead man. Almost. However, even before he finished the thought, the door opened and Prashant stepped out.

"The King is waiting for you in the throne room, Lord Senganan. I am to escort you to see him."

Despite the potentially ominous meaning for this, Senganan didn't hesitate to follow Prashant, but he immediately noticed the entry hall and outer room of the palace was deserted. Normally, there would be at least a dozen people, mostly men but a sprinkling of women who fulfilled the same purpose for Karikala's queen as their male counterparts did for Karikala himself, hanging about and engaged in quiet conversations that were usually little more than gossip about their peers. In this respect, while Senganan had no way to know it, the Chola, Pandya, and other kingdoms of India were virtually identical to other kingdoms in different parts of the world, where an ambitious few members of the upper classes, however they were styled, congregated around the seat of power, always competing and jockeying for a position of favor from their monarch or chieftain. To a certain degree, this described Senganan as well; he was the eldest son of one of the most powerful non-royal nobility families, and his father had sent him to the capital to protect, and to advance, the interests of that family. Where Senganan differed was in his sheer competence, having earned the confidence of their King with that quality, along with his utter loyalty to Karikala, all of which now hung in the balance. The absence of fellow courtiers rattled his already unsettled nerves, and when Prashant reached the closed double doors that led into the large chamber that served as the place where Karikala held his audiences while seated on an ornately carved mahogany chair with an extremely high back so that the figures of the range of deities that the house of Karikala worshiped could be seen, Senganan forced himself to take several deep breaths to calm himself. Like the outer room, as Senganan stepped inside, he instantly saw that it was empty, save for his King, who was seated on his throne, although he didn't even glance in Senganan's direction. Another change was the lack of light; the windows, that normally remained open during the daylight hour were closed, but there were only a handful of lamps lit, forcing Senganan to squint to make out more detail.

"Your Highness," Prashant broke the silence, making Senganan jump slightly, "Lord Senganan is here."

Another unusual moment occurred when, without waiting for Karikala to respond, Prashant turned and exited the room, closing the door behind him and prompting the thought: Well, at least he's not staying here to execute me...yet. Senganan stood there, waiting to be told by Karikala he could approach, which was the custom, but as his eyes adjusted to the gloom, he saw that the king seemed to be fixated on a spot on the floor in front of his throne. After a dozen heartbeats where the king neither spoke nor moved, Senganan began to cautiously approach, but when he finally got close enough to get a good look at Karikala, he immediately wished he hadn't done so. What he was looking at was a man who had visibly aged, almost literally overnight, and for whom life was clearly a burden. His shoulders were hunched in the manner of a man two decades older than Karikala's forty-five, and while the king had had lines in his face that came with his age and exposure to the broiling sun and weather, now those lines were deep crevices, but it was the abject apathy Senganan saw in his monarch's eyes that struck him with the force of a punch to his stomach.

"My King," Senganan dropped to his knees, lowering his forehead to the mosaiced floor, "I can see that you have learned about the tragic death of your son, Prince Divakar, but I assure you, he died bravely, leading our men from the front."

"My son," Karikala's voice was a raspy whisper, "was a fool." He heaved a sigh that was almost as terrible to hear as his appearance. "I have known that for some time, but..." he shrugged, and his voice cracked from a grief that Senganan prayed he would never know, that of a parent who has outlived a child, "...he was still my son, and I loved him, fool that he was." For the first time, Karikala lifted his head to look directly in to Senganan's eyes, and the nobleman saw a flicker of the king he had known, served, and feared, while his tone became sharper. "But it does make me wonder how is it that, when my son, Lords Ajay, Sanjaya, and Vijaya all perished, yet somehow

Caesar Ascending – The Ganges

here you are, alive and," he made a show of examining Senganan, "apparently unharmed."

And, there it was. Senganan now had a choice, one that he had been wrestling with for days now, yet he was no closer to a decision when he had entered this room. As he saw it, his choices were to admit to cowardice, or the real reason, knowing that, as Karikala had said himself, his son was a fool who was essentially committing suicide when he refused to wait. The fact that, now that Senganan had seen what he had, understanding that, even if Divakar had waited, not only would their attack have ended in defeat, it would almost undoubtedly have meant even more destruction of their most powerful asset in the elephants made it even more complicated.

Without making a conscious decision, Senganan began, "As you said, Your Highness, Prince Divakar was...unwise." He settled on the kinder word. "But," he had to swallow twice before he could continue, "what I can assure you is this. Even if the Prince had waited and not ordered our attack prematurely, while it is hard to believe, I'm certain that our losses would have been even greater."

He wasn't surprised when Karikala offered a dismissive wave at this, scoffing, "There is no way that you can know that, Senganan!"

"I can, Your Highness," Senganan replied, respectfully but firmly. "In fact, the reason I was delayed was because I met with the invaders. And," he took a breath, "I have made arrangements for a truce that will allow me to prove it to you."

When Senganan departed the palace, his legs were as shaky as they had been when he entered, but this time it was from relief that he was allowed to leave alive. He understood he was still in terrible danger, and he hated the idea that he was forced to rely on both the Pandya and Romans to convince his King and save his own life in the process. Nevertheless, he was certain he was doing what was best for Chola.

As they had agreed with Senganan, the invading army halted five miles from Madoura, building their huge camp across several fields belonging to Chola farmers, all of whom had fled for their lives to the nearby village at the approach of the Roman army. The day after their arrival, Senganan returned, but this time, he was on horseback and had an escort of royal bodyguards, numbering fifty men, but while this hadn't been discussed, Caesar made no mention of it when the Cholan noble was escorted to the *praetorium*.

"My King will arrive here at midday tomorrow," Senganan had informed Caesar and Nedunj, both of whom hid their relief, but Senganan wasn't through. He hesitated, bracing himself for a negative reaction, "He also insists on bringing his army with him, fully armed and armored."

Of the two, Nedunj reacted most strongly, leaping to his feet to point down at Senganan, although he directed his words at Caesar, "I *told* you these dogs cannot be trusted, Caesar! That was not part of the agreement! And," he insisted, "why would Karikala need to bring his entire army unless he intends to challenge us to battle?"

Since he had spoken in Greek, Senganan understood, although just by Nedunj's reaction it wouldn't have mattered, and he snapped, though in Tamil, "So says the hyena who used these Romans to come skulking across our border!"

"We only did that because your fool of a crown prince chose to attack our ally, in direct violation of the agreement that was made!"

Senganan was about to retort, when Caesar raised a hand. Despite not liking the Roman's presumption that he would heed a nonverbal command like this, Senganan snapped his mouth shut.

"Your Highness," Caesar's tone was reasonable and in stark contrast to the heat from his Pandyan ally, which was directed to Nedunj, "what does it matter if this is what King Karikala needs to feel secure? We know our intentions, but he does not, so it is understandable that he would feel it necessary to take this precaution." Then, he switched to Latin. "Besides, if he's as foolish as his son, wouldn't it be better to have a possible enemy in one place, and with us in our camp, to finish this? You could," he finished dryly, "find yourself the King of both Pandya and Chola."

All Senganan understood was the reference to his own kingdom, and he felt a stab of anxiety at being ignorant of this

Caesar Ascending – The Ganges

last bit of conversation between his two adversaries, and the fact that whatever Caesar had said to the Pandyan dog was enough to get him to subside; if anything, Nedunj looked somewhat abashed as he dropped back down onto his stool.

"Tell your king," Caesar resumed in Greek, "that this is acceptable."

Senganan left, leaving Caesar and Nedunj, and Caesar called his senior secretary Apollodorus, telling him to summon the Legates and Primi Pili.

After the secretary left, Caesar said, "If Karikala feels the need to make a demonstration of his own, then I think that it will be to our advantage to modify what we have planned for tomorrow."

Once the other officers arrived, Caesar informed them of Senganan's visit, although they already had been informed through their network of spies, then explained what the Cholan king intended to do in bringing his entire army.

"Because of that, we're going to make some changes in what we have planned," he explained, then spoke for the next few moments.

By the time he was through, the consensus was almost evenly split, with men like Hirtius, Batius, and a few other Primi Pili of the opinion that the next day would devolve into a battle, but none of them voiced any objection to the idea, such was their confidence in the tactics they had developed, and were still perfecting. At that moment, Pullus was one of them, but it wouldn't be long before he changed his mind, something that he made sure to remind his fellow Primi Pili in the near future.

"I don't think there's going to be a fight," Scribonius said at their evening meal. "In fact," he swallowed his mouthful of rice seasoned with the black peppercorns, "I'm willing to make a bet that what's going to happen is the opposite, that these Chola will break and run without us throwing a javelin."

"*Gerrae!*" Pullus scoffed. Using his hunk of pork to point at his friend, he allowed, "While I think they're going to fight, I'll admit it's possible they won't. But, break and run without us doing anything?" He shook his head. "I don't see that happening."

"I didn't say we won't do anything," Scribonius replied with a grin. "I said we won't be involved. And," he added, shutting the door on where Pullus' mind was going, "I don't think Nedunj's elephants will be involved either."

"All right," Pullus sighed, resigning himself to having his mind changed, which almost always happened when he heard his friend adopt this tone. "Tell us why, Socrates."

Ignoring the jibe, Scribonius did as Pullus bade. "Do you remember what happened outside Muziris? When Alangudi showed up with the Pandyan elephants?"

"I'm old, but I'm not that old." Pullus laughed. "So, yes, I remember."

"Those elephants hadn't actually experienced what naphtha does to them," Scribonius said quietly. "The ones this Karikala is going to bring tomorrow, they have."

For the first time, Pullus showed a glimmer of doubt, but he wasn't quite ready to capitulate.

"But that's only a small number of elephants, Sextus," he pointed out. "How many of them got burnt to a crisp? Four? Five? The others were either killed by Nedunj's beasts, or their..." he fumbled for the word, "...*mahoos* had to kill them, like what happened at Bharuch."

"That's true," Scribonius allowed, "but what's your point?"

"My point is that there will be only a half-dozen of those fucking things that were there the other day and were close enough to see what happened to their leaders." Pullus laughed again, teasing, "What, you think those animals are going to tell the others, 'Stay away from that naphtha stuff, it will turn you into charred meat'?"

This made both Balbus and Diocles laugh, but while Scribonius chuckled, he shook his head.

"They're herd animals, Titus," he pointed out. "Which means that it won't take all of them panicking at the sight of those jars bursting into flames. Actually," he amended, "now that I think about it, we may not even have to launch any of those jars. We know their eyesight is *cac,* but we've also learned that they have a sense of smell that's at least as keen as a dog's. One of the animals that was there might smell the naphtha when our *immunes* prepare the jars to be launched, and that could be enough to start a panic."

Pullus didn't say anything immediately, if only because he didn't want to admit that his instinct had been right, that as usual, his closest friend had made an argument that was too persuasive to resist. They *were* herd animals, Pullus acknowledged to himself, and while his 10th Legion hadn't been selected as the one that might actually serve as crews, he had talked to Felix, Cartufenus, and Flaminius, the Primi Pili of the 6th, 28th, and 30th respectively, who, along with their Legions, had spent the winter in Muziris becoming accustomed not only to working in concert with the animals, but to serve as crews in the *howdahs*, although Caesar hadn't decided about whether to actually use them in battle at that point. And, from them, he had heard enough to have a better understanding of the way the animals' minds worked, which supported Scribonius' point. Finally, he broke the silence.

"All right," he grumbled, "you convinced me. Now," he grinned, "I've got to figure out a way to goad Balbinus and Torquatus into taking a bet about it."

Even to anyone who had witnessed it before, the spectacle created by King Karikala leading a quadruple column of armored elephants south was one not soon forgotten. Because of the wide-open terrain, all of the trees that had once grown in this area having been cut down to create farmland, the assembled Roman-Pandyan army could see them coming three miles away, although at this point, it was nothing more than winking golden fire created by sunlight reflecting off of polished bronze. Originally, Caesar had deemed that his Legions, while wearing their armor and carrying their shields and javelins, would form up in the camp but then wait until Caesar deemed it necessary, but, given what Karikala insisted on by bringing his army, he had decided that it would be better instead to show the Chola what faced him should he refuse what was being offered. Consequently, work had begun early in the morning, with the artillery crews leaving the camp with their pieces, setting them up a distance of three *stadia* from the *Porta Praetoria*, and arraying them on either side of the main road that bisected the Roman camp, which had effectively choked off what little traffic there had been. The people of the nearest village situated a bit more than two miles east of the main road, and to whom the fields the Romans were occupying belonged, hadn't ventured more than a few dozen paces from their collection of hovels. Now, however, they could see that something potentially important to their existence seemed to be happening, so the boldest of them had walked across the fields to within perhaps a quarter mile from the camp's *Porta Principalis Dextra*, the right-hand gate on the side nearest to their village. Once the pieces were positioned, other men, using the two-wheeled carts that they had first encountered in Parthia but which now constituted a quarter of the baggage train, traveled north on the main road, to a distance of three hundred paces from the *ballistae*, and two-hundred fifty paces from the line of scorpions. Almost certainly, their task of unloading each cart of its cargo, in the form of what would appear to be jars, would have confused the Chola peasants. As they watched, the men set each jar down on its overturned crate with an exaggerated care that only deepened the mystery, along a line that paralleled the line of artillery pieces, with each jar directly in front of a scorpion. Once finished, they returned to the camp, and for a third part of a Roman watch, there was no further activity outside the camp, so some of the villagers returned to the village, while about a dozen refused to move, dropping down to sit in between the rows of furrowed dirt where they had just recently planted part of their crop for the coming season. There wasn't anything to see, but they were close enough to hear that something was happening within the dirt walls as they could hear strange-sounding horns blowing, and occasionally, a thin shout would drift across the air. It was shortly after one of the more sharp-eyed villagers who had been idly gazing north in the direction of Madoura first spotted the winking shine that he knew meant elephants that there was a renewal of activity. This time, however, the foreign invaders didn't just emerge from the gate facing north, and when a group of armored men carrying shields that were far larger than any they had ever seen and all painted red emerged from the gate nearest them, the villagers leapt to their feet, and to a man, turned and fled back to their village.

"They can run fast, I'll give them that," Balbinus commented to his *Aquilifer*, Lucius Petronius, Aulus Figulus' replacement, who had perished during the 12th's assault on Muziris.

The *Aquilifer* laughed, and the villagers were soon just moving specks, while Balbinus led his Legion out of the *Porta Principalis Dextra*, their orders from Caesar being to occupy the right wing of what would be a line of four Legions. Normally, the right wing was reserved for the Equestrians, something that was a source of unending irritation to the other Primi Pili, which wasn't helped by the men of the 10th constantly reminding them of this fact. As far as Balbinus was concerned, his fellow Primus Pilus was as bad as his rankers; despite considering Titus Pullus a friend, and a relatively close one, he still had an irritating streak of what someone like Clustuminus would call hubris. The problem with the 8th's Primus Pilus' judgment, as far as Balbinus was concerned, was that Pullus could, and at least to this moment, had always backed up his boasts with the kind of deeds that had made him a legend even before Caesar's army boarded their ships at Brundisium. Always, when he thought about this, for Balbinus, hard on the heels of that one would be the thought, that was now more than four *years* ago! In some ways, it seemed a long time, yet in others, it felt as if the days had flown by, and now here they were, still in India. Another thing that didn't help Balbinus' frame of mind when thinking about Pullus was that, deep in his bones, he knew the huge Roman was right about Caesar's ambitions, but it had also been Pullus who had made a point that resonated with Balbinus.

"If we can take care of these Chola without having to fight them the way we did with Bharuch and the Pandya, that's not only better for us in terms of losing men, but it means that we'll turn north sooner rather than later. And if we can do that, then we're going to reach the Ganges that much sooner. And," Pullus had finished, "once we do that, then Caesar's dream of outdoing Alexander will come true. And then, maybe we can go home."

It certainly made sense, and Balbinus had instructed his Centurions to make this argument to their men, but at the same time, Balbinus made his own, private decision not to ask Pullus if his friend really believed that. But now, in the middle of the morning, with the Chola army slowly approaching, the job was to make this first part happen. Anyway, he thought, I'm just happy that I'm going to be taking Pullus for fifty *sesterces*. As Pullus had believed before he talked with Scribonius, Balbinus was certain that, while it would certainly be a potent display, the idea that all of the Cholan elephants would suddenly turn tail and stampede away because a few jars of naphtha exploded was ludicrous.

The reason the 12th was on the right, with the 25th next to them, was because the 10th would be next to the 25th, with the 15th on the left of the Equestrians. By doing so, it placed Caesar's most trusted Legion directly in front of the *Porta Praetoria*, while Caesar, his Legates, and King Nedunj would be in front of them. Caesar's orders called for a double line of Legions, but rather than evenly divided, Papernus' 21st and Crispus' 22nd would be in the second line, staggered in between the 12th and 25th, and the 10th and the 15th. And, instead of the *acies triplex*, the Legions would be in a double line of Cohorts, moving the Fifth Cohort to the front line, with the Eighth, Ninth, and Tenth Cohorts moving up to join the Sixth and Seventh. As Caesar had explained it, he wanted a wider front to present to the Chola, and while it would be the artillery providing what would hopefully be the clinching argument that convinced Karikala to accept his and his people's fate, such as it was, he also wanted to present an overpowering presence in the form of the Legions. Caesar also placed the first line Cohorts behind the scorpions, but ahead of the *ballistae*, which would partially obscure their presence for any Cholan not on an elephant, but the *ballistae* were there only as a precaution; as it had been with Alangudi, it would be the more accurate scorpions who would provide the punctuation to this event. Normally, Caesar would have avoided having his men wearing armor and helmets at the height of the day's heat, but this couldn't be helped, and it had occurred to the Roman that perhaps this Karikala was more cunning than he had been portrayed to be by Senganan. When the Cholan noble had returned from Madoura, he had portrayed his king as a broken man, one who wanted to avoid further loss and devastation to his army, and to his people. This demand of his that he bring his elephants, Senganan had insisted, was one last, empty gesture by a defeated man who wanted to save face; what Senganan had no way of knowing was that, of all the men to whom he could speak about this, there was no other person who understood the importance of a man's *dignitas* better than Gaius Julius Caesar. While he didn't think that Karikala had something planned, he felt that it was worth the discomfort his men would be feeling from the broiling sun if it dissuaded the Cholan king from doing anything rash and destructive. There was another change, however, one that personally effected Caesar, but when he had walked over to mount Toes, Nedunj, from his *howdah*, had called to him.

"Caesar, I think you would be better served to ride up here with me," Nedunj said. This clearly surprised Caesar, but when he asked why, Nedunj explained, "Because King Karikala is more likely to take you seriously if you are aboard an elephant. In this world," Nedunj gestured around him, "a man of our caste isn't considered a real man unless he rides an elephant."

It made sense, Caesar instantly realized, although he couldn't say he appreciated the idea that, because a man rode a horse, he wasn't considered as worthy as one who rode the back of one of these beasts. Fortunately, Caesar had actually ridden with Nedunj on Darpashata several times, so the huge elephant was accustomed to his scent, and when Sekhar tapped the elephant to kneel, Darpashata obeyed, and Caesar climbed into the basket of the *howdah*, then called for Achaemenes, who did the same, much more reluctantly. Once aboard, the elephant stood, then lumbered away from the *praetorium*, heading for the *Porta Praetoria*. His fellow animals were at that moment leaving by the *Porta Principalis Sinistra*, although this was something of an inconvenience. It had taken a bit of persuasion on Caesar's part, but he had at last prevailed on Nedunj to not insist on having his own camp. Unfortunately, every effort to convince the Pandyan king of the superiority of the organizational layout of a Legion camp had come to naught. Therefore, in a compromise, what Caesar proposed was that the camp be divided in half, with the *praetorium* serving as the dividing point, where the Pandyan could arrange their camp as they saw fit, while the Romans improvised by adjusting their own layout without the *praetorium* as the center of their tent streets. Essentially, it was two camps, but surrounded by the same ditch and wall, and while it was certainly awkward, and required for the Romans in particular to adjust, it was the best solution with which Caesar could come up. Under normal conditions, Caesar would place his cavalry on the right wing, but now that he had, in effect, two formations of cavalry, the horsemen of the army would be leaving the *Porta Decumanus*, then would ride around the camp to place themselves to the right and behind the 12th, while Lord Sundara, commanding the elephants, would array to the left and behind the 15th. In another compromise, command of the horse cavalry had been given to Lord Vira, but this was only because Caesar was reasonably confident that this arm of his force wouldn't be going into battle, and he wanted Hirtius with his group. While he briefly toyed with the idea of having his subordinate Legates, Hirtius and Volusenus, share an elephant, he dismissed it; they would be on horseback, along with the Tribunes, Bodroges among them, and Caesar's bodyguards. Neither Gundomir nor Teispes were happy with Caesar's decision to ride an elephant, which he put down to the difficulty they would have controlling their mounts if they had to get close to Darpashata, but this couldn't be helped, and Caesar put it from his mind, but he did order Achaemenes to join the pair, the Parthian obeying readily enough but clearly not altogether comfortable clambering aboard. By *cornu*, he was informed when his Legions had all exited the camp, and were now in place, whereupon he turned to Nedunj.

"Your Highness," he actually grinned at the Pandyan, "let's go give King Karikala something he will never forget."

There was a boyish quality to Caesar's demeanor that made Nedunj laugh, and matching Caesar's tone, he said, "By all means, Caesar, let us do that."

Then, he gave Sekhar the command, and Darpashata began to move across the large forum, heading for the *Porta Praetoria*, and, both men hoped, what would prove to be a fruitful endeavor.

Caesar Ascending – The Ganges

Pullus, sweating profusely, silently cursed Caesar, as he was certain that every man in the ranks, with perhaps the exception of the new Pandyan *Tiros,* was doing at the same time. His head felt like it was on fire, even with the cooler padded cotton liner that had replaced the one made of felt, and he could see at the bottom of his vision the sweat dripping from his nose, which just served as yet another reminder of how foreign this place was. For the love of the gods, he thought, I was born and raised in Hispania, and it was certainly hot compared to places like Gaul, but *this* is different. He hadn't believed Hyppolita when she had assured him that, as hot and wet as Bharuch was, it was even more so here in the southern tip of India, but he had quickly learned how wrong he was. This thought of the Queen of Bharuch, which, as it always did, came unbidden and by surprise, felt like a stab in his heart, and he ruthlessly shoved the memory of her face out of his mind; at least, he tried to, but in this, like always, he was unsuccessful. It was maddening for Pullus; after all, he had been in love before, with Gisela, with her deep red hair, her full lips, dancing blue eyes, and a figure that still haunted his dreams, but what he felt about Hyppolita was different, and had proven to be much, much harder to dispel. Now, as he tried not to dwell on his physical misery, his mind had clearly betrayed him by introducing these thoughts, which were as miserable in their own way as standing there, trying to appear impervious to the heat while sweating his balls off. It was, he thought bitterly, just like the gods to fuck with him in this way.

"What did you say, Primus Pilus?"

He tried not to jerk in surprise at Paterculus' question, unaware that he had said anything aloud, and he lied quickly, "I was just saying I wish this *cunnus* Karikala would hurry up."

He could tell Paterculus didn't believe him, but the *Aquilifer,* who had been in that post even before Pullus became Primus Pilus, was wise enough not to say as much.

More to divert a potentially awkward moment, he asked Pullus, "What do you think is going to happen, Primus Pilus?"

While he would never know it, Pullus was as relieved as Paterculus to have something else to talk about, and he replied,

"I think I'm going to be a hundred *sesterces* richer by tonight, that's what I think."

Not surprisingly, this only confused Paterculus, but Pullus refused to say anything more. Both men were saved by a commotion from behind, and since they were at *otiose*, like his *Aquilifer*, Pullus pivoted to look back in the direction of the camp, but while the chorus of gasps and exclamations would have normally drawn a reprimand from him, Pullus was caught by surprise just as much as his men.

"Why," Valerius, Pullus' *Cornicen*, asked, "is Caesar riding on that elephant? What's his name?"

"Darpa...something," Paterculus supplied, which elicited a ripple of snickers from the men who heard him, while Pullus smiled.

"It's Darpashata," he told Paterculus. "It's one of their gods."

"Is it the one that has the body of a man but the head of an elephant?"

"No, that's Ganesha."

Every man who heard this turned to look at the man who had said it in surprise, Pullus included, but Vespillo only shrugged, and said defensively, "I asked Nila about it, that's all."

"She has your balls in her hand, and she's squeezing them right now!"

This came from Gnaeus Numidius, who happened to be Vespillo's close comrade, unleashing a chorus of raucous laughter and good-natured taunts, and while Pullus didn't say anything, he was laughing as hard as his men.

"Oh, lick my ass." Vespillo had to raise his voice to be heard. "You're just jealous that she chose me and not you!"

"I thank the gods every day that she didn't," Numidius hooted. "She's likely to give me something that I can't scrape off!"

Predictably, this insult delighted the other men, who wasted no time in urging Vespillo to come up with a rejoinder, but Pullus knew that this was the sort of thing that had to be stopped before it incited even more trouble.

He was opening his mouth, but from slightly behind, and

more importantly, above him, a new voice said, "Is this how the Equestrians behave when their general isn't present, Pullus?"

Of all the things Pullus could have uttered, he knew that there was no comparison to the sound of Caesar's disapproving tone, and he spun about to see Caesar standing there in Darpashata's *howdah*, Nedunj next to him, staring down with his lips set in the kind of thin line that signaled that he was deadly serious.

"No, Caesar, it's not," Pullus assured him, but when he spun back about to glare at his men, they had discarded their *otiose* to come to a rigid *intente*, every man staring straight ahead, not moving a muscle.

What happened next would streak through the ranks with the speed, and the power, of a lightning bolt as Caesar called out, "Vespillo! I believe I saw you in Karoura with this woman, what is her name?"

Because he sensed Pullus glaring at him, Vespillo didn't move, but while he stared straight ahead, he answered loudly, "Nila, sir. Her name is Nila."

"You," Caesar replied, "are a man blessed by Fortuna then, Sergeant Vespillo! Truly blessed!"

Nedunj, who was able to follow the conversation, hid his amusement as he spoke quietly to Sekhar, and Darpashata resumed his progress past the 10th, leaving a beaming Vespillo, a chagrined Numidius, and their comrades eager to chatter about what had just happened. For Pullus, his predominant thought was one that was a mixture of amusement and resentment. You cunning bastard, he thought, you did it again. This, Pullus understood, was how Caesar was able to keep his men under his power, even when they were countless miles away from home. Although it was true that he had lost control of these men in the immediate aftermath of the fall of Bharuch, since his return from Parthia, he had struck the right notes on the harp that he was playing to beguile the rankers who comprised this army. How he did it, however, was something Pullus would never fully grasp, and he wasn't alone in this; it was one of the great mysteries for the men, of all ranks, who marched for Caesar.

Despite the defiant tone struck by Karikala's insisting on bringing the remainder of his elephants, it was Nedunj who quickly discerned that it was an empty gesture.

Nudging Caesar when Karikala and his own animal were a bit more than a quarter mile away, Nedunj pointed. "See that canopy, Caesar?"

The truth was that Caesar had seen *something*, but he had been unsure what it was, forced to squint as he tried to make out what he saw was something that he hadn't seen before with the war elephants of India, and he instantly saw Nedunj was right.

"What does it mean?" he asked the Pandyan, who glanced at him and smiled.

"Nobody going to war is going to use a canopy like that, Caesar. My father," the thought made Nedunj's smile fade, "liked to use one when he was touring the kingdom. But he would *never* use one if he intended to fight."

Caesar sensed that Nedunj was right, but all he would say was, "May the gods make it so."

Karikala stopped his animal just then, but they quickly saw that it was to enable his four-wide column to behave similarly to the Roman Legions arrayed in front of him, and they watched the gray beasts behind him split, with two elephants turning to their right, and the other two to their left. It took some time, but finally, there was a double line of elephants, which Nedunj took the time to count.

"He still has one hundred twenty elephants left, Caesar," Nedunj said, unaware that Caesar had been counting, which he learned when the Roman replied, "One hundred twenty-four, to be exact, Your Highness."

Biting back a retort, Nedunj instead said nothing, waiting for what came next, and both men stood there in their *howdah*, watching as Karikala's elephant remained motionless. They could see behind the elephants what appeared to be a sizable force of horsemen, though not nearly as large as their own cavalry, while behind them marched spearmen, identifiable only because of their weapons held vertically, which they could just glimpse. While both sides waited, Karikala was joined by another elephant, which Nedunj immediately recognized.

"That's Karna, Senganan's elephant," he said, and now it

was Caesar who was irritated because he had seen this as well, though he said nothing to indicate it.

Both leaders remained in place, as the Romans waited for what constituted the rest of the might of the Chola kingdom's Southern Army, including the thousand men of Karikala's royal bodyguard, who were the last to arrive and aligned themselves across the road, directly behind their King and his elephant. Of all the Chola troops, aside from the elephants, these men were the only part of their army who presented a uniform appearance, with every man wearing a helmet, and what Caesar and the Romans had learned was a shirt made of stiffened leather, upon which iron, not bronze, scales were attached, a sign of the kingdom's wealth.

"Those are Karikala's royal bodyguards," Nedunj commented, but while Caesar had assumed as much, he didn't say so, choosing instead to comment, "They appear formidable. It's a good thing there are only a thousand of them."

"They are," Nedunj answered grimly, "and I agree. My father talked about his last campaign against the Chola, when Karikala was a newly crowned king, and how their arrival tipped the battle in their favor."

Caesar found this intriguing, his mind already thinking about how he could exploit this information, but he set it aside for the moment because his eye was drawn to something else.

"Does the king have two other men in his *howdah*?"

"Yes," Nedunj answered with a frown. "They're attired like his bodyguards, so I assume he has a pair of them with him. That," he turned to Caesar, his tone disapproving, "was not what was agreed!"

"Nor was him bringing his entire army," Caesar replied, turning about as he did so, to scan the ranks behind him.

It took less than a heartbeat of time for Caesar to find who he was looking for, but he had to almost shout, "Primus Pilus Pullus! Attend to your general!"

Nedunj's initial reaction was one of startlement, but then his eyes widened slightly, although it was the small smile that signaled his approval.

However, all he said in a light tone was, "Are you sure there will be room for the three of us along with the Primus

Pilus, Caesar?"

This made Caesar chuckle, and he allowed, "That's a good question. But," he turned and grinned at Nedunj, "there's only one way to know, eh?"

Pullus had arrived by this point, but he had abruptly stopped his quick trot as he approached the massive hindquarters of Darpashata, and even with the tension of the moment, both Caesar and Nedunj were amused by the look on the Centurion's face, his reluctance to get close to the huge animal clear to see.

Nevertheless, while it was at a walk, Pullus reached Darpashata's left side and rendered a salute, "Yes, Caesar?"

"It appears that King Karikala doesn't trust us," Caesar explained. "He has two of his royal guards in his *howdah* with him, and I need you with us to dissuade them from any mischief."

Although it had been some time since he had last done so with his general, Pullus' immediate reaction was to stiffen to *intente*, and play the role of the Stupid Legionary, one of the most common methods that rankers had to exact a small revenge on their superiors.

"Sir? I'm not sure I understand," Pullus said, keeping his eyes fixed on one of the scales of Darpashata's armored blanket, since the Stupid Legionary called for the ranker to stare at a spot above their superior's head, which in this case, would have called for Pullus to stare almost directly at the sun.

Normally, Caesar was amused when one of his men fell back on this, but this time, he snapped impatiently, "You know perfectly well what I'm telling you Pullus. Or," he asked mockingly, "have we finally found something the mighty Titus Pullus is scared of, riding an elephant?"

The only reason Pullus didn't go red was because his face was already flushed from the heat, but despite being irritated at Caesar's jibe, he also thought to himself, You should have known better.

"No, Caesar," he sighed. "I'm not scared of riding an elephant." As Sekhar gave Darpashata the command to kneel so that Pullus could climb up, he muttered to himself, "Not much, anyway."

His frame of mind wasn't helped when, as he stepped onto the elephant's huge knee, his eyes met the one of Darpashata, and later, Pullus would swear that the beast once again looked amused, although it would only be after several cups of *sura*. In a small act of defiance, he ignored Caesar's outstretched hand, and instead leapt up and over the side of the *howdah* in much the same way he vaulted over a parapet, but he almost knocked Nedunj out of it in the process, forcing him to murmur an apology while ignoring Caesar's glare.

Caesar didn't say anything to Pullus, instead calling to a nearby ranker, "Gregarius! Bring me your two javelins!"

Startled, the ranker hesitated, but his comrade next to him snarled something and gave him a shove, and he came trotting over, then extended the two missiles, butt first up to Caesar, who handed them to Pullus.

"Put those down in the *howdah*, but be ready with them," he instructed Pullus, who did as he was ordered, but protested, "Caesar, I haven't thrown a javelin since I can remember!"

"Well, hopefully, you *do* remember," Caesar answered, but before he could say anything, he was nudged by Nedunj, who was pointing in the direction of the Chola, and Caesar saw that, finally, Karikala's elephant began to move in their direction, with Senganan's Karna following.

"Hirtius, you know what to do," Caesar called down to his Legate. "Wait for my signal."

"Yes, Caesar," Hirtius replied, then assured Caesar, "the men are ready, and everything has been prepared."

Darpashata had begun moving, so Caesar didn't turn to acknowledge Hirtius' words, but he did nod, although Pullus did turn about to look down at the friend who was closest to him, and as he expected, he saw Scribonius offering him a cheerful grin and a wave as if he was going on a voyage. "Oh, go piss on your boots," Pullus grumbled silently, knowing that this would be fodder for amusement for the foreseeable future. While he would never admit it, especially to Pullus, Caesar was every bit as miserable as his Primus Pilus, ruing the fact that he had chosen to wear his helmet from the moment they emerged from camp. In some ways, the normally fastidious Caesar loathed what was essentially a common condition, where his tunic, not cotton but the even cooler silk, would be soaked in a matter of heartbeats after emerging from his quarters, although it was the sweat streaming down into his eyes that was the most irksome. He had taken to carrying a small cotton cloth that he kept tucked in the general's sash around his waist, and he used it now to dab the moisture from his forehead, not wanting his vision obscured, nor did he want to do this again when he was facing this Cholan king. Caesar hadn't noticed until they drew closer, but he saw now that Karikala wasn't actually standing in his *howdah*, but was seated on a chair that had been elevated to a point where the upper half of the king's body was visible. Behind him were the royal bodyguards, although if they had spears, they had placed them in the bottom of the *howdah* where they wouldn't be visible.

"Now do you see why you're with us?" Caesar asked quietly, though he kept his eyes straight ahead as he stood side by side with the Pandyan king, both of them holding on to the wall of the *howdah* as Darpashata swayed.

Because of his height, Pullus could indeed see the two bodyguards, and while he didn't think the chances of them trying anything were high, he did assure Caesar that he would keep his eyes on them.

"Oh, and Pullus?" Caesar still didn't turn, but Pullus saw by the manner in which his cheeks moved that the general was smiling, "Look fierce, if you would."

"Fierce?" Pullus repeated, slightly baffled. "How do I do that?"

It was Nedunj, who was also smiling, who replied before Caesar, "Actually, that will be easy. Just stand there looking like you normally do. That will be sufficient."

In something of a blessing, Pullus was suitably distracted trying to determine if, when he was simply standing there, he appeared fierce, although he wasn't sure what that even meant, so he forgot the acute discomfort occasioned by his first elephant ride, which had forced him to spread his feet wider apart, almost as if he was on the deck of a ship. Both parties were moving at a slow walk, but inevitably, they reached a point where they were perhaps fifteen paces away, and by an unspoken signal, both sides stopped. Immediately, a silence ensued that, fairly quickly, grew awkward, especially for Pullus, who had an instinctive dislike for such moments when both sides refused to be the first one to speak, and he was on the verge of muttering something to Caesar when, finally, it was Senganan who broke it.

"It is customary," he said in Greek, "for the party who requested a meeting of this type to begin the discussion."

"That," Caesar spoke, also in Greek, before Nedunj could, "is true." He paused for an eyeblink, then continued, "But I believe your king will agree that this is an...unusual situation."

For the first time, Karikala spoke, but he addressed Senganan in a low tone, and when Caesar whispered to Nedunj to ask what they were saying, the young king whispered back in frustration, "I can't tell. They're not speaking loudly enough," and Achaemenes affirmed that he couldn't either.

Caesar wasn't surprised at this, but it was irksome nonetheless, and he was about to interrupt, when Senganan gave his monarch a shake of his head, then returned his attention to Caesar.

"My King suggests that we dispense with the formalities that are required between kingdoms here. He says he is unfamiliar with your customs, and that you may be..." Senganan had to search for the word, "...unaccustomed to these conventions."

"He's calling us barbarians," Caesar whispered, although he sounded more amused than offended. Aloud, he replied, "Please tell your king that this is a wise decision. Although," he added, "from the time I have been here, I have learned our customs are not all that dissimilar in such matters."

Before Senganan could reply, for the first time, Karikala spoke, but he was also pointing in their direction as he asked, in even better Greek than Senganan, "Who is that man? What is his name?"

Thinking that Karikala was attempting to insult him, Caesar replied, "I am certain you know this already, Your Highness. I am Gaius Julius Caesar, Dictator for Life..."

Karikala abruptly nodded his head, which took Caesar an eyeblink to recall meant the opposite of how Romans used the gesture, but before he could speak, Karikala said impatiently,

"Not you. Him. The giant."

Suddenly, Pullus, who, as Caesar had directed, was keeping his attention on the pair of bodyguards, both of whom were glaring back at him, realized that all eyes were now on him, though he took small comfort that Caesar and Nedunj seemed as mystified as he was as to why this Cholan king was so interested.

"Tell him who you are, Pullus," Caesar said softly, but before Pullus could, Nedunj whispered, "Caesar, while Karikala obviously understands Greek, it's impossible for him to understand your tongue."

Along with the flash of irritation Pullus experienced was the amusement, which he saw Caesar shared with him. It was actually a common occurrence, albeit usually from Romans of Caesar's class, the assumption that a man from the Head Count wouldn't speak, or read, Greek.

Rather than reply to Nedunj, Caesar gave Pullus a nod, and, using the lungs that had been developed from a decade of bellowing orders, Pullus was the one who replied, in a Greek that was much better than Karikala's and betrayed that his tutor was a native Greek.

"My name is Titus Pullus," he spoke more loudly than necessary. "And I am the Primus Pilus..." Instantly realizing the error, "...The Centurion who commands Caesar's 10th Legion."

Karikala didn't reply, and instead did something that only became clear later, turning to look at Senganan, who shook his head.

Only then did Karikala turn back, and for the first time, there was emotion in his voice as he pointed again, except even from that distance, they could see his finger shaking, "You are the demon who burned my son alive! It was you, was it not? You killed my son, the Crown Prince of the Chola!"

Pullus wasn't sure if the hiss of indrawn breath was his own, or one of the other three men, barely noticing Achaemenes' glance of obvious surprise. Caesar, while he was looking at Karikala, moved one hand behind him and held it up to Pullus in a silent command, intending to assure the Cholan king this wasn't the case. The truth was that nobody knew exactly who had been responsible for immolating Divakar and his elephant, simply because they never knew exactly who Divakar was among the first slain, and in fact had only learned that the prince was dead from Senganan later on his first visit to the camp.

"Your Highness, I can assure you that Primus Pilus Pullus did..."

"Caesar!" Pullus hissed, but he also reached out and grabbed Caesar's *paludamentum*, and his general stopped in midsentence to turn around and glare at Pullus, who said quickly, "No, don't tell him that it wasn't me! If he needs someone to blame, then I don't want him sending someone with a blade after one of my boys."

Caesar didn't respond verbally, but gave a curt nod, and he smoothly continued, "While I was about to say that Primus Pilus Pullus was not responsible, he just informed me that he in fact was the man who slew your son."

This brought Karikala to his feet, springing from his chair to stand with his lower body pressed against the wall of his *howdah* as if he intended to leap out of it as he replied with a half-snarl, half-scream, "You are a coward! You used a coward's weapon with this demon fire! You are a hyena! Your mother was a prostitute and your father was a slave! My son would have gutted you if you had faced him as a *true* warrior would!"

Now, it was Titus Pullus who actually had to be restrained by Nedunj as the big Roman moved from the rear of their *howdah*, making it clear that he intended to hop out of it and rush across the open ground, but it was Caesar who snapped, "Hold, Pullus! You will *not* do anything! Is that clear?"

In what was the most potent sign that Pullus was truly enraged, he didn't even glance at Caesar, but he did relent, his body relaxing slightly, then in an unconscious reaction, he looked down at Nedunj's hand grasping his bicep, then looked back into the Pandyan's eyes. His reaction would be amusing later, as Nedunj snatched his hand away in a manner similar to someone touching a hot surface, although what the Pandyan experienced when their eyes met was the opposite, a cold fear that made him think that Karikala had lost his wits for rousing whatever it was inside that lurked inside Titus Pullus.

Taking a breath, Pullus relaxed and took a step backward, but his eyes never left Karikala, while Caesar took control of the moment, speaking in a calm, measured tone, "While I understand your grief, King Karikala, you would be foolish to antagonize my Centurion further, and I can assure you that Centurion Pullus did not need what you call the demon fire to slay him."

Karikala, still wide-eyed and shaking with fury, nodded his head as he sneered, "That is easy to say, but the fact is that he *did* slay my son in a foul and cowardly manner! And," he pointed again, but at Nedunj this time, "you and your puppet king invaded my kingdom, without any cause!"

"Actually, Your Highness," Caesar replied coolly, "I was informed that the spot your son chose to launch an unprovoked attack is a matter of dispute as to the ownership, is that not true?"

"Is that what that Pandyan hyena told you?" Karikala scoffed. "You have chosen to ally yourself with yapping curs, Roman! Nothing a Pandyan says can be believed!"

"So says the king whose son lost half of his army," Nedunj snarled, and now it was Caesar who had to put a restraining hand on the Pandyan.

The difference was that Nedunj immediately subsided, and indeed looked slightly ashamed, murmuring, "I apologize, Caesar. I should not have lost my temper."

"It's understandable, Your Highness," Caesar assured him. Raising his voice back to a normal level, Caesar addressed the Chola, "This is getting us nowhere, Your Highness. The purpose of this negotiation is to assure you that, while we came here with peaceful intentions, we also possess the capability to ensure the destruction of what remains of your army."

Karikala stiffened; just as he opened his mouth, Senganan spoke again, keeping his tone low, but this time, Nedunj could hear him, and translated for Caesar and Pullus, "He's begging the king to subside in his threats and listen to what we have to say."

"I think," Caesar's voice was only loud enough for the other two men to hear, but Pullus didn't miss the coldness in his tone, "it will be better to show him, rather than tell him."

Caesar Ascending – The Ganges

As Senganan and Karikala were engaged—to Pullus, it didn't seem as if the king was disposed to listen—Caesar turned and raised a hand in the air, neither of the Chola noticing.

"Pullus, I want you to keep your eyes on Legate Hirtius," he instructed. "Let me know when he signals."

When they discussed it later, everyone involved agreed that the fact that Senganan and Karikala were so distracted by what had become a heated conversation that they didn't notice the activity just ahead of the long front rank of the Legions, as four men instead of the normal three hurried to their scorpions, helped increase the impact of what was coming. Over the span of a hundred heartbeats, Pullus didn't actually need Hirtius' signal, having seen the crews make their preparations that, out of sheer desperation and unable to think of another way to keep his men from being slaughtered, Titus Pullus had stumbled onto what was now another new tactic adopted by the undisputed masters in such things. Over the winter months, the process had been refined, and one change that was the most striking was that the commander of the piece, who would pull the cord that released the pin, sending the bolt hurtling on its way, and his assistant who carried the bolt, around which was a long strip of cloth soaked in naphtha, both wore the vinegar-soaked leather sleeves the Romans had developed to protect the men who assaulted Susa when facing their former comrades of the *Crassoi*, while the fourth man's only duty was to stand ready with a bucket that, rather than water, contained vinegar.

"Caesar," Pullus said urgently, "the Legate just signaled."

"Your Highness!" Caesar raised his voice above the level he had been using in the exchange with Karikala.

Karikala responded, jerking his head sharply back to Darpashata, and even with the space between them and never laying eyes on him before this, Pullus could see the rage in the man's expression, and while he wasn't certain, what he assumed was a powerful grief. Rather than say anything now that he had Karikala's attention, instead, Caesar vigorously, and with what Pullus thought was a bit of an overdramatic flair, thrust his hand into the air. Afterward, Pullus chided himself for not thinking to count how long it took after Caesar swept his arm down for him to win his wagers, but he was certain it wouldn't have been past the count of two hundred.

Chapter Four

"You bastard," Balbinus complained, although he was smiling, and more importantly, he was handing a stack of coins into Pullus' outstretched palm, who was grinning broadly.

Torquatus was next, but he wasn't any happier, and it was his former 10th comrade who demanded of Pullus, "How did you know that would happen?"

For an instant, Pullus was tempted to lie, but he quickly realized that, sooner or later, it would get back to Scribonius, since he was on good terms with Torquatus as well.

"Scribonius," he answered simply. Seeing this wouldn't suffice, he explained, "I was originally of the same mind as you were, that since most of those beasts weren't there, they wouldn't react the same way as the twenty or thirty who were. But," he shrugged, "he reminded me that elephants are herd animals, and it only takes one or two to lose their wits for the rest to follow."

"Tell Scribonius I owe him for that," Torquatus grumbled, then the pair left Pullus where he was standing outside the *Porta Praetoria*, watching as his Legion filed past and wound their way through the dirt gate.

It had been a success, certainly, but Pullus wondered if even Caesar was surprised at how quickly, and dramatically, what King Karikala had once thought of as his invincible elephants turned into a panicked mob of animals who only had one thought, to escape what had quickly become a wall of fire. Since all eyes had been on Caesar, standing in his elevated spot on Darpashata, everything began moving very rapidly when he thrust his arm into the air and brought it down to point at the Chola, prompting the third man who was responsible for lighting the strip of cloth, once the second man had placed the bolt in the channel, to perform his duty, ending with the leader pulling the cord and sending thirty missiles streaking at the same time towards their targets, the jars of naphtha that had been placed above the ground on the crate that carried them. It hadn't been perfect, certainly; Pullus, naturally, had been focused on his artillery *immunes* of the 10th, and he was disappointed to see that two of his crews missed with their first shot, one overshooting the jar, the other striking the ground a few paces in front of it, but the majority of the bolts, some twenty-four out of the thirty, struck their targets with the first bolt. Even in the bright sunshine, the explosion of boiling flames made the men shield their eyes, the sight accompanied by a barely perceptible delayed shattering sound, followed instantly by a deeper rumbling, but even over that noise, Pullus heard Karikala give a shout that was more of a keening moan. To his surprise, Pullus felt a stab of sympathy, as did Caesar, whose eyes had never left the Chola king.

"I can't even imagine what he's feeling right now, knowing that this was how his son died," he said, almost to himself.

While Nedunj didn't feel as sympathetic, given that this was a foe he had been taught to hate almost from being weaned, he did look shaken. With a second volley from the four crews who missed, there were now thirty columns of black, oily smoke rising in the air, partially obscuring their view of the elephants in the Chola ranks, so they only heard the first higher-pitched trumpeting call, the elephant who made it immediately joined by more than a dozen animals. More importantly, despite the obscuring smoke they saw the sudden movement that seemed to originate from a spot off to their right, across from the 12th, and Pullus wondered if the elephant who moved first, trunk raised in the air in much the same posture that Caesar had been in with raised arm that began this conflagration, had been present at the failed ambush. Not that it matters, he thought; yet, while this was the first animal to react, despite its *mahout* frantically using his goad, jabbing it repeatedly into the side of the elephant's head, the beast was quickly joined by its comrades. Once again, as those men with experience knew was always a danger, and as the Romans gaped in openmouthed astonishment, the five men aboard each Chola animal were reduced to frightened passengers aboard a huge beast whose mind was only on escape. In its way, it was an even more impressive sight than what had taken place at the ambush, because the ground was flat and open here, enabling the witnesses to see dozens of elephants pivot about, and again displaying an agility that belied their lumbering appearance, go to their version of a gallop as they fled north to where the walls of the city were visible only as a darker line on the horizon. It was a cacophony of noise, the staccato trumpeting of terrified animals almost overwhelming the alarmed, shouted commands of the men aboard them.

If it had been in a drier climate, somewhere like Parthia, the dust would have obscured everything, but here, the Romans were watching through a veil of the black smoke created by the flaming naphtha. The jars had been placed ten paces apart, which meant there was theoretically enough space between the irregular circles of flame from the shattered pots for an elephant to pass between, but not one of the animals was heading towards the flames...just as Scribonius had predicted. The next part of the Cholan army to react was their spear-wielding infantry, to a man suddenly turning and running perhaps fifty heartbeats after the first elephant panicked, and the only reason they didn't outstrip their four-legged comrades in their flight was, appearances aside, as Pullus and all of the other men of Caesar's army saw that day, the animals ran faster than men. As Pullus would be informed later, while his attention was drawn to the first of the animals to signal its reluctance to remain in the presence of this fiery substance, several others along the front rank closest to the flames bolted as well. The result of this would be the cause of much bickering around the Legion fires about which of the animals actually triggered what became a stampede, each man arguing for the beast closest to their spot in the ranks being the one that broke first. More quickly than anyone, including the Centurion who had predicted this would the outcome, had anticipated, suddenly, all that remained of

Chola's might were two elephants and the men of the royal bodyguard, although their horse-born cavalry, who followed behind the infantry, did regroup about a half-mile away once their riders got their mounts under control, as one group of herd animals responded to the panic of another.

Even with all that was happening, and the noise created by it that made it hard for any man to concentrate their attention, Pullus still admired the skill with which the two *mahouts* remaining on the field kept their animals under a semblance of control, although Karikala's elephant, like all but Karna, had spun about, clearly intending to flee with its brethren. Somehow, the *mahout* managed to keep the animal from lumbering away, but the result was a sight that would provide fodder for the rankers, as no less than three times, Karikala's *mahout* managed to turn his elephant back to face Darpashata, while Karikala sat in his chair, clutching the arms with a death grip, only to have the animal insist on turning back around. To the Romans, including Caesar and Pullus, who were the pair closest to the Chola king, it almost seemed as if this was some sort of demonstration put on for them to display the agility of these animals as it spun around, finally stopping after the third revolution, which prompted Pullus to say something that, even in the moment, caused Caesar and Nedunj to burst out laughing.

"I wonder if their king is dizzy now," he muttered. "I know I would be."

Even as Caesar laughed, his eyes remained fixed on the Cholan king who, to his eyes, did appear a bit unsteady once the animal under him subsided, but it was the expression on Karikala's face that he was studying. Certainly, the gleaming dark beard that covered the lower half of his face made it more challenging, but Caesar thought he saw in Karikala's eyes the expression of a man who has finally been forced to confront, and accept however bitterly, his impotence.

This was confirmed when Karikala asked in a defeated tone, "What is it that you require of the Chola and their King, Roman?"

As expected, Caesar was prepared for this, and for the next several moments, described what he sought from Karikala.

"As Lord Senganan told you, while it is not our intention

to subdue the Chola, as you've seen, we are perfectly capable of doing so." Gesturing to Nedunj, he adopted a reasonable tone, "All we are asking is that you show the same wisdom of King Nedunj and recognize this as a fact."

From where Pullus was standing, he saw Nedunj stiffen slightly, prompting the thought, He doesn't like being reminded of *why* he's standing here right now. For this, Pullus didn't blame him, although his concern for the mental well-being of the Pandyan king extended only to the extent of how he treated his wife and Hyppolita's other children back in Karoura, but nothing he had seen in his time around the young king indicated he was the type to take his frustrations out on those weaker than him. Oblivious to the internal musings of the Roman, Karikala's eyes nevertheless seemed to shift back to him, even as he was listening to Caesar speak; once the Roman was finished, he nodded his head in a sign of disbelief.

"You are telling me that you do not intend to exact any further reprisals, or cause any more devastation and destruction in my kingdom? And that you will not be here long?" Karikala stroked his beard, which Senganan knew was the sign that his king was deep in thought, then he abruptly asked, "What does that mean, exactly, Roman? How many cycles of the moon will you infest my kingdom?"

If Caesar took offense at the characterization, it was impossible to tell, but to Pullus, it was a good question, because his general had been extremely closemouthed about his intentions for the Chola, and Caesar replied equably, "My hope is that it will only be a matter of two, or perhaps three weeks." Seeing Karikala look over at Senganan in confusion at the unfamiliar term, Caesar hurriedly added, "By that, I mean a half cycle, or perhaps a few days after the half moon."

"Then what?" Karikala asked bluntly, "And why?"

"What comes next," Caesar answered coldly, "is only your concern as far as it might impact your kingdom, Your Highness, and much depends on you. As to the why," Caesar paused, which Pullus suspected was intentional and done for impact, "what you see arrayed before you is not my entire army; it is roughly only half. The other half is conducting a campaign to the south, on the island that we refer to as, although you know it by a different name. I do not anticipate that it will take my general Pollio long to accomplish his goal."

Karikala's reaction at the news that Caesar's army was not only even larger came in the form of a gasp that was clearly audible but that, despite Caesar's statement of desiring peace, presumably at that moment, part of the Roman's army was at the very least asserting control over the Chola of a strategically valuable island, while Senganan appeared almost as alarmed, which was understandable, since this was the first he was hearing it as well. And, Pullus thought with grim humor, you haven't seen our fleet yet.

There was nothing said for quite of span of time as the Chola king went through the meaning, and more importantly, the implication and impact of hearing that he had at the very last just lost dominance over a crucial part of his kingdom, against a force that, as he had seen with his own eyes, his army couldn't hope to defeat, all of which was displayed on his face for Pullus to watch. Consequently, it took two attempts before Karikala, all signs of defiance gone with this news of a level of power that, just a few moments before, would have been unimaginable, managed, "May I ask what your goal in seizing a part of my kingdom is?"

Caesar seemed to consider this, but only because Pullus was so close did he see the slight shrug that indicated his general thought there was no harm in answering, "We only intend to construct a supply base on the island that will serve as a shipment point for both supply for my army, and for the purpose of abiding by the trade agreement I have concluded with King Nedunj, upon whose kingdom I have conferred Friend and Ally status."

"What does this 'Friend and Ally' mean?" Karikala asked, suddenly wary at this new term.

Caesar, instead of replying to Karikala, turned to Nedunj.

"Your Highness, would you care to explain it from your point of view?"

While he wasn't certain, Pullus suspected that this had been prearranged, because the Pandyan king didn't appear surprised, and answered immediately, "It means that if my kingdom is attacked, I can count on Caesar and his army to provide me the support to repel the invaders. *If,*" he added, with a touch of haughtiness, "I require it." Karikala didn't respond to this provocation, but his expression was enough for Nedunj, who continued, "It also means that my kingdom has a new market, and Caesar's plans for Ravana," using the name used by the native kingdoms instead of the Greek name, "include a large port that can take our goods to Rome and their provinces around what they call their sea, and expand our trade to the Han."

For the first time, Karikala seemed animated, amusing Nedunj by what the Pandyan interpreted as an avaricious gleam in his eye, asking, "How much?"

While Nedunj and Caesar, since they hadn't switched to Tamil, knew exactly what the Cholan king was asking, Nedunj responded innocently, "How much what?"

"How much gold? How much silver?" Karikala snapped.

"Oh," Nedunj shook his head, "yes." He rubbed his chin for a heartbeat before answering, "While it is still early in our relationship, and as I am certain you know, between using the western part of the Silk Road, then the time it takes for a roundtrip journey to Rome, my kingdom has already received one thousand pounds of gold, and two thousand pounds of silver." Using the universal gesture, he shrugged as if this was a trifling amount. "But as I said, it is early."

Even for a wealthy kingdom, this was a staggering sum, and Karikala struggled to keep his composure when he returned his attention back to Caesar to ask, with seeming indifference, "Is this what you are proposing with my kingdom? This Friend and Ally status?"

"No," Caesar replied firmly, and Karikala stiffened, while Senganan looked similarly discomfited, and Caesar modified, "At least, not immediately, Your Highness. Over time, perhaps, but as of now, all we require is that you suspend further hostilities with my army, that you do not interfere with our activities. As," he stressed, "we will not interfere with yours as long as they are peaceful. Merchants may come and go as they please, your people will be left unharmed and unmolested by my army for the time we are within your borders. And," he finished briskly, "of course, as custom requires, we will require hostages of a high rank, preferably at least one to whom you are related by blood."

It was impossible to miss that Karikala was torn between pride and pragmatism, but the fact that he was essentially alone, with two elephants and only a thousand bodyguards, and all because of a simple demonstration of Rome's power meant that pragmatism won out...to a degree.

After a whispered conversation in Tamil with Senganan, Karikala addressed Caesar, "This is acceptable." Like Caesar, and Nedunj, Pullus visibly relaxed, though it wasn't destined to last, because Karikala then said, "But I have one condition."

"Condition?" Caesar asked, his tone going cold again. "Do you mean request?"

"No," Karikala nodded, "this is a condition. And," in direct contrast to Caesar's frigid reaction, the passion was impossible to miss in the king's voice, "if this condition is not met, I will fight you. Yes," he held up a hand in a peremptory gesture that Pullus knew Caesar loathed, if only because he did as well, "I have seen what you demons are capable of, with that..." his mouth twisted, but he didn't utter the word, choosing instead to point to the nearest column of smoke where the naphtha was still burning, "...but for this, Roman, I am willing to sacrifice my entire kingdom! I am willing to watch all of my elephants burn, my women to be raped, and my men enslaved! And, while you will no doubt crush me and subjugate my people, you will lose many, many men. And," he turned to Nedunj, "this Pandyan cur and his animals will suffer as well."

By the time he was through, the original vehemence he had shown with accusing Pullus was back, which was why the Centurion suddenly realized that he had an idea of what the condition might be.

If Caesar understood, he gave no sign, replying tersely, "State this condition."

It was when Karikala pointed directly at him that Pullus' suspicions were confirmed, the Cholan king demanding, "I want this...*beast* to pay for the foul slaughter of my son, the Crown Prince Divakar! I want his head to place on my table!" Dropping his voice back to a reasonably normal level and tone, he finished, "Only then will I agree to all that you require."

Caesar Ascending – The Ganges

When Caesar swiveled his head to look up at Pullus, he saw that Caesar was as unsurprised as he was, but there was a look in the general's eyes that threw Pullus into doubt. An instant before, he had been certain that Caesar would reject this out of hand, but now, looking into Caesar's ice-blue eyes, and more crucially, the expression he was seeing on his general's face, meant that suddenly Pullus was in doubt. It's as if, he thought, he's a butcher sizing up how much of a piece of meat to slice, with no more emotion or concern than wondering whether his knife is sharp enough. Following hard on the heels of this was another; it made sense for Caesar to accede to this request. After all, he was one man, and if Karikala was sincere, and Pullus believed he was, his comrades would suffer as a result of Caesar's refusal.

This was something Pullus couldn't endure, and while his stomach had suddenly twisted in knots, he broke the silence with a voice suddenly gone hoarse, "If you decide that this is the best way for you to proceed, Caesar, I won't fight it." Before he could stifle it, he gave a short, humorless laugh. "I won't be fucking happy about it. But," he made sure to look Caesar in the eye so that his general could see Pullus meant what he said, "if this will help you and my boys get back home, then I'll do it."

Since they never spoke of it, Pullus would never learn that, despite Caesar's stoic demeanor as he listened to Pullus, internally, it was a far different story, and if he had divulged his feelings in the moment, Pullus would have learned that Caesar's stomach was twisted into as many knots as his own. Like Pullus, Caesar instantly grasped that, on its surface, this was a small price to pay, the life of one man, especially when measured against the likely cost of refusing, and also like Pullus, he was reasonably confident that Karikala was deadly serious. However, what Caesar was looking at wasn't a mark on a piece of vellum, or an incision in a wax tablet containing the names of the men who had departed Brundisium and wouldn't be returning; he was looking at a flesh and blood man, and not just any man. A series of images flashed through Caesar's mind, of a huge teenage boy who Gaius Crastinus had brought to the *praetorium* after, according to his Centurion, he had singlehandedly saved two Centuries during the 10th's first campaign; his glimpse of Pullus, the Secundus Pilus Prior of his best Legion, at Alesia, leading his men over the turf rampart created by Vercingetorix and his Arverni, *gladius* already covered in blood; their time in Alexandria, when he had sent Pullus to escort Cleopatra, who would become the mother of his son, to stand before him, but always, it was Pharsalus that Caesar would remember, when this giant Roman had chosen loyalty to him over a lifelong friendship with Vibius Domitius, Pullus' Optio at the time. All of these events paraded in front of his internal eye in the span of the four or five heartbeats of time after Pullus finished.

Caesar didn't reply, to Pullus at least, turning back to Karikala to say, "I have a proposal to make."

At first, it appeared that Karikala would rebuff Caesar, then Senganan whispered something, prompting the Cholan king to ask warily, "And what is this proposal?"

Pullus watched Karikala carefully, saw the king's eyes narrow in thought, then one more time, stroke his beard.

It was only when Karikala answered abruptly, "This is acceptable" that Pullus realized he had been holding his breath.

"*What?*"

"I said," Pullus repeated patiently, "I'm going to have to fight some *cunnus* before that Cholan *cunnus* will agree not to force us to slaughter the bastards."

"But, fight him how?" Scribonius pressed.

"Is it going to be like a gladiatorial bout?" Balbus asked, earning him a glare from Scribonius, who snapped, "You don't have to sound so fucking happy about it."

"I'm not!" Balbus protested, though without much vigor, then his scarred face twisted into his version of a grin. "But you have to admit, it will alleviate the boredom. Besides," he tried to sound indignant, "I know who's going to fucking win." He pointed to Pullus first, who was munching on a piece of bread without any apparent concern, before jabbing his finger in Scribonius' direction, "Why don't you have any confidence in Titus, eh, Sextus? The man hasn't been born who could beat him!"

Instead of addressing Balbus, Scribonius turned to Pullus.

Caesar Ascending – The Ganges

"You're loving this, aren't you?"

Pullus' answer was only a grin around a mouthful of bread, but Scribonius had two allies this night, as Diocles and Porcinus, who had accepted his uncle's invitation to share a meal, sat there, one of them glaring at Pullus, while his nephew just looked unhappy. Seeing that he wasn't going to be allowed to eat in peace, he sighed, and set the bread down.

"He originally just wanted my head," he explained. "It was Caesar who challenged their king to let me face a man of his choice instead of just turning me over to him."

"And what would he have done if Caesar just refused?" Scribonius challenged, then answered his own question, "Nothing, that's what. He had just witnessed his most powerful weapon running like scared rabbits because of the naphtha, so he knows that we would slaughter them." He lifted his hands, palms up. "Why would he sacrifice all of that just for one man's head, even if he did think you killed his son? Which," Scribonius reminded him, "you didn't. If anyone, it *might* have been Vespillo, or one of the other men of the naphtha detail that day."

While all this was certainly true, Pullus was unmoved, which he explained by saying quietly, "You weren't there, Sextus; I was. I saw him, and he wasn't a king; he was a father who wanted vengeance for his son and was willing to burn his world down for the chance to get it." When he saw Scribonius wasn't going to respond to this, he still hammered his point. "And, when all is said and done, what's my life compared to the number of boys we'd lose because a father is mad with grief and doesn't care what happens to him, or to the people he rules? No," Pullus finished emphatically, "Caesar not only made the right choice, it's a choice that at least gives me the chance to see another sunrise."

He picked his bread back up, and they ate in silence for a bit, then Porcinus spoke, for the first time. "When is this going to happen?"

"As soon as we march from here to Uraiyur," Pullus explained. "It's on a river, called the..." his face screwed up as he tried to remember, then shrugged, "...I don't recall the name, but it's wider than this one, and Caesar believes that Pollio can

179

bring the fleet up it. Then," he shrugged, "I'll fight whoever the bastard sends out the next morning."

"Inside or outside the city?" Scribonius asked.

"Outside," Pullus, knowing where Scribonius' mind was going, assuring him, "that was a requirement by Caesar."

"You'll win," Porcinus said confidently, which Balbus echoed with the same degree of enthusiasm. "Who knows?" His nephew actually grinned. "I may actually put some money on you!"

This made the others laugh, although Balbus, correctly as it turned out, scoffed, "As if anyone in this fucking Legion would dare bet against your uncle."

Of the five of them, only Diocles remained silent, though not because of his technical status of slave and body servant, but because he found the very idea of his master and friend being forced to risk his life for his men, and for the men of the other Legions, troubling in the extreme. Oh, he knew that Pullus risked his life for his men every time they went into battle, but this was different, and he wondered about how formidable Pullus' opponent might be. Unlike the others, he had ways of finding out more, and he resolved to leave once the meal was over to begin gathering that information.

The march from Madoura to Uraiyur took three days, with King Karikala insisting on traveling in a separate column separated by several furlongs, but when he tried to place himself, his royal bodyguard, and horse cavalry at the head of the column, the march was delayed by a spirited but brief debate, which was only settled when, pointing up to where Nedunj and two others were standing atop Darpashata, Caesar asked, "Do I need to remind you that you have given me your solemn vow as the King of the Chola that you will do as I direct, until we leave your kingdom?"

Caesar didn't raise his voice, nor did he make an explicit threat about the fifteen-year-old boy, Kumaran, and his thirteen-year-old brother Karthikeyan who were now in Caesar's custody, which made his words all the more chilling, but the intent was clearly communicated, and only then did Karikala relent.

"King Karikala," Nedunj called down to him, "may I make a suggestion?"

"What do you want, Pandyan?" Karikala snapped, but it was the younger instead of the elder man who retained his composure.

"My suggestion," he said quietly, "is that your elephants march in the column with mine, so they will they have their fellow animals around them."

While tempted, he didn't point out what had happened the day before, if only because he was sure that it was still very fresh in the Cholan king's mind.

"That," Karikala said grudgingly, "is not without merit."

Their exchange had been in Tamil, but it was because Achaemenes was sitting astride his horse next to Caesar that Nedunj had known the Parthian would translate, and Caesar signaled his understanding by saying, in Greek, "Very good! Then it's settled. And," Caesar lied, "I had planned on you and your household troops being with me in our marching column, which is just behind the vanguard Legion, Your Highness."

The truth was that he had planned on attaching the Cholan king at the end of the column, ahead of the baggage train, a train which, Caesar thought ruefully, seems to grow with every king I collect. With this settled, the massively long column began to move, which meant that the drag Legion, the 22nd on this day, waited for almost two parts of a watch before they set out. Thankfully, the rugged terrain was behind them, and while it was still the same combination of hot and wet, because of the openness of the ground, there was a steady breeze that, the Romans were told, came from the great ocean to the east. This was their ultimate destination, and would be where, at last, the two parts of the fleet and the two parts of the army converged. It was now early May; once again, from the perspective of the men, Caesar's Luck had held with this early capitulation by the Chola, although what that meant was not only unclear, but was a matter of intense speculation by all ranks, which included the men from the other nations now marching as members of Rome's Legions. This was especially true for Mardonius, a Parthian in the First Century of the Eighth Cohort, marching for Pilus Prior Ausonius, although he was more commonly referred to as Cyclops by his fellow Centurions, and behind his back by his men, of which he was completely aware. Marching next to him was Aulus Percennius, who had become his close comrade after the fall of Bharuch and Mardonius had lost his first one, Gnaeus Pacuvius, on what had been a horrible night when Caesar's men first took the city, then rebelled. It had taken months for Mardonius to stop having a nightly dream where he relived the feeling of snatching at the sleeve of his friend's tunic, a javelin hurled by a Bharuch warrior protruding from Pacuvius' chest in the span of less than the heartbeat Mardonius had to save him before Pacuvius toppled from the roof down into the fiery maelstrom of burning flesh of man and animal, only to be tackled and bodily pinned to the rooftop by the man marching next to him. Not for the first time, as they trudged along in the scorching, moist heat, Mardonius reflected on all the changes that had been wrought in his life over the previous three years, when he had been among the first of the men who had served in Parthia's infantry who took Roman silver to serve in the Legions. The first few months had been absolutely miserable, but Mardonius was sufficiently removed from those days that, now when he thought about it, he found himself grinning, and while it certainly hadn't been a source of amusement then, it had been the ranker next to him who had been his most consistent tormenter, refusing to trust that a man who, scant weeks before, had been trying to kill Percennius and his comrades. It had been the dead Pacuvius who had been the first to offer the young, scared, and confused Parthian what could be considered friendship, if only to admonish him about something he was doing wrong, but by the time they were lying flat on a roof on a street in Bharuch, battling the rampaging elephants that, even now, scared Mardonius, he had proven himself to the point that, when Pacuvius had been stricken and Percennius saw Mardonius bending out over the edge of the roof, arm outstretched to try and save their comrade, the Roman wasn't willing to lose both men. Now, their relationship was much like the one Mardonius had formed with Pacuvius, with the rough-edged, sometimes cruel humor that fighting men indulged in, no matter the age, the one difference now being that Mardonius' Latin was much better, making it more difficult for his native Roman comrades to catch him out. On this day, the 10th was just behind the command group, although it was much larger than normal with the addition of the Chola, and the Fates had decreed that, as every wise Primus Pilus did, it was the turn for the Eighth Cohort to be the first one of the Equestrians in the part of the column comprising the 10th. Thanks to their spot in the First Century, the pair had a good view of the three elephants, riding side by side but with the one they knew bore the Chola king in the middle, swaying side to side as they marched northeast towards Uraiyur.

"They look like we do when we're at sea," Mardonius observed, which earned him a surprised look from Percennius.

"*Gerrae!*" his close comrade exclaimed. "How do you figure that? We're on solid ground!"

It reminded Mardonius that, while a solid veteran, and a man he had learned he could depend on to the death, Percennius wasn't, as he had heard their Primus Pilus say, the brightest spark in the fire.

Using his free hand, he made a rocking motion with it. "Because that's what they are doing, rocking back and forth like we do when we're at sea."

Percennius, who had learned, and for the most part accepted, that his Parthian comrade was one of the cleverest men in the Century, looked back up at the animals, and it didn't take more than another three or four heartbeats to see what Mardonius was saying as he watched the men in what he had learned was called the *howdah* sway back and forth.

Still, he wasn't quite ready to acknowledge this, muttering, "They're going back and forth faster than we do when we're aboard one of those fucking boats."

"I wonder how long we're going to be on them this time?"

Both rankers glanced over to their Sergeant, Fibulanus, who was two spots down from Percennius, in the middle of the five-wide column, but it was the Parthian who answered, "I don't know, Sergeant, but I hope it's not as fucking long as it was from Caesarea."

This was met with universal agreement for those within hearing distance; while they would never know it, one of Mardonius' proudest accomplishments was in becoming accustomed to using curses and epithets like his comrades.

From his spot to the right of the marching column, next to the front rank that Mardonius and the others were in, Cyclops spoke up for the first time. "What if it's farther?"

As he knew it would, the idea that their Pilus Prior offered this as a possibility was instantly accepted as being fact, and there was a ragged chorus of dismay from the front part of the Century, although they were joined quickly by the rest of their comrades once men turned and relayed this over their shoulder.

"Is that true, Pilus Prior? Do you swear it on Jupiter's Stone?"

"How long will we be on a fucking ship, sir?"

"I'd rather clean out the *cac* in the latrines than spend more time on a fucking boat!"

"How much farther, Pilus Prior?"

Cyclops had turned his head slightly, as if he was surveying the ground off to their right flank, but it was so they couldn't see his smile as he thought, If you can't torment your men from time to time, what good is carrying a *vitus*?

Aloud, he answered the voice he had recognized as belonging to Mardonius, who had asked the most important question, and in the process, had signaled his acceptance that they would be once more covering a vast distance over water.

"Nobody knows for sure, Mardonius," he answered. "But it could take another week, maybe more." Only then did he turn his head to look at the men of the first rank, as he asked with mock seriousness, "Why? Did you have plans for the rest of your life?"

Of all the things he could have said, Quintus Ausonius encapsulated the reality of this existence they had chosen, marching under a standard of Rome, and in the process, subtly reminded them of a reality that, back when he had been in their *caligae*, their Primus Pilus had learned to accept, albeit with considerable difficulty, that there was no sense in wasting time and energy worrying about those things over which rankers had no control.

For Barhinder Gotra, who at least had the luxury of riding a horse, while he was more comfortable physically than the men

Caesar Ascending – The Ganges

around him for whom this wasn't their native land, there were other challenges that seemingly cropped up every day. It was true that he was more accustomed to his new life now than when he had first begun serving these Romans who, every so often, he still regarded as conquerors of his native Bharuch. However, as one of the relatively few men from Bharuch who served the Roman army, he never forgot how well treated he was when compared to some of his compatriots serving in other Legions. No, they weren't whipped, nor were they mistreated, at least any more than men of his caste would have been in Bharuch, but it was through the Greek who had dragged him out from under a pile of corpses that meant Barhinder was truly blessed. By this time, going into his second year now serving Rome, he had accepted that his brother Sagara, who had served in the Bharuch phalanx, had perished, meaning that he considered himself responsible for the rest of the Gotra family. And, through the mentoring given to him by a man who was supposedly a slave yet was so much more, he had already seen more money, and more of the world, than he ever dreamed possible. While his bond was strongest with Diocles, Barhinder, while there was a part of him that still feared their giant leader, had come to regard Titus Pullus with a level of affection and devotion that he would have thought impossible at the moment when they had first met, when the huge Roman had suddenly materialized on the earthen rampart created by what was now a permanent canal on the northern side of his native city. If he had been asked to describe his emotions when he saw what was one of the largest human beings he had ever seen, his sword already bloody, standing, feet apart on the rampart, he would have scoffed at the idea that he would feel anything but hatred and fear of Titus Pullus, especially in the heartbeats after a horrified young man who had joined the Bharuch army in emulation of his older brother and who had dreamed of glory and heroism, had seen his best friend Agathocles dispatched with what, even now that his emotions had cooled, he thought was a contemptuous ease by this giant Roman. The idea that he would be serving him would have been impossible for him to accept; that he would feel devotion to Pullus was unfathomable, yet that was what he felt as he sat astride his horse, just behind and to the right of the large Roman, who still disdained riding a horse but chose to walk with his men.

The First Cohort was behind the Eighth, meaning that the sight of the three elephants was from a greater distance, but unlike Mardonius, as a native of these lands, Barhinder was more aware of the incongruity of the sight of Pandyan and Cholan monarchs riding side by side than his new comrades. He spent the first part of the march watching intently, convinced that, at some point, one or the other would suddenly leap from their *howdah* to attack their lifelong enemy. However, by the time of the first rest break, nothing like that had happened, and only then did he begin to relax, thinking that perhaps it wouldn't happen after all. Barhinder, like the men marching to his left, was eager to learn what their future held, but for him, and for some of the others of Bharuch for whom the gods of their Macedonian conquerors weren't the ones they worshiped, the idea of seeing the sacred Ganges was a prospect that was so exciting, it almost erased his fear of another ocean voyage. It didn't help that he had learned from the Romans that the voyage from Bharuch to Muziris, which was lashed by a storm during which Barhinder was certain he was fated to die, was much shorter than the one they had made from Parthia, and this one was likely to be even longer than that one. Since he was literate thanks to Diocles, although he still struggled with writing in Latin, because of his access to the Primus Pilus' quarters, he had seen what he had been informed by Diocles was a map, and the Greek had explained the meaning of the lines and all the other markings, which meant that, like Cyclops, he had a better idea of just how long their voyage would be. He also knew, although he understood that he wasn't supposed to, that their general Caesar had yet to decide how much of their progress northward would be aboard ship, and how much over land. Barhinder also had another secret, one that not even Diocles knew about, and while the knowledge of it terrified him, at the same time, it made him feel an ever stronger bond of loyalty to Titus Pullus, and he had sworn to himself that he would rather die than give it up. Of course, this silent oath didn't extend to Pullus, because, in his innocence, Barhinder assumed that the Primus Pilus already knew that he had a son in Bharuch, which, while not unusual for the men of Rome's Legions, the fact that the mother was no less than Hyppolita, Queen of Bharuch, was certainly something that made the infant's existence unusual. More than once, he had almost worked up the nerve to approach Diocles, who he also incorrectly assumed knew of Pullus' secret, yet it had always failed him, although his purpose would have been only to assure both the Greek, and their Roman master, that they could rip his tongue out and cut off his genitals, but he would never betray what, despite his youth and political naivety, he understood was an explosive secret.

His secret knowledge began on their last night before departing Bharuch, and Diocles had given Barhinder leave to go visit his family one more time before the army left.

"It will be our secret, though," Diocles had warned him. "If Master Titus finds out..." He didn't finish because he knew he didn't need to, since this was still when Barhinder only feared the giant Roman, although he did add a shudder that he thought would help reinforce the point.

"I will never speak of it," Barhinder swore.

"And," Diocles said, adopting the tone he used when he wanted to convey to Barhinder this wasn't a suggestion or request, "you need to be back by the midnight watch, do you understand? Master Titus will be waking up extra early in the morning, and the last thing either of us needs is you walking in as he's coming out of his quarters."

That had been why he was hurrying back, trying to beat the *bucina* signal of the change of watch at midnight, careful to stick to the shadows along the streets on his way back to the Primus Pilus' quarters. The fact that they were located in the palace compound and had been where the commander of Bharuch's royal bodyguard and his family lived meant that he was moving along the street that paralleled the southern wall, when, out of the gloom ahead of him, some motion caught his eye. Freezing in place, he dropped into a crouch, and completely by accident and as he was about to discover, directly across the street from a secret door in the southern wall, the existence of which he only learned when a dark shape suddenly stopped, and while it was done softly, he heard a rapping noise.

Even in the darkness, Barhinder knew that there was something about the dark form across from him that seemed familiar, though it would take him a few more heartbeats to make the connection. He had to stifle a gasp when a part of the wall seemed to vanish, taking him a heartbeat to understand that it was a door being opened, but it was when the figure stepped into the doorway and had to duck his head that Barhinder realized that it was Master Titus. The door was quickly closed, and while Barhinder knew that he should resume his journey and mind his own business, his curiosity was too overwhelming. Making sure to look in both directions for one of the pairs of Legionaries who walked the streets as part of their guard duty, he moved quickly and as quietly as he could across the street to the doorway. His heart was pounding so heavily that he could hear it in his ears, so he pressed one against the doorway, and he quickly learned that it could beat even more quickly now, at the sound of two voices. Although the voices were too muffled to make out the words, he instantly confirmed by the timbre of his voice that it had been Master Titus who had just entered through this secret door, but it was the second one that made his knees go weak, thinking for a horrified heartbeat he would collapse unconscious on the ground. The only reason he recognized the second voice was due to the fact that he had been chosen by the Primus Pilus to be on a working party, a malodorous one involving shoveling the huge pile of elephant manure behind the large structure that was part of the enclosure where the royal war elephants of Bharuch were kept. As menial as it seemed to be, it was the presence of the Queen of Bharuch, Hyppolita, whose voice he heard through her veil and who was the person who led Master Titus and his working party to the pile, beneath which were heavy wooden crates, heavier than anything he had ever lifted, taking four of them to muscle it out of the large hole, that he had cause to remember. Queen Hyppolita hadn't spoken much, but he heard enough to identify just by the tone he was hearing now that it was her; the fact that he lingered there long enough to hear the other sounds the pair began making further informed him what they were doing. Despite the seriousness of what was taking place, the consequences of which he was only dimly aware, Barhinder felt his mouth turn up into a grin and he had to stifle a snigger, a reminder that he was, after all, still a teenage boy. After several moments, his titillation slowly turned into guilt, of the type he felt when he and Sagara would listen to their parents and giggle about what was happening in the next room, and he correctly assumed that Master Titus wouldn't be spending the rest of the night there; nevertheless, it was with a bit of reluctance he resumed his progress back to their quarters as his fear of Master Titus warred with his curiosity. Slipping in, when he walked over to his pallet in the corner, he saw Diocles' form on the Greek's cot, and he listened to his breathing for a moment, trying to determine if he was asleep.

He almost jumped out of his skin when, out of the darkness, Diocles informed him grumpily, "No, I'm not asleep...now. You make as much noise as one of those elephants."

Whispering an apology, Barhinder lay down, but he didn't fall asleep immediately as he tried not to think about what he had just witnessed, in a manner of speaking, and what it meant. Fortunately, with the call to rise, he was too busy to spend any time dwelling on it, and he quickly forgot about it.

He was reminded almost a year later, when, just before their departure from Karoura, a merchant caravan from Bharuch arrived, although it was totally by accident that Barhinder had been sent on an errand into the city to purchase some items for Master Titus that weren't readily available in the shantytown that had been constructed outside the Pandyan capital to accommodate the needs, mostly of the flesh, of the thousands of men with Caesar's part of the army.

"Gotra! Gotra!"

Hearing his name called amid the babble of voices of people negotiating the price of an object, or more commonly, arguing about it, Barhinder turned in the direction of the call, but it took him a moment to spot the man, who waved to him. What was his name? He tried to think of it, knowing that he was a friend of Barhinder's father, a merchant who specialized in spices that, while commonplace here, Barhinder had learned were considered exotic and were highly prized by the faceless mass of people that Barhinder thought of as Romans, far away.

The man was smiling as they approached each other, while Barhinder offered the ritual greeting of their people as the man said more loudly than necessary, "I told your father that I would look for you when I came to Karoura, but I honestly didn't expect to find you, especially so easily!"

As the man spoke, Barhinder recalled more details, the most relevant being that his father had talked about what a horrible gossip the man was, and how anyone who divulged a secret to him was making a huge mistake, but of more immediate relevance, he at last recalled the man's name just in time.

Aloud, and with only partially feigned eagerness, Barhinder asked, "And, how is my family, Euthymius?"

Like his dead friend Agathocles, along with countless other citizens of Bharuch, the merchant was a product of the intermingling of Macedonian and native Indo-Scythian cultures in that he had a Greek first name, and he assured Barhinder, "They're doing well, young Gotra. And," he lowered his voice, adding, "I know that it's because of the money that you're sending them that helps them."

It wasn't the words as much as the tone the merchant used that bothered Barhinder, detecting a false note that he interpreted as Euthymius' attempt to show Barhinder that he was in his father's confidence, which he knew to be untrue, and he also was positive that his father wouldn't appreciate this man talking about a matter such as this. In their world, fathers supported sons, not the other way around, and Barhinder loved his father; more importantly, he respected him.

Nevertheless, he answered politely, "I'm happy to do what I can for them, Euthymius." Then, seemingly out of nowhere, he felt a stab of an almost physical pain as he said, "Now that I'm certain that Sagara is dead, it's my responsibility to help."

"Yes, yes," Euthymius said with clearly counterfeit sympathy, "it is very sad. We lost many fine young men to the invaders. But," he smiled again, and gave Barhinder what he supposed was meant in a friendly manner, "at least something good has come out of all this, yes? You're in their pay now, and that's a good thing, isn't it?"

Caesar Ascending – The Ganges

While Barhinder also didn't care for the manner in which the merchant had characterized it, neither did he want to argue, so he simply nodded, in the Greco-Roman fashion, which at times was confusing to remember, depending on with whom he was conversing. With the pleasantries out of the way, Barhinder quickly became convinced that the merchant was far less interested in Barhinder's situation and far more eager to do the very thing the youth's father had warned him about.

Making an exaggerated show of looking around to see if anyone was listening, which Barhinder could see at a glance they weren't, Euthymius lowered his voice, taking on a conspiratorial air. "And, as it turns out, you're not the only one who's receiving something from the Romans. Or," he grinned, "should I put it another way, that before they left Bharuch, a Roman plowed a field, and the crop has borne fruit."

Immediately comprehending the merchant's meaning, Barhinder's initial reaction was one of indifference, which he explained with a shrug, "That's no secret. From what I've heard, there are many women who took up with Romans and now are having their children."

"Yes, very true," Euthymius seemingly agreed, then his smile took on a leering quality, "but I'll wager one hundred *drachmae* with you that you'll never guess who one of those women who lay with a Roman might be." This was Barhinder's first presentiment that he might know the answer, but he was only partially right, and after he only offered a shrug, the merchant whispered triumphantly, "Queen Hyppolita!"

It took all of the youth's discipline to appear unaffected by the news, which, judging from Euthymius' expression, he did well, and he said with yet another shrug, "I heard a rumor about that, but I also know that when King Abhiraka returned and tried to take the city, he spent time with the Queen before he died. And," he tried to sound as if he was experienced in such matters, and even offered the merchant what he hoped was a manly grin of his own, "it doesn't take that long, does it? Especially under those circumstances."

It was the triumphant expression on Euthymius' face that warned him, "Yes, that was the story, but someone I trust and who was there that night in the palace assures me that King and

191

Queen were only together for a very short period of time, and that they only embraced briefly and exchanged nothing more than a kiss." When Barhinder still didn't respond, the merchant added, "I also happen to know that one of the Queen's ladies had a child, also by a Roman, but nobody seems to know who the father of that one is."

It was the way Euthymius said this that made Barhinder feel certain that he wanted the youth to ask him, and with his heart in his throat, he did so, "But you *do* know who the Roman is who fathered the Queen's child?"

Now, positively beaming, the merchant leaned even closer, and whispered, "Why, Caesar of course!" Barhinder had to again rely on his self-control, this time not to sag in relief, but there must have been something in his expression that Euthymius interpreted as doubt, because his smile faded, and he sounded a bit offended as he insisted, "Who else could it be, eh, Gotra? She wouldn't lie with a man from a lower caste, whatever the Romans call them," he gave a wave of disgust at the very thought, "so who else could it be? Oh," he allowed, "they tried to pass the babe off as the one belonging to her lady, and they told the palace servants that there's only one babe there, but a woman who serves the Queen in the kitchens is my cousin, and she told me that there are now two inside the palace, not one. And," he reminded Barhinder, "we already know he whelped a bastard on that Egyptian queen, Cleopatra."

Seeing an escape, Barhinder said as convincingly as he could, "I'm sure you're right, Euthymius. And," he attempted another manly grin, "perhaps this Caesar will leave a trail of queens' bastards behind him, eh? It will make him easy to find."

"Indeed!" Euthymius bobbed his head, laughing at the jest.

Before the merchant could continue, Barhinder said politely, "While it's wonderful to see you, Euthymius, I'm afraid I was sent here for several things, and I can't tarry. As I'm sure that you've already heard, the army is leaving very soon, and there are still many tasks my master has for me to perform."

"Of course, of course," the merchant agreed, then offered his hand. "May your gods look over you, young Gotra, as you serve these Romans."

"Thank you," Barhinder replied politely, then hurriedly thought to add, "and please, when you return to Bharuch, I'd be indebted to you if you'd let my parents know that you saw me, that I'm well, and that I'll send word to them as soon as I am able."

With the merchant's assurance that he would do that, Barhinder turned away from Euthymius, quickly losing himself in the crowd, but, while he was honest about the things he had to do, he still needed a moment to himself to think matters through. Ducking into an alley, he leaned against a wall, his head spinning as he forced himself to concentrate. While he considered the possibility that the merchant was merely relaying inaccurate gossip, Barhinder felt reasonably confident that Euthymius was speaking the truth about Hyppolita having a child, but where he was wrong was in the identity of the father, for the simple reason that he knew that the Queen had only seen the Roman general on a handful of occasions, and always with witnesses around, including Master Titus. Coupled with his knowledge of his master's seeing the Queen on the night before they had departed Bharuch, which was just a bit less than a year earlier, he felt confident that his supposition about the identity of the father was the right one. But there was another piece of information that, again, Barhinder had stumbled onto by accident, when he had overheard Master Titus inform his nephew Gaius, who Barhinder liked a great deal, that the Lady Amodini had borne him a child. While this certainly wasn't as potentially dangerous as the knowledge that the Queen of Bharuch had borne a child fathered by what, Barhinder knew, many of his people still considered as nothing but invaders, the pair of secrets wore equally heavily on his troubled shoulders. Now, as they were marching towards Uraiyur, Barhinder's eyes lingered on the huge Roman, wondering what would happen if he learned the truth, that he was leaving a child behind as he marched wherever Caesar was taking them, because, while he never discussed it with Diocles, nor was his opinion solicited, Barhinder sensed that the Romans in Caesar's army would never be returning from wherever they were going.

On their arrival at the city that served as the Chola capital,

Caesar's army behaved accordingly, constructing their huge marching camp, which engendered more conflict because Karikala objected to the occupation of some of the more fertile fields in range of the city. It had been a decidedly tense march, with Karikala offering the bare minimum of what could be called courtesy on those occasions where he was forced to have any congress with Caesar or one of his Legates. Consequently, the burden of ensuring that there were no incidents between these two separate and distinct forces fell on Senganan's shoulders, but he found an unlikely ally in the young Pandyan king, and it was further aided by the common bond between the two kings in their elephants. The idea of sharing the Roman army's marching camp was out of the question during their three-day journey, but Nedunj did prevail upon Caesar to allow both Pandyan and Chola animals to be kept together, and outside the dirt walls of the camp. It certainly wasn't the case that the Pandyan was friendly, either to King Karikala or to Senganan, but it was by a matter of degree, and whether Nedunj sensed that Senganan felt the same affinity for these animals that, aside from gold, silver, and jewels was the most potent sign of a kingdom's wealth in their world and decided to exploit that, Senganan would never know. It wasn't until the final day of the march, when word was relayed that the Roman scouts had sighted the walls of Uraiyur, that there was a conversation between the two enemies that wasn't about elephants and their care.

It was during the brief rest stop, when after relieving themselves, the pair found themselves temporarily alone and out of obvious earshot, prompting Senganan to ask bluntly, "Your Highness, can Caesar be trusted?" Hurrying on, he said, "I'm speaking to you now not as a Chola and you a Pandyan, but as a man of India. These Romans aren't of our world, just as Alexander wasn't of ours either, and I'm afraid that we may have let a *Naja* into our midst, just as the northern kingdoms did with the Greek king."

Because of a combination of factors, and coupled with the fact that Nedunj himself had wrestled with this question, it enabled him to say with some confidence, "Yes, I believe so." Making sure to look Senganan in the eye, he spoke quietly,

"Everything that Caesar told me he would do, he has done. And," he pointed out, "as you saw for yourself, as long as they're in possession and have a supply of that naphtha, or until we can teach our elephants not to fear fire as they do, the Romans are here."

Although this confirmed Senganan's suspicions, he was still struggling with coming to grips with this reality, and he said unhappily, "I'm concerned that King Karikala isn't going to see things the way you have, Your Highness. After all," he pointed out, and Nedunj understood perfectly, "he's older, and he's been king for more than fifteen years now." Nodding his head, he finished sadly, "I'm afraid for the Chola people, that these Romans will force them to submit to their strange customs and gods."

On this subject, Nedunj felt more confident, and he informed Senganan, "While I appreciate your concerns, if only because I shared them, nobody has been more surprised at the manner in which these Romans have treated my subjects. And," he thought to add, "me." Seeing Senganan's expression, Nedunj explained, "Caesar, and by extension, his army, doesn't seem all that interested in turning us into Romans like them. In fact," the thought occurred to him, "this past winter, when their men tried to come into both Karoura and Muziris to find women, rather than allow his men to take whomever they pleased, he had his men construct an entire town outside our walls where women who chose to do so could go and ply their trade. And," he added, "these Romans *love* to drink intoxicating beverages, and they had never experienced *sura* before." Even with the gravity of the subject under discussion, Nedunj grinned at Senganan, who returned it, each of them reliving in their minds moments where, in the grips of whatever it was that was in this fermented concoction, they had experienced moments that they would relive in their memories, and the Pandyan went on, "By isolating his men from my subjects who didn't wish to have any business with them, whatever disturbances there were happened in this small town that Caesar created. And," he finished ruefully, "as I learned, my own soldiers weren't immune to the attractions offered there."

"What's the name of this town Caesar had built?"

Senganan asked, but all Nedunj could offer was an explanation accompanied by a shrug, "I know the men in the ranks call it something, but it doesn't make sense to me. They call it the shantytown, and from what I've learned, it's because of the kind of construction they use in its creation." Before he said more, Nedunj took a quick glance around to ensure there were no Roman ears within hearing range. "Apparently, the Romans allow camp followers, and whenever they stop for an extended period of time, these camp followers use whatever they have to build a permanent settlement outside the camp."

In their world, this was nothing short of scandalous, although Senganan saw nothing in the Pandyan king's expression to make him believe that Nedunj was having some fun with him, so he signaled his acceptance with a shake of the head.

"That," he said, "is quite strange. But," he added bitterly, "it obviously works for them."

"Many things work for them, Lord Senganan," Nedunj replied quietly; now it was his turn for the bitterness to reveal itself, "which I learned when they arrived at Muziris."

Sensing that probing further would disrupt this fragile rapport between them, Senganan tacitly accepted this by moving on, asking suddenly, "So, who do you think will be the victor between their giant Roman and whoever my King selects to face him?"

They had begun moving back to their elephants, who had been watered by their *mahouts*, and Nedunj glanced at Senganan in surprise. "You mean you don't know who King Karikala will select?"

"Not with any certainty," Senganan allowed, "but if I had to wager on it, it will be Prashant, or perhaps Yogesh, because Yogesh is the only man we have who is close to his size, and he's a fearsome warrior. But," he decided, "I think it will be Prashant."

They had reached their animals, both of them kneeling; Karikala hadn't left his *howdah* and, as had been his habit the entire march, chose to engage in quiet conversation with his own *mahout*.

As Nedunj lifted one leg to step up on Darpashata's knee,

he looked over his shoulder and said simply, "It really doesn't matter who your king chooses, because he's going to die."

Senganan stiffened, not liking the manner in which Nedunj so casually dismissed the chances of one of Chola's finest warriors to defeat this Roman brute, but then he recalled his examination of the Roman during their meeting, and he felt a shiver run up his spine. What, he thought dismally, will Karikala do if Prashant or whoever he chose didn't emerge victorious from this? Would he follow through on his threat to sacrifice it all in his quest for vengeance? This troubling thought occupied his mind for the rest of their day's march, which stopped outside the walls of Uraiyur. While he would never know it, Nedunj was similarly troubled, albeit for different reasons. He wasn't a duplicitous person by nature, so it didn't come naturally to lie to Senganan in the manner in which he had; one way or another, Pandya would control Chola, and while it didn't make him particularly happy about lying to a man he was coming to not only respect but to like, it wouldn't stop him from achieving his aims. Not even Caesar would stop him.

When the sun came up on the army's first full day outside Uraiyur, emotions were running high through the entirety of the Roman portion of the army, with one notable exception. When Pullus rose from his cot, he was yawning, and to Diocles, behaving in a bizarre manner, if only because his master seemed completely unconcerned about what he would be facing shortly.

"Is the porridge ready?" Pullus asked, and fortunately, Diocles was prepared, placing the bowl on the table that, by virtue of his status as Primus Pilus, was large enough to seat four, and was carried in his personal wagon.

Watching Pullus shovel the food in his mouth, Diocles placed a half-loaf of bread from the meal the evening before next to the bowl, then demanded, "Well?"

Forced to swallow his food first, Pullus looked up at the Greek, clearly surprised, "Well what?"

"You're about to have to face some barbarian brute, that's what!" Diocles snapped, unusual in itself.

Rather than explode, Pullus instead sat back from his bowl,

and with a smile playing on his lips, he countered, "Do you really have such little faith in me, Diocles?"

"Of course not!" Diocles fought a surge of panic at the thought that this man who he served, and loved, thought he doubted Titus Pullus, but neither was he willing to drop it. "If it comes down to a matter of skill, Master Titus, I have no doubt, at all, that you'll prevail, no matter who Karikala selects. But," his voice softened, "it's not always a matter of skill, is it? Sometimes, it's the gods, who decide for their own reasons to tip the scales, isn't it?"

"That's true," Pullus agreed, but then resumed spooning food into his mouth so that he could grin up at his Greek, showing his mouthful of food as he did so, "but the gods love me."

Knowing this was going nowhere, Diocles turned away, grumbling, to consume his own meal. Pullus, however, was destined not to enjoy an uninterrupted repast, as first Balbus, then Scribonius, who brought Porcinus, showed up at his tent.

"I always said that I never had a mother," he finally said in exasperation, after submitting himself to the same treatment that he had endured from Diocles, "but no more. Now I know what it's like. Besides," he grumbled, "I know that you bastards are just hanging around to go through my things if I don't beat this *cunnus*, whoever he is."

Understanding that it was time to relent, Scribonius turned to more practical concerns, using Pullus' comment as an opening, "Did Caesar tell you who that bastard chose?"

"No," Pullus shook his head, "but it doesn't matter. Now," he stood and gestured to Diocles, "help me get ready, then go get Barhinder, and the rest of you go find a spot to watch."

That, at least, had been decided on. Since Caesar refused to allow this fight to take place within the walls of Uraiyur, Karikala had reciprocated, refusing to agree to a bout in the camp forum. The compromise was a spot, roughly equidistant between city and camp, so that people could watch from the walls of both, with the only source of agreement between the two being that the rankers of both armies wouldn't be allowed to leave their respective spots. While it would be plainly visible, the only men in immediate attendance would be the Cholan king, Lord Senganan, and a handful of other noblemen who had remained in Uraiyur, while on the Roman side, it was Caesar, Nedunj, Achaemenes, the Legates, the Primi Pili, and to what had been Diocles' dismay, the personal attendant that each combatant was allowed, who for Pullus was Barhinder. As Pullus had expected, Diocles resisted this, but in one of the rare instances where his giant master presented an argument that Diocles couldn't refute, he had relented.

"You don't speak Tamil, Diocles," Pullus had said in what, for him, was a gentle tone. "Caesar doesn't trust that *mentula* Karikala, and neither do I. Once I kill the *cunnus* Karikala has chosen, Caesar thinks that he'll try something, and I agree. With Barhinder there, listening, he's more likely to pick up something that you'd miss."

When expressed that way, Diocles couldn't summon an argument, but he didn't pretend to be happy; for his part, Barhinder's emotions were at war with each other. On one part, he was proud that Master Titus demonstrated his trust in a manner that couldn't be mistaken or argued, while at the same time, he was terrified that he might miss a sign, or misinterpret something one of the Cholans said. As it turned out, following behind Pullus through the camp, the *Via Praetoria* lined several rankers deep on both sides with those men who hadn't secured a spot on the rampart, pride won out. Everyone else would be relegated to viewing from a distance, and from their respective walls, but Barhinder would be there to serve Master Titus, and what finer thing could there be for someone like him?

Not surprisingly, it was the men of the 10th who claimed the best viewing spot along the dirt rampart, but since that stretch couldn't accommodate every man in the Equestrians, the four officers of each Century claimed precedence, while those rankers who were relegated to congregating down on the ground inside the camp or standing on the wall but so far away, it was impossible to see clearly were forced to rely on their comrades to apprise them of events. There was an atmosphere similar to what one would find at a gladiatorial contest, with one very notable exception. While men under the Roman standard were notorious, and rightly so, for wagering on seemingly anything and everything, the men for whom this was a profitable side business discovered very quickly that they couldn't find any takers who were willing to bet against the Primus Pilus of the Equestrians.

As one ranker in the 12th put it to Balbinus before the Primus Pilus left with the observing party, "If the boys in the Equestrians ever find out that one of us bet against Primus Pilus Pullus, you'd find us in the baths with our throats slit."

Otherwise, aside from the wagering and the fact that there were no vendors selling wine and meat pies, there was an air of eager anticipation, competing with varying levels of anxiety. Scribonius, Balbus, Porcinus, Cyclops, and Diocles were standing together, and with the best vantage point, but their conversation was desultory as they watched the party of Romans striding out of the Porta Praetoria, with Caesar leading the way aboard Toes.

What quickly became obvious to Scribonius, just from glancing around, led him to comment with some amusement, "This is probably the only time Caesar's not the center of attention. I can't imagine he likes it very much."

However, it was the truth; all eyes were drawn to the only unmounted man, dressed in his *hamata,* and with his helmet on, walking a few paces behind Caesar's horse, his *gladius* already drawn, which he held at his side, point down as his hand made small circles.

It was Porcinus who noticed this and pointed it out to the others, prompting Scribonius to comment ruefully, "Yes, every time we sparred, when I saw him doing that, I knew I was probably going to be sore the next morning."

He said this loudly enough for the other Centurions and Optios around them to hear, and there was a ragged chorus of agreement, and commiseration, because one of the standards for being considered worthy for promotion to the Centurionate and Optionate in the 10th Legion was facing their Primus Pilus in the sparring ring. Pullus was followed by the rest of the party, also mounted, which, along with the Legates, included a pair of Caesar's bodyguards, but by this time, they were all accustomed to the fact that, wherever Gundomir went, the one-eyed Parthian Teispes would be with him. It was also Porcinus who noticed, and pointed out, that Barhinder had been given the duty of carrying a Legionary shield, and despite the circumstances, his observation that it was almost impossible to see the Bharuch youth even on horseback was met with laughing agreement. On the opposite side of the Roman camp, the city gate was opened, and a similarly numbered party emerged; like the Romans, the party was restricted to a small group of men, and while they were mounted, it was on horses, this being another requirement of Caesar's, that there be no elephants. Unlike the Romans, none of them were walking, so it wasn't until the two parties met before the identity of the Chola champion was revealed. Senganan's first guess that it would be Prashant was the correct one, which the Romans learned when the royal bodyguard slid off his horse. The two parties, without any discussion, silently created the boundary of what was for all intents and purposes an arena by forming a rough circle, with the Cholan king and his nobles filling one part of the circle, the other half the Romans.

Pullus had informed Caesar of Barhinder's role, the general immediately seeing the wisdom and the cunning of his Primus Pilus, and on the short ride, it was arranged so that, when they dismounted, it was Barhinder who was closest to the Cholan delegation on one side. Only Pullus and Prashant were wearing their armor, while the others were all armed only with a sword, the Primi Pili included, all of whom were also clutching their *viti*, which the Cholans, like the Pandyans before them, had to be informed of the meaning of the symbol of the Roman Centurion, suspicious that it was some sort of weapon with magic powers. On a signal, Karikala dismounted at the same time as Caesar, while the Cholan king was accompanied by Senganan, and Caesar by Nedunj, while Pullus and Prashant stood there on opposite sides, eyeing each other. Before he took his position, at Pullus' direction, Barhinder had handed the shield he had carried to Primus Pilus Torquatus, and he was standing just behind Pullus and a bit to his left, prepared to hand him his shield while the youth used the horses as a screen to move into position closer to the Chola. When the two parties reached the rough center of the circle, with all of those men who had been mounted now on the ground and holding the reins of their animals, it was Caesar who broke the silence.

Only using his head, he indicated Prashant as he asked Karikala in Greek, "This is your champion?"

"Yes," Karikala replied tersely. "His name is Prashant..." he paused for just a heartbeat, "...Paraiya."

This meant absolutely nothing to Caesar, but Nedunj not only went stiff, his eyes going wide, he gave a small gasp that, while he had no idea why, Caesar knew it meant that the young king considered this important.

Karikala, however, was clearly amused, and in Tamil, he said, "Tell this pale Roman what that means." Before Nedunj could respond, Karikala added, with a sneer, "So, you see, Pandyan, there is an opportunity for all men in my kingdom to better themselves."

Clearly knowing something potentially important was happening, Caesar turned to Nedunj, asking sharply, "What is happening, Your Highness? Why did this man's name make you react that way?"

How, Nedunj thought miserably, do I explain centuries of custom in the span of a few heartbeats?

Thinking frantically, his countenance brightened as he finally stumbled on an explanation, which he offered to Caesar, "A man who carries this name belongs to our lowest caste, Caesar. Do you remember when you explained to me about your system? About men of what you call the Head Count?" Caesar nodded, and Nedunj, now accustomed to this strange habit of the Romans in using a gesture opposite to theirs, went on, "That means that this Prashant has clearly elevated his status to be considered worthy of being a member of King Karikala's bodyguard." He also felt compelled to add, "It is much more complicated than that, but I will try to explain later. But, Caesar," suddenly, Nedunj switched to Latin, and while not fluent, he was able to relate, "this also means that Prashant must be a mighty warrior to have climbed so high, which means he is a very dangerous man."

"What are you saying, Pandyan?" Karikala interrupted suspiciously, in Tamil.

Despite knowing this wasn't the time, Nedunj couldn't stop himself from deliberately hesitating as if he was debating

Caesar Ascending – The Ganges

whether this was worthy of a response before he replied coldly, "I am explaining to Caesar that your...*champion*, is unclean and of our lowest caste. Which," Nedunj challenged, "is nothing but the truth, isn't it?"

While this back and forth was taking place, which Pullus caught most of since it was predominantly in Greek, he was also studying his opponent, as Prashant was doing with him. The Roman noticed the scar, of course, but what he had seen immediately was the lithe grace with which the Cholan moved, and Pullus was certain that this man would rely on superior speed to try and kill him because he wouldn't be able to match Pullus' power. For his part, Prashant was studying Pullus, seeing a man who was much larger than his Roman compatriots, but large, even compared to the men of Chola. In fact, Prashant had been surprised when his king had selected him and not Yogesh, because Yogesh was not only a fierce warrior in his own right, he was closer to the Roman in size. While his initial thought was dismissive, recalling his victories over the men he had faced who were anywhere near this dog's size, because in his experience, they were uniformly lazy in their skill with a sword by relying on brute force, Prashant also didn't miss the scars that, while not as distinctive, were more numerous. *Remember that these vermin have managed to conquer not just Pandya, but those northern tribes as well*, he reminded himself, *so he's not to be taken lightly*. Prashant followed even less of the exchange, not knowing a word of Greek, and while he heard his king's demand to know what the Pandyan was saying to the pale Roman general since it was in Tamil, that was all. *Not*, he thought, *that it matters*, using the time to stretch his legs and arms, because Pullus had guessed correctly, that Prashant intended on striking as quickly as lightning, and in a similar manner, bring this giant down in the time it took for a bolt to fell a tree. Then, he drew his sword, which was slightly curved and longer than what the Roman had in his hand, which he considered to his advantage, then accepted the shield from Lord Venkata, who served as the ostensible commander of the royal bodyguard because of his status. What Karikala hadn't mentioned when he had taunted the Pandyan king was that, while Karikala was content to allow a member of the unclean to serve in his bodyguard after proving himself, starting as a spear-wielder, the heights Prashant could reach were limited. While neither of them would ever know it, the two men facing each other on behalf of their respective leaders had more in common than either of them did with the men whose bidding they were doing. Not, if they had known and both would have freely admitted, that it mattered.

With the formalities done, Caesar strode back to face Pullus, his face a mask, but Pullus was completely unprepared for his general to step close to him to whisper in his ear, "Whatever gods or *numeni* you summoned on that hill in Hispania, Pullus, you need to call on them now."

Pullus' surprise showed on his face, but it was only because he didn't think that Caesar would have remembered that, but of its own volition, he felt his mouth moving to say the words, "I understand, and will obey, Caesar."

"I know you will." His general gave him Caesar's Smile then, bestowed on few but never forgotten by those who received it, but then his face took on an expression that, while unusual for his general, Pullus immediately recognized as that belonging to a warrior, and Caesar hissed, "Now, go show these savages what it means to be a Roman!"

For those who wanted to see an extended battle, where both combatants exacted damage on their opponent, and were evenly matched so that the spectators could comment on the relative skills of the pair, it would prove to be an extremely disappointing contest. What it did achieve was to reinforce to his men that Titus Pullus was, in simple terms, the greatest warrior they were certain the world had ever seen, and even those who were disappointed that it didn't last longer, if they were Roman, joined their voices with those of their comrades who roared in a savage exultation when the Cholan warrior dropped to his knees as he watched his lifeblood fall in a scarlet rain into the damp, green earth.

"He never saw anyone use their shield like that," had been Balbus' comment, and indeed, it was a unique and distinct difference that, to this point in time, none of their foes had demonstrated, using a shield as both an offensive and defensive weapon.

"I knew he was dead when I saw Uncle Titus making those fucking circles with his *gladius*," had been Porcinus' comment.

He had to practically shout this to be heard, as the rankers of the 10th had just been informed by Scribonius, who had been providing the narrative of what he was seeing, when the Centurion suddenly offered an inarticulate bellow that needed no explanation.

Hundreds, perhaps thousands of fists were spontaneously thrust into the air, and as men shouted their elation, and pride, it quickly turned into a chant, a chant of a single name, because, even if they couldn't see him, and they weren't in his Legion, they knew Pullus had upheld the honor of Rome, and even more importantly because of the increasingly polyglot composition, this army, *their* army. What relatively few men knew was that, with this victory, the Primus Pilus of the Equestrians had essentially saved many of these men's lives, but every one of Pullus' fellow Primi Pili were acutely aware of this, and, in private of course, they would commiserate with each other that Pullus would become more insufferable. To their collective surprise, this prediction turned out to be inaccurate, because for the entirety of a campaign that none of them knew would consume several more years, Pullus never mentioned his victory that day or what it meant. Regardless of their personal feelings, none of them were particularly surprised that Pullus had slain the Chola's champion, but the speed with which it happened served as a reminder to them that there was a reason that, when not on active campaign, Titus Pullus devoted a third of a watch of every single day behaving in much the same way as a new *Tiro*, with *rudis* in hand, executing the thrusts as taught to countless men under the standard.

For the other onlookers, and one man in particular, what he witnessed was so utterly shocking, and demoralizing, that Karikala remained standing in his spot, seemingly unable to move even after the Roman party turned away to mount their horses. And, being king, it meant that Senganan and the other nobles that had accompanied their monarch from the city had to remain there as well. The Roman who had caused his dazed and demoralized state barely glanced at the Cholan king, and had already handed his shield to a youth that Karikala assumed was a slave and begun walking away, disdaining the slave's offering of his horse for the giant to ride. Karikala's eyes were fixed on Prashant's corpse, now lying facedown after he toppled forward, the ground around his head stained a darker shade in a pool as the last of his bodyguard's blood drained from his body, and he couldn't seem to tear his gaze away. He was forced to when a shadow suddenly blotted out the sun, causing him to at last look up to see that it was the Roman Caesar, with the Pandyan pup next to him, both on horseback.

"Your Highness," Caesar's tone was formal, "I expect you to abide by the terms of our agreement, that you will refrain from any more hostile action for the time we are waiting here. Do you understand?" When Karikala didn't answer, choosing instead to give the Roman a look of pure, venomous hatred, Caesar's voice hardened. "Do I need to arrange for another...demonstration of what will happen should you choose to violate our agreement and bring dishonor onto your house? This one involving one, or both of your sons?"

It took all of the Cholan king's willpower not to draw his own sword and attack this arrogant, pale invader, and almost as much for him to answer, in a choked voice, "No, there is no need. I will abide by the terms of our agreement. Provided," he added, "you and your cur here do the same."

Nedunj kicked his horse and it was moving forward, the Pandyan king's face twisted into a mask of fury, but he was close enough for Caesar to reach out with his free hand and grasp the younger man's arm. That look of rage briefly transferred to Caesar, which he returned with a cool gaze, not long, but enough for Nedunj to relax slightly, then shake his head. Most importantly, his horse had stopped after taking only the first step. Seeing that the Pandyan was under control, Caesar returned his attention to Karikala, although he was surreptitiously watching Lord Senganan, who was standing next to and just behind his king, trying to gauge the nobleman's reaction.

Sensing that he had an ally in the Chola nobleman, Caesar resumed, "I can assure you that none of my men," then added meaningfully, "or those men and animals of my ally will behave in an aggressive manner." He was about to turn Toes away, then something seemed to occur to him, and he stared down at Karikala as he asked, "And can I assume that you will not be so foolish as to try and exact vengeance on Primus Pilus Pullus? That you accept that your gods, as well as mine, have deemed this business to be finished with the death of Prashant Paraiya?" It was a small thing, but it would stick with Karikala for the rest of his time on earth that this foreign invader deigned to remember his champion's name. As if reading his thoughts, Caesar's tone softened slightly. "Your man fought with courage today, Your Highness, and I will make an offering to our gods to honor him. And," he said, "know that Primus Pilus Pullus is...unique. There is no shame in your champion's defeat."

Despite the kind words, hearing them coming from this pale foreigner was bitter gall to Karikala, but seeing that the Roman was expecting a response, he answered bitterly, "Yes, it is finished. I will take no action against that...man."

Satisfied, Caesar did turn Toes away then without waiting for Karikala to respond, and he wouldn't have been Caesar if he didn't add in an almost careless manner, "And he's unique even for a Roman, and we are a unique people."

It would become a lingering question in Caesar's mind if it had been this last remark that caused the trouble that would ensue, or if Karikala had been lying all along. The Cholan king remained standing there, now reduced to glaring at the retreating backs of the departing party, which meant that he saw when Nedunj, who was just slightly behind Caesar and out of his range of vision, looked over his shoulder, and offered his fellow monarch a smile that Karikala correctly interpreted as gloating.

"Your Highness." Karikala turned to Senganan, unaware that the nobleman had addressed him twice before he finally responded. The other man's countenance was grave, and appeared as shaken as Karikala was, but he spoke calmly, "May we carry Prashant's body back into the city to prepare him for the burial rites?"

The king nodded his head as he said with a quiet vehemence, "No. He failed Chola, and he failed me. Let the hyenas and vultures have him."

Only then did he move, turning and leaping up onto his horse, yanking its head and going immediately to the canter, without looking back, leaving the rest of his party to scramble to their own mounts to catch up. Senganan was the last to mount, because he walked to the slain man's body, and in their manner, offered up his own prayers to their gods; only then did he mount his horse, forced to go to the gallop to catch up before Karikala witnessed what, in his present mood, the Cholan king would undoubtedly view as an act of defiance. It was later that night, under the cover of darkness, that a small party of men emerged to retrieve Prashant's body, all of them members of Karikala's royal bodyguard and each of them offering oaths to never speak of what they were doing, knowing that Karikala would view it as disobedience to his orders, and would undoubtedly incur severe punishment. They took precautions to remain unobserved, but in this they were unsuccessful, as Senganan saw everything from the spot on the city wall, but these men would never learn this, because it was something Senganan never spoke of for the rest of his days, nor the fact that he had been the man to issue the order.

"I'm sorer from being slapped on the back than I am from the fight," Pullus grumbled, but none of his friends were sympathetic.

"Oh, be quiet," Scribonius scoffed. "You love being the center of attention, you always have since we were in Scallabis."

Pullus didn't even try to protest, just offering the others a grin, a grin that was partially lubricated by a couple cups of *sura*, which had replaced wine for most of the Romans of Caesar's army as their favorite method of getting drunk. Normally, he eschewed the intoxicating beverage when they were actively campaigning, but deemed that it was acceptable this night, given that it was a celebration that he wasn't dead, and the army wouldn't march until Pollio and the rest of the army arrived. Balbus had had no such compunctions; the days that he did imbibe far outnumbered the days he didn't, but from his earliest days under the standard, the scarred Centurion had consumed copious quantities of liquids that had the capacity to get a man drunk, and it had never impinged on his ability to perform his duties. The fact that he was sitting there as the Primus Pilus Posterior, second in command of the Legion, attested to his ability to do his job, even with a ferocious hangover, something that his men had learned to watch for carefully, knowing that their day would be correspondingly bad, and the running joke in the Second Century was that there were far more bad days than good.

"He clearly didn't expect you to be that fast," Scribonius commented, returning to the original topic of what had turned out to be not much more than a sparring session for Pullus, albeit with deadly consequences. "But," he allowed, if a bit grudgingly, "he was pretty quick himself."

"As quick as Vibius," Pullus replied shortly, in a tone that the other four men knew was a signal that, while he could mention his childhood friend, it was a forbidden topic for them. He fell silent, but then he went on, "Vibius is still the fastest man with a *gladius* and shield I've ever faced. So," he shrugged, "once he made his first attack, I knew what I had to do."

More than anyone else at the table in Pullus' tent, Scribonius knew the deeper meaning of what Pullus said, yet despite knowing that he was treading on dangerous ground, he felt compelled to explain to two of the others, which he did in the form of a question, although he knew the answer since he had been present on one occasion when Pullus had used the maneuver.

"Was it what you did with Vibius before we joined, when Cyclops was training you?"

Pullus nodded, but said nothing else, preferring to lift the cup to his lips, which, rightly or wrongly, Scribonius took as silent permission to tell the others the story.

He began by saying, "I heard about this from Vibius, back when we were *Tiros*, and I saw it myself when our first Optio Aulus Vinicius paired up Titus and Didius the first day we started sparring." Before he continued, he glanced at Pullus again, who was still sipping from his cup, but he saw the upward curve at the edge of Pullus' mouth, so he continued, addressing himself more to Porcinus and Diocles, "You've heard us talk about Didius, of course. He was a surly bastard, and," he acknowledged, but with a smile of his own at the long-ago memories, "he was a fucking cheat, especially at dice, but more than anything, he thought that he was better than," he didn't say his name, just jerked a thumb at Pullus, "and he'd been running his mouth from the first day. So, our Optio took care of the problem by pitting the two of them together."

"I was in the First Cohort," Balbus spoke up, "so I didn't see it, but we heard about it." He made a raspy sound that was his version of a chuckle. "By the gods, did we hear about it. We already knew who Titus was because, well," he shrugged, and like Scribonius, pointed at his friend, "he's Titus. But, we also had learned by then how the story of these things...grow over time, so I didn't think much of it. Until," now, he laughed openly, "I saw Didius the first time after it happened."

"His nose looked like a ripe plum," Scribonius took the tale back up, but also laughing. "But it was the way Titus did it, like today, and I remember Vibius telling me right after it happened with Didius about what Titus did just a couple years earlier when Cyclops was training them."

"You mean when he punched his shield, but down instead of straight ahead?" Porcinus asked, and his uncle nodded, then explained, "Yes, Gaius. It was something that I did the first time by accident, but I saw what happened, so I had been experimenting with it whenever I fought with Cyclops, but it never worked with him because he's too good. Although," he grinned at the memory, "I came *this* close once." He held one hand up with thumb and forefinger no more than a couple inches apart. "But once I saw the Chola moving, and when he made his first couple of thrusts, I knew that I had two choices, and one was to wear him down. Or," he finished simply, "use the Vibius move."

"The 'Vibius move'?" Scribonius echoed with obvious amusement. "It has a name?"

"Only in my head," Pullus protested. "I've never said it out loud."

"Until now," Diocles spoke for the first time, then pointed to the two Centurions, "and you know these two will never let you forget it."

This elicited laughter from all of them, while Pullus

acknowledged this, then with a rueful tone said, "I *knew* why I quit drinking *sura*..." he paused, then with a broad smile, "...but I had forgotten."

The others laughed, but none of them more than Pullus himself at his own joke, and once it subsided, they fell into a silence that wasn't uncomfortable, but to Porcinus, it seemed as if the three older men had suddenly left the tent, returning to a land of memories, and he offered a silent prayer to the gods that he lived long enough to be able to visit that faraway place of the past, and of comrades, friends, and rivals as they did.

The silence was broken by Diocles, who, while not wanting to ruin the celebration, still felt compelled to bring up the thing that preyed on his mind by asking, "Titus, do you think that the Cholan king will uphold his agreement not to come after you?"

"No," Pullus replied, flatly and with no doubt in his voice, "I don't. Remember," he reminded the others, "I was on the back of that fucking elephant, and I was close enough to him to smell him, but it's what I saw that matters. As I told Caesar," he shook his head, "what I saw wasn't a king, or a nobleman, or anything other than a father driven half-mad with grief and hatred for the man he thinks killed his son. So," he finished with a sigh, "no, I fully expect him to send men after me."

While this confirmed the Greek's suspicion, what troubled him was Pullus' seeming unconcern, but he quickly learned it was shared by the others, because it was Porcinus who voiced his own thoughts.

"You don't seem very worried, Uncle," he chided.

"I'm not." Making a vague gesture that encompassed their surroundings, "Look at this camp. We're not like fucking Gauls, or the Parthians when they're on sentry duty. Whichever Legion has the guard duty is going to be on alert. Not," he stressed, "because they're worried about me. We're camped next to a city full of people who fucking hate us, led by a king who's not only lost a son, but who's been humiliated in front of the kind of enemy like how we viewed Carthage for generations. That," he added, "is why I'm not worried. I know he'll try, but whoever he sends will have their guts spilled long before he gets to me. Besides," he finished, gesturing to the camp around them again, "the only people who would know where the 10th is at are other Romans. These barbarians have no idea how we're organized."

All of this was true, and it made perfect sense, but it was once again left to Scribonius to point something out.

"Titus, you're forgetting one thing."

"Oh?" Pullus suddenly looked wary, knowing from long experience that he wouldn't be likely to be happy about what his friend had to say.

Scribonius pointed like Pullus had, but in only one direction, in the direction of the city as he warned, "Those walls are high enough for them to see down into the camp from the southeast corner. And," he needlessly reminded his friend, "you're pretty easy to pick out, even from a distance. So, I wouldn't put too much faith in the idea that, if they get past our ditch, wall, and the guard Legion that they'll get lost stumbling around the camp."

"You," Pullus grumbled, then reached for the pitcher to refill his cup, "have always been able to find the rat turd in the honey."

Chapter Five

"Your Highness, I can't stress enough that I believe this is a bad idea."
As anyone who served King Karikala learned very quickly, while he was willing to listen to his councilors, once he made a decision, it was either a very brave or very foolish man who persisted in trying to dissuade him from whatever course he had chosen, and this extended to the dead crown prince. Senganan was acutely aware of this, but he felt as if he had no choice, if only because the other men Karikala sought out for advice had been so timorous in their resistance to their king. As he had learned, to his unsurprised disgust, while his fellow nobles assured Senganan that they agreed that the path Karikala was intent on taking was dangerous, when standing before the king, suddenly, their opposition was offered in carefully couched language that, Senganan was certain, was designed to avoid drawing their king's wrath. While it was understandable, and if Senganan was honest with himself, a tactic he had employed himself before, the stakes this time had never been higher. Despite all that had transpired; the crushing defeat at the ambush, the loss of his oldest son, then the overwhelming display of Roman power that had caused the remnant of the Chola military in this part of their kingdom to dissolve, literally and in the span of time that could be counted in heartbeats, and culminating in the brutally efficient dispatching of Prashant by the giant Roman Pullus, Karikala made it clear that he was still intent on exacting some form of retribution. The fact that he had

narrowed his focus to just one man and not in a manner that would require risking the rest of his military was a small blessing, and it was also a sign that Karikala hadn't completely slipped into madness that he didn't even consider making an attempt on either Caesar or the Pandyan king, but it wasn't what Senganan had seen when Pullus and Prashant had met, it was the sound that, even dampened by dirt walls, and reduced by distance, was clearly audible, the roaring of thousands of men celebrating their champion's victory, that had convinced him that Karikala's insistence of assassinating the Roman Centurion would be disastrous. Without specific knowledge to this effect, Senganan correctly intuited that, by virtue of his massive size compared to his countrymen, and his deeds that culminated in his slaying of Prashant, Pullus was a symbol of great importance to the thousands of Romans in the ranks. Karikala had at least been dissuaded from his decision to summon what the Chola referred to as the Northern Army, led by Karikala's younger brother, Lord Kavirathan, from where it was semi-permanently located in the northernmost city nearest to their border with the Andhra kingdom, Chennai. The credit for this Senganan gave, grudgingly, to Lord Venkata, who had offered a simple but powerfully persuasive argument.

"Your Highness, I don't think that the elephants in our Northern Army will fear fire any less than those here in Uraiyur."

This had earned the nobleman a hard stare from Karikala, seated on his ornately carved throne that was a larger version of the one in Madoura, and for the balance of several heartbeats, none of the men present dared to draw a breath or otherwise draw attention to themselves before, with a sharp hissing noise, the king abruptly sat back.

"You are...correct, Lord Venkata," Karikala said through clenched teeth, but the most important part was when he added, "so I won't summon the Northern Army."

It was a victory for those Cholan nobles who sought a more prudent path, but it proved short-lived, and over the course of a Roman week, Karikala had constructed a plan of sorts, which he announced at their council the day before Senganan made what would be his final plea.

Caesar Ascending – The Ganges

"I am sending men, in pairs, who are skilled in stealth and killing with a blade into the camp of the Roman hyenas and their Pandyan minions," he had spoken calmly, in an almost offhanded manner, which he might have used when discussing the weather. "I intend to send in four such pairs, at different points along the camp boundaries, and at slightly different times on a night to be decided. Of the four, only one of them will be sent to the tent of the giant Roman Pullus, while the other three are to cause a disturbance in different parts of the camp. The last pair will also be the last to get into the camp, and will be taking the shortest path to the tent where Pullus sleeps."

He paused; whether it was for questions or to gauge their reaction Senganan couldn't tell, but it was Lord Venkata who, completely unaware he was doing so, confirmed Scribonius' guess by asking, "Your Highness, how do you know where this Roman's tent is located in such a large camp?"

The smile the king offered could only be described as smug, and Senganan felt certain that Karikala was boasting at least as much as he was explaining, "That is a good question, Lord Venkata, but that's why I haven't revealed my plans until now. I have had men watching the camp from the southeastern corner of the wall for the last several days, and while it's too far to make out a man's features, the camp is close enough to judge his size compared to the other Roman dogs. And," he actually chuckled, presumably at the thought that this would an indirect cause of Pullus' demise, "that Roman is very easy to spot."

While this was certainly true, Senganan was convinced that it was equally true that an attempt on Pullus' life, especially if it was successful, would evoke a response by Caesar, and most importantly, his battle-hardened army. Although he hadn't witnessed it during the ambush, even here far to the south, word had traveled to their ears about the Romans' extensive use of artillery, of which there was hardly any usage by the kingdoms of this region, and he correctly assumed that they had devised a method of launching those flaming pots that had been so devastating to Divakar and the rest of the army even greater distances, making it easy for him to imagine the fiery substance literally raining down on the streets of Uraiyur, the very idea making him shudder. This was what found him making his third attempt, after asking for a private audience with the king, but while there were none of the usual assortment of councilors and hangers-on that Karikala liked to keep around for his amusement, and for them to flatter him, they weren't completely alone. With Prashant's death, the actual command of the royal bodyguard had fallen to Yogesh, who stood just behind and to the side of the throne, arms crossed, his bearded face, with features that bespoke of his fondness for brawling, wearing an expression that was impossible to read. While Prashant had been judged to be more skilled with weapons, and was ruthless in combat, Senganan had learned he was quite intelligent, something that would never be said about Yogesh, but along with that was a streak of cruelty in the large Cholan's makeup, and Senganan knew that Karikala used Yogesh as his chief torturer.

One of the more memorable things Senganan recalled was when Karikala had commented at a state banquet, "While I can count on Prashant to do what's necessary to...extract information, I much prefer Yogesh, because he truly enjoys the work."

This memory wouldn't seem to leave his mind as he stood there, waiting for his king to reply, but when he did, Karikala didn't sound particularly annoyed, instead sighing, "Yes, Lord Senganan, you've made that clear. And," he held up a hand as he acknowledged, "you're not alone. Lords Venkata and Sanjaya have both made their case that what I'm doing is ill-advised."

"I agree with them, Your Highness," Senganan said quietly, but he also had more experience working with Karikala, and believed he knew the best way to make his case...and walk out on his own and not with Yogesh. "May I tell you why?"

"Of course, Lord Senganan," Karikala seemed genuinely surprised. "By all means."

For the next several moments, Senganan spoke, and he was certain that never before in his life had he been more persuasive. He had decided that he would deliberately steer clear of anything that resembled criticism of Karikala's decision itself, but stick only to what he viewed as the likely outcome of an all-out Roman assault on Uraiyur.

"Your Highness, I believe that while Caesar may be sincere in his statement that he has no intention of doing to Chola what they have done to Pandya, the northern kingdoms of Pattala and Bharuch, and Parthia," he began, "can the same be said for King Nedunj? After all," he pointed out reasonably, "he's a Pandyan, and just like us, they have been raised from birth to hate us. We've been struggling with the Pandyans since the time of our grandfathers and even before that. So, while Caesar may be speaking truly, I believe it's a certainty that, perhaps at this moment, Nedunj is dripping poison in his ear." An idea came to him, and he lied, "Surely you've seen the same thing that I have, Your Highness, between those two!" The smile he offered was meant to be lascivious, "They're clearly *very* close."

He was heartened to see Karikala's face light up, a rare smile coming to his lips as he shook his head emphatically, declaring, "Yes! I thought perhaps I was imagining things, but I saw it too! The looks they gave each other were those of lovers!" His expression turned thoughtful, although the smile was still there. "We know that the Greeks openly engaged in pederasty and all manner of foul acts between men. Alexander and one of his generals Hephaestion were lovers, after all. There are certainly similarities between the Romans and Greeks; I wonder if this is one of them."

Realizing that, if he allowed it, Karikala could be diverted onto this topic for many watches, Senganan said hastily, "I believe you're undoubtedly right, Your Highness. But what's important is, no matter why, I believe that Nedunj has influence with Caesar that could prove troublesome for us." He was relieved when Karikala shook his head in agreement, and Senganan went on, "We agree that it's highly probable that Nedunj is already trying to persuade Caesar to take offensive action against us, but even if your plan is successful, and you strike down the giant Pullus, it's also very likely that Caesar would be in a much more receptive frame of mind." Another shake of the king's head, and with this established, Senganan hurried on to the part of his argument that he hoped would be the most powerful and had been the source of his nightmares ever since it came to him. "Your Highness, we have both seen the destructive power of the substance they call naphtha. I have made some inquiries, and I've learned that the Romans don't just have the ability to throw pots as they did at the pass, or to use the artillery pieces they call scorpions that fire those missiles that they wrap with rags soaked in the substance to ignite jars from a distance."

Now, Karikala looked, if not concerned yet, wary. "Oh? And what else can they do with this...substance?"

"They have artillery that is superior in range to even what the Macedonian king possessed, and they have modified their pieces to hurl jars of naphtha great distances." Senganan's tone turned intense. "Your Highness, they can hurl these jars above our walls, and down into our city. It will rain fire down on your subjects, and while many of our larger buildings are made of stone, their roofs are made of wood, and there are enough wooden structures that will undoubtedly catch fire. It will be a conflagration the likes of which this kingdom has never seen, Your Highness. And," he held his hands palms up, "only Shiva knows how many lives will be lost, and how much destruction will be wrought." As powerful as he hoped this was, he wasn't through, "And, if I was Caesar, I would wait for the rest of my army to arrive before I did so. If he's being honest, that what we've seen is only half of his army, it won't matter if the Northern Army comes to our aid. Chola," he finished quietly, but firmly, "will be destroyed."

He was heartened to see how Karikala had gone visibly pale as he spoke, and when he was finished, the king suddenly slumped back on his throne, clutching the arms as he stared at Senganan. *I've done it!* The thought flashed through his mind, and he had to struggle to retain an expression of grave concern, which was easy enough to do, knowing that he couldn't be the one to speak next. No, now it was up to Karikala to do so, and the silence stretched out for many heartbeats.

Finally, the silence was broken, by the king, in a voice suddenly hoarse, as he admitted, "You have made a very persuasive argument, and I see now the likelihood that my plan might; no," he raised a hand and amended, "I'm certain that the Romans will react in the manner you describe." He fell silent, but when he resumed, the change in his voice was so subtle that Senganan at first missed it, making his reaction slightly delayed when Karikala continued, "But things will proceed as planned."

It took several more heartbeats for Senganan's mind to register the king's words, but the instant they did, before he could stop himself, he gasped, "But...why?"

"Because," Karikala replied simply, "I am King. I sit on this throne because the divinity has deemed it to be so, and I will not be gainsaid in this decision." With every word, Karikala's tone grew in intensity; he leaned forward, radiating his rage, and his power, as he pointed at Senganan. "Because I will have my *vengeance on the vermin who killed my son!*"

By the time he was through, Karikala was on his feet, bellowing at the top of his lungs, and Senganan knew that not only had he failed, but he had sealed his own fate. That thought wasn't nearly as distressing as it would have been not long before, not now that he saw that Karikala was determined on this course, reasoning that it wouldn't be such a bad thing to be dead to see it. Oh, he had regrets that he wouldn't see his wife and family again, but if this was fated to be, then perhaps it was for the best. Karikala was panting now, standing on the raised platform, glaring down at Senganan, who, in an act of quiet courage, refused to avert his glance from his king.

Whether this was what caused what happened next, he would never know, but Karikala's rigid posture suddenly relaxed, and his voice returned to a semblance of normal as he said, "But I thank you for your counsel, Lord Senganan, and I value it, I truly do. You," he at least sounded sincere, "are one of the few of my councilors on whom I can rely to speak the truth, and not what you think I want to hear." He turned then, to Yogesh, and ordered, "See Lord Senganan out, Yogesh."

The guard, of course, did as ordered, and in the back of Senganan's mind was how it had registered that, not once, when Senganan was speaking, and when Karikala was shouting, had Yogesh's expression altered, and he wondered if perhaps the brutish guard was more simple than it was rumored. He also half-expected that, once they exited the throne room and the door was closed, that he would be seized by Yogesh, but instead, the man abruptly turned about and reentered the throne room, leaving Senganan in a world of despair. Uraiyur, he thought grimly, is doomed, and so are the Chola.

At roughly the same time, another private meeting was taking place, in the *praetorium*, and the topic was identical to that between Karikala and Senganan, and while he would suspect as much but never know, Senganan was more right than he knew about the collusion between a young king and the most powerful Roman, and man, in their world. However, what he had miscalculated was the roles between the two, because it was Nedunj who had requested the meeting to discuss his reservations.

"Caesar, do you really think that it is wise to use your Primus Pilus as bait for Karikala? And," he asked practically, "are you certain that Karikala is so addled by his grief he would take such a large risk?"

"I'm not certain of anything, Your Highness," Caesar replied genially, his arms crossed as he sat on the edge of his desk, inwardly amused that his one certainty had been this visit by a young king having second thoughts. Adopting the tone that Pullus loathed, something Caesar knew very well was shared by the other Primi Pili, his Tribunes, and probably at least one Legate, he asked reasonably, "Can you think of another way to achieve the ends that you desire, Your Highness?"

Nedunj didn't miss the manner in which Caesar characterized matters as being an end only Nedunj wanted, and he wasn't fooled, knowing the Roman well enough by this point to understand that Caesar wanted the same end result for reasons that had nothing to do with making Nedunj happy, nor was he about to betray that knowledge.

And, no matter the reason behind it, it was a fair question, prompting Nedunj to admit, "No, I haven't come up with anything." He hesitated, getting to the nub of what truly bothered him, and without planning on it, he blurted out, "But I know what Primus Pilus Pullus means to you, to his Legion, and to the rest of the army, especially after today. Why would you put him at such risk?"

For the first time in their association, Caesar looked discomfited, and he didn't respond for a long moment; when he did, Nedunj heard a hint of an inner turmoil that he would have never guessed Caesar was capable of feeling.

"It is," the Roman admitted, "a risk, and not an insignificant one. And," Nedunj would never know how sincere Caesar was in this moment, "I do know that Pullus has become almost as much of a symbol of the entire army and our success as I am." There was, after all, only so much Gaius Julius Caesar would bend when acknowledging another man's status when compared to his own. "And," he continued, "you're also correct that I am...fond of Titus Pullus, and not just because he's of such value in his post as Primus Pilus." Suddenly remembering something, Caesar smiled then. "I even had plans on elevating him to the Senate on our return from Parthia, if only because of how much it would vex Cicero and the other *Boni*," the smile vanished as quickly as it had come, his tone contemptuous now, "at least, those who still survive."

As tangential a reference as it was, Nedunj had been assiduous in learning as much about Caesar, and by extension, the world of Roman politics, so it wasn't the first time he had heard Cicero's name mentioned, although none of Caesar's fellow Romans who Nedunj had subtly interrogated, or so he believed, had ever referred to this self-named group who attempted to take matters into their own hands on a day the Romans called the Ides, in the month they called March.

Oblivious to Nedunj's internal musings, Caesar's demeanor softened again, "So yes, I'm aware that this is a risk that I would otherwise not take. But," now he did look at Nedunj, "like you, I haven't been able to think of another way to achieve the ends that suit us both." Just as quickly as the contempt for the *Boni* had appeared, it vanished as Caesar asked seriously, "Do you know why I have been so successful in war, Your Highness? Why I am considered to be at least the equal of Alexander?"

Nedunj's immediate thought was that, from anyone else, this would have been a boastful comment and one that displayed what he had learned from his days as a young pupil the Greeks called hubris, but as quickly as it came, he dismissed it, for one simple reason: Caesar *was* now considered to be at least the equal of the Macedonian. He had backed up his words with deeds that, Nedunj was sure, would be talked about for at least as many centuries as Alexander's exploits had been. More than anything, however, Nedunj did want to know the answers to those questions, and he had to hide his eagerness, remembering to nod his head instead of shake it.

"A general," Caesar said quietly, "can't afford to view any of his subordinates, no matter how valuable they may be, as indispensable. I have sent so many men off to their deaths that I'm afraid that if I knew the number, it might render me ineffective, but it was always to a larger end." He hesitated, as if trying to frame his thoughts, then continued, "My officers, all of them from Legates Pollio and Hirtius, to Titus Pullus, Batius, Balbinus, and the other Primi Pili are all pieces on the board of that game we Romans call tables. Some pieces have more value than others, but none of them are indispensable, and depending on the prize on offer, are to be sacrificed if necessary. That," Caesar leaned forward, his tone intense as he looked Nedunj in the eye, "is what it means to be Caesar...and to be a King." He paused, gauging the Pandyan's reaction; seeing the thoughtful expression, Caesar suddenly smiled as he added, "Besides, our gods love Titus Pullus almost as much as they love me. I think that he'll be fine, whenever Karikala decides to move. You saw what Pullus did to their champion."

"I did," Nedunj agreed soberly; the memory was still very fresh. "And I do see what you are saying, Caesar. It is good advice that I will try and heed."

Caesar stood up from the desk in a silent signal that the meeting was over, and as he walked Nedunj to the partition that served as the door, he said, "Waiting is always the hardest part, Your Highness. But, I'm as certain as I can be that Karikala will act, not as a king, but as a father."

In a sign that the Chola weren't completely impotent, the attempt on Pullus occurred the day before Pollio, and the Legions with him sailed up the river to Uraiyur, which had been tracked by Chola scouts sent to the coast by Karikala almost immediately after they arrived in the city. It also happened to coincide with a moon that was only two days from being full, far from ideal conditions for anyone trying to penetrate a guarded position, but Karikala's choice in men had been cunning.

Caesar Ascending – The Ganges

When he had first broached his plan with the nobles, one of them had asked, more from curiosity than any concern, "Your Highness, this is obviously a highly dangerous endeavor. How did you find men who would be willing to even attempt this, and what did you offer them?"

Being asked clearly pleased the king, who replied jovially, "Why, I offered them their lives, of course."

Like with any large city, there were men who found that crime was a more attractive way to make a living than honest work, and Uraiyur and the Chola kingdom was no exception. In an eerily similar manner to Rome, what constituted a prison for those offenses that didn't automatically earn a death sentence was essentially a large hole in the ground. The difference was that, unlike Rome, where the Tullianum was a large cavity in the native rock, Uraiyur's location on a large, flat plain meant that the pit was manmade. This had been done long ago, but as the city and the kingdom grew, the men who had been consigned to this place had, through a variety of means, managed to not only enlarge it, but had burrowed what served as small cells in the walls of the hole. It was a brutal place, where men were given the bare minimum needed to survive by the handful of men who eked out a living serving as guards. Escape was a practical impossibility after an early attempt, where desperate men had carved out hand and footholds in the dirt wall to climb up to freedom, but now, the upper half of the circular wall was dressed in smooth and finished stone, making it impossible for a man to find a purchase for the final ten feet to freedom. There was a wooden frame over the opening, by which the prisoners were lowered after receiving their sentence that also enabled the guards, using a pulley and rope, to lower the daily water ration in buckets, in exchange for the buckets of waste produced by the prisoners, while the rations were simply dropped down into the hole. It was from this place that the men who were to kill Titus Pullus came, and it had slightly surprised Karikala when Yogesh had reported to his king that there had been no shortage of volunteers, despite the knowledge that their chances of survival were next to nonexistent.

Senganan would have been shocked to know that it was the taciturn Yogesh who had supplied the reason to Karikala, saying simply, "For these men, this is a tempting proposition. If they succeed and survive, they're freed, and if they die in the attempt, they're also free."

The king had also offered what, even to a member of the higher castes, was a fantastic amount of gold for every man, contingent on their success in their part of murdering the Roman and, of course, provided that they survived. They had been given tunics and trousers dyed black to replace the filthy rags they had been wearing since the day they were thrown into the pit, which ranged in time from several months to four years for the longest-term man who had survived. To the king, this man's survival was a testament to his cunning, and most importantly, his ruthlessness in an environment where only the strongest survived to see another day. Karikala was completely aware of the conditions in The Pit, and how the men who served as guards, all but one of them a member of the same caste from which Prashant had come, that man serving as their commander, made extra money from bribes from the handful of prisoners who had family willing to keep them alive. His instructions to Yogesh, who he put in charge of selecting the eight men out of the slightly more than one hundred prisoners, was to find men who had families, which had a dual purpose, the first being that these men were going to be in slightly better physical shape, the second that their families could be used as a tool to ensure the men didn't just skulk off into the night. Ultimately, Karikala was relying on greed, deliberately offering an amount that would enable each of these men to never work a day for the rest of their lives, and while Yogesh didn't explicitly promise it, the bodyguard had followed his king's instructions to strongly infer that the men would be considered worthy of elevation out of their caste, something practically unheard of in their world. The consequence of this was that Yogesh and a dozen guards escorted the eight men, now dressed in black, with black turbans, each of them armed with two daggers, one short one, and one that could have almost been considered a short sword thrust into their waistbands. In a last-moment change, they also were freshly washed when it was determined that, even in the darkness, it was easy to locate the men because of their collective and pervasive stench, so they had first been taken to one of the communal troughs fed by the wells located throughout the city.

Now, they gathered at the southern gate which, although it didn't provide the shortest path to the camp, was a compromise between security and distance. As the plan called for, the pairs were sent out in a staggered fashion, each pair released after a slow count to a thousand, culminating in the final pair, which was led by the longest-surviving prisoner, who called himself Harisha, and in whom Yogesh recognized a kindred spirit, that of a man who was willing to do anything to survive and not be troubled by how he did it. It also helped that Harisha had been thrown into The Pit for murder, but because it was another man of their lowest caste, he wasn't considered worthy of the time it would take to separate his head from his shoulders. Whereas the first three pairs would attempt to infiltrate the camp at three different points of the Roman half of the camp, they were all nowhere near the location of the giant Roman's tent. It would fall to Harisha and his companion, Manoja, to creep down into the ditch, and climb the dirt wall at the spot nearest to the tent belonging to the Primus Pilus of the 10th. Manoja wasn't his real name but a mocking appellation since it meant someone who was wise, and Manoja was a simpleton, but he was a simpleton who was brutally strong, and more importantly, who faithfully served Harisha in the small but savage society down in The Pit. They were held until last, the idea being that, even if one or all of the other pairs of men were discovered before they could enter the camp, there would be an uproar that would draw the attention of the Romans manning the ramparts in the area Harisha and Manoja would be infiltrating away from their immediate area. Personally, Yogesh didn't think any of the pairs had a chance, but not only was he not asked by his king, it wouldn't have mattered, because for Yogesh, it was sufficient that King Karikala willed this to be so.

He did think to remind the pair, "Remember, the only way you'll be rewarded is to return with proof, and that proof the King requires is the Roman's head. But, if you succeed, you'll be showered with gold and you'll be able to live the rest of your days in comfort and leisure, and your children will be wealthy."

Harisha answered by patting the empty cloth sack hanging

from his waist, promising the bodyguard, "I will return with the Roman's head in this sack."

I doubt it, Yogesh thought, but aloud, he mouthed the words of a ritual blessing before sending them out into the night. Now, he thought as he watched them skirting the southern wall in the direction of the camp, we wait.

As the days had passed, and no attempt had been made on Pullus, the men most concerned about this began to relax, and Diocles thought that, perhaps, he had been overly cautious in worrying about his master. It was true that, while it wasn't as tense in the camp as the first two weeks of their time in the shadow of Uraiyur's walls, the men of the guard Legion were still alert as they either stood at their posts or walked them down in the camp itself. Later, some of Caesar's Centurions would recognize that the Chola had used the Romans' rigid adherence to matters like guard duty against them, never knowing that this was what Caesar had been counting on. Yes, the watchword was changed every day, but what didn't change was the method and pattern of how the guard duty was performed, following the same ritual that had been in place for more than two centuries by this point. What became obvious in the aftermath of this night was that the Chola had been paying attention to every aspect of camp life as carried out by the Legions of Rome, where everything was done according to a system that, through observation, the Chola had learned was divided into four distinct and separate periods for day, and four for night. This meant that the men sent to carry out the killing of Pullus had been informed about how much time they had before the current guard shift was relieved, and what would happen when it occurred, thereby timing their attempt for the period of time roughly in the middle of the watch that began at midnight. It was a cunning and intelligent plan, but it had one flaw, although in fairness, it was an impossible thing to predict, that the night chosen to try and kill Titus Pullus was the night the 10th Legion had the guard.

Because of the size of the camp, it required two full Cohorts per watch instead of the normal one, and although the Pandyan half of the army had been allowed to position their tents and shelters in any manner they saw fit, the men patrolling the rampart for the entire perimeter of the camp were always Legionaries. This was something that was nonnegotiable when Caesar and the young Pandyan king discussed it, but the truth was that Nedunj didn't put up much, if any, fight, displaying the same kind of attitude as the other kingdoms and nations that were non-Roman or Grecian, viewing it as a tedious and not altogether important duty. That night, it was the lot of the Third and Ninth Cohort to share the first night watch, when they would be relieved by the Second and Eighth, with the First and Tenth performing the last watch before the *bucina* call that sounded the official start of the daylight hour. Of the three, the least favorite for men of all ranks was the second watch, because it meant a period of interrupted rest, and the Chola had chosen this watch to make their attempt, unaware that they were attempting to infiltrate when Pullus' best friend, and his former tutor in Cyclops, were in command.

Because of the unusual configuration and size of the camp, instead of having both Pili Priores at the *Porta Praetoria*, Pullus had followed the example set by other Legions who had previously stood guard duty, and directed that they split up, with Scribonius at the main gate, while Cyclops stood at the *Porta Decumana* as their Optios performed the tedious duty of making an endless tour of each standing post, with the men paired up, all along the dirt wall. It was left to the *Tesserarius* to monitor the walking posts, which, in the beginning of the alliance between Pandya and Rome, had led to some false alarms when a bleary-eyed Pandyan would stumble out of their tent to see dark figures seemingly wandering through their encampment, since this was unknown to them. By this time, however, the two allies had become accustomed to each other, with the Pandyans accepting the presence of Roman rankers in their midst while they slept, and the Romans learning how to navigate what were serpentine paths through the small city of tents of varying size and design. There was one part of the Pandyan half of the camp where the Romans were expressly forbidden to enter, although this was perfectly acceptable to the men, and that was the quarter of the camp where the war elephants were kept, each one secured with a heavy iron ring around one massive leg, attached to a length of chain that was attached to an iron stake several feet in length. Their *howdahs*, after they were taken off, served as the sleeping area of each animal's *mahout*, the wooden box being large and sturdy enough to protect the humans who served with these animals from being crushed underfoot as the animals inevitably moved about during the night. It had definitely taken some time for both elephants and Romans to get accustomed to each other, the elephants learning to accept their presence during the night, and the Legionaries who had the misfortune to be assigned to the walking posts in the Pandyan part of the camp learning that the chuffing noises, the deep rumbles, and the clinking of chains was as normal to their allies as the snores, mumbles, and flatulence of their own kind was to them.

The first attempt to penetrate, while nowhere near the animals, was nearer to the Pandyan side of the camp, as the pair of Cholans actually made it to the ditch unobserved, aided by the partial cloud cover that obscured the moonlight, only moving when the silvery light was dimmed. A consequence of this caution was that it took them longer to get to the ditch; this was perhaps the reason that the first of the Cholans moved across the bottom of the ditch without feeling his way first, so he had gone only two paces across the fifteen foot width that had been the standard for the Legions who marched for Caesar since his days as a Praetor, when his foot plunged through the mat of woven material covered with just enough dirt to disguise it, the sharpened iron spike of one of "Caesar's lilies" punching through the leather sole of his boots. Even if he had expected it, the likelihood he could have endured the agony of a sharpened piece of iron penetrating completely through his foot, punching through bone to plunge up into the muscle tissue of his calf was highly unlikely. The relatively quiet night air was pierced by his shrill scream, immediately followed by cries of alarm from up above on the dirt rampart, where the nearest pair of Legionaries were standing watch.

It was Mardonius who spotted the dark form down in the ditch, off to his and Percennius' left, shouting, "Down there! On the far side!"

Percennius responded by turning and bellowing at the top

of his lungs, "Alert! Alert! Percennius' post!"

This triggered a series of events, some of them official, while the others were by the men of the 21st Legion whose tents were nearest to that spot, roused from sleep by the alarm, making for a small riot of noise as men rolled from their cots, fumbling for their *gladii* before rushing out to get a better idea of what was happening. On the rampart, Mardonius had snatched up one of his javelins, then glanced up at the clouds obscuring the moon, judging how much time before they drifted past, the first step in deciding whether or not they needed to light the bundle of sticks, held together by a strip of cloth soaked in oil, that would be thrown down into the ditch. It wasn't long, perhaps a span of two heartbeats before the last of the obscuring clouds drifted past, and when he looked down into the ditch, it took him another heartbeat to understand why the figure he had spotted wasn't moving.

Thinking quickly, Mardonius called to Percennius, "That one is stuck on a lily!"

Without waiting, he ran down the rampart, arriving just before the other pair of sentries reached the same spot from the opposite direction, so it was Mardonius who spotted a second figure, clinging to the sloped surface of their dirt wall as he pressed himself flat in a vain attempt to avoid being detected like his comrade. It was done without thought, as Mardonius' arm moved back, hovered there for a span of an eyeblink before it swept forward, sending the javelin unerringly to pierce the man's left side with enough force that it was only stopped because of the weighted ball at the base of the iron part of the shaft. Rather than a scream, he heard a wet, burbling moan, the sound betraying that the man's lungs had been punctured, and while the man moved, it was because he had released the handfuls of dirt as his body relaxed, which then went tumbling awkwardly down into the ditch, landing with a meaty thud. The pinned man's screams were still continuing, but they were cut short when Percennius killed him, although it took both of his javelins to do it, something that Mardonius and the rest of his section wouldn't let him forget. By the time their Optio had come sprinting up the dirt ramp, both Cholans were dead, and one of the other pair of sentries had ignited the bundle and thrown it down into the ditch, where it was now providing more light. It wouldn't last long, but it gave them enough visibility to perform a search of their immediate area, which they were finishing by the time the Optio arrived.

"How many others?" the Optio snapped, only then leaning over to catch his breath, listening as Percennius replied, "Only two, Optio, at least where we can see."

Straightening up, he followed Percennius to the edge of the rampart next to the staked parapet, pointing down, first at the man Mardonius had slain, who was lying in a shapeless huddle in the bottom of the ditch closest to them, then to the second man who, in a grisly imitation of the Optio just a moment before, was held upright by the lily but was bent at the waist, while the butt of the second javelin that had pierced his chest propped his upper body up, his arms and head dangling limply in the total relaxation of every muscle that came with death.

"Who killed that one?" The Optio pointed to the man Mardonius had slain, and when Mardonius claimed him, the Optio glanced over at Percennius with a raised eyebrow. "You missed the first time, eh, Percennius?"

He was pointing to the javelin shaft protruding from the far wall of the ditch, less than a hand's width away from the dead man as he asked, but it was Mardonius, standing just behind the Optio who spoke first, a broad grin on his swarthy face, "It only took me one to kill that *cunnus*, Aulus."

"Mine was farther away!" Percennius protested, which only earned him a derisive snort from the Optio, who countered, "And he was stuck in place like a training pole." Shaking his head in an exaggerated manner, he added, "When I tell the Pilus Prior, he's not going to be happy. You know how he feels about wasting javelins. I think," he said solemnly, although he wasn't serious, "someone has some *cac* detail in their future."

Percennius opened his mouth to protest, but the Optio couldn't maintain his sober demeanor any longer, making the ranker realize that he had been the butt of the kind of joke officers loved to play on their men, prompting him to grumble, "That wasn't funny, Optio."

"It was to me," the Optio replied cheerfully. His expression turned serious again. "Now, I need to go let the Pilus Prior know that..."

He got no farther, because, while it was fainter, they clearly heard, "Alert! Alert! Sido's post!"

Predictably, this prompted another, louder uproar from men roused from sleep, these from the 25th, while the Optio asked, "Sido? Isn't he in the Third Century?"

"I believe so," Mardonius replied, while Percennius disagreed, "He's in the Fifth."

"That's right," the Optio agreed with Percennius, while Mardonius' close comrade shot the Parthian ranker a look of triumph, happy that he at least had something with which to counter Mardonius' mocking his prowess with a javelin. "I need to go report to the Pilus Prior. Stay alert." The Optio had descended the ramp when he turned to call out, "And, Percennius? Let Mardonius throw the javelins next time."

"Oh, be quiet," Percennius muttered to his smiling comrade, who hadn't said a word, knowing there was no need.

The second pair, which Percennius had correctly identified their attempted infiltration being in the Fifth of the Eighth's part of the rampart, had actually navigated the ditch without incident, and it was after they clambered out and, like their one predecessor who had made it that far, dug their hands and toes into the packed dirt of the wall. What betrayed them was one of them losing his purchase, sending him sliding down the steeply pitched wall, bringing a cascade of dirt with him, the noise of which alerted the pair of sentries who heard it and had walked over to investigate. The Cholan who had managed to retain his grip was just swinging a leg up over the rampart, and his trousers caught on the point of one of the stakes, the ripping sound as he pulled himself free enabling the Legionaries to pinpoint the spot. He was cut down, not by a javelin but with a quick thrust, after the ranker, indeed Tiberius Sido as the Optio had guessed, dodged the wild swing of the long dagger the Cholan had pulled. His companion now down in the bottom of the ditch managed to keep his head and not just flee back across the ditch, but instead hugged the near wall as he ran along it as quickly as he dared, hoping to reach a spot outside of the area where men were now shouting the alarm. It was a cunning thing to do, though it only extended his life for a matter of moments when, deciding he had reached a spot that gave him the best opportunity to try again, he resumed his attempt to infiltrate the camp. He had briefly considered abandoning his effort and using the darkness to flee away from Uraiyur, but he thought of the wife and three young children he would be leaving to Yogesh's mercy, of which the bodyguard had none, convinced him to try again. Completely ignorant of the method the Romans used to assign posts, the spot he had chosen for his second attempt was where the Third of the Eighth was posted, and his fate was sealed just as he was within arm's reach when he heard a man shout in a tongue he didn't understand, but recognized as being similar to what he had heard when his companion had been discovered. Even as the realization came to him, he experienced a savage flash of pain as the javelin plunged into his back, then....nothing.

From his spot at the *Porta Decumana*, Cyclops had just received the second report from the Optio of the Fifth Century when, for the third time, there was a shout of alarm coming from the direction of his Third Century, which prompted his decision that it was time to use his *Cornicen* to sound the alarm that roused the entire camp. It was a good choice, and one for which he wouldn't be faulted, either by his Primus Pilus or by Caesar, but it still inadvertently aided the Cholan cause. The notes were still echoing when they were quickly drowned out by the shouts of the Centurions, Optios, and men of the 21st and 25th Legions, those nearest to where the Eighth Cohort was standing post on the rampart. Because of the unusual configuration, while they were at the edge of the camp nearest to the Pandyans, who were similarly rousing themselves, they were also nearer to the *praetorium*, which also meant that, very quickly, Caesar emerged from the tent, wearing only a tunic but carrying his *baltea* with its eagle-headed *gladius*. He was quickly joined by his Legates and several Tribunes, the former having their own tents immediately next to the *praetorium*, while Tribunes shared a tent with another Tribune. This was where Cyclops found them after moving at a pace faster than a trot but not quite an all-out run, to offer his report.

Caesar Ascending – The Ganges

Only after rendering his salute did the one-eyed Centurion inform his general, "We've now had three attempts to get into the camp, but it's not in force, Caesar."

"Not in force?" Hirtius interrupted. "What does that mean?"

Cyclops explained how the incursions had been attempted by men in pairs, currently unaware that the third attempt was by the surviving Cholan of the second pair. Even as he was speaking, another alarm went up, but this one came from the opposite side of the camp, at roughly the point where the last Century of the Eighth and the last Century of the Second were located.

Turning to one of the Tribunes, Caesar ordered, "Rufus, I want you to go in that direction and try to determine what's happening. Send a runner as soon as you've found out the details." Turning to another, and one of the only Parthians serving as Tribune, he pointed back in the opposite direction. "You go do the same, Bodroges."

Waiting only long enough to see the two men hurrying away, Caesar returned to Cyclops, saying formally, "You did the right thing, Pilus Prior Ausonius. Now, return to your post, and let's see what these Cholans are up to, and the same goes for you. If there's any new development, send a runner."

With that, Caesar returned to the *praetorium* to put on his armor, which was where both Torquatus and Papernus found him to report that their men were fully roused.

"Are we alerting the entire army, sir?" Torquatus asked, but after a moment, Caesar shook his head, not betraying his satisfaction that the moment that he had anticipated had finally arrived.

"Not yet," he decided. "Let's see what's what before I make that decision."

Among those unaware of Caesar and Nedunj's involvement, it was Scribonius who correctly deduced not only what this was about, but why his part of the camp hadn't sounded an alarm yet.

"I'm going to let Primus Pilus Pullus know what's happening, and what I think's going on," he informed his *Signifer* and *Cornicen*, the pair of men who stayed with the

Pilus Prior in command of the guard.

He only made it two streets in the direction of Pullus' tent when the third pair of Cholans, having managed to actually make it onto the rampart, went dashing into the camp, narrowly missed by the javelins thrown at them by the almost-frantic pair of Legionaries of the Sixth of the Second nearest to them. The other pair of sentries went off in pursuit of the Cholans, as one of the original pair bellowed the alarm. This stopped Scribonius in his tracks, and he spent the span of a couple heartbeats agonizing over what to do. I might be wrong, he told himself, which means that I'm going to waste time warning Titus, while I know that there's something going on with the Sixth. This was what prompted him to deviate from his original path as he rushed towards the disturbance, which meant that he was fated to run almost headlong into one of the Cholans, long dagger in his hand, and in the dim light, Scribonius didn't see that it was already bloody; only after it was over would they learn that a man of the 15th Legion had just stepped out of his tent because of the alarm, and while he was armed with his *gladius*, the Cholan who was rushing past reacted more quickly, slicing into the ranker's throat. Now, the Cholan tried to skid to a stop at the sight of the dark figure ahead of him, and the moonlight reflecting off Scribonius' helmet warned the man that he was an officer like the giant, wearing a crest that ran side to side. Perhaps if he had stood his ground, he might have had a better chance, but while he had slowed, Scribonius hadn't, still rushing forward with his *gladius* in the first position, his *vitus* in the other hand. Roman caught Cholan just as the intruder was turning his body to run away, the point of Scribonius' blade punching into his lower back, slicing through his kidney, and while it wasn't delivered with much power, it was enough that the Cholan only made it another step before collapsing. He was mortally wounded, but he wasn't dead, which Scribonius determined when he used one boot to turn him over onto his back, the moonlight reflecting the whites of the man's eyes, which were wide with the recognition he was dying.

"I wish I knew Tamil," Scribonius muttered, and while he knew that Karikala and the Lord Senganan spoke Greek well enough, making him briefly wonder if perhaps this man did, it didn't matter because the man died before Scribonius could attempt to get information from him.

And at that moment, there was more shouting in the direction of the rampart, and without bothering to wipe his blade on the dead man's clothes, Scribonius hurried that way.

It was the sound of the horn the Romans called the *cornu* that gave Harisha and Manoja their opportunity, when two pairs of sentries from the Second of the Second moved from their spots to meet halfway between them to confer about what might be happening. The result was that there was enough of a gap on the rampart between the two pairs and the sentries on the opposite side who, fortunately for the Cholan pair, were also looking in the other direction, towards where the horn call had sounded. It was a natural reaction, and one that, despite how many times the Equestrian Centurions and Optios warned men about it, even they had been susceptible to at such moments. Nonetheless, it served to the Cholan pair's advantage, as Harisha crawled on his belly across the dozen feet of rampart, which Manoja copied as Harisha slid down headfirst to the ground at the base of the ramp inside the camp. Rather than waiting to listen for a shout of warning, Harisha moved quickly, in a low crouch, reaching the rear of the rankers' tent nearest to the rampart, Manoja following. Inside, he could hear voices, but Harisha could tell by the tone that while the men inside had been alerted by the distant horn call, guessing that they were speculating about the cause, it made them alert yet not alarmed enough to rouse themselves at this moment. He moved in between a pair of tents, whereupon he turned, and without speaking, alerted Manoja before, with an exaggerated motion that he would have used with the other man even if it was broad daylight because of his simple nature, he pointed to the guy ropes and stakes coming from each one, then made a serpentine motion with his hand while indicating himself. To his relief, Manoja nodded, and once he began his own progress, when he glanced over his shoulder, he saw the other man copying him exactly as he had hoped. It was slow, but Harisha knew he had the cover of the tents on either side to shield him, and he reached the opposite end where the flaps were located, although a quick glance at both told him they were fastened shut. He could still hear quiet talking, but it was dying down as nothing else occurred that would indicate to the occupants they were about to be roused, and now, Harisha could see the top of the larger tent, across the street and at the end of what was, in essence, a street block in what for all intents and purposes was a good-sized town.

Instead of moving down the street in that direction, Harisha beckoned to his companion, and once again moving quickly while remaining crouched, crossed the open strip of ground that served as the street which, by this time several weeks into their stay, had become well-worn and, with the daily rains, stayed muddy. Repeating his maneuver weaving in between the ropes, Harisha and Manoja emerged out onto the next street before the Cholans made their turn to move away from the wall and more deeply into the camp, Harisha's eyes fixed on the large tent. Because they were essentially moving more closely to the Pandyan side of the camp, they began hearing the distant shouting caused by the discovery of their fellow prisoners, but it still hadn't seemed to rouse the men in this part of the camp. Reaching the rear of the tent where the giant Roman was sleeping, they squatted down, and as they had arranged before, it was Manoja who drew his short dagger, then carefully thrust it through the fabric of the tent, pausing once his blade had punctured through so they could listen. Just faintly audible was the sound of deep, regular breathing, the sign that their prey was asleep, and Harisha nodded. With just as much care, Manoja moved the dagger up, slowly, creating a slit in the canvas. Once he reached a spot where a crouching man could enter, he turned the blade to make a horizontal cut first in one direction, then the other, which would enable Harisha to enter without tearing the fabric and making noise. Even knowing time was against them, Harisha paused, listening for any sign that their presence was suspected, but all he heard was the same, regular breathing. Miming to Manoja to wait there, Harisha took a breath, offered up prayers to the divinities that, at last, he would once again be free, then placed his foot through the hole, paused, then turned sideways and entered the tent.

Caesar Ascending – The Ganges

Pullus was normally a light sleeper, but for some reason, he hadn't come awake at the sound of the *cornu* call, and while Diocles, who slept in the outer office had, he listened intently for a few moments before he laid his head back down. It was the third occupant, having been given a spot, also in the partitioned outer office but immediately next to the divider between office and Pullus' private quarters, who was lying on his pallet and was now wide awake. Still, he couldn't say afterward what prompted what he did next, because he didn't remember actually hearing something strange from the part of the tent comprising Pullus' private quarters, nor why he thought to reach for the *pugio* that Pullus had given to Diocles lying on his desk, which Pullus had only done recently and in response to his Greek clerk's worry about murderers lurking in the shadows, sent by a vengeful king. When he moved to the flap that served as the door, he didn't thrust it aside, which would have made noise, but this was because, as he had learned the hard way, Master Titus was a light sleeper, and he didn't react well when surprised from sleep.

"From now on," Diocles had admonished him after almost being throttled by the huge Roman, "don't touch Master Titus to wake him up. Just call his name. And," he had finished with a straight face but with an amused gleam in his eye, "make sure you're still out of his reach when you do it."

This was in his mind as he quietly moved the hanging flap just enough to look into Master Titus' private quarters. Everything from this point forward happened so quickly, and in almost complete darkness, that he would never be able to really untangle everything that happened, but what he would always recall was the sight of a dark shape that suddenly seemed to materialize out of thin air at the rear of the tent. It was also the last quiet moment, but Barhinder was barely aware that it was his voice shouting as, without any thought, he burst through the flap and hurled himself at the shape with the *pugio* in his hand. The shock of their collision, which caused a sudden oath that he vaguely recognized was in Tamil, sent the shape staggering backward, stopped only by the wall of the tent, the canvas bulging outward, but the intruder reacted quickly, and it was Barhinder's turn to cry out in pain when he felt as if someone had plunged a burning stick through the bicep of his left arm. Although Barhinder's time in battle had been brief, and he hadn't been allowed to participate in any of the drills that the men of the Legions performed, he had been trained, and it was this that prompted him as, instead of recoiling away, he forced himself to stand his ground as he thrust his right hand forward with the *pugio*, aiming blindly. The sudden resistance to the point was accompanied by a low-pitched grunt, and he was blasted by the odor of rotting teeth, but the still-unseen attacker, like Barhinder, didn't try to move away from him, instead yanking the dagger from the youth's arm, and this time, Barhinder screamed. In almost the same instant, a new force slammed into him and sent him flying off his feet to land on the partitioned wooden floor, where the carpets that covered it only slightly softened the impact and was still hard enough to drive the wind from his lungs. The sound that came next wasn't a grunt, or even a scream, but a wet, strangling sound and he felt as much as saw the body drop to the floor next to him. Less than a heartbeat later, he heard another shout, this one just outside the tent, although he was only vaguely aware of anything else until he felt a hand grasp his left shoulder, the pain caused by it wrenching a moan from his lips.

"Barhinder! Barhinder!" He recognized the voice of Diocles. "Where are you hurt?"

Before he could reply, the sounds of a struggle outside caused both of them to turn their attention to what Barhinder could now dimly make out was a slit in the rear of the tent. There was an audible sound that might have been from a blade being plunged into a body, but Barhinder didn't think so, nor was there any shout or scream of pain, although there was a dull thudding sound of something solid hitting the ground. Then, he passed out.

The immediate aftermath of the attempt on Pullus' life was heavily in the Romans' favor. Of the eight men who comprised the teams of potential murderers, seven of them were dead, while there was one dead ranker from the 15th, and a badly wounded youth from Bharuch who was being called a hero for saving the life of Titus Pullus. That this judgment came from

Caesar Ascending – The Ganges

Pullus himself not surprisingly carried enormous weight, and actually prompted a personal visit from Caesar when Barhinder was in the hospital part of the *Quaestorium*. The visit came after a busy morning, about which Barhinder was completely unaware thanks to the poppy syrup that Pullus had insisted be administered, which wasn't usually done for a wound of this nature. Pullus was unharmed, although he grumbled about the fact that his sleeping tunic was now ruined with the blood from the man whose body was now stretched out in the forum of the camp along with the other six who died. This had been done on Caesar's order, and was accomplished before sunup so that, once it became light, the Cholans who would undoubtedly be watching from the southeast wall could be given the news that, even if the attempt had succeeded, all but one of the men they had sent were now dead.

"Let them wonder about the eighth man," Caesar had decided. "I doubt he knows much if anything, but one never knows."

Manoja, who, after a brief struggle, Pullus had knocked unconscious rather than kill, was now secured and inside the *praetorium*. As they would quickly determine, and mercifully for Manoja, even if Manoja had been approached by King Karikala himself, it was unlikely he would have remembered, and in fact, was completely lost without the now-dead Harisha. Not that it mattered; the presence of eight Cholans in the Roman camp was more than enough to establish guilt, but, although Caesar was certain that the king would deny any knowledge, it also didn't matter, because he and Nedunj now had the pretext they needed for what was to come. Very quickly, an eventful beginning to the day extended into the rest of it when word of a ship approaching from downstream that was quickly identified as Roman was relayed to Caesar by the scouts who had been sent downriver for that very purpose.

"I expect Pollio to be aboard, and we'll learn what occurred at Taprobane," Caesar announced to the hastily called meeting of the Primi Pili. Knowing that, while interested, they were more eager to know about the events of the night, Caesar moved on, "As you all know, there was an attempt on the life of Primus Pilus Pullus," he indicated Pullus, who looked a bit uncomfortable. "And as you all saw by the bodies outside, which," he assured them, "will be removed shortly before they start to stink, most of them were caught before they could penetrate the camp proper." The cause for Pullus' discomfort was made clear when Caesar continued, "However, one pair did manage to make it all the way to the Primus Pilus' tent." Turning to Pullus, he asked, "Have you decided how those men will be punished, Pullus?"

Pullus shifted on his stool, not eager to inform his general of his decision, knowing how Caesar would react.

Taking a breath, he answered, "After hearing from the men, and from their officers, I've decided that none of them will be striped, but they'll be on only rice and water for the next month."

As he anticipated, Caesar's lips compressed in a sign that his subordinates had learned didn't bode well, which was confirmed when he said sharply, "That's very lenient of you, Pullus...perhaps too lenient."

Bracing himself, Pullus replied, quietly but firmly, "I disagree, Caesar. Yes, they had a lapse of discipline, but it was because they were trying to determine what was happening, and it's something that happens all the time..."

"Which the regulations forbid, and they call for punishment when it happens," Caesar interrupted. Relenting slightly, "If this was winter and we weren't on campaign, I would endorse that as a punishment, but we're on active campaign."

Caesar didn't realize it, but he had said exactly what Pullus hoped, and just as Scribonius had predicted, which meant that he was ready with the argument Pullus' friend had provided.

"Caesar, while we may be on active campaign, we're no longer engaged in hostilities with the Chola, are we?" Pullus pointed out. "In fact, aren't they considered an ally of sorts, given we're camped right next to Uraiyur?"

Pullus went no further, and his reward, a good one, was something that rarely happened, Caesar flummoxed and unable to respond immediately, although Pullus only knew part of the reason for his general's consternation, who was unwilling at this point to divulge that the events of the night before were part

Caesar Ascending – The Ganges

of a larger plan. Pullus still braced himself, but suddenly, the general's expression turned rueful.

"That," Caesar allowed, "is true." Then, he gave only a glimmer of a smile as he added, "And I suspect that you didn't come up with this yourself, did you? Did you receive some advice from one of your officers...your Secundus Pilus Prior, perhaps?"

"That," Pullus admitted cheerfully, "is entirely possible."

Deciding enough time had been spent on this and not wanting further discussion that might inadvertently expose a deeper truth, Caesar dismissed the men, informing them there would be another meeting once Pollio arrived. After they left, Caesar sent for Nedunj, and when the young king arrived, he wasted no time.

"Your Highness, the moment we've been preparing for has arrived. Now, it's your decision to make."

It fell to Yogesh to inform his king of the failure to kill Pullus, assuring Karikala that he had stayed on the rampart long enough to spot the giant Roman with his own eyes, and that there were only seven corpses displayed in the large open area of the Roman camp. For the span of several moments, Yogesh felt certain that, just as Lord Senganan felt the other day when he had attempted to dissuade their king from this course of action, his days among the living were at an end. And, the truth was, Karikala had considered it, but in this, the death of Prashant actually worked in Yogesh's favor. Karikala knew he was behaving irrationally, and he understood that with his actions, no matter the result, he had handed the Roman-Pandyan alliance the pretext to unleash destruction on his kingdom that might result in the end of the Chola reign, yet he couldn't seem to help himself. He had loved Divakar, certainly, but while he never said as much to his councilors, nor to any of his wives, including Divakar's mother, who he had set aside but still had a cordial relationship with, it was his pride that had been damaged far more than the loss of a son. He had two more sons, and he had always known that Divakar wouldn't have made a good king, but the defeat, and the ease with which they had been crushed, had shattered what Karikala now understood had been his bedrock belief in Cholan invincibility when compared to their rival kingdoms, particularly their arch rival Pandya. In his mind, the only reason he hadn't crushed the Pandyan insects prior to this moment was because he chose not to, not because of the slightest possibility the Pandyans would defeat them, and now this was no longer the case.

It was the unfairness of it that was most rankling; if those accursed pale invaders hadn't shown up, and if that worm Puddapandyan hadn't died and left his pup on the throne, he wouldn't be sitting here contemplating the end of everything. Nevertheless, as much as a part of him wanted to, he couldn't take it out on Yogesh, not until he had a better idea of what the future held. At roughly the same time as Caesar was informed of its arrival, Yogesh returned to the throne room, where Karikala had banished everyone to sit alone, brooding, to inform him of the single Roman ship that approached Uraiyur. He briefly toyed with the idea of intercepting the ship, although the only vessels at his disposal were small boats the people of the capital used for fishing and transporting small amounts of cargo, but if he sent twenty of them out, loaded with his royal guard, he was certain he could overwhelm the crew and either seize or kill any high-ranking Roman aboard, but he quickly discarded it. Knowing that he couldn't put it off any longer, he summoned his senior councilors, including Senganan, and their universally somber demeanor informed him they had already been informed of the failure of their king's attempt at avenging his son.

"Presumably," he began, "the ship that is approaching is carrying the Roman that the dog Caesar put in command of establishing the base on Ravana. If our gods smile on us, they will have failed thanks to the valor of our troops under the command of Lord Karthik, and given what we know of this invader's plans, it may force them to withdraw to Pandya to regroup."

This, Senganan thought, was certainly possible, but nothing he had seen of these Romans indicated that they were likely to fail at anything they did. He was also acutely aware of his king's mood and knew that anyone who didn't choose their words carefully ran a huge risk, so he had resolved to himself that this time, he would let Venkata and the others do the talking.

"If they've succeeded, however," the king continued, "then we must prepare for the possibility that Caesar will order the rest of his army to march inland, rather than Caesar and his part of the army departing to meet them to resume their movement north." It took a physical effort for him to get the words out. "And, given...what took place last night, it's possible that the Pandyan king will press Caesar to unleash their demon fire. Which," Karikala turned to look at Senganan, making the nobleman's heart seem to freeze in his body, "Lord Senganan, having witnessed this foul weapon twice now, has painted a very vivid picture of what my subjects will be forced to endure if they do."

He fell silent, and it was left to Venkata to finally ask, "And, what will you do, Your Highness, if the Romans attack us?"

"We will fight, of course!" Karikala sounded genuinely surprised, but added quickly, "But not to the last man. We need to show these dogs that if they decide to try and take advantage of...what has happened," Senganan wasn't surprised that the king couldn't utter words that placed the blame where it belonged, squarely on his own shoulders, "...there is a price they will have to pay. But," he assured the noblemen, "I am not willing to see what Lord Senganan so eloquently described to me a few days ago."

Why, Senganan wondered, is he mentioning me in conjunction with the naphtha? Though he remained silent, he also noticed that, while Venkata and the others were eyeing him, by their expressions, it appeared as if they were thankful for what he had done. Whether that would save his life remained to be seen.

As Senganan ruminated on this, Karikala was continuing, "I believe that the next move belongs to the Roman and his Pandyan pet, so we will wait and see what transpires."

In fulfillment of his prediction, it was shortly before sunset that a mounted Roman, dressed in the uniform of a Tribune, and accompanied by a small party of other mounted men, all of them heavily bearded and some with hair the color of saffron, while the only other one of them dressed in a Roman fashion but without armor and helmet held the leafy branch aloft that signaled this was to talk, approached the eastern gate, the nearest to the main gate of the Roman camp. Lord Venkata was alerted by Yogesh, and without alerting the king or the other noblemen, the pair raced from the palace to the gateway, waiting a few heartbeats to calm their mounts and betray their agitation or eagerness, before the gates were opened. As they approached, Venkata noticed that while this man wore the same kind of armor and helmet with black crest that he had seen Caesar wear, he was much darker, although the man next to him was similarly colored. It was the way both men sat their horses that caused Venkata to intuit that these might be Parthians who had chosen to serve Caesar and not fight him; this was when the thought leapt into his mind that, perhaps, there was a possibility that he, Venkata, might find a place on what he was now certain would be the winning side.

It was the second man who was wearing the soldier's red tunic, although a sword hung from his belt, who spoke in accented but clearly understandable Tamil, "Our general summons your King Karikala to a meeting tomorrow, in the morning."

Even knowing their position was untenable, hearing the Parthian, for Venkata was now certain that was what they both were, speak in such a blunt manner, ignited a flare of anger in Venkata, and the hissing sound Yogesh made told him he wasn't alone.

"You forget, Roman...or whatever you are," Venkata said coldly, "that you are in the kingdom of Chola, as visitors here, and visitors do not summon kings; they *request* an audience with him!"

There was a slight delay as the Parthian translated to his countryman, but his reaction was, in its own way, more unsettling than if he had been angered, saying something in a flat monotone that the first Parthian translated.

"The message is the same, Lord..." Slightly embarrassed, Venkata supplied his name, "...Venkata. How you or your king wish to interpret it is of no concern to us," the Parthian said indifferently. "All that matters is that he is here, on this spot,"

Caesar Ascending – The Ganges

suddenly, the Parthian looked, if not confused then uncertain, and he glanced off to the east before saying, "two finger widths above the horizon after dawn."

"And then what?" Venkata demanded. "Surely you don't expect him to enter your camp."

Fortunately for both parties, Achaemenes remembered in time to nod his head as he replied, "No. The reason for the time is that Caesar will need to set up a tent, at the same spot Primus Pilus Pullus slaughtered his champion." For the first time, the Parthian gave Venkata a smile, "There is much to discuss, after all. Better to do it in some comfort than sit in the sun."

Thinking he had an opening, Venkata asked, "And what may I tell my King will be the topic?"

He wasn't particularly surprised when the Parthian replied, "That is not for me to say. It is," he finished simply, "Caesar who will decide."

Venkata gave an abrupt shake of his head, then realizing he needed to verbalize their acceptance, he said shortly, "I will deliver your message to King Karikala. It is up to *him* as to whether he will be there tomorrow."

He was already turning his mount when the Parthian called out, "You need to do whatever it takes to convince your king to accept, Lord Venkata, for the sake of your kingdom and the people in it."

Venkata heard but didn't acknowledge the warning, moving at a trot the short distance back to the city gate, with Yogesh beside him, the bodyguard's battered features revealing none of his thoughts. It reminded Venkata of how, early in his tenure with the royal bodyguard, when Prashant had been in command, he once asked Prashant if the large man was mute, and it made the normally dour bodyguard laugh, unusual in itself.

"He might as well be," Prashant had commented. "If he says five words a day, I'd be surprised."

Now, Venkata understood the risk he was taking, but he felt it worth it, and he broached the subject on his mind to the royal bodyguard.

"Before I return to the palace, Yogesh, I intend to call on Lord Senganan. I would like him to be with me when we speak

245

to our King."

Yogesh had been silent all the way through the gateway and into the city, but just before they reached the intersection where the palace lay in one direction and the home Lord Venkata kept in the capital in the other, he replied, "I think that would be wise, Lord."

Even with all the excitement of the night before, the evening after Pollio's arrival was at least as eventful, if not more so when viewed in the larger picture. It began with the late afternoon meeting, where Pollio joined Caesar and the rest of the senior officers, with the Primi Pili arriving shortly thereafter. By this time, Pullus had visited Barhinder, who was going to be released before nightfall, his arm stitched up on both inner and outer bicep, but it was the tissue damage that the physician had warned Pullus was serious in a long-term sense.

"He will have to work very hard to regain even partial use of that arm," Stolos, the chief *medicus* for the 10th informed him. "Even then, I cannot say it will be strong enough to hold a shield."

While Pullus knew that this was what Barhinder aspired to, to march as a Legionary, which would make him one of a bare handful of men of Bharuch who were in the ranks, he had also seen that there was more to this boy than just wielding a *gladius*.

"I'll do whatever I can, Stolos," Pullus assured him, then offered the Greek the kind of smile his men had seen before and shuddered at. "I'll either make him strong enough for the ranks or convince him that it's not for him."

Sensing there was more to this statement, Stolos regarded Pullus with a raised eyebrow, but the Centurion didn't say anything else, leaving the *Quaestorium* to attend the meeting Caesar had called. Now, with Balbinus on one side and Torquatus on the other, they sat and listened as Pollio gave his report of the campaign on Taprobane.

None of them were that surprised when Pollio informed them, "We caught the Chola garrison at Palaesimundum completely by surprise by arriving just as the sun was coming up, and while the walls are stone, they were in bad repair and barely ten feet high. Using our translator, we informed them that we had peaceful intentions, only wanting to improve the dock and the other facilities, but just as we believed, the Chola didn't accept this, and launched a sortie. The fort was taken before the noon watch, and the civilians in the town were docile, especially once they understood that we weren't there to slaughter them. The only problem," Pollio gave a soft chuckle, "was the same problem we ran into in Pattala. What they think of as Greek, and what we think of as Greek are two different things. But, once we got that straightened out, we left the 6th and 8th behind, and they were able to construct not only an upriver port by expanding what was already there at Palaesimundum and adding four new warehouses, but repair and enlarge the fort to accommodate the Cohorts of auxiliaries that will remain there. With the rest of the army, we sailed to the cape to seize that sea anchorage." He glanced down at his tablet, frowning slightly as he continued, "These Cholans were better led, by a noble Chola named Karthik, who didn't accept our offer to allow us to perform the needed work, and I'm afraid that we suffered heavier casualties than anticipated, particularly with Flaminius' boys in the 30th. However," he looked back to the assembled officers, "we now have an improved anchorage on the coast in the inlet between the mainland and the island, along with a fort that can hold a Cohort. Honestly," he finished, "the men spent far more time working than any fighting, and they're getting bored."

Pollio sat then, and Caesar took over, beginning with, "I won't go back over what happened last night, but what I will tell you is this. Our Friend and Ally Pandya has been given an opportunity here because of Karikala's poor judgment. And," he added with waspish amusement, "it's now easy to see where his son the crown prince got that trait from." There were some chuckles, and Caesar turned to indicate Nedunj, who was present for this meeting, unlike the first one. Also with him, however, were his sub-commanders Sundara and Vira, which was slightly unusual but had happened before. "After speaking with King Nedunj, and hearing his thoughts, I have made him an offer." As was his habit, he scanned the faces of the men seated before him, something that Pullus had learned was a ploy early on, one that he didn't care for, seeing it as Caesar's attempt to build suspense; the fact that it always worked didn't help, although Pullus acknowledged to himself that his irritation was exacerbated by the fact that, thanks to Diocles, he knew what was coming. Resuming, Caesar explained, "We are going to delay our departure from Uraiyur for two more weeks. During that time, the part of the army that is now encamped on the coast will board the ships to sail north. As some of you know, Hirtius has already taken the bulk of the cavalry and scouted to the northern edge of the Cholan kingdom, a distance of about one hundred eighty miles from here. More importantly, they have located the location of what King Karikala refers to as his Northern Army, where they're quartered in the second largest city in the kingdom. It will take five days for the fleet to sail north, another day to unload, and then a second to march to Chennai, where they will be presented with either a decree from King Karikala submitting to the Pandyan kingdom, or that we have reduced and destroyed Uraiyur and slain their king."

This was the last somewhat calm moment of the meeting, which lasted well past nightfall; by the time an exhausted Pullus and the other Primi Pili returned to their quarters, it was with a spinning head and, for Pullus anyway, a reluctant admiration for the scope and guile of what Caesar had done.

"In effect," Scribonius summed it up late that night, after answering Pullus' call to come to his tent, "he dangled a prize so huge for Nedunj that he would have been mad to resist it. The only difference is that we know that he dangled that bait even before we left Karoura, anticipating that we'd be presented with an opportunity somehow. And," he frowned, though not in disapproval, "the only thing we're really risking is our supply of naphtha, scorpion bolts, and perhaps a few of our own men if the reserve Legions are required to help, while what we gain is a king who's indebted to us for the rest of his days for being the Pandyan who finally subdued and conquered the Chola kingdom, while making the entire southern part of India a Friend and Ally of Rome."

"At the same time," Pullus pointed out, "it makes the Pandya the greatest power in India, which in turn forces the kingdoms to their north to worry more about them than us as we make our way to the Ganges. And," he finished with a quiet satisfaction that had nothing to do with the strategical and political ramifications, "since Bharuch is a Friend and Ally as well, there's no need for Queen Hyppolita to look to her southern border, and with Pattala neutralized, her northern. All that's left is to the eastern part of India, but the Andhra are now hemmed in by three kingdoms, all of them wealthy and one of them powerful enough militarily to make them worry about more than us."

"Wait," Balbus spoke for the first time, the part of his mouth that was mobile twisting down into a frown, "what happens if Karikala realizes that he's fucked, and gives in to Caesar's terms?"

"That," Pullus allowed, "is possible, but he won't be getting anything like what Caesar offered King Nedunj, or Queen Hyppolita for that matter." He offered a grin that was, if not cruel, then hard. "I think he's going to have a hard time swallowing the idea that he's now going to be in effect a client king of Nedunj, and have to give up Madoura in the process."

Balbus thought about this, then asked about what really mattered to him. "So if he doesn't, and these Pandyan boys rain fire down on these Cholan bastards with our artillery, what's our cut of the loot?"

With a roll of his eyes, Scribonius asked with mock weariness, "Why do you care, Quintus? Coins don't stay in your purse long enough to get their edges rubbed off."

"What I do with my money is my business," Balbus replied stoutly, but he couldn't maintain his composure, offering his version of a broad smile. "Besides, the ladies would be heartbroken if I didn't shower them with money. Then what, eh? If word got out that I was like," he jerked his thumb at Pullus, "him, I'd never get my prick wet again!"

"The day you start thinking with this head," Pullus tapped his own, then pointed to his crotch, "instead of that one will be the day that I hang up my *gladius*, because I'll know that the end of days is coming."

They all burst out laughing, especially Balbus, who was as proud of his reputation as a hopelessly degenerate debaucher as he was of his prowess with a *gladius*.

Once the laughter died down, it was Diocles who spoke next, "You know," he reminded them, "there are a whole lot of things that have to go right for this to work out the way Caesar intends it to."

"It will," Pullus replied immediately. "Caesar's Luck will hold one more time. And," with this he lifted his cup, "*when* it does, it's on to Palibothra."

The others hoisted their cup as they chimed in, "Palibothra!"

Predictably, it was Balbus who smacked his lips and said, "The richest city in the world!"

Not surprisingly, the rampart of the Roman camp was as crowded with spectators as the day Pullus slew Prashant, all eyes on what was actually a Tribune's tent, constructed in the new style adopted by the Romans, with the sides rolled up and secured so that it acted as a canopy. Underneath was the table that Caesar used in his *praetorium* as his officers' mess and conference table, and where Caesar, the Legates, and King Nedunj were already seated. Behind them stood four of Caesar's bodyguards, including Gundomir and Teispes, now practically inseparable, but after some debate about the inclusion of the Primi Pili, Caesar decided there would only be one.

"Pullus' presence will remind the king that every effort to have him killed was futile, which will hopefully make him see the hopelessness of further resistance," was how Caesar had explained it to the Primi Pili.

The reality was far different, which he had divulged only to Pullus when he kept the Primus Pilus back at the end of the early morning meeting.

Once they were alone, Caesar began, "The truth is, Pullus, I want you there because..."

It was rare for anyone to interrupt Caesar, especially when it was Pullus, but he did so now, finishing for Caesar, "Because you want to enrage him and make him do something rash that will give you the pretext for unleashing King Nedunj."

What wasn't unusual was that Caesar didn't appreciate being interrupted, and while it was petty of him, he couldn't stop himself from snapping, "Is that something else Scribonius put in your head?"

Rather than rattling or angering Pullus, he smiled as he cheerfully lied, "No, this was one I worked out all by myself, Caesar."

Caesar didn't reply, glaring at his Primus Pilus for a heartbeat, then his upper lip twitched in a silent recognition that Pullus had taken the honors in this exchange, while it served as a reminder not to underestimate the brawny Centurion when it came to matters of the mind.

"Yes, well, however you arrived at that conclusion, you're correct. I think," Caesar unconsciously echoed Pullus' own thoughts, "that Karikala is no longer thinking like a king, and is thinking like a father driven mad with grief." Pullus briefly considered assuring Caesar that this too had occurred to him, but wisely refrained, allowing Caesar to go on. "Seeing you standing there as a reminder of what he thinks is the truth should be enough. However," his tone changed slightly, but Pullus recognized this was now the ruthless part of Caesar speaking, "if he appears to have gotten himself under control, you may have to...increase the pressure. Remember," he reminded Pullus, "he speaks Greek, so anything you say that could incite him and push him to a state where we need him to be will be much appreciated."

Consequently, he was now standing behind Caesar as well, almost directly behind their general, wearing his armor, as were the bodyguards, although Caesar, Achaemenes, the Legates, and King Nedunj were attired in non-military garb, with the young king dressed in the Pandyan style, while Caesar and the others wore tunics, not red but white, with Caesar's bearing a broad purple stripe, the borders on both sides of the stripes embroidered with palm leaves. They were also not made of wool, nor cotton, but of unfinished silk, meaning that they were as cool as it was possible to be, and Pullus cordially detested Caesar for it. There were two attendants, both of them Pandyans who were part of Nedunj's entourage, ready to pour the contents of the two pitchers into the cups already arrayed on the table. They had arrived early, but before much time had passed, it became clear that the Chola were late, and all eyes were fastened on the eastern gate, but the double doors remained closed. Like the rampart of the Roman camp, the eastern wall of Uraiyur was packed with spectators, although it was impossible to tell whether they were citizens or part of what remained of the Cholan army. Pullus was getting restless, as were the other men present, save for Caesar, who sat there, seemingly unruffled as he consulted a wax tablet while conversing with Nedunj in low tones, whose own nerves were belied by drumming his fingers on the table.

Hirtius, seated on the opposite side of Pollio, who was to Caesar's left, leaned over, and while he whispered, Pullus heard him plainly ask, "How much longer do we wait before we go back to camp?"

For the first time, Caesar looked up, glancing at the sun, which was barely peeking over the eastern wall; he was opening his mouth to answer when Nedunj spoke excitedly, "Caesar! They're opening the gates!"

The king was correct, but the gates weren't all the way open when a collective chorus of muttered curses and gasps erupted at the sight, but the only one who seemed unsurprised was Caesar, who did what Pullus considered a curious thing. Twisting on his chair, Caesar looked at Gundomir, not saying anything but giving a curt nod, and naturally, Pullus' attention went to the German, and Teispes, who both abruptly turned about and walked to their horses. He's sending them to bring out a Cohort, Pullus thought, yet to his surprise, they didn't mount. Only once they each untied the sack that had been tied to the back of their saddle then returning did Pullus begin to have an idea of what was in them. They moved past Pullus and the other two guards to come to the table, where they set the sacks down, and while they didn't remove what Pullus could tell by the shape were jars from their sacks, the exaggerated care they took confirmed Pullus' suspicions, while Pollio and Nedunj both shifted their seats a bit farther from Caesar in an unconscious desire to distance themselves from the volatile substance, which Caesar noticed.

Sounding amused, he chided the pair, "Neither of you plan on lighting anything, do you? Then, you have nothing to fear. But," he raised his voice, "I anticipated that Karikala might arrive on his elephant, so I thought this should be a reminder of what awaits him since he wants to remind us that he still has so many of those beasts."

It was, Pullus thought, a cunning thing to do, and typical of Caesar's foresight; however, while he held a healthy respect, based on fear, for naphtha, he knew that as long as there wasn't any source of flame that it would be safe enough. What worried him was what might happen if the huge beast somehow managed to get a scent of the contents of those jars, and he did wonder if Caesar was perhaps thinking of slitting open the leather lid that was secured by a thong around the neck of the jar. Yes, the stampede they all witnessed was in the opposite direction, but that was as much from the presence of the flames as any odor, Pullus was certain. Hopefully, just seeing it would be enough.

Karikala's last-moment decision to ride his elephant, Ananda, was what had prompted the delay, and was done despite Senganan, Venkata, and four of the remaining Chola nobles who made up Karikala's council arguing, to varying degrees, against it.

"Your Highness, if you ride Ananda," Senganan had pleaded, then pointed to the *howdah* the king had ordered be placed on its back, which had no canopy and was missing the small throne, "especially attired for war, it will tell the Romans and the Pandyan king that you intend to fight, and we agreed last night that this would be futile!"

"No," Karikala snapped, "you," he pointed to each of them, "and you, and you, and you, *you* all said it would be futile. I did not!"

When Senganan had opened his mouth to continue arguing, Karikala turned and looked pointedly at Yogesh, saying nothing but sending an unmistakable message that prompted the bodyguard to rest his hand on the hilt of his sword. In a small act of defiance, when the king ordered Senganan and the others to prepare their own elephants, in a relatively rare show of unanimity, they all refused. Presumably, Karikala immediately realized having Yogesh behead his entire council wasn't practical, so he had snarled at them about being cowards, but that was the extent of it. When they reached the eastern gate, Senganan and the others were all mounted on horses, but in another departure from their king, who was now dressed in his full, and very ornate, armor, they were attired in their formal tunics, which hung well past their knees, almost hiding their trousers. Following Ananda out through the gate, it was impossible to miss the tension in the air, if only because, unlike on other occasions, the citizens of the city who normally cheered whenever their king was in their presence, calling out blessings to him, along with the occasional desperate request for his intervention in some sort of squabble, now stood there on both sides of the gateway, and above the party on the rampart, almost completely silent save for the buzz of murmurs and what Senganan guessed was speculation on what their future held. There had only been one uprising against a Cholan king in Senganan's lifetime, occurring just two years before, but it had happened, and as he glanced up at the faces looking down on them as they passed through the gateway, what he saw in the expressions of his countrymen didn't bode well for Karikala. The king, refusing to be hurried, had his *mahout* set an even slower pace than normal for a beast that size, another sign of the pettiness that was now, and had been for weeks, on full display, and it made Senganan wonder if Karikala was really all that different from his son when it came to possessing the mettle and temperament to be king. It was a thought that had come to him a few days earlier, and had since blossomed into something more defined, as Senganan realized that, while Karikala had been a competent ruler for his day and world, he also had never been under this much pressure before. In fact, Senganan had come to the realization that the few times something unforeseen had arisen in the past, Karikala's actions had been more extreme than his councilors thought necessary almost every time.

Since the noblemen who had been the first and most vocal to express their reservations about their king's actions were no longer alive, Karikala had managed to quell the survivors' inclination they had to dissent. At the time, and to his shame now, Senganan realized that he had rationalized their king's behavior; yes, it might have been harsh, perhaps excessive, but it was within his rights, and, after all, the problem had been resolved. This, he recognized, was different, because the threat facing them now was existential in nature, and while he wasn't completely convinced that Karikala would bring them to the brink of destruction, he was acutely aware that he and his fellow noblemen would only know if their assessment was accurate in a short time. Arriving a short distance away from the tent, Karikala again took his time in having Ananda kneel, forcing the rest of them to wait to dismount, since their custom dictated in such moments that they couldn't touch the ground before their king. Lingering on Ananda's huge knee to pat the animal's head while murmuring in low tones something that caused the elephant to respond with a low rumble and a slight lifting of his trunk, Senganan took the time to study the faces of their adversaries, stiffening when he noticed that the giant Pullus was present, and the only one of their officers who wore the white crest that signified the commander of one of their Legions. Caesar, he realized with a stab of fear, and fury, is deliberately goading Karikala with Pullus' presence; he *wants* Karikala to lose control. Finally, his king hopped down, and Senganan and the others dismounted, while he kept his eyes on Karikala, seeing his body stiffen when his eyes reached the men standing a few paces behind the table, where Caesar sat, expressionless, watching the Cholans approach. For a moment, it seemed as if Karikala was going to abruptly turn about and remount Ananda, but he didn't, striding jerkily towards the table with his hand on his sword, and doing it in such a manner that a pair of the men with Pullus who Senganan had deduced were Caesar's bodyguards made their own moves, detaching from the rough line, and like the Cholan king had their hands on the hilts of their weapons. Caesar, however, didn't react visibly, nor did he turn to see the pair of men, both bearded, though otherwise in stark contrast to each other, advancing towards the table, but he held up a hand that instantly brought the pair to a halt. Karikala had faltered in the middle of his stride when the pair detached themselves, but it was slight and barely noticeable, although Senganan was certain Caesar had seen it. Once he was within a couple paces of the table, only then did Karikala slow, coming to a stop just behind the chair directly across from Caesar, and Senganan realized that his king was waiting for the Roman, and the other men at the table, to rise. It was not to be; instead, all Caesar did was make a gesture with one hand at the chair, indicating that Karikala should sit, but the king didn't do so immediately, instead turning and with his head, gesturing to Senganan and the others to come fill the other seats. It wasn't long, but Senganan had enough time to see in Karikala's expression that he was already almost beside himself with fury, but when he turned back to face Caesar, he didn't say anything, waiting for the rest of his party to reach the table.

Without turning around, he pointed to the chair to his right and instructed in Tamil, "Senganan will sit to my right, and Venkata to my left. Lords Rakesh and Vimal will sit next to Lord Senganan, and Lords Abishek and Deepak next to Lord Venkata."

Only then did Karikala pull his chair out, then made a show of adjusting his sword before he sat down.

"May I offer refreshment, Your Highness?" Caesar asked politely.

"No," Karikala snapped. Then, pointing at Pullus, he demanded, "What is this...dog doing here?"

When Caesar looked over his shoulder, Senganan assumed it was to order the giant Roman to be quiet; instead, he gave a slight nod.

"I just wanted you to see that your attempt to kill me was such a miserable failure," Pullus replied in Greek, reminding Senganan that this lowborn Roman spoke another tongue. Pullus wasn't through, his voice hard as he stared at Karikala with what was unmistakable and clear contempt, "In fact, I am the one who slew the only man who made it into my tent." Pullus paused for just a heartbeat, his expression indicating to Senganan that he was trying to recall something; whether this was feigned or not, he would never know, but then the Roman said, "His name was Harisha. Did you even bother to learn the names of the men you sent after me, Karikala?"

When Karikala stiffened, making a hissing noise at the same time, Senganan glanced over at his king and saw that he was a shade paler than a moment before, but it was his coming out of his seat that earned a response, the pair of bodyguards who had stepped back to the original position suddenly moving which, yet again, Caesar stopped with nothing more than a raising of his hand. What Senganan couldn't tell was whether Karikala's reaction was because Yogesh, who had undoubtedly made all the arrangements, had informed him of the men's names, or whether it was the slur when Pullus called him by only his name that elicited the response.

It was Caesar who spoke next, when he said in what could almost be called a cheerful tone, "Oh, yes, Your Highness. We learned quite a bit from your man Manoja. He proved to be quite...talkative. You may not have seen for yourself, but surely one of your retainers informed you about our display at sunrise? And that there were only seven bodies? The eighth one was Manoja."

"So you tortured him," Karikala said bitterly, though not because he cared about a man who had been in The Pit.

"Oh, no," Caesar assured him. "We didn't have to, Your Highness. It turns out that he has been unhappy under your reign for some time, and he was more than willing to offer his grievances."

"Grievances?" Karikala snapped, then unintentionally betrayed himself by snarling, "What do I care that a man from the unclean caste has grievances?"

"That," Caesar replied, his tone wry, "might be why he has those grievances."

As Senganan sat listening, he was almost certain that Caesar was lying about the man Manoja speaking freely, if only because the people of the lower castes had been conditioned by centuries of obedience to the rules and requirements of their world that it would be unthinkable for him to utter a word of criticism against his king, or any member of the highest caste. He would never know it, but Senganan was incorrect in his guess that Manoja had been tortured, but his thought process betrayed what so many of the men of his status from Parthia, through Pattala, Bharuch, and Pandya failed to understand, that, while their stockpile of flaming naphtha represented the super weapon of their age in combating armored elephants, perhaps a more potent weapon was that, in a relative manner, these Roman invaders offered the vast majority of those destined to have been born into the lowest class of their respective society

257

a better existence than what they endured under their previous leadership. He would never learn that Manoja had been promised not only the freedom to leave, but he would be given more silver than he had ever seen in his life, although he was currently under guard.

There was a brief silence because Karikala still had his gaze fixed on the large Roman, and for a brief instant, Senganan thought that his king was about to leap across the table; instead, he returned his attention to Caesar, and asked, "What is the purpose of this meeting, Caesar?"

"Thank you, Your Highness." Caesar lowered his head in what might have almost been called a deferential bow, but his words were altogether different. "The purpose of this meeting is to inform you that you are being given a choice to make, a very important one."

For the first time, Karikala indicated that he was even aware of Senganan's presence, glancing over at the nobleman with what he interpreted as one of inquiry, but all Senganan could offer was a shrug, unwilling to risk his king's wrath one way or another.

It earned him a barely audible snort, then Karikala addressed Caesar, "And what is that *you* say my choices are, Caesar?"

Senganan sat, listening, for the next several moments, and with every heartbeat, it felt as if a ball of ice-cold lead was growing in his stomach, while at the same time, his anger started to blossom at an identical rate, creating the most unusual sensation of his life. Most of his ire was aimed at this arrogant Roman who calmly dictated what was the end of an independent Chola kingdom, but a fair amount was at the man seated next to him, whose conceit and blind rage had brought them to this point where, even as he hated it, he recognized that of the two choices being presented, there was really only one if Karikala entertained any hope of ever reversing their current situation in the future.

When Caesar finished, Karikala didn't respond immediately, although he turned his attention to Nedunj, who had yet to utter a word, then returned it to Caesar to say flatly, "So you are saying I would be a vassal of your puppy here, who is a vassal of yours, and that I would no longer be king."

"No," Caesar countered, "you would be allowed to retain your title, and to live in the style in which you currently live. You will have the same servants, the same slaves, you will keep your wife, or wives, if that is your custom. But," Caesar's voice hardened, slightly, but it was noticeable, "you will have as your council men selected by King Nedunj, you will relinquish command of all of your military, and there will be a combination of troops from Pandya, along with a force of those that we call auxiliaries who are loyal to Rome, and," he stressed, "are trained in our manner, permanently residing here. In fact," he indicated the camp behind him, "they will be housed here for the time being, pending the construction of a permanent camp."

"But who makes decisions for Chola?" Karikala queried, acting as if he was actually interested in the answer. Pointing at Nedunj, he sneered, "Him? A Pandyan? A man who has been our sworn and bitterest enemy since before the time of my grandfathers?"

"King Nedunj would make all the decisions," Caesar agreed, "but how much input you have, and whether your counsel is heeded, is largely up to you, Your Highness. If you accept this as your reality, your people will not only be protected, they will thrive. Yes," he allowed, "your power will be much reduced. But, your people will not have to endure what happens when Rome comes, in all of her might, to take what you could have freely given."

"Freely given?" Karikala echoed in disbelief. "You are presenting me with the choice of submitting and becoming a slave or watching you and your...*minion* rain that demon fire down onto the heads of the women and children of my capital!"

At the mention of what the Chola called the naphtha, Karikala pointed at one of the sacks, informing Caesar that he had seen them, and knew what they contained.

"You wouldn't be a slave," Caesar countered, but his tone turned unyielding, "but aside from that, yes, those are your choices."

Senganan sat there, mind reeling, and he heard the desperation in Karikala's tone when he shot back, "You seem to forget something, Caesar!"

"Oh, what is that?"

"Yes, you have done grievous damage to my army," Karikala admitted, "but what you saw arrayed before you a few weeks ago is *not* the sum total of our military might! There is an army..."

"Ah," Caesar cut him off, although it was the manner in which he did it that warned Senganan of what might be coming, "yes. You call it your Northern Army, yes?"

It took two tries, but Karikala finally answered tersely, "Yes."

"And," Caesar continued, "I am going to assume you noticed that the rest of the army I said would join me has not arrived yet." Without waiting for an answer, he went on, "Perhaps you even started to believe that those Legions did not exist. But I assure you that they do, and even as we speak, they are sailing north, and they will land near Chennai, the city where your Northern Army is located, and march there." By this moment, Caesar's tone was cold, and relentless, "Depending on the message that I send them based on your decision, your Northern Army and the people of Chennai will either suffer the exact same fate as your subjects here in Uraiyur, or they will be allowed to thrive."

At first, Senganan thought that, somehow, his king had gone temporarily deaf, because he gave absolutely no sign that he had heard, but then Karikala heaved a deep sigh, and there was a quality to it that made Senganan think that, now, finally, he understood there was only one course to choose. The silence lasted for a period of time that was impossible to calculate for Senganan as, naturally, he and every other man looked to Karikala, their king.

He could actually hear Karikala swallow before he said flatly, "Do your worst."

Standing up abruptly, the king didn't wait for Senganan and the others, turning and stalking away from the table, leaving his councilors sitting there in stunned silence.

"Lord Senganan."

He had the sense that Caesar had called his name more than once when he lifted his gaze from the empty cup in front of him that had never been filled, looking at the Roman dully.

Caesar Ascending – The Ganges

"Lord Senganan, you've given me the impression that you are a sensible man," Caesar said, not with a flattering tone but as a statement of fact. "For the sake of your people," suddenly, Caesar pointed directly over Senganan's shoulder back at the eastern wall, "those people inside those walls, I implore you to counsel your king to accept our terms."

"You would have us debase ourselves and kneel to our longest enemy?" Senganan replied, but to Caesar, it sounded as if he was mouthing the words without any conviction. "You would strip us of our independence, and make us a vassal to the Pandya, a people whose king submitted to Rome?" Nodding his head in a negation of this idea, he finished simply, "My king will never agree to that."

"Lord Senganan," for the first time Nedunj spoke, in Tamil, and without hostility, "what I did wasn't easy, I assure you." While Senganan's eyes were on the Pandyan king, out of the corner of his vision, he could see Caesar's expression, assuming from it that the Roman wasn't happy that they were no longer speaking in Greek. Nedunj went on, "But as you've seen, in matters of war, these Romans are, in my opinion, invincible. At least," he added, "as long as this man sitting next to me lives." As he listened, Senganan was surreptitiously searching Caesar's expression, but he gave not a flicker of recognition that he was now the subject of the conversation. "And, I will say this much," Nedunj allowed, "that to this point the Romans have honored their agreement with Pandya, and as much as I hate to admit it, there have been material changes to the manner in which we do things that have been an improvement."

By this point, Karikala had returned to his *howdah*, while his fellow noblemen were now remounting, so Senganan rose, stepping backward from the table instead of turning his back, and despite the fact that a part of him hated himself for it, he heard the words coming from his mouth, in Greek. "I will do what I can to make King Karikala see things in the way you desire but I do not hold out much hope."

Then, he turned away, but just as he stepped out from under the cover of the tent roof, Caesar called out to him, "Lord Senganan, there was one thing that I wanted to tell King

Karikala but did not have a chance to, and I would ask that you relay this to him."

Despite knowing that it wasn't likely to be to the benefit of the Chola, Senganan still stopped and turned back to face the table, asking warily, "And what is that?"

Indicating Nedunj, Caesar said, "He should know that a week ago, King Nedunj sent orders to the commander of the rest of the army Pandya can field to send them here. They should arrive within the next two to three days. They will be the ones who actually assault Uraiyur, and I will tell you now that I will not risk one Roman to stop your lifelong enemy when they are inside your walls."

The Caesar that Senganan was seeing now was the Caesar of a place he would never know about, the Gallic town of Uxellodunum, where the pile of severed hands of the defenders who refused to yield still moldered, an implacable, ruthless military commander, and it was this image of Caesar that was burned into Senganan's mind.

Chapter Six

"Do you believe Caesar isn't going to let us into Uraiyur once it falls?"

It wasn't the words as much as the disconsolate manner in which Balbus asked Pullus that made him laugh.

"Quintus, what does it say about you that you're disappointed that your boys don't get to run wild?" Scribonius taunted.

"Who said anything about being disappointed for my boys?" Balbus retorted. "I was thinking of me."

Once the laughter subsided, Pullus answered Balbus' question. "Yes, I do believe Caesar. Subduing the Chola was a secondary consideration because he hoped that it wouldn't be necessary, but it appears that Karikala hasn't changed his mind. So..." He didn't finish, just shrugging.

It was the day after the meeting with the Chola king, and such was the tension that most of the men who had lined the rampart of their camp the day before had returned there to stand in the blazing sun, watching for the gates to reopen to allow a messenger to inform Caesar that Karikala had reconsidered. Their interest wasn't based only in their immediate future; the wagering on whether Karikala would finally submit was quite brisk, even among Centurions, with three exceptions; Scribonius, Balbus, and Cyclops, while Pullus didn't wager with the Centurions of his own Legion, but he wasn't shy about laying odds with his fellow Primi Pili, and he had bet heavily on the idea that Karikala was sincere in what was essentially a challenge.

"He said, 'do your worst'," Pullus had related to Balbinus and the other Primi Pili, who had unsurprisingly been waiting at the *Porta Praetoria* for his return from the meeting. With grim amusement, he said, "I think he's going to find out that he needs to be careful what he wishes for. I don't know if their gods include Hubris and Nemesis, but he's about to be introduced to them."

Balbinus, Papernus of the 21st, and Aquilinus of the 15th had, as Pullus hoped, greedily snapped up the bait that he was laying out, counting on his multiple encounters now with the Cholan king and confident in his judgement that, if he hadn't been mad before this, the death of his son had driven him beyond the edge of reason. When nothing happened by late afternoon of the first day, even the most stubborn men retired to the relative comfort of their tents, all of them with the sides rolled up for most of the daylight hour. Nevertheless, when dawn broke the third day, while it wasn't in the same numbers as before, there were men from every Legion back on the rampart, watching the eastern gate while chatting and bickering, and they were unanimous in one respect, that Caesar forbidding the consumption of anything but water until further notice was a bad decision. As far as the Centurions were concerned, as long as these men didn't create any mischief, if they wanted to stand there in the hot sun, that was up to them, given there was nothing much for them to do. They were rewarded, though not in the way they hoped, when the camp *Bucinator* sounded the call that a large party was approaching the camp, but to their consternation, it was from the opposite side at the *Porta Decumana*, and given its size, none of them had the energy or desire to dash across the camp to witness the arrival of the rest of the Pandyan army. They were led by the new Lord of Muziris, Lord Maran, and in some ways what the young king was doing could have been called potentially risky. By stripping his kingdom of all but the garrison troops of his capital and the larger cities of Pandya like Muziris, it could be said that Nedunj was inviting disaster. The reality was much different, as Pullus had understood; the threat to their north had always been Bharuch, which was under Roman control, and their eastern border no longer was an issue because of the Pandyan presence in Chola, and with their location on the western coast of India, their flanks were secure. Instead of subsuming this new force into their current camp, Caesar allowed Maran's force to make their own camp a short distance west of the larger one, and as his men, and the fifty remaining elephants, settled in, Maran went to the *praetorium*, where Caesar and the rest of the officers, including the Tribunes and Nedunj's commanders of their combined nations, were waiting.

Once the formalities were out of the way, and Maran assured his king that the Pandyan force had endured the march well and didn't need much time to recover, Caesar wasted none of his, declaring, "We will begin preparations immediately." Turning to the large piece of vellum created by stitching together smaller pieces that was hanging on one wall of the officers' mess, he indicated a series of marks. "This is where we'll be placing our *ballistae*. Now that we've been here for three weeks, it's given me the opportunity to learn that the Chola don't possess artillery, relying on archers to defend the walls." Pointing to a specific spot, he continued, "According to our information, the *ballistae* placed here will have the best chance of reaching Karikala's palace, although it's at the edge of our range. It's made of stone, as are their temples and the homes of their upper caste, but as we all know, there will be enough wooden structures around each of those to create a conflagration."

It was Torquatus who, noticing something, or the lack thereof, asked, "Are the ladders being constructed now, Caesar?"

The shake of Caesar's head elicited surprised murmurs, but it was with the same hard expression he had offered Senganan that he explained, "We are going to force Karikala to come to us. Which," he pointed out, "is why we have our scorpions concentrated around each gate, and they will wrap the bolts in naphtha since it's likely he will send his animals out first. Comrades," while he would always begin his addresses to the entire army in this fashion, it was exceedingly rare for him to do so with his officers, telling them this was significant, "I'm not going to risk any more Roman lives than I must." He nodded in the direction of Nedunj, who was now flanked by three of his commanders, "The king and I have discussed this, but I'll let him explain."

Nedunj, obviously expecting this, stood, and in a surprise, chose to speak in Latin, which was halting, "I told Caesar that this is our fight. We have been the enemy of the Chola for more than one hundred years, and while I am grateful for the use of your artillery, and what your artillery will be using," he offered a grim smile, "this must be a Pandyan victory. We must make the sacrifice ourselves, because despite our hatred of each other, we are still of the same people."

"How will your animals handle the fire?" Balbinus asked, not hiding his skepticism.

"Our elephants will only be used as a last resort," Nedunj explained. "As you all have seen, my troops have been training to fight like you Romans, and our spearmen now are carrying swords as well. No," he offered a quick smile, "we are not as skilled as your Legions yet, but we have learned the value of the methods that you use. I believe," he finished simply, "this will be enough to defeat our enemy."

He sat back down as the Primi Pili considered what he was saying, but Balbinus summed up the consensus when he whispered to Pullus, "That all sounds good, but I'll wager you a hundred *drachmae* that our boys are going to have to get their blades wet."

Pullus didn't argue this, because he agreed, but he only nudged his friend and nodded towards Caesar, who had risen again.

"We will begin emplacing the pieces this afternoon," he said, "so your artillery *Immunes* need to inspect their pieces and make them ready to move."

"They'll be able to see where we're placing them. Shouldn't we wait until darkness, Caesar?"

The only sign of Caesar's irritation was the thinning of his lips, but he replied to the man who had asked the question evenly, "I want them to see us, Crispus. I want Karikala's men on the walls to report to him exactly what we're doing. I want him to know what's coming." Feeling that he owed them at least a partial explanation, Caesar went on, "While I believe that

Karikala is currently in the grip of madness, I still hold out hope that he'll come to his senses as the moment draws nearer, and anything we can do to dissuade him from bringing destruction onto his people and his city, I will do."

With that, they were dismissed, each Primi Pili heading to his Legion area to alert their *immunes* to begin the process of preparation. The hope that these would be the only Romans endangered varied from one Centurion to the next, with some of them fervently calling on their household gods to make it so that their Legion would be called on to win glory. Neither Pullus nor Balbinus were one of them; as the two most veteran Legions of this group, they had watched their boys suffer enough, and as they all knew, this was the secondary goal for Caesar and his army. Reaching the Ganges and Palibothra was the true, and supposedly final prize for Caesar's army. Whether it would be enough for Caesar remained to be seen, but almost with every passing day, Pullus was becoming more convinced that this wouldn't be the case. First, however, was more destruction and death.

Senganan, Venkata, Rakesh, and Abikesh stood together on the walls, watching mostly in silence at the methodical, unhurried manner in which their enemies went about preparing for the destruction of their city and the slaughter of the people inside it, and in the most horrible way imaginable. When Karikala had refused Caesar, the city had been shut down as if it was under siege, but Senganan was convinced that it wouldn't last long. He had hoped that with the arrival of the rest of the Pandyans, which he counted to be around ten thousand, most of them infantry, and fifty more elephants, that this would convince his king that the threat was not only real, but one that was futile to resist. Karikala still claimed that his opposition would only be token, that after the Romans lobbed a few jars of that demon fire, he would capitulate, but Senganan didn't believe a word of it, and in whispered conversations, he learned that most, if not all, of what remained of the king's councilors held the same opinion. It was this group who, offering the reason they wanted to observe the preparations that had begun that very afternoon of the Pandyan arrival, were now both watching while talking in quiet tones. The only others now allowed on the walls were members of the royal guard, and they made sure not to be overheard, not wanting a man to report to Yogesh what they overheard.

"What do we do if our fear turns out to be true?" Venkata finally broached the subject.

Of course you'd be the one to ask the question, so you don't have to be the first one to answer, Senganan thought scornfully. That way, if we get out of this somehow, you can claim you were coerced by us. Whether Karikala would believe this there was no way to know, but at this moment, Senganan was certain enough to answer first.

"We must do whatever is necessary to protect the people of this city, and this kingdom," he said firmly.

"Yes, but what does that mean?" Venkata persisted, but before Senganan could reply, it was actually Rakesh, the youngest of these men whose father's position he had inherited just a year earlier, who came to Senganan's aid, asking disdainfully, "Why don't you tell us, Lord Venkata?"

"I was only asking a question!" Venkata replied, seemingly angry, but Senganan was sure he heard something else there, and while his tone was more polite, his response was no less pointed, "Yes, but that seems to be all you're doing. It's almost as if you want us to speak our minds first before you do. Not," Senganan assured him, completely unconvincingly, "that you would do anything like that."

It was the angry glare Venkata gave the other two that confirmed to Senganan they had been correct, but after a pause, and seeing that they were waiting for him to speak next, he muttered, "I think that we will have to step in and keep our King from making a horrible mistake."

"And, do you think Yogesh will just stand there and let it happen?"

This came from the fourth nobleman, Abikesh, and it reminded Senganan that, while Abikesh had participated in battle before, he had been a reluctant warrior.

It was, nevertheless, a valid question, which he answered without hesitation, "No, he won't. Which means that before we intervene with our King, we must neutralize Yogesh." At this, he turned to Venkata, "And you would be the logical choice to do that, Lord Venkata."

Venkata laughed, but it held no humor, admitting freely, "I wouldn't last more than five heartbeats before Yogesh cut me in two. You may not have seen him fight, but I have."

This was also true, but Senganan wouldn't be swayed.

"Then," he said quietly, "you must find another way. A more...subtle way."

At first, Venkata didn't understand, but then he gasped, "What do you mean? I *poison* him?"

"Unless you have a better idea," Rakesh countered, "then that seems to be the only alternative to trying to kill him outright."

Sensing he was outnumbered, Venkata was still reluctant, but said grudgingly, "I will investigate how to do this."

"You need to do more than investigate," Senganan snapped. "Unless Yogesh is out of the way, our chances of doing anything to Karikala are nonexistent."

"The question," Abikesh put in, "is at what point do we determine that our King is intent on allowing that pack of hyenas to burn Uraiyur down around us?"

This was something Senganan had thought about, so his answer came readily, "He said that once the Romans had set two or three buildings ablaze that he would send one of us out to capitulate." While he was determined on his course, he was still reluctant about it, and he finished quietly, "I believe we owe our King that much."

After a few heartbeats, heads began to shake in agreement, but it was Rakesh who said something that, later, Senganan would have cause to remember.

"At least the King has ordered barrels of water to be placed in every street so that we can minimize the damage."

Again, this was met with agreement, but it was one based in ignorance of the substance that would be used to ignite those fires, something they would be learning sooner rather than later.

Despite Caesar's promise that the Romans wouldn't be involved, Pullus and the other Primi Pili gave the order to don armor, although they were allowed to keep their helmets off, and were allowed to remain in their area if they chose, waiting for the call to assemble. Once again, most men chose to make their way to the rampart, or to a spot in the camp where the top of Uraiyur's walls were visible. The Primi Pili were with Caesar, who was also on the rampart of their camp, albeit with the best viewing spot, and the Romans watched as King Nedunj arrayed his troops, dividing them equally to cover the three gates that were suitable for a sally by Chola troops. The fourth gate was located barely a furlong from the river, which was lined with a series of small piers, while the boats moored there were all small, the largest being about the size of the Liburnian that had transported Pollio. This ship had been joined by three others of the same type, effectively blocking the river downstream, but this was a minor precaution in the event that the king actually tried to flee by the only means left to him. Nedunj had Darpashata prepared, but the elephant was kept separate from the other animals and behind the formation of Pandyans outside the eastern gate, while Nedunj made a tour of the positions on horseback. Pullus wasn't alone in thinking it strange that Caesar was content to leave this to Nedunj by remaining in the camp, but he didn't comment on it, nor did the other Primi Pili. Stopping before each formation, they weren't in position to see the western side, and only had a partial view of the southern, but they could hear the roaring of the Pandyan warriors drifting across the distance, then Nedunj came into view from around the southeast corner at the canter, where he stopped in front of the nearest group. They watched, barely able to hear his shouting, as he waved his sword over his head with one hand while pointing dramatically to the walls of Uraiyur, prompting another bellowing cheer that was much louder because of the distance as the Pandyans first thrust their spears into the air, then began beating them against their shields.

"He seems to give a good speech," Torquatus commented, and the other Centurions agreed, although Papernus muttered, "Now let's see if his boys can fight like he talks."

Nothing was said, yet while Pullus understood why Papernus was skeptical, his Legion hadn't borne the brunt of what the Pandyans could unleash, while he had, vividly remembering standing in knee deep water from an incoming tide because they couldn't fight their way off the beach, and it had been at the hands of the young king who, they learned later, had devised this tactic on his own, and even decapitated one of his father's noblemen who balked at implementing it. No, Pullus wasn't worried about Nedunj; this was going to come down to how much punishment Karikala was willing to let his people absorb.

Caesar had lent the Pandyans another group of Romans, both his personal *Cornicen* and from the 15th and 21st, each of them with one of the Pandyan groups, and they saw Nedunj turn to Caesar's *Cornicen*. A heartbeat later, a long, single note sounded, and then within a half-dozen heartbeats after that, the first of the *ballista* crews went through the elaborate but necessary process of placing a jar in the iron basket that the now-dead Greek Anaxagoras of Seleucia had created especially for flaming naphtha, lighting the rag, cut a uniform length, and releasing the pin. The instant the first crew successfully sent its smoking jar streaking through the sky, there was a chorus, seemingly equally divided between shouts of joy and howls of despair, yet one more sign that the men of the Legions had found something worth wagering about.

On the part of the rampart with Caesar, there was a similar if smaller scene, as it was Balbinus who whooped with delight, and while Pullus didn't shout, he did groan as Balbinus hooted, "I *told* you my man Tullius would beat your boy Murena!"

"Go piss on your boots," Pullus grumbled, then reminded his friend, "and keep in mind this isn't the only wager we've got."

Because of their bickering, they both missed that, as expected, the first jar didn't clear the wall cleanly, shattering on one of the crenellations, but while they were too far away to hear the shrieks of the unfortunates who happened to be standing within range of the splattered flaming naphtha, they could plainly see three men begin streaking away from the center of the explosion, one of them clearly already blinded, colliding with a comrade a few paces away who wasn't able to dodge out of the way in time. There were other near misses before the first jar cleared the wall by a matter of three or four feet, leaving a smoking trail as the tumbling jar plunged out of sight. Less than an eyeblink later, a roiling column of flame thrust up above the wall, the sign that the jar had struck a taller building, and although it was the first, it was far from the last. With a ruthless efficiency, and just as Caesar had promised, tumbling pots of naphtha brought fire and destruction down onto the heads of people who were quaking in terror, huddled inside those buildings that they hoped could withstand the onslaught. Some of them would, but even those stone structures were vulnerable, not only because of the need for pitched roofs that were required because of the rainfall, but never in their wildest imaginings had these people conceived of the kind of catastrophe that was developing now. Inevitably, the pernicious substance struck some of those wooden roofs, but the situation was made worse when, following the instructions given to them by their King, teams of men dipped smaller buckets into the larger barrels, then tossed the water onto the spots on fire, whereupon they learned what their Roman foes had discovered, also the hard way, that water didn't extinguish the flames but spread them. By the time a third of a Roman watch had passed, most of Uraiyur was wreathed in smoke, both gray and black, while the ramparts had been almost completely abandoned, leaving Caesar and his army to watch and wait.

"Your Highness, the Temple of Murugan is on fire, and the priests tell me they don't think they can save it! There were people who fled to it when those demons began their attack, and some of them are trapped," Venkata reported, still breathless from rushing into the throne room.

Karikala, seated once again on his throne, was whispering something to Yogesh, but it was impossible for Senganan to hear even the topic they were discussing. With the appearance of the Pandyan forces arrayed around the city, the king had ordered that every man of his royal bodyguard, and the remaining infantrymen and archers all prepare for battle, sending a separate order to prepare Ananda and the other elephants. He didn't respond until he was finished with the bodyguard, who bowed then hurried out of the throne room, leaving Senganan to give Venkata a glare that he hoped communicated his displeasure that his counterpart hadn't done anything to eliminate the man, but all he received was a helpless shrug.

Karikala, now that Yogesh was gone, finally replied, "Temples can be rebuilt, Venkata."

"But, Your Highness, Murugan is the god of war!" Venkata replied, sounding desperate, "Couldn't that be a sign from the god?"

"It could be," Karikala seemingly agreed, but Senganan's stomach clenched when he said, "but it also could be that the god is angry with me that I didn't act sooner and send out my army to crush these insects!"

This was the moment that Senganan knew what had to be done, and a glance at Rakesh and Abhishek informed him that they understood as well, but with Yogesh alive, it meant that even if they were successful in striking down their king, they were all likely to die. Senganan had been listening to the muttered conversations between the rankers of the royal bodyguard, and while it was only a few men he overheard, they all seemed to be of a like mind, that resistance to the Pandyans and their Roman allies would only bring destruction and ruin to all of them. Whether that meant that if Yogesh was eliminated, they wouldn't be disposed to exact vengeance for their king, or this was just normal soldiers' grumbling, would only become apparent after the deed.

It was the turn of Vimal, whose father had been the king's closest boyhood friend, and he pointed in the direction of the door, pleading, "Your Highness, listen. We can hear the screams of the people from your chamber, and the shutters of every window have been closed. And, this is only the beginning. These savages aren't going to stop; the Roman Caesar said as much." Senganan could see Vimal swallowing twice, as if the words had stuck in his throat, as he finished, "How many of your subjects will you allow to die a horrible death before you capitulate as you said you would?"

It had been some time since King Karikala had sat astride Ananda and ridden his elephant into battle himself, but Senganan was reminded that, by the time he had reached his dead son's age, he had already forged a reputation as a formidable warrior. In fact, the name he went by now wasn't the one he had been born with but had earned, and it commemorated a time he had singlehandedly slain an elephant with nothing more than his sword, despite being terribly burned on one leg. Even if Senganan had remembered, he couldn't have anticipated the speed with which Karikala leapt from his throne, crossed the three paces' distance between himself and Vimal while drawing a long, slightly curved dagger from the jeweled sheath tucked in his sash, and in one smooth movement, executed a horizontal slash across Vimal's throat. Blood sprayed in a fine mist from the gaping wound, spattering Karikala's bearded face and chest as the dying nobleman stood there, his heart beating its final few beats, eyes wide as his hands went to his throat in a vain attempt to stem the flow. Even if Rakesh, who was nearest to his fellow councilor had reacted instantly, he wouldn't have been in time to stop Vimal from collapsing to the polished stone floor, still clutching his throat, eyes wide in an expression that sent the message he was begging for help. Senganan's attention was so fixed on the prone body that he didn't really notice Karikala, without any haste, stepping backward to drop back down on his throne, but when he finally tore his gaze away to stare at his king, the first thing he noticed was that Karikala had made no attempt to wipe the blood from the bare skin of his face and upper chest, while his neatly trimmed black beard that now had streaks of silver that was normally carefully oiled, now gave off a scarlet sheen. Whether it was a coincidence, or the king had sent Yogesh to bring them, he entered the throne room with ten other bodyguards behind him, all of them with swords drawn, though they weren't holding them in readiness.

"Do any of you have anything you wish to add to Lord Vimal's plea?" Karikala asked, his pleasant, almost cordial tone a jarring juxtaposition to the scene of a corpse lying in a pool of blood, but it did have one effect; Senganan was now firmly convinced that Karikala, King of the Chola, had lost his mind. Outside the palace, Uraiyur burned, and it wouldn't be long before any decision was taken out of any of their hands, when the citizens of the city made their own choice between loyalty and survival.

Caesar Ascending – The Ganges

It began at the eastern gateway, when the twenty bodyguards, all of whom had retreated from the rampart to take refuge in the high arched stone gateway, were suddenly beset by a throng of panicked citizens, fleeing from the fire. In that unthinking way of a mob, there was an unspoken but collective decision that remaining trapped within the walls of their capital spelled their doom, preferring instead to take their chances with the Pandyan and Roman invaders now waiting outside. Armed only with their frenzy and desire to escape, even after the bodyguards chopped down dozens of them, by sheer weight of numbers and driven by panic, they were quickly overwhelmed, their bodies either torn asunder, or mercifully, stabbed with their own weapons. Throwing the locking bar aside, the gates were pushed open, and the people, many of them in various stages of undress, while others were clutching sacks of hurriedly gathered belongings, came pouring out of the city.

"Pluto's thorny cock! This is like Avaricum!"

The comparison came from Torquatus, though only because he beat Pullus to it, but he was watching Nedunj, still mounted and in front of his troops, which prompted him to comment, "Let's see if King Nedunj does what we did and rush in."

"He already is," Caesar replied, though his eyes also were on the Pandyan, pointing to Nedunj, once more waving his sword above his head, but then turning his mount and going to a trot, while his men, with a huge roar, began a headlong rush.

Heading towards each other as they were, the distance closed with an astonishing rapidity, and Pullus involuntarily winced as the two opposing forces collided, expecting to see the men of Pandya indiscriminately chopping down anyone in their path, whether they were man, woman, or child. However, while there was some of that, mostly what occurred reminded him of water flowing around a rock, as the majority of the people veered out of the path of the armed men, and before the count of one hundred, Pandyans were at the gate. There was a brief stoppage, but none of the Romans could tell whether it was because the narrower gateway was still clogged with fleeing Cholans, or there was some sort of organized resistance. What mattered was that, after another brief delay, they resumed their movement forward, the last ranks of the Pandyans disappearing into the city. Whereupon Pullus, and the other Primi Pili witnessed Caesar's mistake when, out of habit, he turned to address his personal *Cornicen*, intending to have the man sound the call for the artillery to cease their bombardment, only to realize that he had loaned him to Nedunj, although he immediately saw that Potitus, his *Cornicen,* had obeyed Caesar's instruction to stay put, and was standing where the elephants still waited. Too far away to shout, Pullus and his fellow Centurions were treated to the sight of their general frantically waving his arms in an attempt to get Potitus' attention. Fortunately for Nedunj and his column, Potitus happened to glance up only a few heartbeats after Caesar started, and immediately understood, playing the notes that signaled the *ballistae* crews to cease operation. It was out of their sight on the western side, but they learned later that there had been a mishap with one *ballista*, when a jar cracked open when it was being put into the basket. Thanks to the combination of the sleeves and the buckets of vinegar, the crewmen escaped with minor injuries, but the *ballista* was destroyed, prompting conversations around the fires about whether Caesar felt the loss of one of his beloved artillery pieces as much or more as he mourned the loss of one of them. Once the Cholan civilians were clear of the city, and after the Pandyans had disappeared, the collective panic began to subside, even as the Romans watched from their ramparts, and like any mob without a leader, suddenly, the people—Pullus guessed there were at least a thousand of them clustered together—seemed at a loss what to do next. Surprising no one, they didn't move in the direction of either the Roman camp or the new Pandyan camp, nor did they approach the Pandyan elephants, many of them starting to show signs of impatience with swishing tails and flapping ears, their *mahouts* performing their particular ritual that helped calm their animal. Finally, a lone man began walking north, in the direction of the river, then, first one by one, then in pairs, and finally in small groups, the crowd started moving in that general direction.

"I'm surprised none of them are attacking our boys manning the *ballistae*," Aquilinus commented, shading his eyes as he watched them shambling away.

This had never occurred to Pullus, but now he split his attention between the eastern wall and the mob. There were now several columns of smoke towering in the sky, the black smoke created by the naphtha slowly dissipating as the other flammable materials inside the city caught fire. For the next third of a watch, the Romans were nothing but spectators, discussing among themselves what was taking place inside the walls, and while it wasn't the first time, once again, Pullus realized he missed Spurius, because he was the only other Primus Pilus with whom he shared the unique experience of being inside a city where naphtha was a principal weapon. To this day, more than four years later, it still made him shudder to think of it, while his thoughts inevitably moved on to his men, and those of Spurius' 3rd who had been the first victims of what had become their most potent weapon and who had survived, all of them left behind in the twin cities of Ctesiphon and Seleucia, where they were joined the next year by similar victims from the siege of Susa, although they were blessedly fewer in number. He had often thought about it, wondering if it would have been better if all of the horribly scarred men had perished instead of living the rest of their days not only in pain, but horribly disfigured, which many Romans of the lower classes claimed was a sign that the afflicted was disfavored by the gods, or even being punished for some earlier sin. The next topic of conversation was about which gate Nedunj would either lead his men, or more likely, send a small force to, in order to open it for one of the other columns of their countrymen. This naturally engendered more wagering opportunities, although Papernus argued that not only was it more likely that the Pandyan king would open the gate nearest to him, which was the southern gate, but even if it wasn't, there would be no way to know since the other gate on the western side wasn't visible. It was in this manner that, for the first time in recent memory, the Legions of Rome were nothing more than spectators to a battle.

It was the change in the quality of the noise that alerted Senganan and the other noblemen who, when all was said and done, were being held prisoner in the throne room, that something important had happened, but when Senganan had tried to point this out to Karikala, the king wasn't interested. Before, the shouts and screams of the people had been a clear mixture of men and women, but while it was gradual, the background sound took an a more masculine quality. It also had become noticeably warmer in the throne room, while the smell of smoke continued to increase until Senganan realized that his eyes were watering. Even so, he couldn't seem to tear his gaze away from the congealed pool of blood, although Vimal's body had been unceremoniously dragged off and dumped somewhere out of sight. The most potent sign came when Yogesh whispered something to one of the other bodyguards, who hurried from the throne room, and Senganan wondered if the man had been sent to summon whatever remained of the bodyguard to return to the palace.

Whether his thoughts were obvious, or Karikala was a mind reader, for the first time since he had slain Vimal, the king said with a withering scorn, "Don't worry, Lord Senganan. Goutham has been sent to bring every available man to the palace. When the Pandyan hyenas try to skulk in, they will be cut down like stalks of grain."

It was impossible for Senganan to tell whether the king actually believed that they would be able to fight off an assault on the palace, or if he was just saying it because that was what a king should say.

Deciding to try a different approach, he asked quietly, "What about your wife and concubines, Your Highness? Have you made provisions for them?"

As befitted a king, Karikala currently had twenty women who served him in a variety of ways, but it had been his first wife, Divakar's mother, who the king had relied on for counsel over the years, and she had died two years earlier. His new wife was barely out of her teens, and Senganan had had enough contact with her to know that she wouldn't be filling that role for Karikala. All of them were on the second floor of the palace, while the various attendants and lower-ranking courtiers had fled, some of them the day the Romans had arrived, despite the fact they must have known that deserting their king was a death sentence. Not for the first time, Senganan found himself wishing that he had ordered Shanu to turn Karna to his estate to say goodbye, because at this moment, he was as certain as he could be that he would not live to see another sunset. Even during the course of this exchange, the smell of smoke had grown stronger, and now he could hear shrill, feminine voices upstairs, which was what had prompted his question.

"I have assured them that they will not fall into the hands of any of the vermin, whether they be Pandyan hyenas or those pale creatures," Karikala answered indifferently. "I have already sent Khal and Ojas to stay with them and make preparations."

Just as the smoke was growing thicker, despite all windows being shuttered and outer doors barred, the noise from outside was increasingly harder to ignore, and every man in the room, with the exception of Karikala, now had a weapon in hand. The king sat on his throne, but like the other fifteen men in the room, all eyes were on the entrance into the chamber that consisted of double doors, which were still open.

"Your Highness," Senganan approached Karikala, though he was careful to remain just out of reach if the king suddenly drew his sword in the same abrupt manner that he had slashed Vimal's throat. "I implore you..."

His plea was cut short by a tremendous noise, the sound echoing in the high-ceilinged entryway that Senganan instantly knew, as did the others, meant that there were men outside trying to batter their way in.

"Goutham has obviously failed to bring reinforcements in time," Karikala said, and if the circumstances had been different, he could have been making a comment about the weather or some other inconsequential subject.

What happened next occurred so quickly that none of the men involved had time to think, but it began when, with a splintering crack that was instantly drowned out by the sound of voices bellowing in triumph they all knew signaled that their enemy had battered down the outer doors, followed by clashing metal and almost at the same instant screams of agony, Yogesh, with his back to the throne shouted the order to close the doors to the throne room. It meant that the man the noblemen considered the biggest threat didn't see Venkata rushing across the few paces between them to plunge his blade into the bodyguard's back, the man letting out a gurgling moan as he collapsed to his knees. For less than a heartbeat, every other man was frozen in place by shock, but it was Karikala who recovered more quickly than anyone else.

Leaping to his feet, he pointed at Venkata, bellowing, "*Traitor! Naja! Kill him!*"

They were the last words Karikala, king of the Chola, once a feared warrior but now a man broken by grief and rage, was destined to speak. While Karikala had recovered his senses the quickest, Senganan was a shade behind him, and the king's focus on Venkata meant that the king didn't have time to draw his sword since he had unthinkingly pointed with his sword hand. Nevertheless, it was still dropping to the hilt when Senganan made a thrust of his own, driving the blade just under Karikala's breastbone, burying it to the handguard. Karikala tried to say something, his eyes fixed on Senganan in a stare that he knew would haunt him the rest of his days. It wasn't the accusation that he read in his king's dying gaze, but the hurt that prompted Senganan to use his free hand around Karikala's shoulders to guide him to the floor in a jarringly gentle manner given what he had just done, withdrawing his blade as he did so.

"I'm sorry, my King," Senganan whispered, "but this was the only way to save our people, and your living sons."

Senganan didn't know if Karikala heard him, but he doubted it. Only after he let the body fall the rest of the way to the floor did Senganan turn to face what he was certain would be enraged guards, but he immediately saw they had other concerns. They had arrayed themselves across the doorway in a double line, but even as Senganan turned to face in that direction, he saw that of the original ten, only seven were still standing, battling furiously with the Pandyans who were pressing with equal ferocity. It was the identity of one of the Pandyans, standing in the front line, using his sword and with a small round shield in his hand, shouting something that Senganan couldn't make out that prompted his action. Considering the noise, the sound of his sword clattering on the stone floor wasn't enough to be noticed, so he began shouting, in Tamil.

"*King Nedunj! King Nedunj!*"

It was something taught to young warriors from their very first lessons, that they shouldn't be distracted by something unusual shouted by an enemy combatant, because it was almost always a trick, so Nedunj's eyes never left his foe until, whether out of carelessness or from fatigue, his Cholan opponent dropped his own shield just enough for the Pandyan king's blade to shoot out in a hard thrust just above the top, taking the man high in the chest. Only then, as the man, who had been in the second line, collapsed atop his comrade that Nedunj had dispatched first, did the Pandyan king shift his gaze to where Senganan was standing, hands outstretched in a symbol of surrender. What helped his cause was that Venkata, Rakesh, Abhishek, and Deepak all copied Senganan, throwing their own weapons down. Another Cholan bodyguard of the remaining four was cut down before Nedunj, shouting at his men repeatedly, stopped the bloodshed. Uraiyur had fallen.

The Romans of Caesar's army who secretly held out hope that Caesar's order that his men wouldn't be allowed to partake in the sacking of Uraiyur would be rescinded had them dashed, but their unhappiness was a shade compared to the Pandyans who participated in the taking of the city. In a manner similar to the Legionaries in the aftermath of Abhiraka's attempt to retake Bharuch by igniting the stores of the naphtha that had proven so devastating, at least as many Pandyan warriors were tasked with putting out the fires that had started. Unlike their Roman allies, who had not anticipated that a desperate king would be willing to start a conflagration in his own city, Caesar had provided Nedunj with several barrels of vinegar. Relaying what they had learned from experience, the Pandyans used the vinegar only where there was the largest concentration of the flammable substance on a surface, identified by the different color of the flames and the smoke it produced. While this was true in itself, Caesar's real reason for passing this along was because of the finite nature of the supply of the only thing they had found that would extinguish burning naphtha. Even now, ships were making the laborious journey from Pattala, which because of its location, and the Greek influence on it, was the only part of India where the soil, temperature, and relatively dry climate was conducive to the growing of grapes. While it was Caesar's hope that advancing north, albeit a thousand miles east of Pattala, they would be able to replenish their supply of not just vinegar but wine, until he knew, he had ordered that all available amphorae be diverted to his army. However, once the fighting was over and the flames were quelled, with about a tenth part of the buildings in the city destroyed, including the temple devoted to one of the Hindu gods, Murugan, while another tenth were damaged to one extent or the other, the Pandyan king deployed his royal bodyguard to patrol the streets of Uraiyur, ensuring that his men didn't run wild and sate their lusts, whatever they may have been. It was a lesson Nedunj had learned from Caesar, when his Legions had refrained from any widespread mayhem in Muziris, although the circumstances were different, since Nedunj had the advantage of at the very least fighting the Romans to a bloody draw in their first encounter. Nevertheless, just as the Parthians, the Pattalans, and Queen Hyppolita, all kingdoms, Nedunj had noticed, unlike Rome, and to their collective bemusement, had witnessed either the ambivalence, or in the case of the Parthians under the short but brutal reign of Phraates, outright acceptance of their Roman occupiers. What Nedunj knew of Karikala as a ruler was that he had been firm, bordering on harsh, and had taken the more conventional route of expanding his kingdom by a series of wars early in his reign, subsuming smaller kingdoms, whereas Nedunj's father Puddapandyan had favored a subtler approach, the evidence being his own marriage to Aarunya, daughter of King Abhiraka of Bharuch. The truth was that, when Caesar had broached the topic of annexing Chola, his answer had been an impulsive one, brought on by a lifetime of conditioning that these were the mortal enemies of his people, and in the end, only one kingdom could prevail. Now that he was on the brink of success, the young king was grappling with the multilayered complexity of how to achieve a subjugation where the people being subjugated either didn't recognize it was happening or ensuring that their lot in life was actually improved, making them more amenable to the change.

As Caesar had pointed out, "It's almost always the members of the upper classes of any society who fight change," he had told Nedunj during one of their private dinners, which had turned into a weekly affair, and on this occasion, he had added with palpable bitterness, "and I include Rome in that. I spent several years struggling with men of my own class who fought every change I tried to implement to help the people of the lower classes improve their circumstances."

Despite the fact that Nedunj was more amenable to new ideas because of his youth, and for his people, he would have been considered enlightened, this idea of pandering to the lower classes, since that was what he thought it was, bemused him. When he had expressed this to Caesar, before he answered, Caesar pointed towards an open window where, because the palace in Karoura was on a hill, they could see the permanent camp of the Legions beyond the city wall.

"My uncle, a man named Gaius Marius, changed the Legions," Caesar explained, "by opening enlistment to citizens who belonged to what we call the Urban tribes, meaning that they don't possess enough property to have a vote individually."

Puzzled, Nedunj asked, "You mean your poorest caste wasn't allowed to fight for Rome?"

"No," Caesar answered, remembering not to shake his head but nod it. "Before Rome grew, the only men who were allowed to serve in the Legion were men of property, and they were divided into four different lines." Realizing this wasn't the time to give the king a history lesson, he hurried on before Nedunj could press for an explanation of that, "But what matters is that now, for more than fifty years, the men of our poorest class have been allowed to enlist in the Legions, and it's a wise leader who listens to the people of the class who provides the men who will do the fighting for their country or kingdom." Nedunj considered, and while he had questions, he indicated he accepted the basic premise, and Caesar continued, "What matters to the people of the lowest class, anywhere, is," he held up a finger, "can they feed themselves and their family," another finger, "can they and their wives and children sleep at night in safety," and finally, a third, "and can they be secure in the knowledge that a member of their upper class won't arbitrarily take what's theirs, up to and including their lives and freedom?"

It was an ongoing process, but over time, King Nedunj began to comprehend the importance of these three points, albeit in a very basic manner. Most importantly, he did see how, from the perspective of the lower castes, what was important to them was their lot in life, and what they could expect each day to bring them. If they were able to earn enough to pay for their food, or if they farmed themselves, were allowed to keep enough for themselves to feed their families, and weren't constantly scanning the horizon, looking for galloping riders who would swoop in and take their property, or their lives, then who it was sitting at the top of their particular heap didn't really matter to them. It was only men of the noble class, men whose status depended on their ability to defend their holdings, usually given to them by their more powerful king, who cared about things like the fate of Pandya, or who their king was, and whose pride caused them to resist foreign incursions. If a man's life didn't change, or it actually improved, it made conquest easier, at least in a general sense. There were still aspects he wasn't sure he agreed with, but in a broad, nonspecific way, Nedunj had come to accept the wisdom of Caesar's approach, and this was what he was trying to emulate in his investment of Uraiyur. True, there was still the matter of the Northern Army, but on this, Caesar was firm.

"That is your problem to handle, Your Highness," he had said. "According to my information, the Northern Army is about a third smaller than King Karikala's part of the army at full strength, and we destroyed the Cholan army holding the island of Taprobane. And, as you said yourself, now that your men are more familiar with our methods, they didn't have any problem defeating the Cholans defending Uraiyur. I'll leave you with enough artillery to use them either for defending the walls of Uraiyur, or if you choose to take the fight to the north, you can transport them with you. You have enough men who my *immunes* trained, and I will leave you with a hundred cases of naphtha." For the first time, Caesar confessed, "I'm afraid that we may have exhausted the supply with our last shipment, so that hundred cases is a tenth of the total supply. And," he admitted, "I don't know if we'd have enough even if we didn't leave you with any."

This didn't make Nedunj happy, but he didn't feel he was in a position to argue the point. On another matter, however, he felt obligated to resist Caesar's pressure to show clemency to the surviving councilors to Karikala, particularly Senganan.

"He slew his King. That means he can't be trusted."

Although it was Lord Maran who uttered the words, he was merely echoing his own king's sentiment. However, at the moment, he was content to let Maran fight this battle with Caesar, resolving to add his voice only if necessary.

"That," Caesar agreed, "is true, Lord Maran. But doesn't the reason *why* he did so matter? He saved not only his people more suffering, but Karikala was willing to fight to the last man, and while there was no doubt of the outcome, you would have suffered more losses than you did."

"So he says," Maran replied, unmoved. "It is just as likely that he thought to seize the throne for himself."

"When your king was battering down the doors of his palace?" Caesar asked, clearly amused, and even with Maran's dark coloring, Nedunj saw that he was embarrassed, but he was also unwilling to yield.

"We do not know what his plans were," Maran insisted stubbornly. "He was disloyal to his king, so perhaps he thought that you would place him on the throne in exchange for killing Karikala."

The atmosphere unmistakably changed in the *praetorium*, which Nedunj deduced was a strategic choice by Caesar, who now stared at Maran coldly, while there was a subtle shift in posture by the other men attending, with the room evenly dividing between Pandyan and Roman, as if they were prepared for some sort of physical confrontation. Caesar held Maran in his gaze, his blue eyes somehow more noticeable, which Nedunj had observed before and wondered if there was some internal change when the Roman was angered that physically altered the shade. When he spoke, however, his tone was even, although those who knew him well, like Pullus, would have warned Nedunj that this was Caesar at his most dangerous, if he had been disposed to do so.

"Lord Maran, is there anything that I said I would do in relation to your king and his kingdom that I haven't done, or anything that I didn't mention that I have done that could be construed as against your interests?"

For the first time, Maran's eyes went to Nedunj, but while Nedunj didn't speak, he did give him a barely perceptible nod of his head, which Maran interpreted correctly.

"No, Caesar," he admitted, triggering a palpable release of tension in the room, "you have done neither of those things. You have upheld your word in every way."

"So, when I tell you that I have no ulterior motive with Lord Senganan, or any ambitions to back him as a contender to sit on the Cholan throne, that is what I mean," Caesar said flatly.

This prompted Maran to take his seat, but true to his normally contrary nature, Sundara, who had been the most troublesome Pandyan noble, both when he had been with Maran after the death of their king, and with Nedunj, decided to speak up.

"He is a Cholan," he said emphatically, "which means that he is a serpent who cannot be trusted. And," his tone became that of a man who is convinced he has produced a winning argument, "a man who cannot be trusted cannot be allowed to live!"

"Lord Senganan lives."

If it had been Caesar who spoke, it was practically ensured that he would have continued to argue, but this had come from Nedunj, who, sensing that Caesar's interest in this Cholan nobleman was for a reason, decided to trust the Roman's judgment. Consequently, Sundara was left standing, his mouth opening, then closing before he sat down without saying anything else.

Nedunj wasn't through, and what he said next was as much of a test of Caesar's resolve than any real driving desire on his part, but he tried to sound firm as he continued, "However, the same does not apply for the others. They must die."

For a moment, he thought he might have miscalculated, because Caesar's eyes narrowed and his lips thinned in a sign

Caesar Ascending – The Ganges

that Nedunj had learned meant that he was not pleased, and the pair engaged in a silent battle of wills where their eyes were locked, while everyone else forgot their temporary relaxation, watching the pair intently.

Finally, after a long silence, Caesar answered tonelessly, "Very well, Your Highness. It will be as you desire."

There was some obvious consternation on the part of the Roman contingent in the room, none of them particularly caring for a young barbarian king seemingly dictating terms to the most powerful man in their world who also happened to be Roman like them, but Caesar quelled them with a glance in their direction that they correctly interpreted. After this, there wasn't much disagreement on some of the details, and all that was left was Caesar's announcement.

"My army will be departing in two days," he began. Since Nedunj had been forewarned, there was no surprise at this, but then he continued, "We'll rejoin the rest of the army who have been encamped on the coast, and once we're reunited, that's when we resume our movement north."

At first, Nedunj believed he had misheard, asking in puzzlement, "Do you mean you are going to reunite with the ships that will be taking your part of the army to join with Legate Pollio's part that already sailed north and should be waiting near Chennai?"

"No," Caesar replied. "They're still where Pollio left them when he came upriver, Your Highness."

"But you told King Karikala that you were sending them to be in position near the Chola Northern Army." He frowned, and in a manner that suggested he was beginning to get an idea of what he might hear next, which was confirmed when Caesar said simply, "I lied to King Karikala."

"And you did not tell me!" Nedunj exclaimed, showing his first signs of agitation.

Caesar, in contrast, maintained the same demeanor, affirming emotionlessly, "No, I didn't."

"Would you care to give me a reason?" Nedunj retorted, then added, "Perhaps it slipped your mind?"

Inwardly, Pullus was torn between amusement at seeing this young Pandyan, who he actually had come to respect, if only because of how his wife Aarunya clearly loved him, and wincing at what was in essence the hubris of anyone challenging Caesar's memory.

Nor was he surprised to see this clearly irritated Caesar, who snapped, "I can assure you that it didn't slip my mind, Your Highness."

"Then, why?" Nedunj challenged.

"Because I had already decided that I had no intention of wasting the lives of my men unnecessarily on what wasn't a primary goal, Your Highness."

"But it was *your* idea that Pandya annex Chola!"

"It was," Caesar agreed, "but it was never my intention to subdue and subjugate your enemy for you, Your Highness." In a slightly softer tone, he said, "I presented you with an opportunity because I knew that you would take advantage of it, King Nedunj. That's all that I did."

Suddenly, Nedunj felt a bit foolish, not as much for being used but for not seeing Caesar's ploy for what it was, yet despite not caring for the manner in which the older Roman had essentially manipulated him down a path that met Caesar's goals, in that moment, he decided that, after all, he had achieved what neither his father nor his grandfather had been able to do, conquer their lifelong enemy.

"I...understand, Caesar," Nedunj said finally, "...in every sense."

"Do you think Nedunj is going to kill Karikala's other two sons?"

Pullus' only reason for hesitation to Porcinus' query was to swallow his food, then answered confidently, "He'd be a fool not to."

Although Porcinus understood that this was how such things went, he didn't like it; neither did Pullus nor Scribonius. Not even Balbus cared for the idea of killing children, for any reason, but he was more indifferent about it than having any moral qualms.

It was with this in mind that Porcinus asked a question that the others at the table would have cause to remember a few years later, "Do you think someone would do that to Caesar's boy Caesarion?"

However, in that moment, this was quickly dismissed by Pullus.

"Not as long as Cleopatra draws breath," he answered, then added, "or Caesar for that matter. Anyone who touches that boy isn't long for this world."

It was Scribonius who asked curiously, "Why are you asking this about Caesarion?"

Porcinus hesitated, but since it was so rare that he had anything to contribute during their meals together that was more than gossip but not quite serious conversation, he decided to roll his dice.

"When I was in the *Quaestorium* today with Dentatus getting him a new pair of *caligae*, while we were waiting, I overheard that Tribune, Rufus, I believe?" Pullus nodded. "He was talking to that Parthian Bodroges, and he was saying that he thinks that at some point in the future, Gaius Octavius is going to cause Caesar trouble, and that he's going to eliminate anyone who has a closer tie to Caesar than he does."

"Trouble?" Pullus asked, clearly skeptical. With a shake of his head, he said dismissively, "Octavius worships Caesar, and the gods know that Caesar thinks highly of the boy..."

"He's twenty-two or twenty-three now, Titus," Scribonius pointed out.

"So?" Pullus countered. "He's still green as grass."

"According to what I heard from Apollodorus," Diocles spoke up, "Caesar was very impressed with what he did at Ecbatana."

For the first time, Pullus displayed a bit less certainty, which was explained when he admitted, "Actually, Papernus told me the same thing. He said he was skeptical about...him," he omitted "boy," "but he and Figulus of the 14th are good friends, and he said that Figulus told him that while it didn't last all that long, it was a brutally tough campaign, and that when it was time for them to take the walls, Octavian led the way." Although he viewed Porcinus' information more seriously, he still was unconcerned. "Still, I don't see him having the iron in his soul and the balls he would need to do something like that. Besides," he finished, "how old is Caesarion now? Six? Seven?

No," he shook his head, "I think that Rufus is trying to cause trouble for Octavian. I don't know what happened, but I know that there's some sort of bad blood between them that led him to request to come with us when we left Parthia."

Considering this settled, they moved on to the next topic, the coming march. It wasn't going to take more than three days to get to the coast, where the fleet and the rest of the army would be waiting, but what was still an open question was exactly how long they'd be stuck aboard a ship to get to Palibothra. Not surprisingly, the wagering was quite spirited.

Although most of the innovations and new ideas that were developed, either by Caesar himself or at his direction, and going all the way back to the use of the sharpened lead missiles that proved so devastating to the *cataphractoi* of Parthia, not everything was a success. However, at the top of the list of failures that, as Caesar suspected, was a source of secret amusement by his men, rankers and officers alike, was his attempt to safely transport elephants by sea. Although it was bumpy, the winter spent in Muziris by the 5th and the other Legions, teaching them to fight with elephants instead of against them, had been largely successful, both Romans and beasts forming a sometimes uneasy alliance, where rather than the lightly armored Pandyan archers riding in the *howdahs*, there were three Legionaries who had been specially trained in how to fight in the manner that was unique to those men who tried to kill each other from the back of an elephant. The *mahouts* for the animals that were selected with Pandyan input had been taught rudimentary Latin, while the Romans had learned about the same amount of Tamil.

Shortly before the campaign began in earnest, Caesar had been quite optimistic about the prospect of making elephants just another in a long line of weapons and tactics that may have originated with other nations, but that the Romans had adopted as their own and, if not perfected, had at the very least dramatically improved. Then, with six weeks to go before the beginning of the campaign, and after testing them extensively on the Periyar River where Muziris was located, the specially designed transports to carry the elephants were rowed downriver to the real mouth and out into the sea. By this point, the Romans had learned, first from the Pandyans then by witnessing it themselves, that elephants could swim, and surprisingly well, and either on their own in the wild, or when allowed by their handlers, they did so quite often. More importantly, at least from Caesar's perspective, was that the animals could actually swim great distances. On the sea, however, even when within sight of land, the rocking motion of the ships caused by the waves so agitated the animals that the first attempt was a disaster when, of the first five animals out of the total of fifty that Nedunj had agreed to loan to Caesar, they unanimously and very quickly abandoned their craft. Despite their design that maximized stability over speed, every ship capsized, and in the process, several members of the sixty-man crews, all slaves, who rowed in a double tier with thirty on each side, drowned. Because of their proximity to the coast, no elephants were lost, all of them swimming ashore, whereupon Volusenus, who had been given the task of acclimating the animals to seaborne voyage by Caesar, made several more attempts.

Different animals were tried, the idea being that, like humans, some would be more conducive to what was an admittedly foreign environment for the creatures, but with a single-minded unanimity, every single time, the result was ultimately the same, the only difference being that the crews were more prepared, and a *bireme* was there to rescue them should it be needed. In the process, however, the elephants had become quite accustomed to riding in the high-sided, wide, and slow transport, as long as it was on a river. The final result was that Caesar, very reluctantly, had abandoned the idea, but when faced with the prospect of an overland route north to the Ganges that would accommodate the elephants, he was unwilling to do so. Like his failure with them, the reason he abandoned the idea of using elephants was never discussed openly; of course, this didn't mean that men of all ranks didn't speculate about why Caesar seemed so intent on a primarily seaborne route, but those who suspected that the reluctance stemmed from his belief that his army would rebel again, as they had at Bharuch, were correct. As much as the men, which was still primarily composed of Romans, although a full quarter of the Legions who had been with Caesar from the beginning were now non-Romans, loathed the idea of being aboard a ship for any length of time, now that they had also tasted what a forced march was like in this land and climate, especially in the southern part of India, they almost unanimously chose being aboard ship as the lesser of two evils; provided, of course, that they landed at regular intervals. That this was so was also due to another fundamental change, as the crews of Caesar's fleet were no longer Legionaries as they had been when they departed Parthia. Now, the crews were composed of an almost equal mix of slaves and freedmen who were paid what every ship master on Our Sea would have balked at as exorbitant, because Pollio's time on Taprobane had been profitable in other ways. Given its location, Taprobane was one of the busiest ports in that part of the world, serving as it did as a transshipping point between East and West for those who didn't use the overland Silk Road. What all of this meant was that Caesar had been forced to abandon his dream of elephants, judging that by insisting on keeping them as part of his army, he ran the risk of the men rebelling at the idea of marching what his best information told him would be a thousand-mile journey just to reach the Ganges.

In something of a jest, the night before they had departed Muziris, Caesar had informed Nedunj, "Feel free to use the elephant transports as you see fit, Your Highness."

Because their relationship had developed to a degree that Nedunj felt free to do so, he had given the older man a cheerful smile as he reminded him, "I told you that it would not work, Caesar."

Despite Caesar generally not appreciating being reminded of his failures, by this point, he saw the humor of the whole experiment, and while he laughed, it was a rueful one. What he didn't know, and wouldn't learn for some time to come, was that when Nedunj had seen how his animals had adapted well enough as long as it was on a river, he began envisioning all manner of things that might be possible. And, as he stood on the ramparts of his newly acquired city of Uraiyur, watching as the massive Roman army marched east, following the river, his mind was already busy. Once he finished subduing the Cholans, and after enough time passed for his new subjects to learn that, not only were their lives not changing, but would be improved, the possibilities were endless.

The choice Caesar had offered Senganan was a simple one, although it didn't make the decision any easier.

"If you stay behind, you will probably be dead before the new moon," Caesar had told him bluntly.

"But I was told by King Nedunj that I was to be spared because..." Senganan didn't finish because, whether it had been necessary or not, he had committed regicide, but there was no need, Caesar understanding perfectly.

Sparing Senganan, he replied, "And I believe King Nedunj is sincere...but not Lord Maran, or Lord Sundara. And," Caesar pointed out, "if they did go against their king's wishes, does King Nedunj strike you as the kind who would execute a subordinate for disobeying orders in this matter?"

"No," Senganan agreed, somewhat reluctantly. "But that is what Karikala would have done."

Caesar noted the bitterness in Senganan's voice, but he didn't mention it, choosing instead to emphasize, "Which is why I believe that King Nedunj is the right man to lead both Pandya and Chola."

"He may be," Senganan agreed again, again reluctant to admit as much. "But he still has a very large task facing him. While Lord Kavirathan, Karikala's brother isn't as formidable a warrior and commander as his brother was, and the Northern Army is smaller than what our forces were before Prince Divakar's failed ambush, he is also much loved by our people." Despite the circumstances, Senganan still felt a twinge of guilt as he explained, "There are many people, of all castes, who believed that the wrong brother was king."

"I have heard as much," Caesar replied, surprising Senganan, wondering how the Roman had learned this. "But I also have confidence in King Nedunj's ability to defeat Lord Kavirathan and what remains of Chola's army, should he decide to fight and not do the sensible thing...as you did." Senganan felt the heat come to his face, as once more his head warred with his heart, but he said nothing, which prompted Caesar to continue, "The reasons I wish you to accompany us, at least for the rest of this campaign, are twofold, but before I reveal them, I have a question." When Senganan indicated he should go ahead, Caesar asked, "How much experience do you have with the kingdoms to your north, especially those that are on the eastern coast of India?"

"I have some," Senganan replied cautiously. Then, for reasons he couldn't articulate, he expanded, "I have been on two embassies to meet with King Satakarni, second of his name, who is the king of the people we call the Andhra."

"I've heard of him," Caesar nodded, forgetting the convention for a moment. "King Nedunj said that, next to the Chola, the Andhra are the biggest threat to Pandya."

"My king said essentially the same thing," Senganan admitted with a slight smile.

"But you've met with this king?" Caesar pressed.

"As I said," Senganan answered stiffly. "I have met the king on two occasions."

"Forgive me." Caesar held up a hand. "I just wanted to be precise since it's not unknown that when an embassy from a potentially hostile nation is sent, the leader of that nation will have someone else meet with them to send a message of its own."

That, Senganan immediately understood, was true. Mollified, he assured Caesar, "Of course, you are correct, Caesar. But, while Satakarni has done that with our emissaries before, I was not treated so discourteously."

"Which means that you would be the perfect person to represent me in my status as Dictator for Life, which authorizes me to speak in the name of Rome."

Senganan noticed that Caesar said this as if it was the most natural thing in the world, and, Senganan suspected, as if his acceptance was a foregone conclusion.

"Why would I do that?" Senganan asked, his tone suddenly cold. "You and your army have enabled our lifelong enemy to establish a hold over the lower half of our kingdom. And," he was certain that Caesar thought that he was ignorant about Senganan's recognition of the reality of the situation, "you Romans conquered the island you call Taprobane that has been claimed by our kingdom for more than twenty years, which had always been your intention, no matter what you told King Karikala."

Since Senganan's acquaintance with Caesar was relatively short, he didn't recognize the bare flicker of the Roman's gaze that his surmise that Caesar was unaware of Senganan's insight had been correct, but there was no other discernible change in his demeanor.

"The reason," Caesar replied without hesitation, "is that you have already demonstrated that your concern is for the people of your kingdom, Lord Senganan. This Satakarni undoubtedly knows of our presence here in Chola territory by now, and I've received reports from my Legate who remained in Bharuch that the Andhra tested our defenses a month ago by marching west to the headwaters of the Narmada and followed it downstream, attacking from the east. They were repulsed, with a great loss, particularly of their elephants, and I don't have to explain why, do I?" Senganan nodded, albeit reluctantly, and Caesar continued, "In my estimation, it's extremely likely that once Satakarni becomes aware of the...change," he put it diplomatically, something Senganan did appreciate, "...that it's likely he's going to make a similar attempt with your kingdom. Would you agree with that?"

"Yes," Senganan answered tersely. "I believe that is an accurate assessment."

"While I have every confidence that King Nedunj will be able to repulse the Andhra should they penetrate deeply enough into your lands to reach Uraiyur, that will undoubtedly cause a great deal of trouble, would it not?" When Senganan shook his head again, Caesar slightly changed his approach, seemingly asking out of nowhere, "What's Satakarni like? Is he an aggressive king? Cautious?"

Senganan considered a moment before replying, "I would call him opportunistic, Caesar. He is not as aggressive as his father, also named Satakarni, was, but he does not hesitate to take advantage of a situation if he believes that it will profit him and his kingdom."

"So, you would say he's reasonable."

"Yes," now he turned cautious, thinking he was getting a

glimmer of where Caesar was going, "he is reasonable."

Caesar didn't hesitate.

"That's one reason I am asking you to accompany us, Lord Senganan. While I have Pandyans who will represent the king's interests, I also want to have someone who can speak about Chola, and the current situation. And," he emphasized, "someone who has witnessed what Rome can do if it so chooses."

Senganan thought for a moment, but rather than answer, he asked, "What is this second reason?"

"The second reason is because I'm taking Karikala's two sons with me, and I think they would benefit from having a familiar face with them, someone they can rely on," Caesar offered.

"And how long are the princes going to be in your...care?"

Just as Caesar had, Senganan chose a more tactful word than "hostage."

"That," Caesar replied in what seemed to be an offhand manner, "remains to be seen."

This was when it hit Senganan what Caesar was trying to accomplish, and it was a struggle to maintain his demeanor when he asked, "How much time do I have to decide this, Caesar?"

"Unfortunately, not much," Caesar sounded regretful, or at least tried to. "We're leaving shortly after dawn tomorrow."

Deciding to trust his instincts, Senganan said, "Given my situation here, and I believe you are correct that one of King Nedunj's councilors will try to have me killed, if only," he smiled without humor, "because that is what I would do if my king was similarly merciful with a Pandyan, I have only one question." He paused, then asked, "How long would you desire my company?"

Caesar chuckled at Senganan's characterization.

"For the time it takes us to reach the mouth of the Ganges," Caesar answered. "And then, I will make one of my smaller ships that we call a Liburnian at your disposal to bring you back here. Or," he shrugged, "wherever you desire."

"And when this happens, will the princes come with me as well?"

Something seemed to shift behind Caesar's eyes, but there was no discernible change in tone in his voice.

"Perhaps," he answered. "It depends on many things."

Deciding against pressing the Roman, Senganan rose and excused himself, and as he exited the large room of the *praetorium* that served as Caesar's quarters, they would never know that their minds were running on parallel tracks. For Senganan, it was the realization that Caesar's purpose in keeping both princes hostage had as much to do with Nedunj as it did with the Chola, while for Caesar, it was wondering if the Cholan nobleman had discerned that he was taking precautions in the event, that he considered unlikely, that Nedunj would entertain ideas of his own by either cutting off or seizing Taprobane, on the pretext that it had been part of the Chola kingdom.

For Barhinder, the excitement of leaving Uraiyur was tempered by the pain he was still suffering from his wound, but no matter how often both Diocles and Master Titus assured him that they didn't expect him to perform his regular duties, he still felt quite guilty. Yes, his arm was still in a sling, although he was now able to move the limb, though not quite fully straight, and yes, it was so painful that the first time he tried, he passed out briefly, but he felt as if he was shirking, nonetheless.

"If all the boys in my Century were like Gotra, I wouldn't have a *cac* detail," Balbus had commented, to both laughter and agreement by Pullus and Scribonius.

"He is eager," Pullus agreed, eyeing the boy, who was oblivious to the scrutiny because he was busy varnishing Pullus' *baltea*, albeit with just one hand, and because Barhinder was unaware, he missed the fond smile that Pullus gave him.

"I'm just surprised that he's sober," Scribonius observed dryly, which drew another laugh, but this time, Barhinder heard and looked over his shoulder.

"Get back to work, boy," Pullus growled. "Just because you saved my life doesn't mean you can fuck about."

Barhinder grinned and turned back to his task. While Scribonius' jest was humorous, it was also accurate. When the men of the Equestrians learned of Barhinder's role in saving their Primus Pilus, he had been the toast of the Legion, and had been plied with *sura* that, according to Caesar's orders, wasn't supposed to be available in camp, a rule that was completely ignored, not only by the Centurions, but by Caesar himself. As Pullus and the other Primi Pili understood, Caesar's order was a warning to keep the men in hand, not that they weren't allowed to imbibe at all, and they had largely been successful in this, with one notable exception. A few days after suffering his wound, Pullus had been roused in the night by Diocles, who had been awakened himself by someone from the *praetorium*; it was the identity of the messenger that got Pullus up and out of his tent with a haste only slightly slower than if the camp was under attack.

"Caesar said to come and retrieve young Gotra," Apollodorus said, clearly irritated at being up at that time of night, or perhaps because he had been unable to get to sleep in the first place.

Initially alarmed, Pullus gasped, "Why? What is he doing?"

"He's singing," Caesar's secretary said sourly, "and loudly. And," he was speaking to Pullus' back, calling out, "not very well either. It woke Caesar up!"

He hadn't gone to an all-out sprint, although it was close, but when he arrived, Caesar was standing in the entrance to the *praetorium*, arms folded and watching as Barhinder, completely ignorant to the fact that he was being watched by the commanding general himself since his back was turned, was singing as he gazed up at the moon.

Unlike Apollodorus, Caesar was mostly amused, though Pullus heard the edge in his voice as he said, "Pullus, I believe I've found something that belongs to you."

"Er, yes, sir," Pullus mumbled, but he stopped to stand by Caesar for a moment to explain, "I apologize for this, Caesar, but the lad has been invited to tell his story by my boys the last few nights. I think he was Macula and his boys in the Fifth's guest tonight."

"Well," Caesar said, "I can't say that it's undeserved, but enough is enough. Take him with you, Pullus."

"Yes, sir." Pullus began walking away, and Caesar called

out, "And tell him that he's not meant to be a singer."

"Yes, Caesar," Pullus answered, making sure that his grin was gone when he reached Barhinder.

He remembered not to grab the youth or treat him roughly, but he did tap him with his *vitus*, startling the youth, who let out a surprised squawk, then in turning around, tripped over himself and landed on the ground with enough of an impact that it made Pullus wince, worried that Barhinder might have reinjured himself. This seemed to be confirmed when Barhinder let out what sounded like a moan, but when Pullus squatted down, he determined that it was in fact snoring.

"Pluto's cock," Pullus muttered, then with no more effort than if he was hefting a shield, scooped the boy up, slung him over his shoulder, and carried him back to his quarters.

Not surprisingly, the story of Barhinder Gotra's nocturnal serenade to their general flashed through the camp, so that for the next several days, whenever any ranker, from any Legion, saw Barhinder, they'd call out, "Sing for us, Barhinder! Sing us the song you sang for Caesar!"

For his part, at first Barhinder was mortified, and indeed sat in the Legion office the entire next day, nursing a headache and waiting for what he viewed as his inevitable summons and dismissal from the army, which Pullus did nothing to dispel, understanding that this would be a lesson in itself. Finally, in the late afternoon when he could take it no more, he asked permission to speak to Pullus, who was stretched out on his cot, reading a scroll by lamplight because the sides were lowered at that moment since it was raining.

"Master Titus," Barhinder tried to keep his voice steady, but he clearly heard the quaver, "will Caesar have me flogged with the scourge before I'm dismissed?"

It was a struggle for Pullus to maintain a sober demeanor, but he pretended to consider it before saying solemnly, "I don't know, but it's possible." The instant the words were out, he regretted it, because the youth's knees collapsed, and Pullus sat up, saying quickly, "No, Barhinder. You're not going to be striped, not with the scourge and not without it. And no, you're not going to be dismissed from the Legion. But," for the first time, Pullus allowed himself to smile, "you *are* going to be asked to sing every day, probably many times a day. At least," he finished with a laugh, "until someone else does something that tops that."

Barhinder refrained from rushing across the room to embrace Pullus, knowing that it was not only unseemly, but Master Titus would probably smack him.

Now, standing in the predawn darkness watching the last-moment frenzy of activity that he had learned was normal for an army of this size when they were departing, he felt odd not having anything to do, but Diocles had been strict about him refraining from any activity that might harm his recovery. Even more unusually, he had been relegated to the status of passenger on the wagon belonging to Master Titus, although in his efforts to minimize the baggage train, Caesar had deemed that, whereas the Pili Priores normally had a wagon for themselves, and the Primus Pilus had his own wagon, all first-grade Centurions would share one. This had been met with some resistance on the part of some of the Primi Pili, Diocles had confided to him, but Master Titus hadn't been one of them, if only because he had never developed a taste for some of the small luxuries that made life more bearable. While Barhinder appreciated the gesture, he also resigned himself to being in the rear of a column that would stretch for more than a mile, and he was secretly proud of himself that, like the Legionaries of the drag Legion, he stretched out under the wagon to catch some sleep as they waited for their time to begin moving. The Pandyans who had marched with the Romans under King Nedunj were lined along the *Via Praetoria*, watching as their allies departed, leaving the odd sight of a camp where one half of it was still occupied with the shelters and tents arranged in what appeared to be a haphazard fashion to a Roman eye, while the other half was empty of tents, although the outlines were clear because of the trodden earth where each tent had been located, while the grid of streets were now churned mud, leaving black lines that might never fully disappear. King Nedunj, who was now occupying Karikala's palace, under heavy guard, left the city with his nobles to be present for the departure as well, with Nedunj riding Darpashata, although the elephant wasn't equipped for battle, but with what the Romans had learned was the ceremonial *howdah*, while his nobles were aboard their own elephants. Despite becoming accustomed to their presence, more than one ranker eyed the line of animals as they marched past, heading east on the road that would take them to the coast. Only those who knew him well could discern that Caesar was irritated at Nedunj's choice to bring his elephant, but none of them were aware that the cause for Caesar's ire was because he had pointedly requested that, if the king decided to see them off, that he do so astride an animal that didn't enable Nedunj to tower over Caesar. Fortunately, like his two-legged comrades, Toes had become accustomed to the smell and size of the animals, and stood patiently as Caesar sat with Nedunj as the vanguard of his army marched past.

"I will send a courier to inform you when we set sail," Caesar said, and because he refused to be seen by his men craning his neck up at the Pandyan king, he kept his eyes on his Legions as they marched past. "If all goes as planned, that will be about five days from now."

"Thank you, Caesar," Nedunj answered, copying the Roman by looking straight ahead. "And your plan is still to have Legate Hirtius and your cavalry remain on land?"

"Yes. And you're sending Lord Maran and the bulk of your army the day before we sail, correct?"

"That," Nedunj seemingly agreed, "is our plan."

Exercising his formidable self-control, Caesar didn't let the fact that his irritation now flared into anger show, recognizing that the Pandyan was being deliberately vague for a reason.

Forcing himself to use the same tone, he replied, "If there's a change in those plans, I trust that you'll send word to Hirtius? We're going to be conferring at the end of every day, and we have a signal system set up if he needs to alert me immediately."

He hadn't intended to divulge just how tightly coordinated the movement between his land-borne cavalry force and his fleet would be, which he had put in place because of the tenor of his last conversations with Nedunj. The Pandyan hadn't said anything overtly worrisome, but there was a nagging feeling that Nedunj had something in mind that wasn't part of their mutual plan, which was for the bulk of the Pandyan army to march north to confront Kavirathan and the Northern Army, although they wouldn't go on the offensive immediately. First there would be an attempt to reason with the Cholan commander, and while he hoped it wouldn't be necessary, Caesar was prepared to land enough of his army to both augment the Pandyan forces and, if this show of numerical superiority didn't work, conduct another demonstration with his precious supply of naphtha. Of all the myriad things that worried Caesar when it came to the logistical effort required to sustain his army of eleven Legions, ten thousand cavalry, and the five Cohorts of auxiliaries that were now exclusively composed of Parthians, Pattalans, and a Cohort with a mixture of Bharuch and Pandyan, it was his supply of naphtha that concerned him the most. As long as they would be facing elephants, the substance was the most crucial weapon in the Roman arsenal, as much from a morale standpoint as for its material value, so using even a few jars of the volatile substance to help an ally subdue the only force remaining that could challenge the Pandyan conquest of the Cholans was no mean thing.

Now that Caesar was beginning to have doubts about Nedunj's sincerity, he had to reconsider what he was willing to do to support the Pandyan effort. While it was important to his plans, Caesar had also developed a contingency for this moment should it arrive that wouldn't rely on the Pandyans to protect Taprobane in its role as the final link in the chain of supply bases that now stretched from the southern tip of India, all the way along the coastline back to the new port of Caesarea near the mouth of the Euphrates. Thanks in large part to his nephew Octavian, who still served as Praetor of Parthia Inferior after relocating to Susa, there was a series of outposts, small but self-sufficient, that enabled couriers to exchange mounts and riders and resupply, while offering the same for the supply wagons that plodded back and forth connecting Rome with what was now truly a world empire. Even with these improvements, there was a minimum of a two months' lag between Rome and its Dictator for Life, and it wasn't lost on Caesar that, over the span of the previous several months, the frequency of dispatches originating in Rome had steadily decreased. This was certainly worrisome to Caesar; as much as he trusted Marcus Antonius in terms of personal loyalty, when it came to the mundane but crucially important matters of administration, he could hardly be bothered when he knew that Caesar was a matter of weeks, if not months, away. Now that he was farther away than any Roman in their history had gone, he recognized that it was time to make a decision, although not the one his Legates, Primi Pili, Centurions, Optios, and rankers thought it should be, and that was to declare this extraordinary effort would officially over once they achieved his goal of reaching the Ganges and Palibothra.

Much to the surprise of Caesar's army, their march to the coast, where there was already an enlarged camp constructed by the Legions under Pollio's command, not only went without incident, but since it was still early in what the Romans had learned was called the monsoon season that was just beginning now in Junius, there wasn't the kind of daily downpour that would have slowed the progress of the baggage train once the already moist ground had been churned into ankle-deep mud that normally bogged down several wagons a day. It was a reunion of sorts, as their comrades lined the *Via Praetoria*, calling out to men in the arriving Legions they knew, taunting them with stories of all the wealth they had looted from the defeated Chola on Taprobane, while the men under Caesar boasted about slaying elephants whose armor was plated with gold, all of which were lies. As expected, Caesar wasted no time, the boarding process beginning the next day, with each Legion returning to the ships on which they had arrived from Parthia, then sailed from Bharuch to Muziris when possible. Following Caesar's orders, Pollio had established his camp within sight of the walls of the small but important city of Puhar, which straddled the river and served as the primary trade port for the Chola Empire, which had already been invested by a thousand Pandyan troops sent by Nedunj immediately after the fall of Uraiyur. Most importantly, and again by Caesar's order, Pollio had established a strict enforcement prohibiting the men from entering the city, which was naturally the source of much complaining, though not just from the rankers, since he had extended it to all officers, even of Tribune rank. Pollio himself had entered the city, with Volusenus accompanying him, for the purpose of inspecting the docks, but it was quickly determined that they were insufficient for the purpose in terms of the speed with which the army could embark. Consequently, parties had been dispatched to an old-growth forest a mile south and two miles inland, where enough trees were felled to construct three separate piers, each one wide enough to accommodate a pair of ships being loaded simultaneously. While it would have made the process easier by constructing the piers farther away from the southern wall of Puhar, Pollio had made the decision to build the northernmost barely a hundred paces away from where the southern wall terminated at the low tide line.

When Caesar arrived, he explained, "This way, the Pandya can either extend the wall to keep the piers inside the city, or use it as it is outside, and construct a gate."

Pollio wasn't surprised that Caesar instantly approved, and gave Pollio the ultimate compliment, remarking, "I should have thought of that myself, Asinius."

Over the course of the next three days, the portion of the fleet that would carry the Equestrians and the other Legions with Caesar were loaded with the disassembled wagons, which were now constructed in a manner where the pieces were joined with mortice and tenon, although instead of wood, the pegs were made of iron with a large flat head that could be reused. For the watching Cholans, who quickly dropped all of their normal daily duties and lined the southern wall to watch, it was the speed with which these strangers worked that they would remember, although it was accompanied by a great deal of shouting by men whose only job seemed to be waving sticks around as they bellowed some sort of gibberish, and occasionally using those sticks to smack one of the other men, who they all noticed were the ones doing the brunt of the work, leading these simple people to deduce that the workers were from their caste, while the men with sticks were of the upper.

Not surprisingly, it was Scribonius who observed the onlookers lining the wall, musing aloud, "I wonder what those Cholans think of all of this activity?"

Pullus glanced over at him in surprise; while he had noticed them watching, perhaps four hundred paces from the central pier where Pullus was standing, he had only given them a cursory glance, and only then to assess them as a possible threat.

As often happened, Scribonius' query made him actually think about it, and he laughed. "They'll probably tell their grandchildren about the day a horde of pale barbarians descended and, for no reason at all, built these things, then disappeared."

"We're not that pale anymore," Scribonius replied, also with a laugh, then pointed down at first his, then Pullus' arm. "We were never this dark in Gaul or Hispania."

"Or Africa, for that matter," Pullus agreed, but when he glanced down at his own arm, he was surprised at the several white lines scoring his leathered skin, realizing that he had never really looked at himself in that way. Where, he wondered, did I get *that* one? he wondered. Could that be from our first campaign in Hispania against the...He actually had to stop for a moment, trying to recall. Giving up, he asked, "What was the name of that tribe in Hispania?"

"The Lusitani?"

"No," Pullus shook his head. "The ones who held the island that we had to take."

"The Gallaeci," Scribonius supplied, but Pullus shook his head again, sounding irritated, "No, I know, but there were two branches of them."

"Ah, right." Scribonius thought for a moment, then came up with, "The Bracari and the Lucenses."

"Yes! That's it." Pullus nodded now.

He didn't say anything for a moment, the pair content to watch as their men, their cotton tunics soaked through as they hustled about dragging the contents of the supply wagons over to a tall pole with a pulley that served as a crane and was anchored several feet deep in the water about five feet down the pier from where it met the beach. Working in teams, they lashed crates together then placed them on a large net made of lengths of rope, the four corners of which had a large loop, which were dropped over the iron hook that was attached to the line running up to the pulley, whereupon one of the slaves who drove a wagon goaded an ox to plod a few feet, taking the slack out of the line and lifting the loaded net up off the ground.

As they watched the men on the pier muscling the suspended load over, while another group of men who were on the deck of the ship, this one a *trireme*, pulled the load towards them, Pullus asked suddenly, "How many different tribes and people do you think we've fought and beaten, Sextus?"

This startled Scribonius, and again he was forced to think, but this time, all he could offer was, "I've never tried to count them, Titus. But," his voice turned sober, "it's a lot."

"It is," Pullus nodded. Without looking over at Scribonius, he said, "I just hope we're running out of people Caesar wants us to kill."

This was such an unusual thing for Pullus to say that Scribonius felt a stab of concern, looking over at his friend, who pretended not to notice Scribonius studying his features.

"What," Scribonius asked quietly, "brought that on?" Then, to lighten the mood, he chuckled. "Since when have you wanted to run out of people to kill?"

Pullus didn't laugh, though he did smile, but there was something in his voice that Scribonius couldn't identify when he replied, "I suppose there's a first time for everything." His head moved abruptly, his eye caught by something, or someone, and pointing with his *vitus*, he barked, "*Oy!* Corvinus! Yes, you, you bastard! Don't act like you don't hear me! You pull your prick harder than you're pulling on that rope! Do it again, and you're going to be too sore to hold it for a week!"

While it was true that the ranker, a man in Pullus' Century and in the Tenth Section, had been doing a half-hearted job of it, Scribonius was certain that this was Pullus' way of changing the subject, so he didn't pursue it. Nevertheless, he was slightly troubled, thinking, if Titus is nearing the end of his string and is ready to go home, what will the rest of us do?

Oblivious to the musings of the Secundus Pilus Prior about his Primus Pilus' troubled mind, the men of Caesar's army continued working, and in less time than seemed possible, and on the third full day after their arrival at Pollio's camp, the army had reunited and was loaded aboard their assigned ships. Caesar's army, and by extension, Rome, was moving again.

It was on their second day at sea that Barhinder, asleep in his hammock, was awakened by a rough hand. While he came awake immediately, he still had to blink the sleep away, noticing two things: it was still dark, but even in the gloom, the bulk of Master Titus was impossible to mistake.

"How's your arm?" Pullus asked gruffly.

"It is fine, Master Titus," Barhinder replied, although not altogether truthfully.

He wasn't lying, exactly, but while it was much better and he was able to straighten his arm out, he had to think about it and do it relatively slowly, or he would be hit by a shock of pain that would make him gasp.

"I think," Pullus growled, "you're full of *cac*. But, if you say it is, then it's time to get to work."

This brought Barhinder tumbling out of the hammock, which was slung in the master's cabin of the *quadrireme*, named the *Lykaina*, the Greek term for a female wolf, frantic with worry that he had forgotten one of his nightly tasks that he had been assigned by Diocles, although he was certain that he had done them all.

This prompted him to ask, "What did I miss, Master Titus? Tell me, and I will see to it immediately."

With some chagrin, Pullus realized that he had caused the youth needless anxiety, though he hid it well.

"You didn't miss anything," Pullus assured him, amused at the manner in which Barhinder's shoulders slumped in relief, thinking, Let's see how long this lasts. "But since you say your arm is better, it's time we start strengthening it back up." He paused, and he knew he was being somewhat cruel. "Unless now that you've gotten a taste of what it's like getting stabbed, you've decided you don't want to be under the standard."

"No!" Barhinder answered without hesitation. A bit more calmly, he said, "No, Master Titus. I still want to be a *Gregarius*. I want," Barhinder's voice throbbed with the intensity he felt whenever he thought of this, "to be as great a warrior as my brother Sagara was."

Neither Pullus nor Barhinder were aware of just how accurate Barhinder's characterization was, since neither of them would ever learn that it had been Sagara Gotra whose sacrifice in igniting the lone wagon containing the supply of naphtha that in turn enabled King Abhiraka and his Pandyan allies to completely destroy the 7th and 11th Legions more than two years earlier.

"I'm sure he was," Pullus replied. "And we're going to start today. Follow me."

Naturally, Barhinder did so, the pair only pausing to relieve themselves over the side of the *Lykaina* before Pullus walked out on the main deck next to the mast. While it was dark, the eastern horizon was pink, meaning that the fleet was about to rouse itself and shift from sail back to the oars for another long day.

For the first time, Barhinder noticed the large training shield leaning against the side of the ship, and to which Pullus pointed and said, "Pick it up."

As he expected, Barhinder obeyed without thinking, reaching out with his left hand, which wrenched a gasp of pain from him.

"So you lied," Pullus said flatly. "Your arm isn't fine."

Barhinder's eyes had filled with tears from the sudden shock of pain, but now the sting that he knew came from letting Master Titus down was added.

Still, he said stubbornly, "I did not lie, Master Titus. I just..." he searched for the right words, "...cannot make sudden movements without thinking about it."

What Barhinder didn't know was that Titus Pullus, of all the men under the standard, understood Barhinder far better than the youth thought. For months after the battle of Munda, when he had almost lost his life, Pullus experienced the same thing that Barhinder was going through; as long as he limited his range of motion and didn't make any sudden movements, he could pretend to himself that he was close to full strength. Walking over to Barhinder, he saw the apprehension in the youth's eyes, and decided something. Without any warning, Pullus dropped to sit on the deck, then ordered Barhinder to sit next to him, and once the youth did so, he proceeded to tell him that very thing. To an extent and with a level of detail he had never shared with anyone, not Diocles, or Balbus, or even

Scribonius, Pullus described those agonizing weeks, of the fear that he would never be whole again, nor be able to duplicate the feats that had made him Titus Pullus, one of the most well-known men under the standard of his age. Barhinder, naturally, listened intently, not interrupting as Master Titus talked of those days, a bit more than five years earlier, when he had endured the pain as he rebuilt his strength and fought to return to the man he had been before.

"What you're doing is no small thing, Barhinder," Pullus was speaking quietly, but Barhinder heard the intensity there. "And it will take a lot of hard work, a lot of sweat. And," he emphasized, "a *lot* of pain." He paused, then continued, "If I'm being honest, Barhinder, I'm not sure that your destiny is to be a warrior."

If Pullus had punched him in the stomach, Barhinder was certain that it wouldn't have hurt as much, but he was also feeling the first stirring of anger, although he tried to hide it.

"Why do you say that, Master Titus?" he asked stiffly, forcing himself to look up into the Centurion's eyes as he did so.

Pullus didn't answer directly, choosing instead to break his gaze and look away as he said, "Diocles tells me that you're doing very well with your Latin."

"Yes," Barhinder replied cautiously. "He has been very kind to me, and he is an excellent teacher."

"He should be," Pullus chuckled, "since that's what he was before Pharsalus. But," the smile vanished, "he thinks that you have a unique talent, and not just for languages. He tells me that you've developed a very fine hand, and your writing is improving every day."

Suddenly, Barhinder understood, and before he could stop himself, he exclaimed bitterly, "So, you want me to be your clerk, Master Titus? To copy and write all those reports that Caesar wants? What kind of life is that for a free man? That is the work of slaves!"

As soon as he said it, Barhinder knew he had erred, but it was the sudden way in which Master Titus, who had been speaking quietly and reasonably, seemed to emanate a coldness, and, making Barhinder nervous, a terrible anger that he could almost feel in a palpable sense, sitting so closely to him. The fact that he didn't raise his voice was even more chilling.

"Is that what you think of Diocles?" Pullus asked softly.

"N-no," Barhinder stammered, but it was the sudden stab of shame that he would remember. "No, Master Titus. I think Diocles is a good and wise man, truly!"

"And he saved your life, Barhinder," Pullus reminded him needlessly. "If it hadn't been for him hearing you under that pile of bodies, you would have been thrown into a mass grave and buried alive."

Barhinder knew quite well this was true; he also knew that several of those bodies, particularly that of his best friend Agathocles, had been put there by the huge Roman next to him, but this was something that he refused to think about.

"I know that, Master Titus," Barhinder said, softly but with feeling as he remembered the sensation of the crushing weight being lifted and seeing a face peering down at him. "And, I was wrong to say that. It is just that," he sighed, "as much as I thought I never wanted to hold a sword and shield again, it is all I ever think about. I want," the youth turned to look up at Titus so that the Roman would see his sincerity, "to be like you, Master Titus!"

To Barhinder's surprise, in the growing light he could see that Master Titus didn't seem amused, or even flattered; if anything, he looked sad, and this more than anything gave Barhinder pause.

Standing abruptly, Pullus said only, "Be careful what you wish for, Barhinder. This life isn't what you think it is. But," he held a huge hand out to pull the youth to his feet, "if this is what you want, let's get started before the deck is too crowded."

Barhinder forced himself to reach up and take Pullus' hand with his left, grimacing from the sudden stab of pain as the Roman lifted him to his feet as if he weighed nothing.

Once standing, Pullus pointed to the shield and repeated, "Pick it up."

By the time the sun was fully up, and the first shift of men of the First and Second Century was allowed up on deck to relieve themselves and spend time in the fresh air, Barhinder was certain that he hadn't been in as much pain immediately after his wounding, but he was also hopeful that the first day would be the worst. In the ensuing weeks, he would learn how wrong he had been.

Despite pressure from Lords Maran and Sundara, King Nedunj honored his agreement with Caesar to take his army north, resisting the efforts of two of his most senior councilors to persuade him to cease his cooperation with the Romans.

"We have done everything that Roman has asked, Your Highness," Sundara had argued, more than once, though he did allow, "and yes, the Romans upheld their pledge to you. But how long must we be beholden to these foreigners? When will we resume our independence?"

While it was a valid point in some ways, it also wasn't the wisest path to take by insinuating that Pandya wasn't an ally but a vassal, which aroused the ire of Nedunj whenever this was mentioned. That, in his heart, he understood what the Friend and Ally status truly meant, that Pandya was in reality a vassal in all but name, even if the Romans used the term "client state," only exacerbated his irritation at being reminded. Maran, while more tactful, was no less direct in his objection to Nedunj ordering what equated to three-quarters of Pandya's military might to prepare to march north, although his stated reason for doing so was different.

"By moving so quickly after we took Uraiyur, we're going to be leaving while the situation here with the paroled Cholans is still very...delicate," was the word he chose. "The Northern Army and Lord Kavirathan is certainly something that we will need to deal with, but I don't believe there is a hurry. And," he argued, "there might be value in forcing Kavirathan to come to us. As long as we have the capital, if he has any designs on reclaiming his brother's throne and driving us out, he must come to Uraiyur."

As Nedunj knew very well, this was all true, and it wasn't a decision he made lightly, but it was one that he wouldn't be dissuaded from making, although he tried to avoid giving his real reason for making it.

Finally, out of exasperation because of Sundara's refusal to relent, he had finally snapped, "Do you really want to break an agreement with the Romans after we've all seen what they can do?" When neither nobleman answered, he pressed, "And, do you think Caesar will hesitate to exact punishment on me and my subjects if I don't honor my word? No, he may not do so immediately. He's intent on at least reaching the mouth of the Ganges before the end of what they consider their campaign season, if not getting all the way to Palibothra, but you can be sure that once he accomplishes that, and he returns south on his way back to Rome, there will be a reckoning!"

Even Sundara understood that there was no point in arguing, but it was Maran who, while not objecting any further, asked a question that the young king would have cause to remember for the rest of his life, which was destined to be many more years.

"Your Highness, are you certain that Caesar intends on returning to Rome?" he asked quietly. "Or, if he does, he's going to retrace his route? As I understand it from you, the reason that the Romans took this longer route was because they didn't know enough about the overland eastern route from Bharuch." He finished with a shrug, "It's very possible that he will either forge an alliance with the Yavana kingdoms, or at the very least negotiate safe passage west overland from Palibothra since they're all Greek speakers."

This was something that Nedunj couldn't argue, so he didn't try, but it didn't dissuade him from his decision, and two days later, he led his army aboard Darpashata, heading north, but despite his resolve to avoid even the possibility of antagonizing Caesar, Maran's words wouldn't leave his mind. He would have even more cause to remember them in the coming years, when Caesar and his army essentially vanished from their world.

Kavirathan, younger brother of Karikala, was exhausted, both physically and mentally. Ever since the news of the utter catastrophe in Uraiyur, he had been beset on seemingly every side by his councilors and the few remaining high-ranking nobles whose holdings comprised the northern part of the Chola kingdom, each of them with their own ideas that ranged from suggestions to demands about what to do.

Caesar Ascending – The Ganges

"We must march south and attack those Pandyan dogs immediately! Crush them and drive them back to their hole!"

"We need to prepare Chennai for the attack that is surely coming! Break the invaders on our walls!"

"We should seek a truce and determine what the Pandyan king intends before we make a military decision."

The stream of men demanding his time was seemingly endless, but this was only a partial reason for his paralysis as he sat in what served as the headquarters of the Northern Army in Chennai, and he had been in this state of mind even before a messenger had been ushered into his presence to announce what he had been secretly dreading ever since he became aware of their existence.

"Lord, the headman of Ophir has sent me to report that we have seen a fleet of ships! He believes it is those demons they call Romans!"

Despite the fact that he had been expecting, and dreading, this news, it still hit Kavirathan with the force of a punch, but he somehow managed to maintain his outward demeanor of calm as his mind raced. Ophir was a small but important trading port of perhaps two thousand residents a half-day's normal ride from Chennai, and he tried to calculate how long it would be before a sentry on the walls here would alert him the Romans had arrived. Ever since he had been made aware of his nephew Divakar's death, he had tried to learn more about the Roman invaders, and one of his regrets had been his older brother's dismissive attitude about the foreigner's incursion into India. When they learned of their investment of Bharuch a bit more than two years earlier, Kavirathan was of the same mind as his brother, that the southernmost kingdom under Greek influence was sufficiently far away for it to be a matter of minor interest and nothing more. But then, the Romans had landed at Muziris, and for a short period of time, Karikala had almost been beside himself with delight at the prospect of their lifelong foe suffering at the hands of these foreigners. What came next had alarmed Kavirathan, but Karikala had been unconcerned about the problem the unexpected alliance between invader and defender might pose to their own kingdom. It had prompted Kavirathan to leave Chennai and travel to Uraiyur in the Roman month of December, whereupon he had learned that, from his perspective, the situation was even direr when Karikala informed him that the Romans and Pandyans were actively training together. Despite this, his older brother hadn't seemed to be worried, continuing to insist that, should this combined force attack Chola, they would be soundly defeated.

"They must come through the pass," Karikala had insisted. "And when they do, we will stop them just as we always have. Remember, little brother," he had pointed out, "superior numbers don't matter there. We'll choke that narrow road with corpses! Whether they're Pandyan or these Roman dogs doesn't matter." What Kavirathan would remember was the wolfish smile as his brother exclaimed, "Dead men smell the same, whether they're Pandyan or Roman, and their stench will carry for miles, the air will be black with buzzards, and the hyenas will get fat!"

On its face, Kavirathan knew it was true that the pass was a strategic ally in itself, and it was why Pandya had never been successful in their attempts to invade the southern Chola kingdom. That the reverse was equally true, that the Cholan attempts to conquer Pandyan territory beyond Madoura had come to an end in the same place was something Kavirathan didn't mention to his older brother. Never far from his mind was his recognition that, many years ago, there had been another brother, younger than Karikala but older than he was, but that brother had suffered a hunting accident, mauled by a tiger while out on a hunt with his older brother. That, at least, had been the story, but this had been early in Karikala's reign, shortly after their father, the first of his name and the king who had created what was now the Chola empire, had died, and Khakuntal, the middle brother, had made it clear that he coveted the crown for himself. For that reason, Kavirathan didn't really blame Karikala for what he was certain was the murder of Khakuntal, but it served as a lesson, and he had always gone out of his way to let his brother know that he had no aspirations of kingship himself.

Nevertheless, he had still felt compelled to ask Karikala, "And what about this weapon that the Romans have? This fire that can't be extinguished that kills elephants?"

"Surely you don't believe that nonsense," Karikala had scoffed before relenting, albeit slightly. "Oh," he had given a dismissive wave, "I know that they have something, but I'm certain that it's what they call Greek fire. It's very hard to make, so I'm sure that while they have some, it won't be enough to stop our elephants."

Kavirathan had returned to Chennai in a slightly better frame of mind, mainly because Karikala had assured him that he intended to lead their army in the event that the Pandyans and their Roman allies attempted to invade. As he had learned just three weeks before the appearance of the messenger warning him of the approaching ships, not only had Karikala not led his army as he promised, but instead of letting a more experienced commander like Lord Venkata, or even Lord Senganan, lead, he had given the command to what Kavirathan privately believed was the worst choice possible in the crown prince. There was no questioning Divakar's courage, but from an early age, he had behaved in a manner that convinced his uncle that he was only marginally more intelligent than the elephant he rode, and once he learned the details of the crushing defeat at the pass that had cost the prince his life, he realized he had been too generous. While there had been no real communication between the brothers since then, based on what had transpired in the aftermath of Divakar's defeat, Kavirathan came to the belief that the loss of his oldest son had done something to Karikala, and now, Kavirathan and the Northern Army was the last hope of the Chola empire. It was this enormous pressure, and the fact that there was no consensus among the noblemen who were advising him that found Kavirathan, seated on another of the ornately carved wooden chairs that was a symbol of Chola, wondering how long he had before the Roman fleet arrived. He had summoned his advisers immediately after the messenger came, and they were all standing there now, watching, waiting...and judging him, he was certain of that.

"Lord," Nish, the nobleman who had been the most strident in his demand for action, broke the silence, not hiding his impatience, "we need you to make a decision! When are you going to send our army out to face these vermin?"

It was the man's tone, and his attitude of borderline contempt that made Kavirathan's decision for him, and he made sure to look directly at the man as he replied evenly, "We're not. We're going to use the walls of Chennai to our advantage."

"But our elephants will be useless behind these walls!" Nish protested, and Kavirathan saw that, while he had been the most vigorous, he wasn't alone now, at least four other noblemen of the same mind as Nish judging by the manner in which they drifted over to stand next to him while shaking their heads in support of the nobleman.

"Judging from what we have learned, Lord Nish," Kavirathan replied with a calmness he didn't feel, "they would not only be useless in the open, they will likely be slaughtered by these Romans."

For the first time, Nish hesitated, though not for long, recovering to insist, "This terrible weapon these Romans are supposed to possess is only a rumor, Lord Kavirathan. None of us have actually seen it!"

"That's true," Kavirathan replied mildly. "But what we know without a doubt is that the Crown Prince Divakar and all but a handful of our elephants, virtually none of our infantry, and less than half of our horse cavalry survived when they tried to stop these Romans from crossing into our kingdom." Holding his hands out, he asked reasonably, "Knowing that, and knowing that Uraiyur fell and my brother the king was also slain, how else would you explain it?" Before Nish could answer, he pointed out, "Even if this weapon doesn't exist, or is exaggerated as my brother believed, what we know is that the Northern Army is all that's left to defend Chola from this invasion." This was met with silence, if only because when Nish glanced over at the other nobles who had seemed to be sympathetic to his argument, they suddenly became more interested in the tiled floor of the room. Seeing this, Kavirathan said more forcefully, "My decision stands. We will defend Chennai." Feeling that he owed the shade of his brother something, he did add, "And, once we break them against our walls, then we'll unleash our elephants."

It was shortly before sunset the next day when the cry from the sentry positioned on the southeast corner of the wall sounded. By the time Kavirathan arrived on the wall to see for himself, the sea was a gold color from the setting sun, but it was what looked to him to be a veritable forest of trees that had somehow sprouted on the surface of the water, if instead of multiple leaves those trees had just a single large one, identical in shape with the others around it.

Struck dumb by the sight, by the time he gained his voice, the hulls of the leading ships had become distinct enough to make out, but he only vaguely recognized his voice as it asked, "Have you made a count yet?"

"No, my Lord," the sentry replied, then hastened to explain, "I mean to say that I began, but..." When he paused, this got Kavirathan's attention. Glancing over, he saw the expression of shame, so he wasn't surprised to hear the man admit, "...I don't know numbers past one hundred, Lord."

He didn't chastise or embarrass the man, knowing that not only was there no point, but the sentry wasn't unique; most of his comrades in the ranks of the Cholan army were no different in their limited ability to handle large numbers. Consequently, he stood silently, watching and counting, but he stopped at five hundred ships, mainly because the sun had just set by then. More crucially, the leading vessels were now perhaps a mile south and a bit less than a mile offshore, so he used the remaining light to examine them. Kavirathan was familiar with *biremes*, and *triremes*, although they were less common here on the eastern coast of India, and those that were there came mostly from the north, originating somewhere along the Ganges and one of the Yavana kingdoms. He had even heard of the ships called *quadriremes*, but despite the fading light, he understood that what he had imagined it looked like and what he was seeing now were vastly different; that he counted five such ships before it became too dark only reinforced his belief that he and his men would need every advantage. Staying only long enough to determine that the leading ships had come to a stop, turning their bows towards the shore as they anchored, Kavirathan turned to the nobleman he had named his second in command.

"Lord Marish, I want you to rouse the men. I want half of them on the walls immediately." He indicated the fleet, the ships now discernible in the darkness only because of the single lamps that hung from the bow and stern of each vessel, making it look as if what seemed like a thousand small fires had magically sprouted on the water. "I don't think they will do anything tonight, and it appears as if their fleet is still arriving, but we will not be caught by surprise."

For a moment, he considered summoning Lord Nish so that he could see for himself that the Romans had not only arrived, but what it looked like in a tangible form, seeing those sparks of light stretching to the south as far as one could see, but he decided that it could wait until the morning. Let him see what these ships actually look like and how large they are, he thought, completely unaware that he had yet to see any of the *quinqueremes* that were the backbone of the fighting ships available to the Roman Caesar. He was also unaware that, shortly before midnight, another courier would show up outside the southern gate of Chennai, but since he had been unable to sleep, the man was ushered into his presence immediately.

"Lord Kavirathan, I was sent by Lord Deepak." The messenger's voice was hoarse, and he was visibly shaking, although Kavirathan couldn't tell if it was from fear or exhaustion, since the man was clearly near the point of collapsing. "He wanted to warn you that the Pandyan King Nedunj has departed Uraiyur, and is marching here."

Despite expecting this, Kavirathan still experienced a chill, especially now that their Roman allies were offshore, and he was more thinking aloud when he mused, "They will be here in three days, then..."

"No, Lord!" The messenger nodded his head, clearly alarmed. "They will be here tomorrow, probably early in the day!"

"How is this possible?" Kavirathan gasped, trying to appear that he was sitting and not collapsing onto his chair. Suddenly angry, he pointed an accusing finger at the messenger, "Why did you delay in coming here? Surely Lord Deepak sent you as soon as he knew that the Pandyans were moving!"

"He did, Lord," the messenger admitted, seeming to condemn himself, but he explained, "Lord, I had to be very careful in getting here. The Pandyan king has a screen of horsemen spread out for several miles on either side of the

Uraiyur road. I was almost caught twice, but I lost them in the *jangla* both times. That is why I stayed hidden during the day today, because that was the only way I could be sure to evade their scouts, Lord, I swear it!"

Kavirathan didn't possess a suspicious nature like his dead brother, and he acknowledged to himself that the messenger's story made sense; nevertheless, he felt certain that there was something about this man's tale that deserved further investigation. Fortunately for him, the possible duplicity of one man paled in importance to the knowledge that the Pandyans were approaching, and he set the matter aside, thinking that he could revisit the messenger's possible negligence later...provided he survived.

Chapter Seven

"We're only spending at most two days here," Caesar had informed his Legates and Primi Pili after summoning them to his flagship. "And," he stressed, "I was sincere in telling King Nedunj that we will play no role again, other than allowing this Lord Kavirathan to see our fleet."

"If that doesn't scare the *cac* out of him," Balbinus muttered to Pullus, "then we know that idiocy runs in that family."

Proving that his hearing was as keen as his vision, Caesar agreed with a smile, "Very true, Balbinus, and you whisper about as well as Pullus." Pausing for the chuckles the jibe brought to subside, he continued, "But from what I've been told by Lord Senganan," he indicated the Cholan noble who, Pullus had observed, had either placed himself or been placed by Caesar in an unobtrusive corner of the cabin that, while relatively spacious, was still crammed, "Kavirathan isn't as...aggressive as his brother and nephew were, and once Nedunj arrives, and he sees how outnumbered he is just by the Pandyans, I don't anticipate that there will be a fight."

"And if there is?" Clustuminus asked, in an almost challenging manner, "Will you give my boys the opportunity to get stuck in, Caesar?"

Pullus wasn't alone in bracing himself for what he viewed as an inevitable rebuke, since Caesar had already made it clear that his patience had worn thin with the Primus Pilus of the 8th and his seemingly never-ending attempts to prove that his

Legion was at least the equal to the Equestrians, and to a lesser extent, the 12th.

He also wasn't the only one surprised when Caesar replied evenly, "While I appreciate your eagerness, Clustuminus, I'm not going to waste one Roman life on what is ultimately a matter between Pandya and Chola. However," he allowed, "if it's absolutely necessary, I've spoken to Lysippus and he assures me that we can bring at least four of the *quinqueremes* within range of Chennai's seaward wall." Perhaps sensing the concern, Caesar assured the others, "But we will *not* be using naphtha, just our conventional ammunition. I feel reasonably certain that we won't be needed, but if we are, all we'll be losing are a few rocks and scorpion bolts."

Since Pullus' ship had arrived after the sun set, he had been one of the first on deck to examine the walls of Chennai the next morning, although he was quickly joined by Balbus, who still insisted on sleeping with the men and not sharing the cabin with Pullus, which Pullus was certain his second in command did just to irritate him. His examination hadn't taken long; the walls appeared to be a bit higher than those of Uraiyur, although it was hard to judge because he was farther away from the walls of Chennai than he had been at Uraiyur, and it was crenellated. Otherwise, Pullus' opinion was that it was a city that could be taken in no more than two days by the Legions, if Caesar was willing to lose a few more men; how long it would take Nedunj was another question, and since his examination came before the meeting, Pullus was assuming that, if the Pandyan told Caesar that it would take longer than Caesar thought necessary, at least one of the Legions would be going in. Now that he had heard Caesar insist the Romans wouldn't be involved, he returned to his ship content for the Equestrians to be spectators.

"Caesar's more concerned about the Andhra than he is with the last of these Cholans," Diocles had informed him after returning from Caesar's flagship with the daily report two days earlier.

It was a feature of life for a Primus Pilus in Caesar's army, that the meticulous record-keeping that Caesar insisted on didn't stop just because they were separated and floating in the middle of the sea. Under other circumstances, it would have irritated Pullus, but Diocles had pointed out that, because of their separation while at sea, this afforded him the opportunity to speak with Apollodorus, who was Diocles' best source of information for learning what Caesar was thinking and what he was concerned about.

"Why?" Pullus asked somewhat skeptically. "They fight the same way as the Pandya and the Chola, don't they?"

"They do," Diocles confirmed, "but they also have a large fleet of their own, and according to Lord Senganan, they have experience in fighting from ships."

This was concerning; Pullus was a typical Roman, having no love for the sea, although like most of his men, he had become resigned to the reality that they would be spending extended periods of time aboard a ship as Caesar pursued his goal, but fighting aboard ship was something that was completely foreign to him. There had been discussion by Caesar and the Primi Pili of doing something similar with another Legion that had been done with the Muziris Legions in training them to fight from the *howdahs*, but it was quickly discarded because of the impracticality of ensuring that any fighting with a potential enemy navy was only performed by that Legion. However, while it was something to worry about, as Pullus had learned long before, it was something to worry about in the future; now, they would sit and watch their Pandyan allies subdue the last Cholan army. How they did it was the question, and by sunset of the day after their arrival, Nedunj and his army arrived, and as he watched the four abreast column of huge gray beasts, all of them attired in their armor and with their *howdahs* full, from his spot leaning on the railing of his ship, Pullus thought, At least we won't have long to wait.

It was Senganan who made the suggestion.

"I believe I should be there when King Nedunj and Lord Kavirathan meet."

Although it was difficult to catch Caesar by surprise, he was by this, and he asked the Cholan, "Are you certain that is a good idea, Lord Senganan?"

"Probably not," Senganan admitted with a small smile. "It is certainly possible that Lord Kavirathan might strike me

Caesar Ascending – The Ganges

down, and I suspect that King Nedunj would not try very hard to stop him."

While he was unaware of it, Senganan handed Caesar the opening he had been looking for, a pretext to be present at the meeting that the Pandyan king had informed him was arranged, sending Sundara by boat out to Caesar's flagship to inform him shortly after sunrise.

"Then, I'm coming with you," Caesar informed him. "I still need your help with the Andhra, and I can't afford to let anything happen to you."

"That," Senganan replied, sounding sincere despite not believing Caesar, "is very kind of you, Caesar. But," he pointed out, "you told me that you assured King Nedunj that you would not be involved in whatever happened between my people and the Pandya."

"I did," Caesar agreed, "and I intend to stand by that. I will just be there to...discourage anyone who might want to harm you."

In what Senganan assumed was a sign of Caesar's sincerity, after summoning Achaemenes, when the three of them boarded the small boat that was lashed to the stern of the *quinquereme,* before rowing ashore, Caesar directed them to another ship, a *quadrireme,* where the giant Roman Pullus was standing on the deck, waiting, wearing his armor and weapons, holding the stick that Senganan had learned was called a *vitus,* although he was still a bit hazy on why it seemed to have such importance to these Romans that were called Centurions that they carried it with them everywhere.

"Don't drown us jumping in, Pullus," Caesar called up, only partially in jest, but Pullus had almost learned the hard way about the need for someone his size not to make sudden moves in a small boat, so he lowered himself down the rope ladder then stepped carefully into the craft, taking the spot next to Achaemenes facing the other two men, the Parthian giving him a welcoming grin.

"I suppose that my job is to, what did you call it, 'look imposing'?" Pullus asked Caesar with a smile of his own.

"Actually, I said to look fierce, but yes, that's exactly it," Caesar answered cheerfully, in Greek. More seriously, he indicated Senganan. "Senganan's presence with Karikala's brother might tempt him to do something...rash."

"Then why bring him?" Pullus asked this in Latin, and Caesar replied in their native tongue, while Achaemenes, having become accustomed to his role, gave no indication that he understood, in order to forestall being questioned by Senganan later.

"Because I think that, while this Kavirathan might be angry at what he might view as the Lord's treachery, I also think that since he's the only Cholan present who's seen everything from the ambush to our demonstration, and he was with Karikala at the end that he's going to be the most powerful weapon we have to convince Kavirathan that resistance is futile and will only end in utter destruction."

Pullus considered this, then, taking a glance over his shoulder to gauge how much time they had before they landed on the beach, where he could see a party of men waiting, he decided to broach the subject that had been lurking in the back of his mind.

"Wouldn't it be a good thing if this Cholan chose to fight?" Pullus asked. "So that Nedunj won't have to worry about this Kavirathan or some other of the surviving Cholan nobles causing trouble in the future?"

"That," Caesar replied in a tone that didn't alert Senganan that they had moved to a potentially dangerous topic, "is certainly one way to go about it, Pullus. But, why did I pursue a policy of clemency with our opponents during the civil war?" Without waiting for Pullus to answer, Caesar went on, "Because I didn't want to lock our people into a cycle of endless retribution that would only bleed us dry more than we already had. That," he finished, "is what I urged Nedunj to do as well, and he says he'll try to arrive at a peaceful settlement with Kavirathan."

Pullus made no comment, hoping that a nod would suffice, because he wasn't about to utter what was running through his mind; even now, four years later, those who were in close contact with Caesar knew to never bring up that Ides of March when he narrowly escaped being murdered. The fact that many of the would-be killers, like Brutus, had sided with Pompeius but had been forgiven by Caesar, only to have him participate in a plot to kill him actually indicated to Pullus that urging Nedunj to adopt a similar policy could have serious repercussions and unleash consequences that were either unintended or unforeseen. Despite his lack of formal education, Pullus was very intelligent, and hard experience had taught him that, of every variety of consequences that could result from an action, it was the unforeseen and unintended that could prove disastrous, especially when they combined. Of course, none of this was verbalized by Pullus as he sat in the boat, choosing instead to occupy himself by trying to identify the waiting Pandyans.

"I think that's Lord Sundara, Caesar," Pullus told Caesar, "and it looks like Lord Vira as well, but I don't see King Nedunj."

"He's probably waiting in his tent until the last moment before he meets with Lord Kavirathan," Caesar replied. "That's what I would do."

Something occurred to Pullus, and he tore his gaze away from the Pandyans because he wanted to gauge Caesar's reaction to his question.

"Does King Nedunj know that you're planning on attending?"

Caesar didn't look guilty, exactly, if only because Caesar never felt guilty about any of his actions, and although he didn't hesitate to answer, there was a hint of awkwardness in his tone that Pullus noticed.

"No, not exactly." Before Pullus could press on what this meant, he explained, partially, "I did mention to him that I might want to personally meet Lord Kavirathan, but I wasn't specific about when."

Pluto's cock, Pullus thought, not with alarm but with a fair amount of apprehension, and for the first time, he wished that at least Gundomir and Teispes had accompanied them, in the event that Nedunj felt the need to express his newfound independence from Rome in a manner that Caesar wouldn't appreciate. Not that he thought it likely; from what he had observed about the young Pandyan king, he was levelheaded, and most importantly both for himself and for Rome, pragmatic.

Nevertheless, Pullus also knew what could happen to a young leader who was surrounded by councilors who were dripping poison in his ear as they advanced their own agenda, and he had seen enough of Sundara in particular to know that he represented potential trouble for their alliance. His thoughts were interrupted by the sudden scraping of the bow of the boat on the sandy beach, which was a dirty brown in color given its closeness to a river's mouth, and Pullus made sure to leap out first, taking advantage of his height so that he could wade the rest of the way to stand with his back to the boat, folding his arms in a manner he knew accentuated the size of his arms while watching the Pandyans as Caesar, Senganan, and Achaemenes more sensibly walked to the front so that they could set foot on dry land first.

Caesar was in the process of dismissing the boatmen, but Pullus, hearing him, turned and said, "Caesar, if you don't mind, I'd like them to stay here for now." Since his face was turned away from the Pandyans, he added, in Latin, "In case we need to leave...quickly."

Caesar actually looked amused, but he didn't disagree, saying only, "Very well, Pullus."

Then, he approached the two Pandyan nobles, behind whom were four men that Pullus recognized as belonging to Nedunj's personal guard, and he was slightly encouraged when one of them, whose name he knew was Narasimha, gave him a nod that, while not overly friendly, wasn't hostile.

Sundara, whose Greek was atrociously bad, barely acknowledged Senganan and demanded of Caesar, "Why have you come, Caesar? King Nedunj did not tell us that you would be attending this meeting."

Ignoring the hostile tone, Caesar said airily, "Oh, I decided to come because I was curious to see this Lord Kavirathan with my own eyes." He paused, then in a slightly harder tone, asked Sundara, "King Nedunj doesn't have a problem with my attendance, does he?"

"No, Caesar." It was Vira who assured him, cutting Sundara off. "We are just...surprised."

"I also thought that Lord Senganan might be of use as well," Caesar explained, now pointedly ignoring Sundara, who was glaring at the Cholan nobleman with a poisonous hatred. "Given that he is the only one of us who actually knows Lord Kavirathan, I believe that he might be able to...persuade him to see reason."

Rather than respond to Caesar, Sundara turned and pointed directly at Pullus, a sneer on his face that made Pullus' *gladius* hand itch.

"And why is *he* here?"

For the first time, Caesar addressed Sundara directly, and this time, there was no mistaking that this was Caesar, the conqueror, the greatest general in the known world, his voice as cold as Pullus had ever heard it.

"He is here because I want him here. In the event that someone does something...rash, and foolish, Primus Pilus is here to remove that fool's head from his shoulders." He lifted a hand in a manner that made it clear he was displaying it. "And all I have to do for him to obey is to lift this hand. Now," Caesar tone instantly changed into something almost cordial, "is there a problem with that, Lord Sundara? Because if there is, I will let you take it up with the Primus Pilus himself."

Pullus was grimly satisfied seeing Sundara's swarthy features visibly pale, but he said nothing, choosing instead to pivot about and stalk off, leaving Vira to offer an apologetic shrug before turning to follow his counterpart. Caesar fell in behind Vira, the other three men following suit, the party arriving at the large tent that, while not quite as large as the Roman *praetorium* tent, was actually quite a bit taller, just in time for Nedunj to emerge. To Pullus' surprise, he wasn't wearing armor, and in fact was garbed in what the Romans had learned was the equivalent of a Roman or Greek tunic, except that it was more of a vest that, while it could be buttoned, Nedunj wore open, and he wore not one but several necklaces of gold, along with the loose fitting trousers that flared out but were tighter at the ankles. It wasn't the attire itself—by this time, Pullus and all the men of the Roman army had become accustomed to the different style of dress worn by the people in the southern part of India—but the fact that he had chosen this instead of his armor, or even the state robes that he wore for formal occasions was what Pullus thought unusual. He was wearing a turban, but with his crown wrapped around it, while his beard had been oiled, and somewhat to Pullus' relief, he saw that Nedunj was wearing his sword.

He didn't look surprised to see Caesar, although neither did he look pleased, which he explained, "I thought you might come, Caesar. But I assure you, I know what must be done."

When Caesar wanted to, he could disguise his supreme authority, and he did so now, telling Nedunj, "Your Highness, there was never a doubt in my mind. That's not why I'm here." Indicating Senganan, he said, "I brought Lord Senganan, not because I don't trust you, but because neither of us know Lord Kavirathan, but Lord Senganan does. That," he finished with a shrug, "is the only reason I'm here."

Pullus didn't know if Caesar convinced Nedunj, or whether the Pandyan decided not to argue the point, and he proved to be equally adept at the duplicity that seemed to be a requirement when high-ranking men sparred.

"That is a good idea, Caesar, and I should have thought of it myself," Nedunj said, and while he wasn't overtly hostile to Senganan like Sundara, there was no mistaking the coolness when he turned to the Cholan nobleman. Then, he looked at Achaemenes, and his tone wasn't nearly as friendly as he asked pointedly, "And why did you feel the need to bring Achaemenes, Caesar? Do you not trust me to interpret what is said between myself and the Cholan?"

"Not at all, Your Highness," Caesar lied. "I assumed that you would be more comfortable conversing with Lord Kavirathan in Tamil, and rather than slow things down because you have to explain to me what is being said, I brought Achaemenes along to speed up the process. Besides," he added with a smile, "Achaemenes has been after me to give him opportunities to practice his Tamil since he is not as fluent in it as he is in Sanskrit."

Again, whether he believed Caesar or decided it wasn't worth arguing about, Pullus didn't know.

What mattered was that Nedunj said, after a glance up at the sun, "It is time."

Then, without waiting for any response, Nedunj began striding away, though not in the direction of Chennai. Instead, he headed for where Darpashata was standing, already armored, and when he was a few paces away, Sekhar made the "tut tut" sound that Pullus had learned was the command for the animal to kneel, which he did immediately, just in time for Nedunj to hop up onto his huge knee, then with an ease that Pullus envied, jumped up into the *howdah*. What Nedunj did next convinced Pullus that the Pandyan wasn't happy, nor was he accepting, of Caesar's presence, because he gestured to Sundara and Vira, both of whom scrambled up to join him in the *howdah*. Then, in a manner that left no doubt, he spoke to Sekhar in Tamil, the *mahout* making the "hut hut" sound that told Darpashata to rise, before Caesar could climb up and join them.

"Follow us," Nedunj said peremptorily, not waiting for an answer as Sekhar tapped the elephant on the top of its head with the goad, twice in rapid succession, leaving Caesar to stand there, seething with rage and embarrassment.

Suddenly, Pullus wasn't quite as happy to be part of this, and he and Achaemenes exchanged a glance that communicated the Parthian was of a like mind.

"Let's go," Caesar said tersely, Senganan hurrying to follow, while Pullus and Achaemenes, by unspoken consent, decided to linger a couple of heartbeats before following.

"This," Pullus muttered, "should be interesting."

In fact, the meeting between King Nedunj and Lord Kavirathan was somewhat anticlimactic, although it didn't start out that way. In a manner similar to outside Uraiyur, Nedunj had a large canopy set up instead of a tent, while the table had been confiscated from one of the dwellings scattered outside the walls of Chennai. Like Nedunj, when the gates opened, Lord Kavirathan was astride an elephant of his own, one that rivaled Darpashata in its size, while he was accompanied by two men in his *howdah*, leading Pullus to assume that this was arranged beforehand. Neither side seemed to be in a hurry, and in fact, Nedunj ordered Darpashata to stop about a hundred paces away from the canopy in a clear attempt to force Kavirathan to arrive first. This led to something of a standoff, compelling the Romans to stand in the searing heat, which didn't help Caesar's mood any.

It didn't do much for Pullus either, who had to keep blinking to keep the sweat from clouding his vision, and he finally muttered, "Pluto's thorny fucking cock. Would these two stop measuring their pricks? It's fucking hotter than Hades."

Caesar didn't turn around, but he snapped, "I'm not any happier than you are, Pullus, but complaining about it won't speed things up."

You don't know that, Pullus thought mulishly, but finally, it was Kavirathan who broke first, resuming his progress towards the meeting place, and when the animal reached a spot about twenty paces away, the *mahout* stopped it and, in imitation of Darpashata, it dropped to its knees. Only when Kavirathan, clearly reluctant, swung his leg over the wall of the *howdah* did Nedunj order Darpashata to resume, and they reached the spot, also twenty paces away on the opposite side of the canopy, where the elephant came to a halt. Caesar got his revenge when Sekhar stopped Darpashata by taking advantage of the amount of time it took for the elephant to drop to its knees, and for Nedunj and the others to climb down, striding past the animal to reach the table, taking one of the three seats on the Pandyan side, though not the one in the middle.

"Oh, Nedunj will *not* be happy with that." Pullus chuckled, although he kept his voice down.

Achaemenes was equally amused, while Senganan looked as if he had no idea what was expected of him.

Caesar was turning to indicate the wooden chair on the other side when Nedunj, who, as Pullus expected, was as irritated as Caesar had been, snapped, "That chair is for Lord Sundara, Caesar, not this Cholan."

For the span of perhaps three heartbeats, it looked to Pullus as if Nedunj was going to demand that Caesar vacate his spot; the fact that instead, Nedunj glanced over his shoulder to look directly at Pullus, who stared back just as directly into his eyes, he didn't think was an accident, nor the fact that Nedunj didn't say anything. Once this little drama was over, Pullus turned his attention to the Cholans, starting with the man he assumed was Lord Kavirathan, who was seated in the center seat, and like Nedunj, wasn't wearing armor. The truth was that, to Pullus' eye, they looked almost identical in their dress, the only differences being that Kavirathan wasn't wearing a crown over his turban, and if anything, had even more gold draped on his body, with not just necklaces, but several golden arm rings and bracelets. He appeared to be in his late thirties, making him perhaps a decade older than Nedunj, while his facial features were even, and Pullus could see that his cheeks were pockmarked from some affliction. His eyes were his most arresting feature, and to Pullus he looked...sad, and while he understood why a Cholan in particular would not be in a happy frame of mind at the moment, he had the sense that this was his normal expression. *I wonder if he wanted to be king*, Pullus thought, *but his gods made him a second son.* Somehow, Pullus didn't think that was it, but there was definitely an air of melancholy in Kavirathan's demeanor. There was another surprise coming to Pullus when he broke the silence with a voice that was deeper even than Pullus' own, although he spoke in Tamil, of which Pullus only knew a smattering of words, and all of them having to do with someone's mother, along with a request for certain services.

It was left to Achaemenes, who dropped to one knee so that he could whisper in Caesar's ear as the Roman leaned over to listen, whispering, "He says the reason he agreed to this meeting is only because of his concern for his people, and he wants to know what King Nedunj wants to discuss."

Rather than answer Kavirathan, Nedunj actually turned to stare at both Caesar and his Parthian translator, expressing his feelings quite eloquently without saying a word.

When he did speak, however, it was to ask Kavirathan, in Greek, "Do you speak the Greek tongue?"

"I do," Kavirathan answered immediately, then continued, "along with Sanskrit and Telugu, along with several local dialects. I even," he said with obvious pride, "know some Latin. Although," he added hurriedly, "not enough to be conversant."

Before Nedunj could reply, Caesar said with apparent sincerity, "That is quite impressive, Lord Kavirathan." He paused, then, "May I ask how you came to learn our native tongue?"

Without hesitating, Kavirathan replied, "I only began

learning it recently, Caesar." The smile he offered was a grim one to Pullus' eye, "Once we learned of your arrival in India, actually."

"I congratulate you on your foresight," Caesar replied. Then, in a clear signal, he said, "But this is a matter for you and King Nedunj to decide. I am only here as an observer."

The slight bob of his head was the only thanks Nedunj offered, but he didn't hesitate, staying with Greek. "I will not belabor all that has happened, Lord Kavirathan, because I know there is no need, and we are where we are, here at this moment." Leaning forward slightly, Nedunj asked, "What I need to know is this: do you intend to continue to resist me and my army?"

Kavirathan didn't answer immediately, and the silence stretched out for several heartbeats.

When he broke the silence, it was to ask, "Why should I not? What exactly are you here to offer Chola?"

Over what Pullus estimated was the next sixth part of a watch, Nedunj spoke, sometimes passionately, sometimes with a flat, matter-of-fact tone, and despite his ambivalence about the young Pandyan, Pullus was impressed. Perhaps the most noticeable thing for the huge Roman was recognizing that Caesar's influence over the young Pandyan had been profound, because what Nedunj outlined was essentially the same Friend and Ally status that Caesar had bestowed on Pandya. Allowing the Cholans to keep their pride, Nedunj stressed that the people of the kingdom would be allowed to continue living their lives, and that there would even be improvements, but what struck Pullus was how Nedunj wasn't sparing in giving Caesar credit for showing him that there was a way to acknowledge what was, in actuality, a bitter reality, that the Pandyan had the ability to crush the Cholans. What Nedunj didn't do, Pullus noticed, was communicate that his newfound military power was due directly to the pale Roman sitting next to them, who sat there listening impassively, never revealing his thoughts as the exchange went back and forth. For his part, Kavirathan proved to be, in many ways, similar to Nedunj, with a pragmatic streak that was devoid of any kind of partisan fervor that, as Pullus had witnessed, seemed to be one of the few universal beliefs that men held, that *their* kingdom, *their* people, were destined to rule. As intelligent, and as introspective, relatively speaking, as Pullus was, like all mortals, he possessed a blind spot, because even as he thought about this, he never doubted that, in fact, Rome and all that it represented *was* destined to rule the known world, and in his defense, he would have simply pointed to the fact that he was standing there, thousands of miles away from the city for which he and his comrades marched, where no Roman had ever set foot, as proof of his belief. It was only after this long exchange that, for the first time, Kavirathan turned his attention to Senganan, who was standing behind and to Caesar's left, putting the Cholan next to Pullus, and there was nothing even remotely cordial in his gaze.

This coolness was communicated even more clearly when Kavirathan asked, "And what do you have to say for yourself, Lord Senganan?"

Senganan clearly wasn't surprised at the reception, but he didn't hesitate, replying, "I have nothing to say, Lord Kavirathan." He stopped then, and it was long enough for Caesar to begin to turn in his chair, an annoyed expression on his face, but before he could admonish the Cholan, Senganan resumed, "Other than that I have seen with my own eyes what the Romans are capable of, Lord. I watched your nephew consumed in flames, and our entire corps of elephants panicked at the sight of only four of their fellow elephants that perished in the same manner as Prince Divakar's did, and it allowed King Nedunj and his animals to take advantage of their terror and slaughter them." It was clear to Pullus that Senganan was trying to maintain his composure while delivering what, in many ways, sounded like the kind of report Pullus himself would give Caesar after a battle, but it was impossible to miss the raw emotion as he continued, "I know that we have discussed our mutual concerns about your nephew Prince Divakar, Lord, but while it is true that he behaved rashly, he also showed great courage, and no man should die in the manner in which he did."

Kavirathan had been listening with an impassive expression that didn't betray his thoughts, arms folded, but when Senganan paused, he asked in a slightly less hostile manner, "And you witnessed my nephew's death with your own eyes?"

"I did, Lord."

"And," Kavirathan asked as if it was a matter of minor curiosity, "how far away from the Prince were you when you saw this awful thing happen?"

Pullus' eyes were on the table, but he sensed Senganan suddenly stiffen, alerting him that there was more to the question than appeared on the surface, but the Cholan didn't hesitate to answer.

"I was on my Karna at the edge of the forest where we had been waiting," he said quietly.

"And not at my nephew's side?" Kavirathan snapped, sounding angry for the first time.

"No, Lord," Senganan admitted, and Kavirathan demanded, "And why not?"

"Because, Lord, even if the Romans did not use that vile substance that they call naphtha, we would have been defeated." Senganan's tone was flat. "Prince Divakar launched our attack when the first Roman soldiers," he suddenly turned to indicate Pullus, "led by this man, were still in the narrow part of the pass. I counseled him to wait, as did Lord Ajay, but he refused to listen."

While Pullus didn't particularly care that this Cholan nobleman sitting on the opposite side of the table was informed of his own role in what in reality had been little more than a skirmish for the Equestrians, even as gruesome as it was roasting men and animals alive, he was interested to see that one of the Cholans next to Kavirathan who had been introduced as Lord Nish suddenly look at him intently. *So you* do *understand Greek, you little bastard,* Pullus thought with sour amusement.

It was Kavirathan who spoke, however, starting with a sigh before he said, "I told my brother several times that Divakar was not intelligent or disciplined enough to succeed him, but Karikala refused to listen. Still," his voice hardened, "it was your duty to remain by his side, Lord Senganan, just as those lords did."

"I do not deny that, Lord," Senganan replied, not flinching even as Nish and Marish glared at him, making no attempt to hide their hostility. "But that is an action that I cannot undo. All

I can do now is to assure you of what I have seen."

For a long moment, Kavirathan didn't respond, but he finally broke the silence. "That is true. So," he gestured at Senganan, "please tell me all that you have seen these Romans do."

Senganan did so, but when he switched to Tamil and Achaemenes crouched behind Caesar to whisper what the Cholan was saying, their general stopped him with a wave of his hand.

"I'll know what I need to know by the way he reacts," he whispered, and Pullus saw that Caesar's gaze was fixed on Kavirathan.

While Pullus only learned the basics of what he said from Achaemenes later, in the moment. he saw that Caesar's judgment about being able to discern the impact by watching Kavirathan was borne out, as the dead king's brother grew progressively paler, his mouth dropping in shock on at least two occasions, while Senganan's tone remained flat and matter-of-fact. which, ironically, seemed to have more of an impact than if he had spoken in more dramatic tones.

Finally, Senganan switched back to Greek, speaking more formally now as he finished, "That is why I made the judgment that our people will suffer more than they ever have before, against any other of our enemies, my Lord. The Chola kingdom would be completely destroyed, and there would be only ashes on which to build. Of course," he assured Kavirathan, "you are free to make the decision for yourself, but also remember that Caesar still holds Karikala's last two sons as hostages, and he has asked me to care for them as he and his army sail north."

To Pullus' surprise, it was obvious that Kavirathan had either been unaware of this or had forgotten, because he turned his head to stare at Caesar, and although Pullus couldn't see his general's face, he was certain that Caesar was returning that stare. He braced himself for Kavirathan to demand that Caesar release his two young nephews, who were aboard Caesar's flagship, but he didn't, and Pullus deduced that he had read Caesar's expression and recognized that it would be futile.

Instead, he said dully, "I accept the terms that you have offered, King Nedunj..."

Before he could get anything else out, the Cholan Nish leapt to his feet, shouting in Tamil, but Pullus didn't need any translation, nor did he need it for Sundara, who began bellowing at Nish, the pair pointing first to their respective leaders, then at each other, making Pullus realize the wisdom the Pandya and Chola leaders had shown in barring their subordinates from wearing weapons. Pullus' own hand had dropped to the hilt of his *gladius* when, for a brief moment, the two adversaries turned their attention to Caesar, who was still sitting with his arms crossed, seemingly only slightly interested in what was taking place, but then Sundara said something that brought Nish's attention back to the Pandyan, and Pullus saw him suddenly thrust his hand down into the wide sash wrapped around his waist. What happened next occurred so quickly that Pullus didn't get his *gladius* even partially out of the sheath: when Kavirathan stood, drew his own sword, and swung it in a backhand swing because Nish was to his right, the blade slicing into the Cholan's throat, though it didn't sever his spinal column, making Nish's head drop backward at a grotesque angle as blood sprayed up in a scarlet fountain for the bare instant the dead man remained standing. Sundara was showered in his foe's blood, some of it landing in his open mouth, and he staggered backward, gagging and pawing at his eyes to clear the ichor away. Nedunj hadn't gotten to his feet, nor had Caesar, although the Roman was far enough removed at the opposite end of the table not to be spattered, and the Pandyan had his hand on the hilt of his sword as he watched Kavirathan. Nish had collapsed down into a heap, but when Kavirathan leaned over, Pullus used the moment to draw his *gladius,* which he held point down, his eyes fixed on the Cholan nobleman. Pullus' assumption was that Kavirathan was going to search Nish's sash, but instead, he loosened it and pulled it free, although he had to use his foot to move the body to do it, and Pullus saw the dagger, in a sheath that he was certain was made of solid gold, fall to the ground. Kavirathan gave it barely a glance, interested instead in the sash, which he used to wipe his blade clean. The silence was total, as all eyes were on the Cholan, and since he was the only other man whose face he could see, Pullus glanced at Lord Marish, whose eyes were wide and, to Pullus, appeared to be frightened by Kavirathan, although the Cholan didn't even look in his direction, seemingly absorbed in making sure all the blood was wiped from the blade. Finally satisfied, he sheathed his sword, then sat down, and only then did he return his attention to his shocked audience.

"I apologize for Lord Nish's behavior, King Nedunj," Kavirathan spoke at last, making it sound as if the dead man had spilled a drink on his guest. Pullus saw him swallow, then take a deep breath, but he looked directly at Nedunj. "As I was saying, I will accept your terms, but only for the sake of my people. And," his voice hardened slightly, but it was his gaze that Pullus would remember, "know this. If you prove that the Pandya are the people we Chola believe them to be, and you break this agreement, I swear on my dead brother's life that I will finish what he started, and make sure that you have nothing to rule over but ash and corpses."

Pullus had to stifle a groan, thinking that there was no way the young Pandyan king would accept this kind of language, especially from an essentially conquered foe, and for a long moment, Nedunj said nothing.

"And I swear on the life of my wife and family that, as long as the Chola abide by the terms, so will we."

Pullus could tell by the sibilant quality that Nedunj was speaking with his teeth clenched, but what mattered was that when he stood and extended his hand, it was empty.

Caesar was true to his word, the fleet departing the next day, but not without some resistance from Pollio.

"Do you think it's wise to leave Nedunj and Kavirathan behind? It's a tinderbox right now," he told Caesar the night before their departure. "Letting tempers cool while we're here is surely something to consider."

"It is," Caesar seemingly agreed, "and I did. But," he put a hand on Pollio's shoulder, "we're not staying another day. The sooner we sail into Andhra territory, the sooner we'll know what kind of reception to expect, and then we can plan accordingly."

It was the gentle but firm squeeze that Pollio had learned was the signal that Caesar's mind wouldn't be changed, so he didn't try, but he wouldn't have taken much consolation from the fact that he was far from alone in his concern about leaving an unsettled and potentially volatile situation effectively in their rear. Yes, with Taprobane established, the Romans could receive resupply by sea, and neither the Pandyans nor Cholans had anything resembling a navy that could stop the transport ships, which were now guarded by a dozen *biremes* and three *triremes* that were now permanently detached from the larger fleet. Nevertheless, it wasn't only Pollio who was nervous about the situation.

"I wouldn't be surprised if we have to come back here a month from now, if not sooner," Pullus had complained. "These are people who have hated each other for generations, one of them just crushed the other, the Cholan king is dead, and we're supposed to believe that Kavirathan is being sincere?"

"I thought you said he sounded like he meant what he said," Diocles countered.

"I did," Pullus agreed. "But I'm worried that once he thinks that we're too far away to come back to help Nedunj, he's going to have second thoughts."

"Does it really matter?" Diocles asked quietly, knowing this would be the last thing Pullus would expect the Greek to ask.

He was rewarded by the look of surprise, but when Pullus automatically opened his mouth to reply, nothing came out of his mouth as his mind turned over what Diocles had said.

"No," he finally said slowly after thinking about it. "I don't suppose it does. We," he sighed, "aren't coming back this way until we've reached Palibothra."

It would be only days later when this straightforward goal became much, much more complicated, and would present Caesar with yet another challenge.

The lead ships of Caesar's fleet entered Andhra waters when they sailed past the mouth of the river the Greeks had named as the Tynnas (Penna) River early on the second day of the voyage, the river marking the boundary between the Chola and Andhra Empire. Caesar ordered the fleet to anchor, while his small boat was sent ashore to retrieve Hirtius, whose cavalry had been busy, with at least two or three *alae* of cavalry sent west to scout the northern part of the Cholan interior, while a smaller group had been sent across the river, but with orders not to penetrate more than twenty miles into Andhra territory, and to try and avoid detection. Hirtius came to the *quinquereme* to deliver his report, for which Caesar summoned the Primi Pili.

"The good news," Hirtius began, "is that the Northern Army of the Chola was the only force of any size in this part of their kingdom. We came across several small villages that, frankly, aren't that different from Pandya, or Bharuch for that matter. And no," Hirtius assured Caesar, "I didn't allow the men to do any looting, and I gave silver for everything we took for our food." Seeing Caesar nod his approval, Hirtius continued after consulting one of the tablets he brought with him, "We did have two...incidents, I suppose is the best way to put it, and one of them involved men from the upper caste of the Chola. It was something of an accident, when Decurion Frontinus' *ala* ran into an armed party of Cholans with five elephants."

"What do you mean 'ran into,' Aulus?" Caesar asked, causing his Legate to redden slightly.

"I apologize, Caesar, I should have been more precise. It turned out that one of the villagers in the village Frontinus had just passed through ran to the estate of his local lord, and he roused his warriors. They came looking for us, but since Frontinus was on unfamiliar ground, the Cholan took advantage of his knowledge of the land and was able to approach through one of the patches of *jangla*. The first Frontinus knew about it was when two of his troopers were shot out of their saddles by the archers in the *howdahs*."

"How did their horses not smell the elephants?" Batius spoke up. "What we learned when we were training with those beasts in Muziris was that you have to train horses to tolerate them. Surely in an *ala* of cavalry, there were enough horses who smelled them before Frontinus and his men saw them."

"It was raining," Hirtius replied, his tone even, but Pullus could see that the Legate didn't care for Batius' line of questioning. "Remember, it's now monsoon season. While horses still have a good sense of smell, the downpour meant that they had to be much closer than normal." Hirtius looked at

Caesar, who indicated with a nod to move on. Looking back at the tablet, he picked up where he left off, "The second incident I'm afraid was north of the Tynnas."

"Which means the Andhra," Caesar interjected.

The nod Hirtius offered was reluctant, but it was about to get worse, "I'm afraid that we lost our translator, Arjan Udayar, and by lost, I mean he was either captured. Or," he hesitated, "he deserted."

Even a man with as formidable a memory as Caesar had his limits, and he was forced to ask Hirtius, "Refresh my memory, Aulus."

"He was one of the first of the Bharuch men who took the job," Hirtius explained.

It was Pullus who spoke next, realizing the reason the name had sounded familiar.

"Caesar, he's friends with Barhinder Gotra. When I get back to the *Lykaina,* I'll ask him about Udayar. He might be able to at least tell us if he was someone who might desert us."

Caesar nodded, but while this was good information to know, ultimately what mattered was that he had undoubtedly been questioned by the Andhra.

"Did anyone see who it was who might have taken him?"

"No," Hirtius shook his head. "At least, not clearly. It was a small village not more than two miles north of the river, and Decurion Brennus sent Udayar to talk to a man who was in his field just outside the village. Brennus swears that he told Udayar to remain in sight, but then he saw the farmer point in the direction of the village, then turn and walk in that direction, and Udayar followed. He was too far away for Brennus to yell, and he didn't want to have his *Cornicen* sound the recall to bring Udayar back. He said he waited to a count of a hundred, then he took a *turma,* and they went into the village. Udayar wasn't there, but one of Brennus' men spotted movement on the track that leads north from the village, and they could tell that it was horsemen. The trooper swore that he recognized Udayar's horse. But," he finished with another shake of his head, "whether he went willingly or was captured we don't know."

"It doesn't matter." Caesar frowned, but while he was

looking down at his own tablet, his mind was working furiously. "We must assume," he said finally, "that either way, the Andhra now know more about us and our organization than we know about them." For the first time, he acknowledged Senganan's presence to ask, "How much farther to their large port? Kantakasylla?"

"Kantakossylla," Senganan corrected Caesar, but it was done absently as he tried to calculate the distance, missing Caesar's glare at him. After a pause, he answered, "It is about as far from here to there as it was from Chennai to here."

"So, a hundred miles," Caesar mused. "Which means that we will be there late tomorrow, unless there's a storm. Lysippos tells me that our chances of making it all the way to the Ganges without a major storm where we'll have to put in or find a protected cove of some sort is next to nothing." Those who didn't know him might have thought he was praying, his head bowed as he stared sightlessly at the tablet. Finally, he said, "We're going to operate on the assumption that, whether it was willing or not, Udayar has divulged most or all of what he knows about us, and they clearly know that we're coming." Turning to Hirtius, he ordered, "Aulus, you and your men are going to match our speed on land. I know," he cut Hirtius' groan off with a raised hand, "that your men won't care for this, but I don't want us to be in a position where you come under attack by the Andhra, and we aren't in a position to land to support you. Which," he finished, "is also why you need to ride no more than a mile from the coastline. Only deviate and go deeper inland if there is no other choice." Turning to address the Primi Pili, Caesar's expression was grim. "So have your men prepared for the possibility that we may see some sort of excitement tomorrow, although only the gods know when."

Satakarni, second of his name and the fourth king of what would become known as the Satavahana dynasty, had eschewed the relative comfort of riding his elephant from his capital of Garthapuri to Kantakossylla, choosing to ride in his personal chariot instead to reach the port city as quickly as possible. He had been anticipating the arrival of the Romans for some time, but now that the moment was at hand, there was an urgency to his preparations that found him racing along the royal road that, while not paved in the Roman fashion, was still well maintained. His chief advisor, Lord Jyani, was already there and had been inspecting the defenses of the city that, while not the only port, was the most important because it wasn't only a seaport, but the river the Greeks called the Maisolo and was the Krishna River by the Andhra was similar to the river Narmada, which flowed out to the Arabian Sea, being navigable for much of its length by larger ships. Because of its location, the Andhra had more contact with the Yavana kingdoms to the north under Greek influence, and Satakarni's father had actually lured a Greek experienced in ship design to help construct what was the most powerful fleet on the eastern coast. However, what Satakarni had learned from a captured scout, who hadn't been Roman, but from Bharuch, his bitter rival to the west, was that not only was this Roman fleet more numerous, his ships wouldn't last long against the massive power the foreign invaders brought with them. The bitterest blow came when, shortly before he died, the enemy scout had described the fifteen *quinqueremes*, a design that he had never heard of before this moment, as the man gasped out a description of a ship so massive that it had five banks of oars. He was familiar with the *quadrireme*, but there was only one in the fleet that had been under construction when his father, also called Satakarni, had died and he had ascended to the kingship. The rest of his fleet was composed of forty *triremes* and fifty *biremes*, and it had proven more than sufficient to patrol the eastern coast to thwart the ever present swarms of pirate ships that preyed on the slow moving, sail-powered transports that carried the goods that was the lifeblood of the Andhra.

    Because of its location on the eastern coast, the merchants of Andhra did the most business with the faraway Han, who had proven to have sufficient resources to buy most of what the Andhra produced, while the Andhra coveted the silk, jade, and a number of other items that came from the lands of the Han. All of this fueled the ambition of the man currently sitting on the Andhra throne, providing him with the gold needed to maintain what was a large standing army, although like its western neighbor Bharuch, the Andhra favored what was an amalgam of the military style of East and West. He had five thousand men for whom the spear was the primary weapon, but organized and armed in a style that the late King Abhiraka, and all of the northern kingdoms would recognize, one of the many influences that still impacted India even now, almost three centuries later after the death of Alexander. These men were considered the elite warriors of his kingdom, and any man who sought to serve his king in this manner had to undergo a grueling process where he learned how to cope with the hardship brought on by the combination of being heavily armored while in the stifling heat and crushing humidity of their land. And, also like Bharuch, the Andhra had elephants, although he had learned through bitter experience that with the appearance of the Romans, they brought with them something that, unbeknownst to him, his fellow monarchs in the lower half of India had been unable to counter. While Satakarni hadn't led the attempt, he had sent his ablest general and a quarter of his elephants westward to Bharuch, in an attempt to probe the extent of the defenses now that his rival Abhiraka was dead and the foreigners were in control. Having the Andhra kingdom stretch across the entirety of India had been a long-held ambition, starting with Satakarni's great-grandfather, the first king of what was now known to the Greeks as the Andhra, and Satakarni had seen an opportunity in what he assumed would be the turmoil and chaos of a kingless Bharuch. Not only had he lost almost half of his elephants, he had lost Lord Khaj when he had gotten too close to the walls of the city, and while he had been informed of the gruesome nature of his death, he was unaware that in this, Khaj and the Crown Prince Divakar of the Chola shared the same fate. It was a bitter blow, damaging in both a material sense and to his own prestige, but it had also been instructive to the king, which was what found him in a chariot, surrounded by five hundred mounted men of his royal bodyguard, racing to Kantakossylla, hoping that Lord Jyani had acted prudently and not blindly ordered what he now understood was a tiny fleet out to sea to meet the advancing Romans. It would be better to know their intentions before making what could be an irrevocable and costly mistake.

Fortunately for Satakarni, Caesar's intentions were similar to his own, which was why, when Lord Jyani behaved as Satakarni feared, sending three of the *triremes* and five *biremes* out of the protected dock on the Maisolo, rowing a mile out to sea before arraying themselves perpendicular to the coast in a manner that made their intentions clear, Caesar's order to only engage if attacked meant that for a span of time, the leading ships of the Roman fleet were drifting, facing north, with the Andhra fleet pointed in the opposite direction doing the same thing. This impasse had an unexpected benefit, because it enabled a fleet of ships that stretched for several miles to coalesce, particularly the warships, and out of which five *quinqueremes* rowed north to array themselves in between the leading edge of Roman ships that were already present. It made things cramped, and would have been detrimental in the event that the Andhra ships suddenly began rowing to attack, but as Caesar had surmised, just the sight of the massive vessels was enough for the Andhra nobleman who had been given command by Lord Jyani to order the ships to backrow and retreat back to the Maisolo, although they stopped and dropped anchor in a line across the river mouth.

Pullus, standing on the rear deck of the *Lykaina*, now drifting two hundred paces behind their own first line of ships and to the left of Caesar's flagship commented to Balbus, "It looks like they might want to talk rather than fight."

"Wouldn't you if you saw all that?" Balbus pointed to the five massive ships, each of them armed with two *ballistae* positioned amidships, with a pair of scorpions at the bow and stern.

"Yes," Pullus agreed, then movement off to his right caused him to turn to see Caesar's flagship was now rowing past the other motionless, drifting craft. "And it looks like Caesar is about to do just that."

Balbus nodded, but his mind was elsewhere, pointing again to the line of ships ahead of them. "Where is he going to fit? There's no room between any of them for that big bastard to fit."

It was, Pullus saw instantly, true, but before he could begin to speculate, they got their answer when the *quinquereme* in the center essentially copied the Andhra ships by backrowing to move itself out of the way. As often as he had seen it done by this point, it never failed to impress Pullus at the skill of the *navarchae* who served as the masters of these massive vessels, this one moving with a ponderous grace that reminded Pullus of how elephants maneuvered when they were packed together. He was about to mention this to Balbus then thought better of it, not wanting to endure his friend's derision for thinking such thoughts that he was certain Balbus would have ascribed to Pullus being influenced by his Greek clerk.

"You know," Balbus commented as he watched along with Pullus, "they remind me of elephants a bit in the way they move around." Looking over sharply at Pullus' groan, and unaware that their thoughts had been running along the same line, he said defensively, "What's that for? It's true!"

"I know," Pullus considered having a bit more fun at Balbus' expense, but he was too distracted by the sight of Caesar, who had emerged from his quarters to stride down the deck just as his ship was sliding past the *Lykaina*. "Caesar is dressed for war," he observed. "Let's see if that's just a precaution or if he's changed his mind."

He was about to order Balbus and his Optio Lutatius to rouse the men; in a slight variation of Caesar's orders for the men to be prepared, Pullus had allowed them to delay putting on their *hamatae*, knowing how close the air was down below, but once Caesar reached the bow, he bent down and picked up what served as a signal of intention. When Caesar stepped up onto the side, Pullus winced at what he viewed as Caesar's recklessness, but his general had a firm grasp of the high prow with one hand while he thrust the leafy branch into the air, then waved it back and forth. After a delay of a few dozen heartbeats, Pullus saw movement at the bow of one of the Andhra ships, barely able to pick up the flash of green, and he felt his body relax.

"It looks like we talk first," he said to Balbus, but the Centurion had seen it as well, and was already moving to the ladder to inform the men of his Century they had a respite.

Caesar had to transfer to one of the Liburnians, which was

maneuverable enough to come within hailing distance, and fast enough to escape in the event the Andhra had a change of heart, but along with Senganan and Achaemenes, he brought Gundomir and Teispes in the small boat that rowed to the Liburnian, more to quell what he knew would be their complaining.

Before he lowered himself down the ladder, he reminded Pollio, "You know what to do if the Andhra betray us."

"I do," Pollio confirmed, a bit nettled at the unnecessary reminder.

With a lithe grace that belied the fact that Gaius Julius Caesar was now almost sixty years old, the general dropped down into the boat and sat down as the lead oarsman shoved it away from the side of the larger vessel. Once they clambered aboard the Liburnian, Caesar wasted no time, ordering the *navarch* to resume movement, slowly, towards the waiting Andhra. Once they were within perhaps two hundred paces, the man Caesar assumed was the ranking officer stepped up onto the prow in the same manner as Caesar had, but it was the winking of golden fire that caught Caesar's eye.

Senganan glanced over when Caesar shaded his eyes, and made a shrewd guess, saying with some humor, "The Andhra do love their gold, Caesar."

"Do they have gold mines?" Caesar asked, seemingly distracted, but Senganan sensed the keen interest behind the question.

"No, but they have other things that others will offer gold to buy," Senganan replied. "The gold mines are north of the Andhra."

Like Caesar, he had tried to sound offhand about this, but like Senganan, Caesar wasn't fooled, giving him a sidelong glance, with a knowing smile.

"You mean the gold mines happen to be where I'm leading my army?"

"Yes, Caesar," Senganan agreed, but while he had returned Caesar's smile, he added soberly, "And their location is a closely guarded secret with the Gangaridae."

"I'm sure that it is," Caesar answered, but this was all the time he had to devote to the matter, although in the back of his mind, he was thinking about how gold could solve many of his problems with the men. The Liburnian had come within fifty paces of the bow of the ship carrying the Andhra noble, which had also detached itself from the other ships. Gesturing to Achaemenes, he stepped back up on the side and called out to the other man, "Do you speak Greek?"

When the man shook his head, Caesar, assuming that the Andhra were similar to Pandya and Chola, began to introduce himself in Greek, only to have the man hold his hands up in confusion. Muttering a curse, Caesar turned to Achaemenes, who stood on the opposite side of the prow, and repeated Caesar's words in Tamil. This man, who in fact was wearing several thick gold chains around his neck, along with gold armbands and several bracelets, while his turban gleamed in a manner that told Caesar that it was silk, clearly understood, but when he replied, it was Achaemenes' turn to curse.

"He is speaking Tamil, but it is a dialect that I have not heard before, Caesar," Achaemenes said.

Hiding his reluctance, Caesar turned to address Senganan, but the Cholan was already moving to the bow, stopping just behind Caesar, saying quietly, "He says his name is Lord Jyani, and that he speaks for King Satakarni, but that he expects the king to arrive from the interior very soon."

"You heard what I instructed Achaemenes to say?" Caesar asked, and Senganan shook his head. "Good, then will you please relay that to Lord Jyani?"

Changing places with Achaemenes, Caesar just happened to have his eyes still on Lord Jyani, and he saw the man, who appeared to be in his thirties, react in a manner that Caesar was certain meant they had met. He was about to ask, then decided against it, for the moment.

Their exchange finished, Senganan informed Caesar, "Lord Jyani says that, if your intentions are peaceful, that you will be allowed to land so that you can speak to King Satakarni." He hesitated, and Caesar learned why when he said, "But that it can only be you and one other man, to interpret."

Although Gundomir and Teispes didn't fit on the small foredeck of the Liburnian, they were close enough to hear that, but it was the German who objected first, "Caesar, that sounds like a trap! Going ashore with only one man will put you in grave danger!"

Rather than address Gundomir, Caesar told Senganan, "Tell Lord Jyani that I invite King Satakarni to come aboard my flagship."

This surprised Senganan, but he quickly obeyed, prompting a stream of words from Jyani that, while indecipherable to the Roman ear, communicated the essence in its tone, prompting Caesar to chuckle.

Before Senganan could translate, he said, "Allow me to guess, Lord Senganan. He said that he could do no such thing because it would put his king into too much danger, and it could be a trap."

It was Senganan's turn to laugh softly, admitting, "That is essentially what he said, Caesar."

"Then tell him," Caesar turned and pointed to Gundomir, "that is exactly what the commander of my personal bodyguard said."

Senganan did so, while Caesar studied Jyani's demeanor, but rather than be offended, or defensive, although he didn't laugh, he did offer a broad smile as he replied.

"Lord Jyani says that Lord Gundomir makes an excellent point, and perhaps he would like to serve King Satakarni in his royal bodyguard."

Caesar's laugh was only partially feigned, but he had gotten what he wanted from the exchange, and he said calmly, "Tell Lord Jyani that if he allows me to come with two people, I will come ashore."

He wasn't surprised at the uproar this caused, but Caesar had made up his mind.

"This Lord Jyani isn't blind," he explained to his bodyguards, while Achaemenes, who would be the third man, didn't look particularly happy at the idea either. Facing aft, Caesar swept his arm over the vast fleet, most of which now had men standing on the deck plainly visible, watching the scene being played out. And, as Caesar well knew, wagering on the outcome.

Once Gundomir and Teispes determined Caesar wouldn't be swayed, they could only stand and watch as the Liburnian's

Caesar Ascending – The Ganges

navarch lowered the small boat into the water, although it was so small that Achaemenes had to serve as the second oarsman.

"Pollio knows what to do," Caesar called out to the pair who had come to the prow, both of them expressing their disapproval, albeit in their own way. "Don't worry, I'll be fine. But," Caesar was speaking in Latin, and his voice hardened, "if they do betray me, I want Pollio and my Legions to avenge me and leave no doubt that Rome is here, is that understood?"

There was nothing they could do but nod their agreement, and hope that, once again, Caesar's Luck held.

Caesar took it as a sign of that very thing when, even before the *trireme* bearing him, Senganan and Achaemenes returned to its mooring, there was an uproar from deeper in the city that presaged the arrival of the king, who came thundering through the open gates in his chariot. The king stopped only long enough to order the commander of his bodyguard to escort his wife, Queen Charvangi, who had shared his chariot with him, to the stone two-story building that, while smaller, was a copy of the royal palace in Garthapuri. By the time the king arrived at the docks, the ship was being moored, the plank lowered, but while Satakarni had been able to see the vast Roman fleet spread across the natural bay that had been formed over the millennia as the silt carried by the Krishna extended out from the coastline to create a blunt peninsula, upon which Kantakossylla was built, he wasn't present to see a Roman stride down the plank, seemingly completely unafraid, arriving at the docks a moment too late. The first time Satakarni ever laid eyes on a Roman was at the sight of the tall, pale man, accompanied by a man he vaguely recognized and remembered as being part of a delegation from Chola, with a much younger man on the Roman's opposite side who, while dark, bore distinctly different features than any of the people of southern India. Not surprisingly, however, Satakarni's attention was on the Roman, who was wearing a cuirass that, while it was similar to the armor that had been introduced to their world by the Macedonians, was much more ornate, with a pair of rearing horses facing each other, while the leaves of some kind of trailing plant wrapped around them, the horses and the leaves chased in gold. His helmet was also different, with an iron strip just above his eyes and two hanging cheek pieces that were hinged instead of one piece, with a black feather crest that ran front to back, and around his shoulders was a cloak that was a brilliant scarlet, but it was the Roman's eyes that arrested Satakarni's attention, never having seen eyes of that coloring before. Only belatedly realizing that he had come to an abrupt halt, he looked for Lord Jyani, who had been giving instructions to the ship master, and he now came hurrying towards the king, dropping to his knees in front of Satakarni.

"Your Highness, this is the Roman Caesar. I did as you asked and urged him to come ashore, which neither of us thought he would do, but..." Realizing the obvious, he looked up and said simply, "...as you can see, he is here."

Satakarni's eyes hadn't left the three men, and he noticed that the Roman seemed more amused than apprehensive at essentially being in Satakarni's power, but the king had seen more than enough as he approached Kantakossylla to know why the Roman was unafraid; he could see just by the sheer number of ships filling that bay that they would carry enough men to raze the city and slaughter every inhabitant. That, he understood, was why this Caesar was standing there so confidently; nevertheless, it took courage, and Satakarni's respect grew for this strange-looking man.

"Rise and come with me," he murmured to Jyani, but when his bodyguards, who were standing just a few paces behind him made to follow, he stopped them with a gesture, determined to show Caesar that he wasn't the only one who could seem unafraid.

"He speaks Greek, Your Highness," Jyani whispered, "but I pretended I didn't understand him." When Satakarni gave him a curious glance at this, the nobleman shrugged and still whispering, said, "Their ignorance of that might be useful."

Then, they were just a matter of five paces away, and forewarned, Satakarni spoke in Greek.

Indicating himself, he began, "My name is Satakarni, son of Satakarni, second of my name and I am the fourth King of what some call the Andhra, while we refer to ourselves as the Satavahana, after our clan name. And," he made an expansive sweep of their surroundings with both arms, "I bid you welcome to the city of Kantakossylla, one of my *many* ports." It wasn't much, but Caesar didn't miss the change in tone as the king continued, "You are welcome, provided of course, that you come in peace." As if to soften the words, he smiled and addressed Caesar, "And you must be the Roman Caesar."

"Yes, Your Highness," Caesar, always comfortable dealing with royalty, did incline his head, barely, "you are correct. I am Gaius Julius Caesar, of the Julii, who are direct descendants of Aeneas, who founded our city of Rome and was the son of our goddess Venus." You're not the only one who can boast about your ancestors, Caesar thought with some amusement. "I am also Dictator for Life, as appointed by the Senate and People of Rome."

There was a gleam in Satakarni's eye that told Caesar that the Andhra knew what Caesar was doing and why, which he confirmed when he said with obvious amusement, "Now that we have established how important we are and favored by our gods, may I ask your purpose here?"

"Only to talk," Caesar replied. "And," he emphasized, "nothing more, so I am afraid that my visit will be brief."

"Ah," Satakarni tried to sound regretful, "that is a pity. I am sure that we have much to discuss, and to share." Before Caesar could reply, for the first time, Satakarni turned to Senganan, looking slightly embarrassed, "While I recognize you, Lord, and know that you are from the Chola, I am ashamed to say that I do not recall your name."

"There is no reason you should, Your Highness," Senganan replied, and if he was upset at the slight, he hid it well. "My name is Senganan and I was part of an embassy several years ago, just one of many men of to come to Garthapuri to discuss several matters on behalf of our king."

"Yes, I remember you now, Lord Senganan," Satakarni lied, but once more, there was a change in his demeanor, "but I must admit that I am quite curious as to why a man from Chola would be here with a Roman, given what we have heard of what happened between Pandya and your King Karikala."

Despite being certain that the Andhra didn't know that he was in fact speaking to the man who had slain Karikala,

Senganan still felt a surprisingly strong stab of guilt, even as he was certain that he had done the right thing even more now than he had been that day in the throne room.

Knowing this was as much a test as anything, Senganan replied evenly, "I am loyal to Chola, Your Highness, and I always will be."

"I did not mean to imply otherwise, Lord Senganan," Satakarni assured him, and now Senganan was certain he was lying, but the Andhra had turned his attention to the third man.

"I do not recognize your garb," Satakarni said politely, "but I do not think you are Roman."

"No, Your Highness," Achaemenes answered, in Greek, but then switched to Tamil, which Caesar had told him to use at the first opportunity, "I am Parthian, not Roman. But," he turned his head and indicated Caesar, "I serve Caesar, and Rome now."

Satakarni's eyes widened slightly, and his surprise was genuine as he exclaimed, "I have never met a man from Parthia before. Although," he laughed, returning his attention to Caesar, "I had never met a Roman before today." With the introductions done, the king said, "Might I suggest that we retire out of this hot sun? I have a home here, and I can offer refreshment while we become more acquainted."

Expecting this, and as eager to get out of the heat as anyone, Caesar readily agreed. The king, who appeared to be in his mid-thirties, offered something of a tour as, surrounded by his bodyguards, the party moved into the city. While Satakarni had been talking, and just as the king had done when Caesar was introducing himself, he had examined the Andhra king. Most striking was that he was draped in even more gold jewelry than Lord Jyani, who had hurried ahead to prepare the palace, with three armbands on each bicep, which were well-formed and muscular, one stacked above the other, while the gold necklaces were of varying lengths, so the effect was to make his chest, which was bare, appear to be covered in gold so that the bare skin in between his nipples was barely visible. It was the scars on his upper chest and arms that the jewelry didn't cover that Caesar noticed, telling him that Satakarni was a warrior king, and not one in the mold of Nedunj's father. Just like

Caesar Ascending – The Ganges

Uraiyur, Karoura, and Muziris, there were several temples, also with the distinctive spires of ornately carved rock, each one devoted to one of the dizzying array of gods that, even for a Roman, whose pantheon included dozens of deities from nations they had adopted as their own, was an overwhelming number. In fact, it was a source of secret embarrassment to the Roman that, as much as he prided himself on his ability to remember astonishing amounts of information, he had only scratched the surface of the religion the people of this land called Hinduism, and he wondered if he would ever have the time to study it more thoroughly. Caesar was also accustomed to the stares of the common people, although the bodyguards leading the party shoved them out of the way, and they all dropped to their knees and bowed their heads as their king walked by, still pointing out a sight of interest to Caesar. While Caesar appeared to listen, he also was observing everything else, and he noticed how Satakarni didn't acknowledge, or even seem to notice the people who had been going about their daily business then suddenly found themselves on their knees as he swept by. This, Caesar thought, is a man who takes his people for granted, which might be useful at some time in the future. He wasn't particularly surprised to see that what the king had described simply as his home was made of stone like the temples of southern India, was two stories, and dominated one side of the large open square that, even in all of his travels, seemed to be a standard part of the design for all the people he had encountered. Crossing the square, Satakarni bounded up the steps where two guards stood, each one pulling open a door in a manner that suggested to Caesar that when the Andhra king was moving, he was always in a hurry. Making sure to dab his face before entering the palace to reduce the sheen of perspiration, Caesar led the other two men into the cooler interior, which was well lit because the wooden screens over the large windows were raised, while curtains made of a gauzy material that helped keep the bugs out but enabled a breeze were in place, softening the harsh sunlight. Caesar barely noticed any of this, because standing directly in front of the double doors, clearly waiting, was a woman who was strikingly beautiful, and even as the woman stepped forward to welcome Satakarni, their

353

eyes locked. Suddenly, Caesar was reluctant to doff his helmet; he was aware that his men were amused by his attempts to cover his baldness, and he knew that it was his vanity that caused the fact that he was going bald to matter more than it should, but he had long before accepted himself, foibles and all. The woman spoke in Tamil, and Caesar heard Satakarni's name, but his hopes that this was a sister or even a concubine were dashed when the king turned to address them.

"Caesar, may I introduce my wife, and queen, Charvangi."

The pride in his voice was not only obvious, it was clearly unfeigned, and Caesar felt a stab of irrational jealousy, while Cleopatra would have been dismayed to learn that he wasn't thinking of her now, and he hadn't thought of her in weeks; she would have been even more alarmed to learn that, the last time he had contemplated her at all, it was in the form of a potential problem that needed to be controlled, as she would be learning once Rufus arrived in Rome to deliver his message to Antonius sending him to Alexandria, a fact that was unknown to anyone other than Caesar himself.

Glancing over at Achaemenes in a signal to translate, Caesar finally removed his helmet and inclined his head as he instructed the Parthian, "Please tell the Queen that rarely have I seen such beauty, and King Satakarni has truly been blessed by his gods."

When the words were translated, Caesar could see both husband and wife were pleased, but as pleasant a diversion as this was, the Roman also was acutely aware that even now, thousands of men were crammed aboard ships, wondering where their general had gone. Either Satakarni sensed this, or was of a similar mind, because he beckoned Lord Jyani, who had emerged from another room, then rattled off what sounded like instructions in Tamil. When he was finished, Jyani hurried off, and Satakarni extended his arm to the archway that led into the room from which Jyani had emerged.

"I have sent for some refreshment, but am I correct to assume that you have no objection to speaking while we wait?"

Caesar didn't try to hide his relief, remembering to shake his head. "Your assumption is correct, Your Highness."

"Come then, and you can tell me why you have so many

ships floating in my kingdom's waters," Satakarni was entering the next room, so it was over his shoulder as he added, "and why there are almost ten thousand men on horseback on my lands."

It was a bit optimistic, Caesar recognized, to expect Hirtius and his men go unobserved, but he waited until he took a seat on what was similar to a Roman-style couch that the king indicated, and since there was enough room for just one more, Caesar indicated for Senganan to sit, and Achaemenes moved behind the couch.

"The answer to the first question, Your Highness," Caesar began, "should help answer your second."

He stopped only once, when three young slaves entered, one carrying a jug, with the other two bringing cups; that they were all females wasn't unusual, but the fact that they were all topless was, at least to this point in time. While the women of both Pandya and Chola often went seminude in their homes, it had been Caesar's experience that they were more circumspect in the presence of strangers, and he wondered if this was an attempt by the Andhra king to throw him off balance and perhaps reveal something, in a manner of speaking. Pointedly ignoring the girls and returning to his conversation, Caesar outlined his plans in clear and simple terms, but took care to present them as a fact, wanting to make it clear that while he had no interest in any hostilities with the Andhra, neither would he shy away from it.

He paused to sip from his drink, which Satakarni took advantage of to ask bluntly, "You have assured me that you have no hostile intentions, Caesar, but while I will accept that this is true for the moment, it still does not answer the question of why?"

"Why what?"

"Why," Satakarni explained patiently, "you are going to sail along the entire length of my kingdom and beyond? What is your purpose?"

"My purpose," Caesar replied coolly, "is my own business, Your Highness. But," he saw the flare of anger in the king's eyes and held up a hand, "because you have shown us such hospitality and made it clear that you prefer to talk rather than fight, I will tell you. I intend to reach the Ganges with my army."

The look of bemusement on Satakarni's face was replaced, suddenly, by a dawning understanding, "I see. You are attempting to do what the Macedonian king Alexander could not, yes?"

"Yes," Caesar answered, then hesitated before saying, "but I also intend to take my fleet up the Ganges to take Palibothra from whoever is currently holding it."

Satakarni's reaction was one Caesar would never forget; after a heartbeat of silence, when the Andhra king determined that Caesar wasn't jesting...he burst out laughing.

When Pullus returned from Caesar's flagship later that night after meeting with the general, who had returned, unharmed, to the fleet shortly before sunset, he was shaken enough that he sent messages to the ships carrying his Pili Priores, rousing most of them since they had retired for the night. The fleet was now anchored, which required a bit of shuffling so that the ships drew close enough to shore to toss their anchor stones overboard in shallow enough waters, but even at sea, Caesar insisted on organization, meaning that the ships carrying the Equestrians were grouped together. This did save time, but it was still almost a third of a watch later before the nine Pili Priores were aboard, although Scribonius had come onboard first, and Pullus had immediately retired to his cabin with his two best friends to let them know what was happening before informing the others.

"Once the men find out, we might have another Bharuch on our hands," was how Pullus began once everyone was present, crammed into his cabin, with Diocles and Barhinder posted outside the cabin to keep any curious ranker from overhearing. "The Andhra king Satakarni advised Caesar to turn the fleet around now, or if he was absolutely set on it, get us to the mouth of the Ganges and that's it." Pausing to allow for the reaction that he knew was coming, his Centurions quieted down quickly to allow him to continue, explaining, "There are three challenges. The first is that Palibothra is almost four hundred miles from the mouth of the Ganges."

Caesar Ascending – The Ganges

"But Caesar told us that it was barely a hundred miles inland!"

Pullus glared at Metellus, his former Hastatus Posterior and current Tertius Pilus Prior, but he kept his temper in check to reply, "Yes, he did, but his information was inaccurate. But that's only part of the problem with the Ganges. According to Satakarni, only the first two hundred miles of it are navigable for ships of our size. And," he hurried on before anyone could ask what that meant, "you saw the ships these Andhra have. They only have one *quadrireme*, but the king told Caesar that his father tried to lead his army up the Ganges and they only took their *triremes*, and that was as far as they could get because beyond that point the river narrows down and loops and twists and there are submerged sandbars and huge trees that can rip the bottom out of anything that rides that low in the water." He paused again, knowing that as bad as this was, there was worse coming, but he decided to get it over with. "But I said there were three challenges, and the first is the river. The second is the size of Palibothra itself. It's supposed to be about nine miles long and about five miles wide, in the shape of a rectangle, with two sides protected by the Ganges on the short eastern side, and another river along the southern side. They supposedly have more than five hundred towers, and more than sixty gates."

There was a stunned silence, as each Centurion grappled with the scale of a city that they had assumed they would be besieging or taking by direct assault. Even with an army of eleven Legions, and the most veteran and experienced army since Alexander's, this would require a massive effort.

It was left to Scribonius who, despite already knowing the answer because of his earlier conversation, subtly but unmistakably forced his friend to deliver the last, and worst piece of news by asking, "And what's the third thing, Primus Pilus?"

Not fooled in the slightest by his friend's use of his rank, Pullus gave him a scowl, even as he knew that he had been deliberately postponing the final blow.

Trying to keep his tone as even as possible, he said, "Supposedly, the army available to defend Palibothra on the behalf of their king is something we've never faced before, at least in scale. According to Satakarni, he can summon at least two hundred thousand men, but most of them are poorly trained levies that are armed with a spear and shield." Pullus consulted his wax tablet, though he had no real need to do so, but to put off what came next. "He also has twenty thousand cavalry, evenly split between lancers and archers, and apparently still uses two-man *quadrigae*, and has two thousand of those. And," he took a breath, "he uses elephants, but again, it's not the fact that he uses them, it's how many he supposedly has at his command, which is between three and four...thousand."

Judging by their collective demeanors, Pullus could see that his Centurions were in a state of shock similar to what he had experienced not long before, and he couldn't blame them. Even Caesar had been, if not shaken, then in a somber state as he related the information, but the one advantage that Pullus had that Caesar didn't was the fact that there was no map in Pullus' cabin, at least where it could be seen, Pullus having rolled it up and placed it in the chest containing his personal library before this meeting. If he had, then he would have faced the same reaction of the Primi Pili who saw that, with Palibothra so far inland, it would have been far shorter to march up the Narmada from Bharuch to its source before turning northeast, and marching about another three hundred miles.

The silence was broken by the Quintus Pilus Prior Marcus Trebellius, who sounded somewhat dazed. "While I don't know the exact number of jars of that *cac* we have, I know it's not anywhere close to four thousand."

Pullus didn't reply; there was no need to do so. Then Scribonius, in an attempt to help lighten the mood, joked, "Whoever these barbarians are, they must be fucking rich."

"That," Pullus agreed, "is certainly true." Before he could stop himself, he said, "They're the gateway for the Silk Road down into India, and the gateway from all the spices and peppers from the Chola and Pandyan kingdoms that supplies the interior of the Han Empire. And," he finished, "they're the source of all that gold that we've seen these barbarians wearing."

"So," the only non-Pilus Prior present mused, "all the stories about their wealth are true." Balbus' face twisted into his version of a grin, "If we take it, we'll all be as rich as Crassus, that's what I'm hearing."

"That's true," Pullus allowed, "but not even you could buy that many whores and drink that much wine. Or," he amended, "*sura*."

This elicited some chuckling, but it was muted as the Centurions grappled with what was, at a minimum, an important piece of information, if not one devastating to their general's plans.

"You told us the size of Palibothra," Scribonius asked, "but how many people live there?"

"Satakarni doesn't know with any certainty," Pullus replied, "but he says that it is at least four hundred thousand people."

"Pluto's *cock*!" Marcius gasped. "That's almost as big as Rome!"

"No, Rome is twice that size," Scribonius said grimly, "but it's still bigger than anything we've ever tackled before."

Pullus felt compelled to point out, "Caesar doesn't believe Satakarni, at least not completely. He thinks that he's exaggerating the numbers for reasons of his own."

"What reason?" Scribonius countered, confirming Pullus' fear that his friend would point out the flaw in their general's reasoning. "If he's lying, and Caesar believes him, he's got us sitting right here. This Satakarni may not know much about us, but he's got eyes, and he knows that we've subdued every other kingdom we've faced in India, and we've done it in less than two years. If I was him, my concern would be that by scaring Caesar about the power of these..."

Realizing that Pullus hadn't actually offered the name of this tribe, or kingdom, he looked at Pullus, who provided, "They're called the Gangaridae, but I don't know what the name of their king is."

"...These Gangaridae," Scribonius continued, "...and knowing that he's got an army who's probably anxious to get rich before we return to Rome, he's practically inviting us to invade his kingdom."

I hate you sometimes; this was what ran through Pullus' mind, mainly because he suspected that Scribonius was correct, but he felt compelled to say, "Whatever Caesar decides, he can count on the Equestrians. Right?"

He took the time to look at each and every one of his Pili Priores, but when few of them met his gaze, he briefly considered making an issue of it, then decided they had been through enough for the night.

"Right, get back to your ships," he ordered, then warned, "but do *not* let this get out, not until Caesar has had time to think about what to do about it. Is that understood?"

This time, Pullus wasn't content for nonverbal responses, and he didn't allow them to leave until they each assured him, with words, that they wouldn't tell anyone, not their Centurions, or their Optio, or whoever was their normal intimate that, like Pullus himself with Scribonius and Balbus, every one of them had. As far as Scribonius was concerned, he indicated for him to stay, and when Balbus moved to follow the others, he stopped him as well. Waiting until he heard the splashing sound of oars that signaled his officers were returning to their vessels, he turned to Diocles, pointing to the amphora, not the one that held water, but the one filled with *sura*, and Scribonius regarded him with a raised eyebrow.

"Oh my," he said mildly, "there must be worse news."

"There is," Pullus said shortly, dropping down onto his stool at the small table nailed to the deck, ignoring the audible smacking sound Balbus was making as he thrust his cup out to have it filled first by the Greek.

Scribonius decided to not force Pullus to express what he was certain was the thing bothering his friend, but as usual, he did so indirectly, asking as if he was simply curious, "Titus, can I see that map?"

His friend wasn't fooled, however, glaring at Scribonius a second time, but stopping Diocles from going to get it, he got up, opened the chest, and withdrew the rolled piece of vellum that was a smaller copy of the one hanging in Caesar's cabin.

"So you figured it out," Pullus said sourly, tossing the map at Scribonius, but his friend unrolled it before he said, "No, not really. I had an idea, though."

"Would you two tell me what the fuck you're talking about?" Balbus grumbled, his lips shining from downing half of the contents of his cup already. "I hate it when you two make me feel thick."

"The only reason we do," Scribonius countered, though his eyes were now on the map, "is because you are." Seeing it, he gave a nod, then looked up at Pullus. "So, if Caesar decides to go on to Palibothra, we're going almost halfway back in the direction of Bharuch."

"Yes," Pullus agreed miserably, "I was wrong to suggest taking the sea route to Caesar."

"No, you weren't," Scribonius replied firmly, looking Pullus in the eye as he tapped the map with a finger for emphasis. "You weren't wrong at all. You were basing your suggestion on what Caesar told us about where Palibothra was located. And," he stressed, "remember that he had all of those scrolls from the library in Alexandria from Alexander, Megasthenes, Androsthenes, Ptolemy, and Seleucus that he took before the fire. Caesar's at fault for this, not you."

"That may be," Pullus admitted reluctantly, "but it still doesn't change anything. The men have had their sights set on taking Palibothra, but once they find out the truth, I don't see them marching another step for Caesar."

This, Scribonius knew, was nothing more than the truth. Nevertheless, he found himself in the unusual position of being the defender of their general to his friend's pessimistic view of the overall situation.

Consequently, he said, "I think we need to trust Caesar to come up with something that will appease the men and keep them motivated to follow him. After all," he joked, "you know that Caesar won't stand for having the same thing happen to him that happened to Alexander and have his army quit on him. He figured out a way to get the men back on his side after Bharuch, so I'm sure that he's thinking right now about how to keep them going."

Even Scribonius would admit that it was said lightly, but he, Diocles, Balbus, and Pullus would on more than one occasion recall this conversation, and marvel at it.

Despite how events transpired, after Caesar returned to the fleet, if Scribonius had been aware of Caesar's state of mind in the next several watches, he would have never uttered those words. Reeling from the shock of the information imparted to him by Satakarni, he locked himself in his cabin for a span of time that had Pollio, Volusenus, Nero, and Hirtius, who had been rowed from shore, extremely worried.

"I've never seen him like this," Pollio muttered, then amended, "at least since the Ides more than five years ago."

The others agreed, even Volusenus, who had served with Caesar continuously from the early days of the Gallic campaign, but when they pressed the other two men who had been present, neither Senganan nor Achaemenes would divulge what had their general so shaken, albeit for different reasons. For Senganan, it was straightforward; he was as much of a hostage as the two young Chola princes, who were confined, comfortably enough, on one of the *quadriremes*, and while he at least partially trusted Caesar, he wasn't sanguine that his senior officers would view him as charitably. For Achaemenes, it was simpler; on their way back to the flagship, Caesar had asked both of them to not utter a word about the information they had learned from the Andhra king, and for the young Parthian, that was enough. Regardless of this, he was still uncomfortable refusing the other Romans who, to one degree or another, he respected, but finally, Pollio snapped at Nero, who had been the most persistent, to stop pestering him. After a stretch of time that couldn't be measured in heartbeats, while Caesar didn't emerge from his quarters, he did open the door before turning and going back to his desk, his Legates following immediately behind him. In a flat, emotionless tone, Caesar related what he had learned from Satakarni, their own reaction essentially identical to Pullus' Pili Priores, and the Pili Priores of the other Legions who would be summoned shortly to their respective Primus Pilus' ship. Shock, of course, dismay, and a fair amount of fear was the collective reaction of Pollio and his counterparts, each of them focusing on a different piece of information as their cause for concern.

Once Caesar finished from where he was seated behind his desk, his face still pale, it was Pollio who asked the first question that had come to his mind. "Do you believe him, Caesar?"

Caesar Ascending – The Ganges

"Not completely," Caesar admitted, then hurried to add, "though I don't think he was being deliberately deceptive." Suddenly realizing something, he turned and told Apollodorus to summon Senganan and Achaemenes, telling the others to hold their questions. It didn't take long, and once they were present, Caesar addressed Senganan first, asking bluntly, "What is your assessment of Satakarni and what he told me about Palibothra? Do you think he was telling the truth? Or was he deliberately lying to me?"

Put on the spot, Senganan hesitated, then in Greek, he said hesitantly, "While I would not put it past Satakarni to deceive you, in this I do not believe he was doing so."

"Why?"

Since he hadn't had time to think it through, having replied instinctively, it took a moment for Senganan to gather his thoughts, and when he resumed it was more firmly. "Because he has nothing to gain by deceiving you, and much to lose. You Romans," he tried to keep the bitterness out of his voice but was only partially successful, "have completely changed our world, and you have proven that you are difficult, if not impossible to stop should you decide to subdue us. If I was Satakarni, my concern would be that, if I lied about the size and strength of Palibothra and you discovered this, instead of focusing on Palibothra, you would turn your army on my kingdom, if not now then at some point in the future."

"But even if he was telling the truth," Hirtius objected, "he has to know that makes it even more of a possibility." Pointing away from the gathering and in the general direction of the ships floating around them, he argued, "Because of them. We have to assume that he heard what our Legions did when we took Bharuch."

"He had," Caesar confirmed, "and he brought it up." Turning back to Senganan, he asked, "Is there anything else you noticed? Any other thoughts?"

"No, Caesar, other than to say my sense was that Satakarni does not really know and is just repeating what he has heard from others about the Gangaridae."

Caesar signaled his acceptance, then turned to Achaemenes, who was just as nervous about being in this position as Senganan, albeit for different reasons, but he did not hesitate. "I agree with Lord Senganan, Caesar. I would not call what he related to us gossip, but I do believe that he was relaying only what he himself had heard from his father."

"His father?" Pollio asked. "Is he still alive?"

"No," Caesar replied. "His father died several years ago, but Satakarni told me that when his father was a young man and the crown prince, he led a campaign at the orders of his father the king to try and take Palibothra, but they were repulsed with such terrible losses that Satakarni said it took years for the Andhra to recover."

"That was, what, twenty years ago?" Nero's tone was skeptical. "Or more?" With a shake of his head, he said dismissively, "That was a long time ago, and only the gods know how much things have changed with these Gangaridae barbarians."

Of the remaining Legates, Nero was the least respected, not only by his fellow Legates, but by Caesar himself, and more than once he had considered removing Nero from his nominal role as being in command of this huge fleet. However, Caesar was also honest enough with himself to acknowledge that Nero had proven to be a competent commander of what was not only a huge fleet, but for what Caesar had planned, crucial to their collective success, and it wasn't an unreasonable question.

Deciding to use this as the opportunity to broach the other piece of information that had shaken him, and was personally embarrassing, he answered Nero's question by saying, "That's certainly a possibility, Nero, but there's something else that will be the same today as it was then. And that," he took a breath, "is the fact that Palibothra is much farther upriver than we had believed."

As he expected, and dreaded, this caused a reaction, but as the others murmured to each other, Caesar was standing up and turning to the large map hanging from the rear wall of the cabin. He hadn't placed the mark yet, but his time spent alone after coming aboard hadn't been wasted in self-pity, but in poring over the box of scrolls that contained what he had believed was the sum total of knowledge of the East in general and India in particular, looking for something, anything, that he might have missed. Using the information that he had previously relied on, then comparing it to what Satakarni had told him, he had calculated the approximate spot on the wavy line that moved from east to west representing the Ganges. Now, he placed his finger on the spot, eliciting gasps from his officers, and keeping his finger on the spot, he turned to offer them a grim smile.

"That was my reaction as well," he said. He knew these men well, and he could see they were of the same mind, the dismay and concern easy to read, but he forced himself to continue, "This was my error and no one else's, my comrades. I misinterpreted something I read from the account of Megasthenes about Palibothra's location, thinking that it was a bit more than one hundred miles from one of the mouths of the Ganges, when it's at least four hundred miles upriver." When this elicited more silence, he moved his finger, sliding it down and to the left from Palibothra to rest on Bharuch, then tracing another wavy line moving west as he spoke, "And as you can see, the Narmada moves in a northwesterly direction." His finger stopped at the end of the line, pausing because, in some ways, this was the worst part. "But Satakarni informed me that the Narmada is much longer than we knew. In fact, the source originates in the lands claimed by him as the King of the Andhra." He moved his finger several inches, and this time, the reaction was muffled groans as his Legates compared the two points on the map.

"So," it was Pollio who broke the awkward silence, "we would have been better served taking the overland route."

"And this route was Primus Pilus Pullus' idea, I would remind everyone."

Caesar's discomfort at admitting his error instantly turned to anger, and he turned on Hirtius, who had brought this up, acutely aware of the friction between the Legate and Pullus, and he snapped, "Because he was basing his suggestion on the information given to him by me, and I was wrong. So what are you saying, Aulus? He should be blamed for *my* mistake?"

As he expected, Hirtius quickly subsided, only muttering an apology for offending Caesar and not for his attempt to blame Pullus, but Caesar ignored it; he had bigger issues than a petty squabble instigated by one of his senior officers.

"What are we going to do?" Volusenus asked quietly.

"At this moment, Gaius," Caesar admitted, hating the very words coming out of his mouth, "I don't know."

"Are you going to tell the Primi Pili?"

"Yes," Caesar answered Pollio. "I owe it to them, and I want them to be prepared for the moment when I tell the men."

"How are you going to do that when we're all at sea?" Hirtius asked, happy that Caesar's ire at him seemed to be gone when Caesar replied, "We're going to have to come ashore, but I have to find a spot where we can do it and not alarm the Andhra into thinking we're going to invade."

"Why don't we?"

"Because, Nero," Caesar sighed, "I gave their king my word that my intentions were peaceful, and given what we know now, we're going to be on the eastern side of India for longer than we anticipated. I didn't fight the Chola," he pointed out, "until we were forced into it. Which," he did smile, temporarily forgetting the presence of Senganan, "Karikala and his son were kind enough to provide." It was the sidelong glances of his men towards the Cholan noble, who had been standing next to the door, and Caesar added quickly, "I apologize, Lord Senganan."

"There is no need, Caesar." Senganan's tone was even, but as Caesar knew, the man was an experienced courtier, so it was just as likely that he was enraged; which, he thought wryly, is the least of my troubles.

"I'm going to summon the Primi Pili now, so I'd suggest you take a few moments out on deck." When the Legates rose to follow Achaemenes and Senganan out of the cabin, Caesar stopped one of them.

"Gaius," he called to Volusenus, "please stay behind. I have something I want to talk to you about."

Ignoring the curious glances by the others, Caesar waited until Pollio closed the door, but when Volusenus returned to his stool, Caesar stopped him.

"Bring it and let's sit at the table," he instructed. "My throat is dry, and I'm going to be talking even more."

Doing as Caesar directed, Volusenus sat, taking the cup Apollodorus offered him, cautiously eyeing Caesar, but at first, he seemed content to take a long swallow of what had become his favorite drink, the juice concoction to which Nedunj had introduced him.

Finally, he looked directly at Volusenus over the rim of his cup, and began, "Gaius, I have something I'm going to ask you to do. And," he emphasized, "it's not an order, I'm *asking* you, and I swear on Jupiter's black stone that I won't fault you or hold it against you in any way if you say no."

Volusenus knew Caesar well, and his instincts that this was something momentous and of potentially huge consequences were proven sound, and it began when he asked cautiously, "What is it, Caesar?"

By the time Caesar was through, Gaius Volusenus Quadratus realized one thing: there was no way he could have been prepared for this, but what he didn't know was that Caesar had been shrewd in picking Volusenus, because in one regard the two men were almost identical, endowed with an almost overwhelming curiosity about what lay beyond the horizon. This, however, wasn't a scouting trip to Britannia; while it was similar in nature, the scope of what was being asked was staggering.

"When would I go?" he asked, and by doing so, vindicated Caesar's choice.

"As quickly as possible, preferably within the next two days," Caesar answered. "And, I'm going to give you *Philotimia* as your flagship," naming one of the *quinqueremes*, and Volusenus proved he understood Caesar's joke in providing the vessel that used the Greek word for "ambition" as its name by laughing. "And I'm giving you Lysippos as the *navarch*. I'm also giving you two Liburnians, but while you can select the *navarch*, my suggestion is that you rely on Lysippos. He knows his fellow Rhodians better than any of us." Caesar had opened a tablet and was writing in it as he spoke. "This authorizes you to requisition everything you think you will need for at least a month from our supply vessels." Handing Volusenus the tablet, Caesar stood and walked over to one of the four ironbound boxes that had been nailed to the deck, opening one with a key from a drawer in his desk. As Volusenus watched, Caesar rummaged through the contents before extracting an obviously heavy leather bag. Dropping it on the desk, Volusenus knew by the clinking sound that it contained coins, but he was completely unprepared for what he saw when he looked into it.

"All of these coins are gold!" he gasped. "How much of our treasury is this?"

This caused Caesar to chuckle, and he assured Volusenus, "Only a tiny fraction, Gaius. But," he became serious, "since we know so little of what lies east of India, I want you to be prepared to buy supplies when you run low."

"How do we know there are people east of India?" Volusenus asked, and it was a valid question, but Caesar replied, "I said we don't know much, but that isn't the same as knowing nothing. And," he promised, "I'm going to find out more tomorrow when I return to talk to King Satakarni and find out everything I can."

Volusenus nodded, but he still wasn't certain, so he asked, "What am I looking for, Caesar?"

Caesar didn't answer immediately, choosing instead to gaze at Volusenus, making Volusenus think he was considering whether to answer, or what the answer would be, which was exactly the case.

Finally, Caesar said, "You're looking for the fastest way to sail to the Han kingdom."

This was the moment that Gaius Volusenus was certain that, at last, Caesar had lost his mind.

Chapter Eight

If Volusenus had known what was coming, in the form of another passenger to accompany him on the *Philotimia*, he would have viewed this as confirmation that something had happened to Caesar, perhaps the broiling sun had finally cooked his brains, but the addition of Barhinder Gotra wasn't actually Caesar's idea, although he had quickly seen the value. The next morning, when the *Philotimia* sailed, Barhinder had been aboard, and despite Volusenus' early misgivings, within a week, he had already seen the value in the youth, a value that would only increase over the ensuing weeks, when they finally made their first meaningful contact with the Han. By the time they returned to find Caesar encamped on the island in the southernmost of the five mouths of the Ganges, the Legate could confidently report to Caesar that Barhinder was the most knowledgeable member of Caesar's polyglot army when it came to the Han, although Barhinder himself would readily admitted that his familiarity with the people of the Han only scratched the bare surface.

By outward appearances, the week-long pause in the Andhra kingdom was a matter of routine, as Caesar once again worked to forge at the very least an agreement whereby Satakarni would be neither emboldened or provoked into what would inevitably be a foolish and disastrous decision. Even so, the men were growing restless because, despite Satakarni's relatively cordial attitude towards these Romans, he was steadfast in his refusal in allowing the Legions to land and make a camp.

"I'm concerned that if I let Caesar and his men establish a presence ashore, we'll never be rid of them," he had confided to Jyani. "I saw his face when I informed him of the actual location of Palibothra, and Lord Senganan has proven to be valuable, in more ways than one."

For the first time in three days, they were dining without Caesar, or any of his party, as a guest, and the Andhran king was thankful for the opportunity to not only speak freely, but in his native tongue, although, he had acknowledged privately to Charvangi, he now appreciated what he had viewed as a waste of time and nothing but drudgery when his father had required him to learn Greek.

"What have you learned, my love?" Charvangi asked, which would have normally been considered an impertinence for a wife to involve herself in matters of state, but Satakarni and Charvangi had a unique and unusual relationship in that, not only did the king consult his wife on such matters, which was actually quite common with the kings of India, he didn't do so only privately, which wasn't.

It was something that Jyani, along with the other high-ranking noblemen of the Andhra had learned to accept, or at the very least tolerate, at least in public. And, Jyani had acknowledged to himself some time before this, the queen's input, while not always followed by her husband, was always well thought out and shrewd.

"The first thing," Satakarni replied soberly, and with a fair amount of bitterness, "is that we would be absolutely foolish to try and eliminate these barbarians. Oh," he waved a hand; there was only so far he could bend, "we could drown them with our numbers if I summoned every available man and elephant, but there would be so many widows and orphans in my kingdom that it would be impossible to find husbands and fathers for them all, and we'd only have a handful of elephants left." Nodding, he went on, "No, we're not going to resist this Roman Caesar unless it's absolutely necessary for our survival, and I actually do believe that he's sincere in not having any designs on my kingdom."

"Then why are you troubled, Lord husband?" Charvangi asked, feeling a stab of concern on her own part as she thought of their four children, of which only one was a boy.

"It's Caesar's men that worry me," the king replied unhappily. "Lord Senganan managed to tell me in confidence that there is unrest in his army, that they want to return to their homes."

"Do they?" Charvangi asked, seemingly out of politeness, but the king knew his wife well, and he regarded her now, sensing something more.

"What?" he asked bluntly. "What is it?"

"Why," she replied with widened eyes, "I was only talking about what you've told me, Lord husband."

Satakarni wasn't fooled, and while he growled at her, it was with affection.

"Stop pretending you're a simple woman, my Queen. This means something to you."

"How long have they been gone from their homes?" she asked pointedly, but answered her own question, "Four years? Five?"

"About that," Satakarni agreed.

"What have they seen?" she wondered aloud, suddenly looking out the open window. "What have they done during that time?" Returning her attention to her husband, she said, "They have done something that has never been done before, Lord husband. They have traversed from the West and the setting sun, and they have either conquered every nation they have encountered, or they have forged some sort of agreement that's favorable enough to the kingdom they are in that they not only don't resist, they seem to welcome them."

"What is your point?" Satakarni replied, growing impatient.

"My point is that we must not underestimate this Roman Caesar's control over his men, or his ability to soothe them somehow. And," she pointed out, "how many times have you told me that once a man becomes a warrior, it's almost like a sickness of the kind when a man becomes obsessed by eating or smoking the poppy?" Seeing that she had Satakarni's attention, she pressed her point. "This Caesar has managed to keep his men following him even farther East than the Macedonian, yes?" Satakarni shook his head, so she continued, "Alexander's army was what kept him from achieving his goal of reaching the Ganges. While I'm only a woman, and I've only been in this Roman's presence three times, I feel fairly certain that Caesar is aware of Alexander's failings, and," she emphasized by placing her hand on her husband's arm, "why it happened. And nothing I have seen in this Roman makes me believe that he will make the same mistake as the Macedonian king."

When Satakarni didn't respond, it was left to Jyani, who, while his wife was also in attendance, was much more traditional, and she had spent the entire conversation staring down at her hands in her lap as her husband spoke up.

"How would he convince men who only want to return home to see their families, to see their parents again before they die and pass into the eternal bliss to continue to hazard their lives? Especially, as you say, my Queen, after all they have seen and done, and accomplished something that the Macedonian couldn't do?"

Charvangi ignored the condescending tone, and countered by asking quietly, "Have you ever wondered what lies to the East, Lord Jyani? Haven't you ever wanted to actually see the Han Empire with your own eyes? To see where all the wondrous things they produce come from? To see the people, with their yellow skin and slanted eyes? Yes," she hurriedly added, "we've all seen the merchants who come here in their strange-looking ships, but wouldn't you like to see where they come from with your own eyes and wondered what it must be like?"

The brutal truth was that Jyani wasn't in the least bit curious about the faraway Han, just as he had had no interest in faraway Rome until he was forced to take one by their literal appearance in the form of a fleet of ships in numbers beyond counting. However, just as Senganan, Jyani was an experienced courtier, and what he had seen out of the corner of his vision was Charvangi's husband, who was the only man whose opinion counted, shaking his head in agreement.

Nevertheless, and again like Senganan, he was both loyal to his king, but also willing to tell Satakarni unpalatable truths, which was what prompted him to reply, carefully, "I would agree with you, my Queen, that there are undoubtedly men in the ranks who possess that kind of curiosity. But," he asked pointedly, "are there enough of them to convince their fellow Romans to continue to follow Caesar wherever he goes?"

Ultimately, this was what, at this moment at least, was an unanswerable question, and to her credit, Charvangi made no attempt to argue further. Instead, in a subtle but unmistakable message to the courtier, she turned to address her husband.

"You said that your information about Palibothra was a blow to him, Lord husband. Perhaps you might offer him an alternative that doesn't involve taking Palibothra, but is an even richer prize than that?"

She could see for a moment that her husband didn't follow her line of thinking, but then she saw his eyes widen slightly, then he gasped, "You mean the Han?"

"As I recall," she said coolly, "you told me that their Emperor Yuan is heavily involved in a struggle with a rebel general who has gathered a large following? What was his name?"

"Zhizhi," Satakarni supplied, then laughed, displaying even white teeth that were in surprisingly good shape. "Their names are so ridiculous, aren't they?" The smile vanished, but while it wasn't exactly what Charvangi wanted, he did say, "I will think on this, my love. If Palibothra is too much of a challenge, then perhaps letting him know about the troubles the Han are having, and how it's weakened their kingdom is a sound strategy to get them out of *my* kingdom."

In what would turn out to be a journey worthy of Homer and eclipsing not only Alexander but the Anabasis of Xenophon and his Immortals, there were only two occasions where, by a variety of means, Gaius Julius Caesar managed to keep an absolutely explosive secret. And this, the first time when he managed to prevail on his officers, and more importantly, his staff, the true circumstances facing them in the form of the Gangaridae, whose as-yet-unknown king ruled over the entire span of the Ganges, from a coastal city appropriately named Gange, to beyond Palibothra, was only guessed at but never truly known by any of the rankers of the army. It was such a closely held secret that only the Primi Pili and men of Legate rank were aware of not only the distance up the Ganges, but the massive size of the city. Through a variety of means that was unique to each and every man who knew the truth, Caesar cajoled, pleaded, bribed, and threatened those officers to remain silent. He was inadvertently aided in the case of the Primi Pili by the mood of the men themselves, who had indeed become restive being cooped aboard their ships, none of their Primi Pili willing to indulge their own need to unburden themselves with their trusted comrades that they unanimously believed would tip the scale into outright revolt. Despite their silence, men of the ranks are always finely attuned to the moods of their officers, watching and listening for the slightest sign or hint that might indicate what lay in their future.

Some Primi Pili were more adept at concealing their thoughts and emotions from their men than others, but whereas Pullus would have normally fallen into the category that, ironically enough, his men appreciated more because of his difficulty in hiding things, this was one, and one of the only, times he was able to behave in what passed as a normal fashion. Compounding his personal difficulty was the fact that, ultimately, Titus Pullus had grown weary of Caesar's seemingly insatiable desire to achieve what was an admittedly unparalleled feat in the entire history of their world to that point. Even if they turned back at that moment, still well more than five hundred miles from the mouth of the Ganges, they had surpassed Alexander's achievement. That this wasn't enough for Caesar was common knowledge, but thanks to Scribonius, Pullus had become convinced that reaching the mouth of the Ganges, even if they did at least assault Gange, which they had been told by Satakarni was the second largest city of the Gangaridae located at one of the five mouths of the huge river, still wouldn't be enough. Part of Caesar's dilemma lay with the men; over the previous months, and even as far back as Bharuch, the taking of Palibothra had taken on almost mythical proportions. Now that, from their latest information, the city not only met but exceeded the scale to which the men had built it in their imaginations in terms of wealth, and the army that it would take to defend it, Pullus was relieved to learn that Caesar had discarded the idea, but he also understood there would be men who wouldn't feel that way. Confidence in one's skills is crucial for a warrior, no matter for whom he fought, and that truth extends to the larger group of which that man is a part. In the case of Caesar's army, there was not only a confidence in them, there was a pride that Pullus recognized bordered on hubris, a trait that he privately knew he was prone to himself. Not that this pride was unwarranted, and Pullus knew that every one of his Centurions, and all the Centurions and Optios of all the other Legions present felt the same way. They had accomplished more than even Alexander and his Macedonian phalanxes with their *sarissae*, but therein also lay the danger. Never before had Caesar turned away from a challenge to his goals and by extension to his army, and Pullus feared that when what he considered the inevitable revolt came, it wouldn't be because Caesar would lead them up the Ganges to conquer Palibothra, but because he refused to do so.

"He's a victim of our success," was how Scribonius had put it. "The boys think of Palibothra as the end of the road, the last goal before they go home, and he turns away from it?" He had shrugged, but his tone matched Pullus' mood, and his large friend's opinion, when he said simply, "I think we're going to be fucked either way."

The reason for their delay in leaving Kantakossylla wasn't solely based in Caesar's dilemma; through Diocles, Pullus learned that Caesar was negotiating with Satakarni a similar agreement that their general had ostensibly negotiated with the Chola to allow safe passage for a movement of Roman troops. When Pullus was first informed of this development, his initial reaction was to leap up and grab his *vitus* to go and confront Caesar about what Pullus was certain was the abandonment of the seaborne approach to the Ganges. Fortunately for all parties concerned, Diocles managed to stop him.

"It's not for us, Master Titus!" He had to practically shout this at Pullus' back as he strode out of his private quarters.

This did serve to stop Pullus, who spun about, an expression of mingled anger and confusion as he demanded, "Then who's it for? We're the only army Caesar's got!"

"It's for the 14th," Diocles explained, but this only deepened the mystery for the Centurion.

"The 14th? They're in Parthia," Pullus exclaimed, then Diocles saw a slow dawning of understanding. "So Caesar summoned the 14th?" When Diocles nodded, Pullus asked, "When?"

"Before we left Karoura," Diocles said, bracing himself for what he viewed as the inevitable explosion, but when Pullus didn't immediately respond, he felt it wise to add, "And Apollodorus swore me to secrecy about it. And," he hesitated now, then decided to plunge ahead, "some other changes he plans on making."

"Changes?" Pullus frowned. "What other changes. Wait!" His eyes widened, and he gasped, "He's not going to send us back to Parthia like he did with Spurius and the 3rd, is he?" Before the Greek could answer, Pullus began pacing, talking more to himself. "If anyone deserves to go home, it's us. We've suffered more than even the 3rd, and we've got more Parthians and Pandyans in our ranks than any other Legion."

This, as Diocles well knew, was the truth; whereas now almost a quarter of the entirety of the Legions marching for Caesar were newly enlisted, primarily from Parthia and Pandya, the 10th, because of its status as Caesar's favored and most trusted Legion, now had in the ranks of its rear line Cohorts close to half its numbers of these new men. In fact, it had become enough of an issue that, even as they were in Karoura, Pullus in his role as Primus Pilus had ordered that all officers of the Eighth, Ninth, and Tenth Cohorts, Centurions down to section Sergeants, learn a handful of phrases in the native tongues of the men who now composed their ranks. The Greek also knew that he needed to nip this in the proverbial bud, now, before Pullus went storming into the *praetorium*, although he thought that it probably would come down to a coin flip either way whether he'd be successful.

"No, Master Titus," he tried to hide his nervousness, "Caesar isn't sending the 10th. But, he *is* making changes with some other Legions." Deciding to get it all out, the Greek explained, "We're still going by ship, but the safe passage isn't to allow the 14th to march up from Taprobane, it's allowing them to use the same route that King Satakarni used when he tried to take Bharuch last year, but in reverse."

Pullus said nothing at first, Diocles recognizing by his master's expression that he was working through the meaning of this, and to his relief, he saw the giant Roman's shoulders slump ever so slightly, the sign Diocles had learned to look for that the storm that was Pullus' rage had passed them by, for the moment.

"I wonder," Pullus finally asked, "if Caesar has two purposes in this?"

"How so?"

"By finding out the nature of the overland route back to the western coast of India using the 14th, so that when we do return, this time it will be that way and not back on these fucking ships."

To his internal surprise, Diocles realized that this was something he hadn't thought about, and just like Master Sextus, the Greek was reminded that his giant master and friend was more than just a formidable warrior, that he had an excellent if untutored mind.

"I think that's exactly what he's doing, Master. Well done!" Diocles replied, to Pullus sounding like a tutor congratulating a pupil for solving a knotty problem of logic, and he gave the Greek a look that expressed his amusement, causing Diocles to blush deeply.

Fortunately, Pullus didn't make an issue of it, and while it would take some time, they would both learn that Pullus had been right and wrong at the same time, because Caesar had one more surprise in store.

When the fleet departed at the end of their week spent in the anchorage outside Kantakossylla, not all of the ships began sailing north. Because of some worrying information Caesar had received from one of his paid informants who had remained behind serving King Nedunj, Caesar dispatched Primus Pilus Crispus and the 22nd with orders to return to Karoura by way of Muziris and occupy the permanent camp there, in a not very subtle reminder to the young king that what Caesar gave, he could take away, and how unwise it would be for him to believe

Rome was gone. For his part, Crispus made all the right noises, protesting on behalf of his men that they would be missing out on the culmination of Caesar's goal of taking Palibothra, but as far as Pullus was concerned, his fellow Primus Pilus' heart wasn't in it. And, over the course of the ensuing years, he would often think of Crispus and wonder how he felt now, once Caesar and the army who remained with him had done all that they had done. He would never know; he was destined to never see Crispus again, but only because the Primus Pilus of the 22nd would succumb to a fever three years after returning to Muziris. Of course, none of that was known in this moment, and Pullus had stood on the stern upper deck of the *Lykaina*, watching the ships carrying Crispus, his men, and a portion of their precious supply of naphtha vanish over the horizon, thinking, You lucky bastards, even as he knew that he didn't really mean it. For this was the true conflict within Pullus; while he sympathized with and understood those men of the Equestrians who desperately wanted to return to the more familiar surroundings of home, the larger part of him was every bit as eager as he was certain Caesar was to see what was out here, beyond the Ganges, and he knew in his bones that he would follow Caesar, no matter where he went. How many of his men felt the same way, he didn't know, but he was becoming convinced that there would be another reckoning coming.

The tension on every single vessel of Caesar's fleet, save for the portion that was sailing south with the 22nd, was palpable and strong enough that, if they had been in camp, the officers of every single Legion would have had a tablet full of rankers destined for the punishment square. Fights were so commonplace that it only drew comment from the onlookers if blood was drawn, and more than one Centurion wore out their *vitus*, which they had to replace with bamboo now that the supply of twisted grapevines had run out. And, as their men quickly learned, a bashing with a bamboo *vitus* was far worse than what they had become accustomed to with the traditional grapevine. It was a learning process for the Centurions and Optios as well, who quickly found that not only did the sectioned but supple bamboo leave larger welts, if they weren't

Caesar Ascending – The Ganges

careful, they could draw blood. Nobody was immune to the pervasive mood, but what did differ was the cause for it, although the majority of the entire army were of the same mind, their tension building with their belief that, at last, they were nearing the end of their momentous campaign. For a tiny minority, however, their worry was based in their knowledge that what the rankers were counting on happening, the assault on Palibothra, wasn't going to be happening at all, and that, ultimately, as soon as they reached the Ganges itself, after a period of time Caesar refused to define, despite almost constant pressure from his senior officers, they would just be turning around and coming back, emptyhanded. The fact that every man of Caesar's army was wealthier than any of them had ever dreamed when, for whatever reason, they had answered the call for the *dilectus* of their Legion made no difference; it was, as Balbus pointed out, a matter of principle.

"We were promised by Caesar that we would share in the spoils from the last city and kingdom that we'd be fighting," he had declared, with enough fire that he had pounded one scarred fist on Pullus' table. "The boys have sweated their balls off, they've bled, and they've seen their best friends die because Caesar wills it! We've been away from our homes, and our families, for five fucking years now, and we're owed this! And," he shook his head, his scarred face taking on an expression that communicated his grim fear, "if they don't get it, there will be Hades to pay, I can promise you that."

It was only because this wasn't the first, or the fifth time that Balbus had made a declaration like this, nor was it the first time that the Primus Pilus Posterior of the Equestrians had a skin full of *sura*, but Pullus, and Scribonius, knew that, despite his inebriation, their friend was only expressing the current mood of the men cooped up in the stinking confines of their particular ship. Compounding matters was that, for the first time under his command, their general, who had always behaved as if there wasn't enough time in each day to perform all the tasks he wanted done, suddenly took what could only be described as a leisurely pace, anchoring each night rather than remain under sail power. Suddenly, to rankers and officers alike, it seemed as if Caesar wasn't all that eager to fulfill what his men had accepted as his destiny, and by extension, their own, sailing up the Ganges to conquer the city that was now accepted as being the most fabulously wealthy city in the known world. The mood had become so dangerous that Pullus, along with the other Primi Pili, had taken the extraordinary step of holding a meeting, although it wasn't on the *Lykaina,* but on Batius' *quadrireme,* to discuss whether it was a good idea for Caesar to put ashore after five days as he had originally intended.

"You all know what's going to happen." Batius had begun the meeting with this flat statement of fact. "If we let our boys talk to each other, we're fucked."

"Why?" Clustuminus challenged. "I know that none of my boys know anything about Palibothra and that we're not going to take it. What are you saying, Batius? Did you talk?"

For his part, Pullus was just happy not to be the target of the Primus Pilus of the 8th's hostility, and that he hadn't been forced to be the host, his supply of wine long since exhausted and *sura* now perilously low, but he experienced a stab of sympathy for the Alaudae's Primus Pilus.

"No, I didn't fucking talk, you..." Batius just managed to stop himself from uttering a slur that would have required Clustuminus to respond in a manner that guaranteed that the brawling wouldn't be confined to the rankers. "...Primus Pilus Clustuminus. But," he sneered, "my boys aren't fucking idiots, and they know that there's something going on. They may not know what it is, but they know enough to know that they won't like it." Batius turned his gaze away from Clustuminus to glare at the others. "Do any of you deny this? That they're sniffing the wind and know something's gone foul?"

As Pullus suspected, Batius got no argument, just a ragged chorus of murmured agreement, but the large Roman's hope that, for once, he wouldn't be the focus of attention lasted as long as it took Batius to demand, "What about you, Pullus? You're closer to Caesar than any of us. What does he have planned now that we're not going to Palibothra?"

"How should I know?" Pullus protested, but he wasn't surprised to see his fellow Centurions shaking their heads in dismissal. Understanding that they wouldn't stop hounding him until he said something, he did divulge a piece of information

Caesar Ascending – The Ganges

he had gleaned through Diocles. "I think that Caesar's waiting on Legate Volusenus to get back."

"Get back from where?" Balbinus asked, a reasonable question. "I noticed that he left on that ship, what is it? The *Philotemia*? And he wasn't alone, but he was sailing north. Wasn't he just scouting the Ganges?"

Inwardly, Pullus groaned; Titus, you idiot, why did you bring him up?

Aloud, he spoke carefully, "I don't know any more than any of you." He hesitated. "But, Diocles has a good relationship with Apollodorus, and Volusenus' mission isn't to scout the Ganges. I don't know what it is, just that it's not that."

He wasn't surprised that this didn't satisfy any of his fellow Centurions, but he refused to budge, having no intention of divulging Scribonius' guess that Volusenus' disappearance had something to do with the Han Empire, although not because he thought his friend was wrong. When he returned to the *Lykaina*, he moodily recounted the events to Diocles and Balbus, and as the *Lykaina* beat north with the fleet, the mood was growing more sullen by the day, mirroring the collective attitude across the fleet. The monotony of the voyage was broken twice, in the form of two storms, although neither of them posed the kind of threat that had found Barhinder clutching one of the columns supporting the upper deck in Pullus' quarters, praying to every god in the Hindu pantheon he could think of as had happened on the shorter voyage from Bharuch to Muziris, while Diocles was doing the same with his own gods. It was the day after the second monsoon when, by chance, Pullus and Balbus were out on deck, supervising the men who had drawn the lot that gave them the freedom of the upper deck for a watch. Pullus had been staring morosely at the verdant green of the coastline, barely a mile away, when the lookout shouted a warning to the *Lykaina*'s *navarch*, interrupting their conversation about nothing in particular. Glancing up to see in which direction he was pointing, Pullus was sufficiently intrigued to quickly descend from the upper deck at the stern to move quickly to the bow, while Balbus followed, although he stopped to banter with some of his men, or at least tried to, but he quickly determined they were in no mood. Like Pullus, the rankers abovedeck seemed more interest in simply staring at the scenery that was sliding past them with every stroke of the oars. By the time he rejoined Pullus, he immediately saw the cause for the alert, in the form of a Liburnian rowing in their direction, coming from the north.

"I was hoping it would be Volusenus," Pullus commented, not taking his eyes off the oncoming vessel until he was satisfied that his assumption that this was a scouting ship was confirmed when they stopped rowing and drifted, seemingly directly in the path of Caesar's flagship.

"You still think that Sextus is right? That he's out there," Balbus waved a burly arm towards the east, where there was nothing but water, "looking for those Han?"

"I'm not sure," Pullus admitted. "But it's as good a guess as any I can come up with."

"Most of the boys think that he's gone up the Ganges to scout out Palibothra," Balbus' voice turned grim. Lowering his tone to a whisper, he said, "Titus, Caesar is going to have to let the boys know, and soon."

"I know," Pullus sighed. "I just wish I knew what he's come up with so we can prepare for it."

Both Centurions were aware that conversations like this were taking place on every ship around them that carried men wearing the transverse crest, but for Pullus, it was especially frustrating since he normally knew from Caesar directly, or from Apollodorus through Diocles before his contemporaries did. It was only now that he realized he had taken this for granted, and he would remind himself in the future of this moment, back when, for the first time, he had been ignorant of Caesar's plans.

"Maybe Caesar will finally call a meeting tonight," Balbus suggested.

"We'll see," Pullus grunted as he turned away to return to the stern, pleased and unsettled in equal measure at the lengths his men avoided making eye contact with their Primus Pilus as he strode down the deck.

It was always a bad sign; even in the heat of battle, Pullus and his men would have exchanges, sometimes humorous, but now the only sound was the slapping of the oars dipping into the water in the endless rhythm tapped out on the small drum. Even worse, while he didn't acknowledge it was happening, he was acutely aware of the glares at his broad back as he climbed the ladder back up to the stern upper deck. He was just turning around when his eye caught another movement, this one in the form of a piece of red cloth that was run up the mast of Caesar's flagship.

"Fuck me," Pullus breathed, before Balbus had reached his side, but rather than say anything more, he simply pointed at the flapping red pennant.

"Ha! I was right!" Balbus gave his version of a laugh. "I should have baited you into a wager."

"I wouldn't have taken it," Pullus assured him, then turned away to inform the *navarch* it was time to lower the boat to go find out their fate.

He went below to his cabin, but only to retrieve his *vitus*, his last one made of the grapevine that he was determined to preserve somehow, and inform Diocles of what was happening.

"Make an offering to Fortuna," Pullus instructed as he exited the cabin. "I have a feeling that we're going to need her."

The sun was still a couple fingers' width above the horizon when Caesar met with the Primi Pili aboard his ship; that it would be well past dark before the Centurions returned to their respective vessels would serve as fodder for rampant speculation across the fleet. Even with the prevalent mood among the men, the wagering on the cause for the lengthy meeting was brisk, but in a rare occurrence, no money, or whatever was wagered ended up exchanging hands because no man had correctly surmised the cause.

"The Ganges," Caesar began, even as the door to his cabin was closing, with Rufus and another Tribune assigned as guards to stand outside, "has more than one mouth." Although this wasn't unusual, what he said next was enough to create a tiny uproar among the nine remaining Primi Pili. "It has five mouths, and those mouths are spread over a distance of a bit more than two hundred miles."

"Pluto's *cock*!"

As usual, the epithet escaped Pullus' lips before he could stop it, and knowing how Caesar felt about using coarse language at moments like this, he braced himself for a chastisement. Instead, in a sign of his own feelings on the matter, Caesar actually smiled, though not with much humor.

"That is a good way to sum it up, Pullus. Pluto's cock, indeed."

This did elicit a ripple of chuckling, but there was a shaky quality to it, as each Centurion dealt with the meaning of this in their own unique manner, while Pollio, Nero, and Hirtius, who had been rowed out to the flagship while his troopers were still plodding along the coast, had already been informed and, presumably, accepted this new reality.

Turning his back to the assembled men, Caesar removed the cloth that had been draped over the large vellum map to reveal this new information, and each Centurion drew their own comparison with the five waving lines that now sprouted from what had been the single line of the Ganges.

"There are several problems with this, obviously," Caesar commented, picking up the slender piece of wood he used as a pointer. "The first being that we have no way of knowing with any certainty is where the mouths converge upriver. However," he moved the pointer and Pullus noticed a new dot, "*Navarch* Perdiccas and Tribunes Artaxerxes and Asellio managed to locate the city they call Gange. It," he turned back to face his officers, "isn't the size of Palibothra, nor are the defenses anything like what King Satakarni informed us protected that city." He leaned over to consult an open wax tablet, apparently reading verbatim, "It is estimated to have a population of between seventy-five and one hundred thousand inhabitants. There are a total of ten towers, one naturally at each corner of the city walls, but they aren't equally distributed, most of them concentrated along the southern and eastern side, which makes sense given that the city is situated on the northern bank of the fifth mouth of the Ganges."

He paused, although Pullus wasn't certain that it was by design, so it was Flaminius of the 30th who broke the short silence.

"So, if your intention is for us to assault this Gange, we're still almost four hundred miles away from landing."

"Yes," Caesar replied tersely. "That's what it means." For

a second time, he hesitated, alerting Pullus that the bad news wasn't over. "However, until we can perform a proper survey, we don't know whether or not the ground in between the fourth and fifth mouth is suitable for a camp. From their observation," he referred to the tablet again, "while the land is certainly fertile, it also looks to be very soft ground, and I don't have to tell you that locations like this tend to be unhealthy as well because of the various miasmas, swamp vapors, and the vermin that infest it." He actually glanced over at Pullus. "As Primus Pilus Pullus can attest from his time with me on the Nile Delta."

Understanding the message, Pullus nodded, and added his voice.

"And as I recall, the Nile Delta is only about a hundred miles wide, and it doesn't have as many mouths. Was it," he pretended to think, "three?"

"Four," Caesar corrected him, as Pullus knew he would. "Although it's less about the number of mouths as the distance. And," he added, "Perdiccas, who's sailed along the Nile Delta, informed us that, just by looking at it, he believes that the ground along the Ganges is even softer and potentially more marshland than the Nile." Taking a breath, Caesar went on, "Which means that, as of this moment, I can't guarantee just how much longer we'll be sailing. That will have to wait until I'm in a position to send our surveyors ashore to test the ground."

Nor can you guarantee that the men will obey when you give the order to debark and make camp, Pullus thought, but kept this to himself.

"What do we tell the men now?" Balbinus asked, and Pullus didn't blame his friend for the plaintive note he struck with the question.

"That we're now only four days away from reaching the Ganges," Caesar replied calmly. "Which," he turned and pointed to the southernmost mouth, "is true, technically speaking."

"The men aren't going to care about what's true 'technically' speaking," Batius interjected flatly, emphasizing the kind of word a lawyer would use. "We're not orators, or lawyers, or philosophers, Caesar. We're fucking soldiers, and if we tell them that we've reached the Ganges, but are still two hundred fucking miles away from this city, a city which," Batius' tone was growing more forceful, "is actually a substitute for the one that the men have been dreaming about for *years*," the oldest Primus Pilus' tone was growing more forceful with every word, but what Pullus noticed were the heads moving in agreement, and his was one of them, "I can't guarantee that my boys will even get off their fucking boat if they know that."

It was an astonishing moment; neither Pullus nor even Pollio and Hirtius, whose association went back almost as far, had ever heard any of Caesar's subordinates speak to him in such a manner. Caesar was famous for many things, but as other leaders, like King Nedunj had witnessed firsthand, he was almost as well known for the latitude he gave his Centurions to speak their minds, but Pullus couldn't recall anything like this in a setting with this many witnesses.

Consequently, Caesar's response was even more remarkable, because instead of lashing out at the crusty Primus Pilus of the Alaudae, he instead turned to look each Centurion in the eye, one by one, before asking quietly, "Do all of you agree with Batius?"

What wasn't surprising was that, as Caesar looked at each Primus Pilus, who either nodded or offered a muttered assent, he saved Pullus for last, and the huge Centurion saw what, to his eye, appeared to be a silent plea for support in Caesar's eyes, so that, for a heartbeat, Pullus was about to assure Caesar that, just as they had done at Bharuch, the Equestrians could be counted on by their general.

"Yes, Caesar," was what came out of his mouth, hating himself for it. "I'm almost certain that my boys aren't going to turn a spade of dirt. Not," he did add, "without feeling like they've been told the truth. Even then," he offered a shrug, "I don't know if that will be enough."

The Primi Pili were both right, and they were wrong. As Caesar had promised, the fleet reached the southernmost mouth of the Ganges four days after what was the first of several meetings. Determined not to be caught by surprise, Caesar instead began summoning Centurions, not just Primi Pili but Pili Priores, polling them on the collective state of their Cohorts. If he had hoped to find some cause for optimism that had escaped the notice of the Primi Pili, he was quickly disabused of that idea, as one by one, men like Scribonius and Cyclops assured Caesar that his grip over this massive army was tenuous. Not surprisingly, it was the words of Secundus Pilus Prior Scribonius that Caesar would remember.

"When men have built something up in their minds to the degree they have with what Palibothra represents, taking that away from them without any kind of alternative they can focus on leaves them with time on their hands to dwell on their dissatisfaction. We need," he had finished simply, "a new Palibothra."

What the Primi Pili had been wrong about was that, when the order came from Caesar that, after sending his survey party ashore on what was in effect a large island six miles east to west and more than fifteen north to south, that the ground was suitable once a drainage system was dug and a day to allow the ground to dry out, the men actually filed ashore, with their tools, and while the grumbling was a bit darker than normal, it wasn't enough to alarm their officers. It was certainly tense, but Pullus made a point to ignore what he would have otherwise called a man out for, whether it be leaning on his spade a bit too long, or complaining a bit too loudly, and he had given his Centurions the same instructions. The camp was as massive as always, but between their familiarity with the process, and with the number of men providing the labor, the ditches were dug, the dirt which, while moist, was firmer than they had expected, was turned into a wall, with the squares of turf laid on the rampart, and the men were released to wash in the brackish, brown water of the river before returning to their moored ships, before the noon watch. When the rest of the day passed uneventfully and night fell, the men were docile enough to make Pullus think that, perhaps, he and his fellow officers had overestimated their ire. At the beginning of the noon watch the next day, the order was given, and the men returned ashore, but this time, it was the Legion slaves who led the way, starting with the small army of clerks and other servants who erected the *praetorium* first, as the custom that had been in place for centuries dictated. They were followed by the Legion slaves, one per section, who were the first to enter through the earthen gates, moving with the same practiced ease to erect their section's tents, while Diocles, like his counterparts serving the other Primi Pili, erected the larger tent, although with some help since Barhinder was still with Volusenus. It was somewhat unusual; normally, the slaves erected tents and started the fires while the Legionaries constructed the camp, but since that had been done the day before, all that was left for the men to do was to construct the towers and set them now that the ground was dry enough, using the precut pieces of timber that now traveled with them when there wasn't enough standing wood available.

It could have been another day of the hundreds of days over the previous five years, here in the month of Sextilis, just before the beginning of September, the men even accepting the rain showers that came two, three, or sometimes more times a day, using that as an easy way to bathe if the timing worked. When Pullus and the other Primi Pili were summoned to the *praetorium*, men were sitting under the shade provided by their tents, while all four sides were rolled up, playing dice or some other game of chance, arguing about whose version of some past event was the correct one, and it had every appearance of a normal day on campaign. This illusion was shattered when, after Caesar dismissed his officers, having informed them that he would finally be calling the formation where he would reveal the truth, the *bucina* call that played the order for an assembly of all Legions, in the massive forum of the camp sounded. As was his habit, he remained inside the *praetorium*, waiting for his army to assemble, and while it had been an unpopular decision, Caesar had decreed that the sides of the headquarters tent remain down, making it stuffy, which meant that it was his ears that warned him something was happening. More accurately, it was the absence of the noise that inevitably accompanied the movement of almost fifty thousand men into what was a cramped space, even with the size of the camp forum, which rivaled the original Forum of Rome in size, that got Caesar to his feet. He had originally intended to address the army in just his tunic, but an impulse made him call for his body slave, who helped him into his cuirass, and although he eschewed the greaves, he did pick up his helmet, carrying it with him out into the main room of the *praetorium*, where he saw the three Legates who were currently present, standing there, their expressions almost identical.

"It sounds like the men are refusing to assemble," Caesar broke the silence, forcing himself to sound calm, and as if this wasn't anything he hadn't anticipated. Spotting Apollodorus, who had been standing huddled with the other senior clerks of the army, he called to him, and as the scribe reached him, he asked, "Do you have any idea about which Legions are refusing the order?"

"Y-yes, Caesar," Apollodorus stammered, singularly unusual in itself—the Greek usually unflappable—but the most potent sign was that he didn't say anything more.

This was too much for Caesar, and he betrayed his own nerves by snapping, "Well? Have you been struck mute, Apollodorus? How many Legions are refusing the summons?"

"All of them, Caesar," Apollodorus replied quietly, and Caesar heard a gasp of surprise, but instantly saw that none of the Legates looked surprised. Knowing his master well, Apollodorus hurried to explain, "The Legates know because each Primus Pilus sent runners to the *praetorium* right after you sent them back to get their men ready, telling us that they're refusing to move."

"And you didn't think to tell me this?" Caesar didn't shout this, but it was close, except that now he was looking directly at his Legates, all three seemingly interested in the dirt floor, even Pollio, who could normally be counted on to deliver Caesar news, even when it was bad. As quickly as it had come, Caesar's ire dissolved, and he heaved a sigh, then said ruefully, "I don't suppose I can blame you for not letting me know this." Turning back to Apollodorus, he asked, "Even the Equestrians? Them too?"

"Yes, Caesar," Apollodorus replied.

"Caesar," Pollio spoke quietly, uncertain how to approach their general in this situation, "maybe it's better to just...ignore the problem today?"

"Ignore it?" Hirtius broke in, giving his friend an

incredulous glance before turning and addressing Caesar, "You can't just ignore this kind of flagrant disobedience, Caesar! You'll only encourage even more of that behavior down the road! If they think they have you cowed, they'll..."

"Do what?" Pollio cut him off. "Disobey him? They're already doing that, Aulus! Caesar," he didn't try to disguise he was pleading, "I beg of you. If you want to make an issue of it, do it with just the Primi Pili, and in private. But addressing the men when they're in this mood, and reprimanding them would be..."

Rather than say the word—he had almost said "suicidal"—he held his hands out, palms up, hoping that Caesar would interpret it and not force him to finish.

"Foolish," Caesar supplied for him, though not with anything that indicated he was irritated. If anything, he looked thoughtful. Finally, he said, "Very well, we won't be holding a formation today. In the morning, I'm going to reassess the situation." He turned to Apollodorus then. "Send a runner to Primus Pilus Pullus' quarters and request that he attend to me."

If the others noticed Caesar's use of the word, they were wise enough to pretend not to hear it, and they returned to their own tents, relieved for the moment, but still worried about what the next day held.

"It's that bad?"

Pullus didn't reply immediately, choosing instead to regard his cup, which in another sign of the unusual nature of this meeting, actually held *sura*, although it was offered with an apology by Caesar because there was no more wine, anywhere in the army.

Finally, he looked up and answered quietly, "Yes, Caesar. It's that bad. And," he shifted on his stool, uneasily adding, "this is before they find out the truth about Palibothra."

"What do you think they'll do when they find out?"

It was, Pullus thought, a remarkable moment, but there was a part of him that, once again, was angry at Caesar for not seeming to grasp how this moment was practically inevitable. This certainly wasn't the first time he had experienced this feeling; the first had been at Pharsalus, even as he chose loyalty to Caesar over his friendship with Vibius. It had happened again in Bharuch, although that time, his rage had actually been the only thing that kept the Equestrians in check, while the other Legions who had assaulted the city ran rampant, as the giant Primus Pilus stalked the streets where his Legion were sitting, practically daring one of them, any of them, to defy him by participating in the rapine and slaughter that, even for the standard of that time, had been excessive. Now, however, most of the anger he felt stirring was directed at Caesar, and only Caesar, yet somehow, he managed to curb his tongue.

Instead of snapping, "What the fuck did you think would happen?" as he desperately wanted to do, he said more moderately, "I think that it will be at least as bad as at Bharuch, Caesar, if not worse."

Caesar didn't seem to hear Pullus; if anything, he appeared to be copying Pullus' study of the cup in his hands, although it was filled with his juice concoction, but Pullus saw the worry etched into the lines of his general's face, which seemed to have deepened over the course of this conversation.

"I pushed them too hard, didn't I, Titus?"

Even with Caesar's use of his *praenomen,* Pullus wasn't about to reciprocate, but he did feel a stab of sympathy, although it wasn't enough to make him lie.

"Yes, Caesar," he replied frankly. "You did." He hesitated, then added, "And I mean *all* of us." Caesar did react to this, looking up suddenly, staring into Pullus' eyes, but Pullus had never flinched from Caesar's gaze yet, and he regarded his general steadily as he continued, "Caesar, there is no man in this army who has been as loyal to you as I have."

He didn't say it to get Caesar's agreement, but he was gratified when Caesar immediately nodded in agreement.

"I know that, Titus. And I haven't forgotten Pharsalus, or your sacrifice."

"That being said," Pullus chose his words carefully, "I'm just as tired as the men, Caesar. I'm tired of sweating, and I'm tired of watching my boys suffer, and die." He actually gave a quiet laugh, though without much humor. "I've even thought about settling down and starting a family."

While they were destined to spend several more years

together, Pullus would never know just how close Gaius Julius Caesar came to divulging to his best Primus Pilus that, in fact, he already had one, back in Bharuch. Even more than the news itself, Pullus would have been shocked to know how many times over the next years they would be together that Caesar would think about that evening in the camp on the Ganges, and wonder if he had done the right thing. For, of all the things that Caesar would struggle with, the unanswered questions that would haunt him, the one thing he was certain of was that, if he had told Titus Pullus the truth, he would have lost the most valuable piece on his great board, in the game that he was playing of changing the world. Pullus would have immediately demanded to be released to return to Bharuch, no matter what the consequences may have been, and it would have forced Caesar into making a decision that he had no stomach to make. It took a great deal of his formidable self-control not to sag in relief when Pullus changed the subject.

"Scribonius said something to me," he said. "And I've been thinking about it."

"Oh?" Caesar arched an eyebrow. "What does Pilus Prior Scribonius have to say about this...situation?"

Ignoring the slight sarcasm, Pullus treated the question seriously, knowing that Caesar wanted to know what one of the few men in this army, of any rank, whose intellect rivaled his thought.

"Before you tell the men the truth, you need to have an alternative in mind, something that might be just as attractive to them."

Again, Caesar had to hide his reaction, which had been identical to a moment earlier when Pullus veered to another topic, since this was essentially the very thing he had been planning on when he dispatched Volusenus on his quest.

All he said was, "That's certainly something for me to consider."

Pullus left shortly after that, although he wasn't any more enlightened about what Caesar would do than when he entered the *praetorium*.

That night, Caesar wrote a series of orders, all of them on vellum and imprinted with his seal, then sent for one of his

Caesar Ascending – The Ganges

Tribunes, Quintus Salvidienus Rufus.

"I have an important task for you, Quintus," Caesar began once the Tribune arrived in the *praetorium*.

Normally, Caesar didn't refer to Tribunes by their *praenomen*, but this was an important and potentially explosive mission on which he was sending Octavian's contemporary.

"Yes, Caesar?"

Pointing to the scrolls that were lined side by side on his desk, Caesar explained, "You're returning to Susa first, Quintus." Indicating the first scroll, "On your way there, you'll stop in Bharuch and give Legate Ventidius his new orders." Moving to the second, he continued, "From there, you will return to Susa, and give these new orders to Gaius Octavius, and," he pointed to the third, "you will also give Octavius this one, which is for Quintus Pedius, and this one is for Marcus Antonius." His pause was barely noticeable, then he pointed to the last three scrolls, "These are to go to Marcus Tullius Cicero, Gnaeus Domitius Ahenobarbus....and the last is to go to my wife Calpurnia."

Rufus nodded, thinking he understood, replying, "So I'm delivering Legate Ventidius his new orders, then Octavian, and I ensure that Quintus receives his in Merv, then Octavian will send on the rest of them."

"No," Caesar shook his head. "You're to deliver these going to Rome in person, to each of them. And Quintus," he continued, "Octavian will be returning to Rome as well. And," he hesitated, knowing that he was placing an extraordinary burden on the young man's shoulders, "I need you to ensure that Octavian obeys my orders to return to Rome."

Rufus visibly paled, then reached out in an unconscious reaction to touch the desk as if he needed it to steady him, which Caesar understood. Despite the fact that Rufus was just a few years older than his grand-nephew, Octavian had parlayed his attachment to Caesar far more skillfully than Rufus, or Pedius for that matter, something that Caesar had allowed because, in fact, he did have larger plans for his nephew.

"C-caesar," Rufus stammered. "I'm not sure how I could stop him if he decides he won't obey your orders. After all," he

393

pointed out, "he's a Praetor, and I'm just of Tribunate rank!"

"That's true," Caesar nodded, then pointed to the scroll in Rufus' hand, "but in that, I've given you temporary Propraetor rank by my authority as Dictator for Life. Which," he warned, "expires the moment you set foot on the dock at Ostia." Sensing Rufus still needed reassurance, Caesar added, "Honestly, I don't think that Octavian will balk at this, but the task I've given him is not...inconsequential, and I can see how he would be daunted by it. But it's something I've decided must happen in order for Rome to continue to thrive. And you," he finished gravely, "are essential to putting this all into motion, and you will be playing a role in that larger goal."

It was, Caesar knew, somewhat unfair, but in this, Caesar had made up his mind that he needed Octavian back in Rome now more than he was needed in Susa.

Proving that he was paying attention, Rufus frowned as he thought about the details, which prompted him to ask, "Who will replace Octavian in Susa, Caesar?"

"Marcus Agrippa," Caesar replied, "with Gaius Maecenas as his Quaestor. That directive is contained in my orders to Octavian."

Although he would never know it, the face Rufus made mirrored Caesar's thoughts on this matter, knowing that Octavian would be extremely unhappy that his two most trusted friends would be separated from him, but Caesar had become concerned that his nephew had become too dependent on the pair, relying on Agrippa for military affairs, and Maecenas for the subtler but equally important diplomatic and cultural issues that were endemic to any new conquest by Rome. More than that, Caesar understood, Octavian would feel especially vulnerable because of the high possibility that Antonius would see Caesar's orders as a demotion, despite Caesar couching his decision as a massive responsibility, which was true enough, considering what he was asking Antonius to do. Despite his relative isolation, while communication from Rome had dried up, he was still receiving reports from Parthia about events on this side of Our Sea, and what he had learned was disturbing to say the least. It concerned Cleopatra, who was growing increasingly restive, and despite her love for Caesar, which he

Caesar Ascending – The Ganges

was certain was genuine, she was still a powerful ruler in her own right as Pharaoh, and even as heavily as he'd drawn on the treasury of that ancient kingdom, she still had massive resources. Over the course of the winter in Karoura, the shipment of bullion consisting of more than ten thousand talents that was to be used for paying the army, securing the Pattalan wine and vinegar supply, and to hold up his end of the bargain that he'd made with Nedunj that was part of their agreement, had not only arrived late, but was only seven thousand talents. If this was all, it would have been a source of irritation, but he had also learned where the missing three thousand talents had gone, which was why Caesar was making changes. It had been a source of irritation, and mystery, about why, after only one token foray into Parthia, the Armenian king Artavasdes hadn't fulfilled his promise to join himself to Caesar's army. Thankfully, it had turned out that the *cataphractoi* of Parthia could be defeated without having his own *cataphractoi*, and once they arrived in India, it was quickly obvious that those heavily armored horses and their riders would be a liability in the crushing heat and humidity of India, which meant that it was more of an annoyance to Caesar. However, he had learned, from a Roman patrician named Quintus Delius who, under the guise of being just another bored but extremely wealthy Roman who traveled about the area of Our Sea on an extended tour of various historical and cultural sites and had settled in Alexandria for an extended period, informed him that Cleopatra had diverted the three thousand talents to Artavasdes. Why she was doing this was unknown, at least to Delius; Octavian had had no qualms in expressing his opinion even before this, but his antipathy towards Cleopatra was no secret, but to Caesar's chagrin, it appeared as if his nephew's fears had been well founded. This was why he was sending Antonius to Alexandria, both to remind Cleopatra that, while he had been content to maintain the façade that Egypt was an independent kingdom, it was anything but, and it was time to remind her of this.

Those who were aware of these changes, which at this moment only numbered Pollio, Hirtius, and, at least partially, Volusenus, would have ascribed it to Caesar being thorough, creating some stability in their world until he returned from achieving his ambitions. What none of them knew, save for Caesar, was that he was setting up this part of the Roman world to operate efficiently in his absence, because he had no intention of returning, at least not soon. Yes, he was determined to see the Ganges, but with every mile eastward, he had learned more about lands that had long been shrouded in mystery, and there had been one nation mentioned in particular that intrigued him. Romans, at least those of the upper orders who were more worldly, had heard of the mysterious Han, but now that they were much closer, it was the manner in which men like Nedunj spoke of the Han, in much the same way the nations ringing Our Sea spoke of Rome, that had helped form his decision. He would see this mysterious nation and its people for himself; whether he had an army at his back or not, that was up to the gods. First, however, he had to reach the Ganges, then come up with a way to convince his men to continue following him, on a quest that not even he fully understood.

As Caesar anticipated, Gaius Octavius was anything but happy when Quintus Salvidienus Rufus arrived in Susa in late October, bearing the orders from the Dictator for Life that relieved him as Praetor of Parthia Inferior and ordered his return to Rome, the full purpose for which Caesar had refused to divulge, saying cryptically in the orders that once he returned to the city, there would be further instructions awaiting him. His discontent turned to anger when, using his rank as a Praetor as his authority, Octavius demanded to know the contents of the other messages, whereupon Rufus, although nominally a Tribune, immediately after presented Octavius with his own warrant granting him the powers of a Propraetor, meaning that he outranked the slightly younger Roman. It was when, after Octavius then tried to prevail on their past friendship and association, and Rufus steadfastly refused to divulge anything about what Caesar intended for Octavian when he returned to Rome, he was enraged to the point that he briefly considered taking steps to find out what was contained in the satchel stuffed with scrolls that Rufus never let out of his sight, by ordering the slave on Maecenas' payroll who was responsible for caring for visitors to the former palace in Susa that now served as the *Praetorium* to pilfer it.

"How would you go about it?" Agrippa had asked when he was summoned to the former throne room that served as Octavian's office. "I mean, in a way that Rufus doesn't know that you've disturbed them?"

Octavian shrugged, but it was the manner in which he refused to meet Agrippa's gaze that caused his second in command to glance over at Octavian's third, Maecenas; that Maecenas was clearly as disturbed wasn't helped when Octavian finally answered vaguely, "Oh, I'll think of something."

It had been more than two years since Caesar had returned to Bharuch after leaving an army in revolt behind, and in the intervening time, Octavian had grown increasingly comfortable having full autonomy running Parthia Inferior. More importantly, to Agrippa and Maecenas, as the dispatches and orders from Caesar diminished in frequency, Octavian had begun to show increasing signs of an independence that they were both certain the Dictator wouldn't appreciate, if only because the Praetor had been devoting more time and energy to undermining the mother of Caesar's son Caesarion and her rule over Egypt than actual governing, choosing to rely on his two subordinates and friends to deal with the drudgery of governance. For his part, Octavian was unaware that his two most trusted subordinates and friends knew what Octavian was doing, thanks to yet another one of Maecenas' spies, the identity of whom was the most closely guarded secret that the effete patrician held, even from Agrippa, despite trusting him implicitly. In fact, both of his friends were aware that Cleopatra's diversion of three thousand talents of the ten thousand that was supposed to be sent to Caesar had been diverted by the Egyptian queen to pay the Armenian king Artavasdes for his army's potential service, not in an attempt to seize control of Egypt, but to protect it from the ambitions of Gaius Octavius. And, they privately agreed, it wasn't an irrational fear on Cleopatra's part that she saw Caesar's nephew as a threat, not just to her but to her heir and Caesar's son. It wasn't a matter of loyalty or mistrust of Octavian; both men, who were talented in their own ways, especially Agrippa, were completely devoted to their friend who, less than ten years earlier, had been *Contubernales* together with them, young aides who weren't even of Tribune rank, when the pair had recognized that, albeit in a different way, Octavian was a singular character just like his grand-uncle. Nevertheless, they also knew Octavian had his flaws, and that his ambition not only matched Caesar's, but might surpass it, to the point where, because of his relative youth, he might overstep. This situation with Cleopatra was an example of one of Octavian's failings, few as they may have been; as far as they were concerned, he held an irrational hatred of the Egyptian Queen and Pharaoh that made him nearly impossible to reason with when Cleopatra's name came up. Early on, in their private discussions on the matter, they assumed that Octavian's hostility was motivated by a feeling of jealousy, because anyone who was ever in the presence of the couple could see that Caesar genuinely cared for the Macedonian queen, who was somewhat younger than Octavian, but who possessed a charm and intelligence that Maecenas in particular believed was the root cause for Octavian's feelings.

"He's been accustomed to being considered the only one as clever as Caesar," was how Maecenas had explained it to Agrippa. "Now, here's Cleopatra, who can not only match his wits, but speaks even more languages, and she's a woman in the bargain. And," he had added with waspish amusement, "she's rich. No wonder he hates her."

And, at first, Agrippa had accepted this reasoning, but now, as they sat there discussing Rufus, he had developed another belief, that, while Maecenas had accurately pinpointed the original cause for Octavian's antagonism towards Cleopatra, there was a new factor, and that was Caesarion. It wasn't just the name, and that it was Caesar's only son, because Roman law was very clear that full citizenship, and the ability to participate in the *cursus honorum*, had to come from two Roman citizens. When Cleopatra had brought Caesarion to Susa to spend time with his father on Caesar's last time in the provincial capital, Agrippa had gasped aloud when the youngster, a sturdy six-year-old, had entered the room, his first thought: he's *Caesar*!

Caesar Ascending – The Ganges

Certainly, Octavian bore more than a passing resemblance, but Agrippa knew that it was partially artifice on Octavian's part, his friend having studied Caesar's gestures and mannerisms then copying them. And, Agrippa would be the first to admit, it had been effective, up until a young boy had entered the former throne room. Caesarion *was* Caesar, in that undefinable but inarguable manner of fathers and son, and even Agrippa saw the sham in Octavian's imitation; what made it dangerous for Caesarion was that Octavian had immediately seen the same thing. The memory of Octavian's face that day had troubled Agrippa, and his uneasiness continued to this day, but in this moment, he had to dissuade Octavian from doing something rash and intemperate with Rufus, who was resting in the room provided for him after a hard journey.

"Maybe," he spoke up, "you should trust what Caesar has planned for you."

For a long moment, Octavian didn't respond, choosing to look down at the unrolled order, a thoughtful expression on his face.

"He says," he finally broke the silence, "that I'm going to have more responsibilities in Rome than I do currently, and that I should prepare accordingly."

"That's a good thing, isn't it?" Maecenas asked gently, as intent as Agrippa on steering Octavian away from what could be a dangerous, and even worse, foolish mistake. "Clearly it's not a demotion if he's telling you that you're going to have more responsibilities."

"It could be just a matter of scale," Octavian countered. "Just the city of Rome has more people in it than the entire province of Parthia Inferior."

"That," Agrippa allowed cautiously, "is one way to look at it, certainly, but Caesar has clearly been impressed with your performance."

This prompted Octavian to lift his gaze and direct it first to Agrippa as he replied, "You mean *our* performance." He looked over to Maecenas, clearly meaning to include him. "Don't think that I'm not aware that, while I may get the credit from Caesar and from *some* Senators, it's only because of the work you two have done to support me. And," he emphasized, "no matter

399

where I am, I'll never forget it, I swear it on the black stone." He sighed then, and with his next words, both Agrippa and Maecenas understood that it wasn't all about Octavian's ambitions. "That's what bothers me more than what might be waiting for me, if I'm being honest. I'm going to Rome alone, without the two of you, and I don't know if I'm up to the job by myself." Addressing Agrippa, Octavian's expression was shamefaced, and seemed genuine as he apologized, "And forgive me, Marcus, for not congratulating you on being named Praetor of Parthia Inferior. I know that you'll do a magnificent job because," he smiled then, and again Agrippa was certain it was sincere, "you and Gaius have been doing most of the work anyway."

It was, they both agreed later, an astounding moment, at least when it came to the recent past, it having been a few years since their brilliant friend and patron had expressed any kind of self-doubt.

"You're up to it, Gaius," Maecenas said quietly, but with an intensity that emphasized his own earnestness. "I wouldn't say that about anyone else, and I wouldn't say that if it wasn't true."

"Except for Caesar, you mean," Octavian replied, but it was with a grin and both men, understanding and appreciating the deeper meaning, roared with laughter.

"Yes, forgive me," Maecenas managed to gasp, "except for Caesar. We mustn't forget Caesar."

It would be a moment all three would remember, wondering at how prophetic they would turn out to be, when Caesar, and his vast army, seemingly vanished from the known world...at least for the next several years.

Forty days later, Rufus set foot on the docks at Ostia, instantly losing his Propraetor powers and reverting back to the rank of Tribune, but this was the least of his concerns. While Caesar hadn't divulged the details to Rufus, he had deduced that the Dictator for Life had no intention of putting Gaius Octavius and Marcus Antonius in the same room together and equally sharing power. And, despite his antipathy for Octavian, Rufus felt reasonably sure that, if his instinct was correct, Caesar's concern wasn't for his nephew, but for Antonius, if only because of how outmatched he was with Octavian when it came to intelligence. Guile? That was another matter, although Rufus also believed that Octavian was at the very least a match in that area with the older Master of the Horse. Rufus had deviated from his instructions in one regard in not waiting to ensure that the young Praetor accompany him back to Rome, but he had been assured by both Marcus Agrippa and Gaius Maecenas that Octavian would obey, also arguing that it was unreasonable of Caesar to expect his nephew to immediately drop everything and depart from Susa. Consequently, and using his temporary Propraetorial power, Rufus had given Octavian thirty days to settle affairs in the province, then follow behind Rufus, taking the same route that by now, four years later, had become a well-traveled route from what had once been considered the far reaches of their world. Construction on a Roman style road that connected Susa, back to Ctesiphon, then back to Zeugma was still in the planning stages, and it would be a massive project, but with the creation of a series of way stations, each guarded by a Century of Parthian auxiliaries, it had reduced the time it took to travel these vast distances substantially.

Thanks to Rufus' orders; anything bearing the seal of Caesar, even one as cracked and faded as the one on Rufus' personal scroll had become, meant that his delay at Ostia was less than a third of a watch before he was aboard a horse and moving at the trot towards the city. The nerves he was feeling were akin to those he had felt when they went into battle, because unlike Octavian, Marcus Antonius wasn't the master of his temper, it was the master of him, and he had no idea how the volatile Master of the Horse was going to react. There were stories, of course, about him lashing out at the man who had the ill fortune to be the bearer of a message that sent him into a rage, but Rufus continually reminded himself that he was protected by Caesar. Yes, the Dictator for Life was far, far away, but in a nation ruled by laws like Rome, his legal status was insurmountable, and most importantly, all-encompassing. Never far from memory was the Caesar who pursued Gnaeus Pompeius Magnus across Our Sea, and while it would undoubtedly take longer, Rufus had no doubt that if the cause was sufficient, the Dictator for Life would reappear in Rome to punish those who went against his will. The question was, as far as Rufus was concerned, did Antonius share that certainty? Such were his thoughts that he barely noticed how much more quickly he was allowed through the *Porta Ostia* and into the city, simply because he had developed the habit of holding the scroll in one hand so the seal showed to anyone who might want to know by whose authority he was doing such things like going to the head of the line outside the gate. It was also surreal; despite having months to prepare himself for the moment, actually being inside the walls of his home city was almost overwhelming, especially as it finally hit him that he had been gone for more than five years. Beyond that, it was also how much of a world that he knew none of the people hurrying about in front of him and cursing him as they had to hop out of the path of his horse were aware even existed. He, Quintus Salvidienus Rufus, had been to the Ganges River, an achievement that, at this moment, he was the only human not only inside Rome but in the entirety of the Republic who could boast that. This, ironically enough, gave him the confidence to draw up outside the huge villa on the Palatine that had once belonged to Pompeius but was now the property of Marcus Antonius, then stride into the entrance with a sense of purpose that quelled his nerves. Come what may, Quintus, you've been to the Ganges; you've outdone Alexander, while Marcus Antonius was sitting on his ass here in Rome. Make sure he knows that, and that you're speaking for the man who made it possible.

As it happened, Marcus Tullius Cicero was at his villa in the countryside when Tiro, his personal slave and confidante, rushed out into the garden, where the great orator was seated reading a series of Greek epigrams by Meleager that he had just received from Athens.

"Master Marcus! The Master of the Horse is here! He..."

"Where is he?"

Cicero instantly recognized the booming voice, but when he spun about on his bench, he had just enough time to compose his expression.

Caesar Ascending – The Ganges

"Marcus Antonius," he rose with a false smile, but when Antonius roughly shoved Tiro aside, in a rare show of the kind of behavior that could antagonize a brawler like Antonius, he snapped, "How *dare* you! Who do you think you are to manhandle Tiro like that, let alone come bursting into my house as if Cerberus is after you!"

To his astonishment, Antonius actually stopped, and while he didn't look ashamed, he did turn and address Tiro politely enough given his status, "I apologize for that, slave." Turning back to Cicero, he thrust out a scroll, saying only, "Read this."

This had only happened one time before, so even as Cicero reached for the scroll and, without seeing the seal, he felt certain he at least knew from whom the message came. This wasn't nearly enough preparation, and when he heard a gasp, Cicero only dimly realized it was from him as he dropped back onto the bench, his book of epigrams lying on the grass at his feet and completely forgotten.

Finding his voice, he managed, "Alexandria? He's sending you to Alexandria? But why?"

"Keep reading," Antonius answered, noticing that Cicero hadn't unrolled the scroll all the way. When he saw the other man's eyes go even wider, he continued grimly, "It's because of that bitch Cleopatra. Caesar thinks she's up to something, and he says that he only trusts me to handle her, not the boy, who would be the logical choice because he's closer."

There was no need for Antonius to elaborate on who the "boy" was, and Cicero was ignorant that, in one way, Antonius and the young Octavius were remarkably alike: Octavius' loathing of Cleopatra was visceral, while Antonius' feelings for Octavius were almost identical, and for essentially the same reason, each viewing the other as the biggest threat for Caesar's favor. As he got over his shock, Cicero reread the relevant passages again, his tone turning thoughtful.

"And Octavius is coming here, to essentially step into your *caligae*, as it were, although Caesar is explicit about you retaining your title of Master of the Horse, and that your time in Alexandria isn't indefinite, but for at least a year. Which," he mused, "makes sense, given the amount of time it takes for messages to travel from...where is Caesar now?"

403

The smile Antonius gave Cicero was more like a grimace, but it was his tone, one of a grudging admiration that Cicero would understand in a matter of heartbeats that the Senator would remember.

"He did it," Antonius replied. "He reached the Ganges. That's where Rufus came from."

Cicero suddenly dropped back down on the bench, his mind reeling, immediately seeing the larger implications of what was already momentous news in itself.

"So he's done it. He's surpassed Alexander."

"Pluto's cock," Antonius muttered, and unbidden, he walked over and dropped down onto the bench next to a man he normally loathed, who barely noticed. "I hadn't thought about it like that. But," he agreed grudgingly, "you're right. This makes him..."

"Immortal?" Cicero finished for him, now sounding grim. "Especially to the Head Count? Yes, it does. Which means," he sighed, "he's going to be even more insufferable now. Once the people know this, any further word from him will be considered to be akin to coming from the gods themselves."

Antonius nodded, then he said, half-jokingly, "Maybe we should send Rufus back across Our Sea on the next ship now, before he stops at the first *taverna* he comes to and lets everyone know."

Cicero, who had slumped over with his elbows on his knees to stare morosely at the ground in front of him, contemplating a future with a Caesar as demigod, was only partially listening, but this made him sit up and regard Antonius for a moment.

"I don't know much about Rufus, but he doesn't strike me as one for associating with the plebs."

"Normally, he isn't," Antonius acknowledged, then with a chuckle, he added, "but he said that the one thing that kept him going all that way was the thought of a nice Falernian and a dish of tasty dormouse. He as much told me that he was going to stop at the first one he found after he finished his tasks."

"Tasks? What tasks?"

"Oh," Antonius replied in an offhand manner, "he has a letter for Calpurnia to deliver." Cicero wasn't looking at the

Caesar Ascending – The Ganges

other man, but he was warned as Antonius' tone turned thoughtful, "And, he said he has one to deliver to Ahenobarbus...and to you."

"To me?" Cicero gasped, and temporarily forgetting that he was thoroughly intimidated by Antonius, particularly when the brute was sitting next to him, he snapped, "And you didn't think that was important to tell me, Antonius? Have you lost your wits?"

Only later would Cicero appreciate that, rather than explode in a fit of his famous temper, Antonius' reaction was one of abashment, leaping to his feet to gasp, "By the gods, Cicero, I forgot! I was just so surprised that we've finally heard from the bast...him," he corrected himself automatically, "that I completely forgot to tell you. Please, forgive me."

Cicero was surprised, because Antonius actually sounded sincere, and he, grudgingly, allowed that it was an understandable oversight given the larger news.

"None necessary, dear Antonius," he assured him, with only slightly less than complete sincerity. Always finding it easier to think when he was doing so, Cicero began pacing back and forth, his tone thoughtful, "Naturally, he'll go to my villa in the city first." Looking at Antonius, he asked, "And did you come directly here?"

"No, I went to your villa first," Antonius replied, which Cicero had expected.

"So, that means that you're ahead of him by however long it takes him to deliver the letters to Calpurnia and to Ahenobarbus."

"I know where Ahenobarbus is," Antonius said. "He's in the city. He stopped by this morning."

"That means," Cicero stopped pacing as the jumble of thoughts going through his mind began to coalesce in his mind into more concrete form, "that young Rufus is unlikely to stop off at that *taverna* until he's come here. Would you agree?"

"Yes," Antonius replied instantly. "He's very dutiful, that one." Sensing something, he asked warily, "Why?"

Cicero didn't immediately reply, taking a heartbeat to frame his thoughts, then, adopting the same tone he would use when arguing a point of law, he began, "Would you agree that matters here in Rome are stable right now?"

"I would," Antonius nodded, and he wouldn't have been Antonius if he added, "because I've made sure that it is, without any help from Caesar."

"Nobody denies that, Marcus," Cicero assured him, only partly out of his recognition of Antonius' monstrous ego; as loathe as he was to admit it, Antonius had done better than Cicero had expected. "And I know that I'm not alone when I say I'd like to see Rome remain that way."

"Agreed." Antonius nodded. His eyes narrowed, giving Cicero the sense that he was beginning to see where the orator was headed, which was confirmed when he said, "And, through no fault of his own, young Rufus and his news about Caesar reaching the Ganges would create...excitement, particularly with the Head Count."

Knowing that he had to tread carefully—as obtuse as Antonius was in some ways, he would also see through any attempt at flattery for its own sake—Cicero replied, "Well put, Antonius. It would indeed create excitement among those who already half-believe that Caesar is a god."

It was Antonius' turn to pace, but he was careful not to look Cicero in the eye as he spoke, "So it's not really in anyone's interest for Rufus to spread the word about Caesar's accomplishment, no matter how deserved the praise might be." He stopped, and now looked at Cicero. "What if we swear him to secrecy? Forbid him to remain in Rome once he's delivered his final letter to you?"

"That," Cicero admitted, or at least seemed to, "is certainly one alternative." He paused, then asked, "But, where do you send him? And under what authority?"

"I'm still Master of the Horse," Antonius pointed out. "Even if in name only, until I leave the *pomerium*, which I'll have to do in order to obey Caesar's orders sending me to Alexandria."

Cicero picked Caesar's orders back up to reread it, his lawyer's mind parsing the words, and as he usually did whenever reading one of Caesar's missives, damned the man, silently, for his precise wording. What he found especially galling was the man's habit of putting a dot above the last word

Caesar Ascending – The Ganges

of a sentence, although that was only because he hadn't thought of it himself, acknowledging how much easier it made to read.

"The orders specify that you're to depart on the same day as the arrival of Gaius Octavius, whereupon you will transfer your *imperium* as Master of the Horse to him." Which, Cicero thought with a dark humor, was a good idea on the part of Caesar, knowing what was likely to happen if the young Octavius and the volatile Antonius had to spend more than one sunset within the walls of the city together. He continued, "What matters is today. As of this moment, you are still Master of the Horse, and the only person who can overrule an order by the Master of the Horse is..."

"...The Dictator, or through a *Senatus Consultum*," Antonius finished. Thinking he understood, he went on, "So I have the authority to order Rufus to remain silent about Caesar reaching the Ganges. In fact, I can order him to remain silent about *anything* regarding Caesar. The question," he said in a challenging manner, "is whether you have enough control over the Senate to make sure that they don't overrule me."

"They won't," Cicero snapped. "I'm the *de facto* senior Senator, even if I'm not *de jure*."

"What about Censorinus and Albinus?" Antonius countered, naming the two Consuls that Caesar had selected three years earlier when the Dictator had still been in Parthia, this being the last year of Caesar's selections, back when he had given every indication that he intended to return to Rome. "They're completely devoted to Caesar. Even if I send Rufus back across Our Sea to Parthia, they're going to hear that he was in Rome. And," he finished, "they're going to want to know why he was here, and why I sent him away."

"Who said anything about sending him away?"

It took Antonius a long moment to correctly interpret Cicero's quiet question, if only because he would have never assumed that the portly, bald orator had the iron in his soul to even suggest such a thing.

It was, Rufus knew, an egregious dereliction of his duty. He had vowed to himself that he wouldn't succumb to the temptation that he had expressed to the Master of the Horse,

407

who had naturally been surprised to see him. Although Caesar's orders to Rufus hadn't required him to remain to ensure that Antonius actually read the scroll, he had debated about whether or not he should do so; to his relief, it hadn't proven necessary, because Antonius had snatched the scroll, broken the seal, and begun reading within a matter of heartbeats. Rufus did notice that Antonius went pale, but aside from that and a sudden clenching of his pronounced jaw, he otherwise didn't react to whatever was contained in the scroll. Although Rufus knew the bare bones, that Caesar was sending Antonius to Alexandria as soon as Octavian arrived in Rome to assume the Master of the Horse role, he knew Caesar well enough to understand there would be more to it than that, but despite his intense curiosity, he also knew better than to ask. Antonius had asked him a few questions, mainly about the women of India, and what kind of debauchery they indulged in, and his expression of admiration for Caesar's accomplishment seemed genuine enough, but to Rufus, he seemed a bit distracted by the news, although he could understand. He, after all, had spent the last months grappling with all that he had been a part of, so it was a bit much to assume Antonius would absorb this momentous news in a matter of less than a third of a watch. It had been his offhand comment, which he had meant as a jest, about stopping at a *taverna* for a jug of Falernian and a plate of dormouse that he had offered to amuse Antonius that ended up sticking in his mind. He had found Gnaeus Domitius Ahenobarbus easily enough, and Calpurnia had been at Caesar's home that abutted the Temple of Vesta, but it had been Cicero who proved harder to track down, Rufus starting at the newly reconstructed Curia, with Pompey's Theater no longer being used since the day after the Ides of March almost six years earlier. It was when he stopped at The Rostra to inquire of the group of men, mostly out of work lawyers who were always hanging about The Forum, if they had seen their fellow lawyer, that he had learned not only that the Theater was no longer used by the Senate, but that there had been noises about tearing the building down because of its association with the foul deed that had rocked their world. It still stood, but none of the troupes of players, mimes, and assorted other acts who would have normally clamored to use the structure, with its vast audience space, expressed any interest in holding performances there, not after the fate of the unfortunate troupe of itinerant Greek players who had arrived two months after the Ides and tried to rent the space for a series of plays by Aristophanes.

"They were torn to bits," a middle-aged Roman, with a paunch and a shabby toga that could only be charitably considered white, had informed Rufus. "The moment the mob found out that someone wanted to use the place where those foul beings tried to murder Caesar, well," he held his hands out, palms up as he shrugged, "they weren't long for this world. It was ugly to see."

"I can imagine," Rufus said, but while this was interesting, he pressed, "but I really must find Cicero. He's not at the Curia, but do any of you know his whereabouts?"

He asked this of the middle-aged lawyer and those around him, but it was another, younger man, with a slightly cleaner toga and protruding teeth that made him speak with something of a lisp, who called out, "I overheard his slave Tiro telling another slave that they were retiring to his villa in the country for the next two days. The Senate is meeting again in three days. Although," he laughed, "I have no idea why. Everyone knows it's a sham. Marcus Antonius is running things, and he's acting on orders from Caesar."

It was the middle-aged lawyer, who tried an ingratiating grin, who asked Rufus, "So, young Tribune, you clearly are on a mission of some importance." He turned to his comrades, and said jokingly, "Maybe he's come from wherever Caesar is, eh? Bringing orders to Cicero to open his veins, perhaps?"

Stung, both by the joke and the laughter it provoked, it prompted Rufus to snap, "You should go into business as an Oracle, citizen, because that's exactly where I'm coming from. I just arrived in Rome today, bearing orders from Dictator Caesar himself."

He knew the instant he said it he had erred, if only because it would take him several moments to extricate himself from the sudden crowd of people, drawn by the shouts of some of the lawyers standing on the Rostra that a messenger from Caesar was in their very midst, but he also couldn't deny the thrill of pride he felt at being the first man in Rome to relay the news that Caesar had prevailed over all of their enemies and that he and the army had reached the Ganges River. The clamor was such that it drew even more onlookers, and more importantly, some Senators who were holding private meetings inside the Curia. His best estimate was that he was delayed almost a third of a watch and had shouted himself hoarse as he repeated the news more times than he could count, while answering as many of the questions as he could. He was finally forced to use the bulk of his horse to forge a path through the crowd, leaving behind something that, over the course of the next watch, would become something very closely resembling a religious holiday, as word flashed throughout the city, from the Palatine to the Subura, that Caesar not only lived, but had been victorious, surpassing the Macedonian king by reaching the great Ganges River. This was why, once he made it out onto the Via Appia heading south, with a parched throat and a growling stomach, when he saw the roadside inn at the three-mile marker with a sign declaring the tastiest dormouse in the Republic, and the finest selection of wine known to man, he decided that, after all, no one but he would know that he had taken a moment for himself.

By the time he staggered out of the door, it was close to dusk, he was a bit drunk, but he was thankful that it was only another mile to Cicero's villa, and given the time of day and his importance as Caesar's messenger, the orator would undoubtedly offer him a place to rest his weary head. And then, his future was bright, given his appointment as Quaestor, the warrant for which was nestled in his satchel, signed by the most powerful man, not just in Rome, but in the world. In retrospect, it would be something that Cicero at least came to regret, that young Rufus' future wasn't nearly as bright, or as long, as he thought it would be, given that the orator and his coconspirator Antonius were ignorant of the fact that the very news they were trying to prevent with Rufus' sudden and mysterious disappearance was already flashing through the city of Rome, the Republic, and the rest of the world.

Caesar was alive, and he was now the greatest general in the history of mankind.

Made in the USA
Monee, IL
10 July 2022